THE SALAMANDER

Book Two in The Dawn of America series

REGAN WALKER

This is a work of fiction. Names, characters, places and incidents either are the product of the author's imagination or are used fictitiously. Any resemblance to actual events, locales, business establishments or persons, living or dead, is coincidental.

THE SALAMANDER

Copyright © 2025 Regan Walker

Paperback ISBN: 979-8-9997947-0-3

PRAISE FOR REGAN WALKER

"Regan Walker is a master of her craft. Her novels instantly draw you in, keep you reading and leave you with a smile on your face."

—Good Friends, Good Books

"Walker's detailed historical research enhances the time and place of the story without losing sight of what is essential to a romance: chemistry between the leads and hope for the future."

—Publisher's Weekly

"Regan Walker excels at weaving sweeping historical drama with deeply intimate moments."

—Historical Novel Society

"Ms. Walker has the rare ability to make you forget you are reading a book. The characters become real, the modern world fades away, and all that is left is the intrigue, drama, and romance."

—Straight from the Library

"Spellbinding and Expertly Crafted...Walker's characters are complex and well-rounded and, in her hands, real historical figures merge seamlessly with those from her imagination."

—A Reader's Review

ACKNOWLEDGEMENTS

I am grateful to artist Donald MacLeod, who graciously gave his permission to me to use his painting "HMS *Serapis* & *Bonhomme Richard*", which shows the Battle of Flamborough Head in 1779. The one sea captain on the American side in the Revolutionary War to whom Jonathan Haraden is most often compared is John Paul Jones, and this was one of his battles. For more of Mr. MacLeod's art, see https://www.stivesgallery.co.uk/index.html.

Among those who assisted my research were Allan Vaughan at the Salem Marine Society, of which Jonathan Haraden was at one time a member, and Claire Burday and Lucy Hereford at the Phillips Library of the Peabody Essex Museum. I thank each of you for helping bring Jonathan to life in my story. (It was Lucy who found a color miniature of Jonathan that told me he had dark blue eyes.)

My beta readers provide invaluable assistance, including Dr. Chari Wessel, expert in all things nautical, Liette Bougie, my French-speaking Canadian reader with an eye for detail, and my critique partners, Jackie, Mary and Susan. Many thanks!

THE COLONIES IN 1775

HUDSON BAY COMPANY 49°

N S
(to Mass)

PROVINCE OF
QUEBEC

N H

N Y MASS

R I
CONN

PA

N J

MD

DEL

Proclamation Line of 1763

VA

(Spain)

N C

INDIAN
RESERVE

S C

GA

W FLA

E FLA

From the National Atlas of the United States

CHARACTERS OF NOTE

CAPTAIN JONATHAN HARADEN

EUNICE DIMAN MASON, daughter of Reverend James Diman

HANNAH HARADEN, Jon's daughter

POLLY HARADEN, Jon's daughter

REVEREND JAMES DIMAN, Pastor of the East Church of Salem, and his wife, Mary

MARTHA TIBBETTS, the Haraden cook

SILAS TURNER, man of all work at the Haraden home

JOHN FISK, Captain of the *Tyrannicide* and the *Massachusetts*

JOSEPH STOCKMAN, Second Lieutenant on the *Tyrannicide*

BENJAMIN MOSES, Second Lieutenant on the *Tyrannicide* under Jon Haraden, Captain

JOHN MARSH, Chaplain on the *Tyrannicide*

JOHN REED, Cook on the *Tyrannicide*

BENJAMIN LOVETT, Sailing Master on the *Tyrannicide*

HENRY MALCOM, Surgeon on the *Tyrannicide*

JOHNNY DEADMAN, Cabin Boy on the *Tyrannicide*

BOBBY GROVER, Cabin Boy on the *Tyrannicide* and then on the *Pickering*

JOSHUA TRASK, Cabin Boy on the *Tyrannicide* and then on the *Pickering*

ELIAS HASKET DERBY, Salem merchant

GEORGE WILLIAMS, Salem merchant and owner of the *Pickering*

ANDREW and LYDIA HARADEN and their daughters Hannah ("Joanna"), Lydia, Betsey, Peggy, Jane and Polly ("the Gloucester Haradens")

ISRAEL THORNDIKE of Beverly, First Lieutenant on the *Pickering*

JOHN CARNES, Second Lieutenant on the *Pickering*

ROBERT COWAN, Lieutenant on the *Pickering*

ROBERT BOWAN, Boatswain on the *Pickering*

DAVID MCCLURE, Chaplain on the *Pickering*

SIMEON SAMSON, Captain of the *Hazard*

THE PRIVATEERS

They were the daring American seamen who seized British merchant ships during the Revolutionary War. Initially operating in the shadows as a pirate militia of the sea, they successfully disrupted British supply lines to aid the Continental Army. General George Washington encouraged them and American Patriots embraced them. Eventually they were armed with letters of marque, transforming them from outlaws to official heroes, allowing them to seize enemy vessels as prizes of war.

Individual colonies (states after 1776) commissioned privateers, and in March 1776 the Continental Congress began issuing commissions. America's fledgling navy never had enough ships to do all they did without the help of the Patriot privateers. Their success was so profound it led the British merchants to protest the continuation of "the American war". While the ports of Boston, New York and others were blockaded by squadrons of British warships, the privateers managed to slip to sea and spread destruction. Salem, Massachusetts was a critical hub.

THE SALAMANDER

Captain Jonathan Haraden's coldblooded courage earned him the nickname "the Salamander". Like the creature of old, his crew believed him immune to the fires of battle. At the Revolution's outbreak, he joined the militia guarding the seacoast, but his passion for the sea drew him to the fledgling Massachusetts Navy.

A dashing sea captain, tall and handsome, Jon captured hearts as easily as ships, but his own belonged to Hannah, his young wife he lost to a fever as the Revolution began. Devastated, he sets sail with a vengeance, entrusting his young daughters to Eunice Mason, a preacher's daughter and young widow whose quiet strength steadies his home.

Commanding the *Tyrannicide*, Jon seizes British prizes and vital dispatches for General Washington. But chafing at the state's inefficiencies and wanting more freedom, he accepts command of the privateer *General Pickering*, backed by Salem merchants who hail his daring and skill. Adored by his crew and feared by the enemy, Jon soon becomes a legend, capturing ships with unmatched audacity. Yet, he wonders if there will be another chance for love or if the sea will be his only mistress.

"…before the war commenced, the Revolution
was in the minds and hearts of the people; a
change in their religious sentiments, of their duties
and obligations."
– John Adams 1818

CHAPTER 1

*The Old Burying Point Cemetery, Salem, Massachusetts, June
1776*

A RARE FOG, thick with the sea's breath, cloaked the
church graveyard like a shroud, swallowing the early
summer's light as mourners gathered for Hannah's burial.
Even the yellow flowers she would have loved, laid upon
the grave, were veiled as if hiding their joy. Hollowed by
grief, Jonathan Haraden held his nine-month-old daughter, Polly, close, her warmth a faint anchor against the
chill. Seven-year-old Hannah, named for her mother,
clutched his hand, her golden hair like her mother's, her
eyes fierce despite tears. She was his brave little soldier

who had vowed to take care of her sister.

"Will Mama see us from Heaven, Papa?" she whispered, piercing his heart.

"Mama is with Jesus now, sweetheart, visiting Grandpapa and Grandma."

The church that Jon and Hannah had attended offered no solace, reduced to ashes in the fire that swept Salem two years before. And their pastor, Nathaniel Whitaker, was not one for compassion. So, Reverend James Diman of the East Church had come to hold Hannah's service. The plump, black-robed reverend with his bushy white wig stood before the open grave, his expression solemn, as his voice cut through the mist.

"We gather to honor Hannah Haraden, devoted wife and mother," Diman intoned. "A friend to Salem's women. Always smiling, she trusted God through life's trials. She prayed for the colony's liberty and stood by her husband, Jonathan, as he joined the militia to guard our coast."

A sob broke from the crowd; handkerchiefs dabbed at tears. Diman paused, his eyes dropping to his Bible. Then, looking up, he said, "As the Apostle Paul reminded the church at Thessalonica, we do not sorrow as those who have no hope. Jesus died and rose, and when He comes again, He will bring with Him those who have fallen asleep, like our beloved sister, Hannah. We thank God for her time with us and ask Him to watch over her family."

As the coffin was lowered into the ground and the first thud of earth struck the wood, Jon passed the sleeping Polly to Martha, his cook, and rested his hand on little Hannah's head. She looked up at him with tear-stained cheeks. "We'll be all right, sweetheart."

Beside him, Martha muttered, "Grief's a heavy burden, sir, but life goes on. You need to live for your daughters, as the mistress would want. 'Sides, them redcoats won't wait if America's to win this war."

Her tongue, sharp as her kitchen knife, hid the care he knew she had for his family. Without his asking, she had already secured a wet nurse for Polly.

"We'll need to get the young'uns home," she added, winking, "your friends'll soon fill the house with food and sympathy."

Nodding, he walked with Hannah to Reverend Diman. "I hope you will join us for the repast."

"Of course," Diman replied. "Mary will come, too, for she has counsel if you will hear a friend's advice."

"I'd be grateful." He liked Reverend Diman's wife, Mary, and, in truth, he felt adrift with Hannah gone.

The mourners, many of them ship captains, militiamen and their wives, made their way to his home on Charter Street close to the cemetery and a mere block from the harbor. Their boots rang on the cobblestones as the fog thinned, revealing the salt-washed air.

With Hannah's hand in his, Jon and the reverend made their way to where Mary Diman waited. A small woman, she was almost engulfed in her long black gown with white fichu draped around her shoulders and elaborate white lace cap hiding her brown hair. Her smile was welcoming as she joined them to followed the mourners.

By the time they reached his house, it was full of guests and the scent of roast chicken, cod stew and fresh bread. Jonathan released Hannah. "Welcome your friends," he urged her, "be our hostess."

Hannah bit her lip. "Very well, Papa." She curtsied bravely to a friend's mother, then slipped away, clutching her mother's locket. Too young for the role, she nonetheless carried it with fierce dignity. Jon's chest tightened. Both he and his daughter were being asked to step into roles too soon.

A memory broke through his grief, the first time he had seen Hannah Deadman. At seventeen, she had swept into the cooperage where he had become skilled at making barrels. She was looking for a barrel for the merchant she worked for, Joshua Ward. It was as if the sun itself had made an appearance, her golden hair, her blue eyes. Smitten, he had fumbled his tools, knowing even then she would claim his heart. The sting of that memory was too fresh, pulling him back to the crowded room where life pressed on without her.

The reverend was right when he said Hannah trusted God through life's trials. They had lost three sons in infancy and yet she never retreated from her faith.

Martha, bustling nearby, caught his gaze. "You mustn't brood like a fogged in ship, sir. Your girls need you lively."

He returned her a tight-lipped smile, her blunt words softening the ache in his chest.

Silas, his man of all work, more elegantly attired than his usual brown breeches and waistcoat, limped forward balancing a tray of red wine glasses, his gray beard trimmed, his weathered face solemn. "She was a fine woman, sir—sorry for your loss."

"Thank you, Silas." Jon handed glasses to the Dimans before taking one for himself. The wine steadied him though food held no appeal.

Mary Diman smiled up at him. "It is good to see you and young Hannah surrounded by friends."

Around them the crowd conversed, enjoying the camaraderie a wake always brought. Mourners came, spoke brief words, and moved on. Jon stood as if within a fog, though the room was warm with firelight. He heard the thud of earth again, insistent. Yet somewhere beneath the ash and smoke of grief, a small ember glowed, stubborn and alive.

"What are your plans if I might ask?" said Reverend Diman.

For a moment, Jon stared into his wine. Plans? He could scarcely think past the sound of soil striking the coffin lid that morning. Hannah's laugh still hung in the corners of the house, ready to undo him if he turned too quickly.

He cleared his throat. "I…Richard Cabot, son of my old employer, George Cabot, has asked me to serve as First Lieutenant aboard the *Tyrannicide*. It's the same rank I hold in the militia." His voice felt like it belonged to someone else, speaking of a life already far from this dim parlor.

Reverend Diman's eyebrows rose. "You would go to sea?"

Jon's gaze drifted to little Hannah across the room, clutching her mother's locket as though it were a lifebuoy. "It's in my blood, Reverend," he said finally, forcing the words. "My grandfather and uncle were both captains…"

"Who is to be the captain on the *Tyrannicide*?" asked Mary Diman.

"John Fisk, son of Reverend Samuel Fisk."

"Of course," said Diman with a knowing glance at his wife. "He was pastor of the First Church in Salem until he died some years ago. It's a good family. John, the son, has much experience as a seafaring merchant."

"John and I are of an age," said Jon, "just past thirty. But his experience as a master mariner with his own ships will allow me to learn much serving under him."

"If that is to be your decision," said Mary Diman, "and I can see from the look in your eyes it is your heart's desire, then I have a proposition for you."

Jon narrowed his eyes on Mary Diman with sudden interest.

"You will need a governess for young Hannah and eventually for Polly, too. A nursemaid will not do. You need a young lady educated and trained in the graces, who loves children."

"You know such a paragon?" asked Jon.

Mary Diman exchanged a smile with her husband. "I do. I would like to recommend our daughter, Eunice Mason, widowed a year ago when her husband of one year drowned. She is well-read, trained in domestic duties and sings hymns that soothe even the wildest child. Like you, she is in mourning."

Jon's brows drew together. "Martha's capable, and Silas handles odd jobs, but a governess...I'd feel easier knowing my girls had a young woman's care, one you raised, Mrs. Diman."

"Trust me, Jon," said the reverend's wife, "you'll be

glad she's in your home. And Eunice needs a purpose. We'll guide her if needed."

"Providence guides us, I can see," said the reverend.

John Fisk approached, his face grim. "Jon, you have my sympathy for Hannah's loss. Still, I cannot hide the news. The British are raiding our coast. It's time to end your militia duties. I need you on the *Tyrannicide*. She's at the Salisbury Shipyard now and should be here soon. I will send word when she arrives."

Jon's gaze drifted past him to the mourners, their voices soft and respectful in the dim light of the room. The name of the ship stirred something in him, a familiar pull, but grief still pressed heavy on his chest. He took a slow breath before answering. "I thank you for the news, John. But not today."

Fisk's brow furrowed. "I understand. Yet the fight for liberty will not wait for our grief to ease."

Jon's gaze shifted past Fisk to where Hannah stood across the room, clutching her locket. Her golden hair caught the light, so like her mother's. He felt the familiar ache sharpen, then steadied himself. "Then send word when she's here," he said at last. "I will come."

Even as he spoke, he felt the sea's call, constant like the tide, but muffled, as though he heard through the soil of the grave.

TWO DAYS AFTER the funeral, the Haraden house on Charter Street lay hushed. The murmur of mourners had faded, replaced by creaking floorboards and gulls wheeling above the harbor. Jonathan sat at his oak table in his study, a militia dispatch before him, the inked lines unread. His pen hovered over the dispatch, unmoving. From somewhere deep in his memory, her laugh rose like a gull's cry on a summer wind…and was gone.

Sitting nearby, Hannah's head bent over a book, her golden hair a painful echo of her mother's, while Polly babbled to old Silas who crouched next to her cradle. Martha's cod chowder scented the air, but the kitchen was quiet.

A knock stirred Jon. Opening the door, he found Mary Diman, no longer dressed in black but a dark blue dress and a red Kashmir shawl, a young woman beside her. The resemblance between them was plain, the same brown hair and eyes, the same composed bearing. But the younger green muslin gown and plain bonnet lent her a quiet reserve. Eunice Mason, widowed by the sea's cruelty, stood with hands clasped, as if bracing herself.

"Lieutenant Haraden," Mrs. Diman said, "I've come to introduce you to my daughter, Eunice, who we spoke of as governess for your girls."

Mrs. Mason offered a shy smile, like a gentle doe unsure of herself.

Jon inclined his head. "Mrs. Diman, Mrs. Mason. Please come in."

The young woman followed her mother inside.

Hannah looked up, her book forgotten.

Silas rose and bowed to the ladies. "Beggin' your pardon, I'll just let Martha know we have company."

Polly stopped babbling and began to fuss. Eunice knelt beside the cradle, humming a hymn. The melody wrapped through the room like a thread of calm. Polly quieted, her tiny hand curling around Mrs. Mason's finger. Gratitude pricked through Jon's daze. Those gentle brown eyes met his, soft with understanding, before turning to Hannah.

"I am happy to meet you, Hannah."

Hannah nodded but said nothing.

Martha bustled in, wiping her hands on her apron. Her gaze swept over Mrs. Diman's daughter. Turning to the pastor's wife, Martha said, "Welcome, Mrs. Diman. We've chowder if you and your daughter can join us for the noonday meal."

Mrs. Diman glanced at Jon. "If it's not too much trouble…"

"Not at all," Jon said quickly. "Yes, please stay." Her presence would ease her daughter's first hours with them.

Jon picked up Polly who'd fallen asleep and led Mrs. Diman and her daughter into the dining room, the scent of chowder drawing them. Hannah walked behind them, silent and watchful.

The oak table, worn from years of family meals, held four settings, Martha having added two across from Jon and Hannah for their guests. Jon placed the sleeping Polly into a basket set in one corner. "She will sleep," he said. "It's time for her nap."

They took their seats and Martha and Silas hurried into the kitchen, returning with steaming bowls of chowder and bread and butter. Having eaten little in the days before, Jon was suddenly hungry.

"Chowder's hot," Martha said to Mrs. Mason, placing a bowl before her, "if the hymns haven't scared it cold."

A smile flickered across the young woman's face as

she turned to meet Martha's gaze. "I'll save the hymns for the girls, Ma'am. This chowder smells wonderful, and its warmth is music enough for now."

Behind Mrs. Mason, Martha's mouth twitched in grudging approval.

Hannah's fingers tightened on her locket. "You're not my mama," she said sharply, her blue eyes fierce. "We don't need you."

Jon laid his hand over hers. "Hannah, Mrs. Mason is here to care for you and Polly, as your mama would have wished. Be kind and give it time."

Mrs. Mason met Hannah's intense look, her brown eyes gentle but firm. "I know I'm not your mother, Hannah, but I'd like to be your friend. I, too, have lost someone I loved."

Jon exchanged a glance with Mary Diman, whose nod told him she trusted her daughter to weather both his irascible cook and his defiant daughter.

Over the meal, the conversation turned to Salem's readiness for the fight against the British. "So the fight is to move from the land to sea," Mrs. Diman observed.

Jon nodded. "General Washington leads the fight on land. He has encouraged the Colonies to take the fight to the sea as well to interrupt British shipping, even sending a few privateers out himself. Massachusetts now has the beginnings of a navy. With it, we can aid the troops with what we take from the British supply ships."

"That is so important to the cause," said Mrs. Mason in her quiet voice.

When the bowls were nearly empty, Silas entered with a folded and sealed parchment. "This just arrived for you, sir."

Jon broke the seal, unfolded the parchment and read Fisk's neat hand, summoning him to the wharf. The *Tyrannicide* had arrived. He looked up at their guests, "I am summoned to the wharf where my new ship awaits. Martha, perhaps you could show Mrs. Mason the chamber prepared for her and the girls' sleeping room."

Martha, returning from the kitchen, stood with hands on hips. "Tour's fine, sir, but then I've work to do and dustin' that won't do itself."

"I will be happy to do my own dusting," said Mrs. Mason her cheeks flushing faintly.

"That all sounds fine," said Mary Diman, her smile warm. "We thank you for the meal, Jon, and the delicious chowder, Martha. If all goes well, we will have my daughter's things delivered later today."

EUNICE FOLLOWED MARTHA through the narrow hall of the Haraden house, her heart fluttering like a trapped bird. Mr. Haraden's kind insistence that she and her mother stay lingered in her mind. His strong features and his eyes, dark blue like a storm on the horizon, had been clouded by grief. Yet his gentle touch on Hannah's hand, calming her fierce outburst, and the way he cradled Polly, so tender for a man just entering his thirties, spoke of a father's heart.

Losing Thomas just a year into their marriage had driven Eunice inward, her shyness often a cloak against others' pity. The position as governess would force her to rejoin the living. Perhaps God had placed her here to help a hurting family.

The stairs creaked as Martha led her and her mother upward. Young Hannah trailed behind, her hand around her locket. "This'll be your chamber, Lass," Martha said, opening a door to a small but well-appointed room that looked out on a garden below, its sprig wallpaper bright and cheery. "The mistress decorated this chamber herself. The chamber reminds me of her, always smilin', always cheerful. She kept it for infrequent guests, but now it will be yours." A narrow bed bore a hand-stitched green and yellow quilt with a nod to the wallpaper's sprigs, its stitches fine, perhaps a product of Mrs. Haraden's hands. A washstand, chest of drawers and pegged shelf stood against the walls, and a small writing desk fit nicely in front of the window. "The chamber gets the afternoon sun," said Martha, "so you'll be able to sit at that desk then with no need for a candle."

Eunice ran her fingers along the surface of the quilt, its softness grounding her. "It's lovely."

"Aye, the mistress had a needle sharper than my tongue," Martha chuckled, as she picked up a small silver frame holding a miniature painting of Jonathan Haraden. "She often spent time here when there were no guests and liked to have the master's portrait near. She was teachin' young Hannah to stitch when she took sick with the fever. She went so fast, the master had no time to prepare."

"It happens like that sometimes," said Eunice, re-membering how quickly Thomas was taken from her.

"This chamber will serve you well," said Eunice's mother.

"Though your hymns might soothe Polly's naps,"

Martha said, setting down the silver frame, "they won't charm the dust off these shelves, and I ain't scalin' the stairs to chase more cobwebs, mind."

Eunice faced the cook, tempted to smile. She was a sturdy woman in her late forties, her white apron tied over a plain woolen gown, and her mob cap barely taming wiry gray curls. Her hazel eyes, glinting like polished oak in candlelight, softened with crinkled warmth when she spoke of the Haradens, her tough exterior hiding a heart fiercely loyal to the family. "You need have no concerns, Martha. I'll take good care of this chamber and help you with the others when my duties with the children allow." She kept her voice steady, though inside she felt her heart trembling. To serve here, where God could use her, was enough.

Martha's eyes crinkled, a grin breaking through, betraying her approval. "Aye, well, the master's away plenty with the militia, and it'll be worse now he's off to sea with that *Tyrannicide*. Don't expect him hoverin' round."

"I don't mind," Eunice said, her cheeks flushing. "I only wish to care for his girls, to be where God has placed me." Her thoughts flickered to Jon Haraden's kind smile.

Her mother's Kashmir shawl caught the window's light as she smiled at Martha. "Eunice's heart is steadfast. She'll serve this house well."

They stepped into the girls' sleeping room next door, where two small beds flanked a large window. Beneath the window was a wooden chest. A carved wooden cradle sat in the corner. A rag doll lay on the bed she assumed was Hannah's, its button eyes worn with love. Hannah stood in the doorway, clutching her locket, her golden hair framing her sweet face.

"That locket," said Martha, "was the master's gift to Hannah's mama. It never leaves the child's neck."

Eunice nodded, understanding. Thomas had given her small gifts she treasured for his memory. Smiling at Hannah, she said, "I would do the same were I her."

"Polly's a light sleeper, like her mama," said Martha. "That one," she nodded at Hannah, "has her mama's spark—keeps us hoppin'."

Ignoring Martha for the moment, Eunice met Hannah's gaze. "I'll take good care of your sister with you, Hannah, and be your friend when you're ready." Her smile held a prayer, a hope to anchor this grieving home.

Eunice wanted to respect the space their mother doubtless treasured. The appliqué quilts on the beds were charming with flowers and hearts stitched carefully.

"Did your mother make the quilts for you and Polly?" Eunice asked Hannah.

The girl nodded. Her blue eyes flickered, interest piercing her frown.

"I like them," said Eunice. "Your mama had a gift."

Eunice's mother's hand rested on her shoulder. "You'll do well here."

Martha didn't offer to show them the master's bedchamber or the other chambers that lined the hall. Instead, she led them downstairs, muttering, "Well, now that's done, we can get on with the day's work. Hymns settle babes fine enough but they won't clean stoves or bake loaves."

Eunice's heart lifted as she thought of bringing joy to this home where hurt lingered.

"To be prepared for war is one of the most effectual means of preserving peace."
– George Washington 1790

CHAPTER 2

Salem Harbor, late June 1776

JON STRODE ALONG Water Street, passing Salem's wharves, his excitement rising for what lay ahead. The breeze off the water loosened the heaviness of his sorrow just enough to let hope seep in. Each step toward the *Tyrannicide* was a step away from the shadow that had clung to him since Hannah's death.

The tang of salt and fish were sharp in the air, as gulls rose in the sky to shriek overhead. Passing barrels and chests ready to be loaded, he spotted the *Tyrannicide* looming ahead, her single mast tall against the blue sky, her fourteen cannon gleaming under fresh canvas, a sleek sloop of war flying the Massachusetts pine tree flag.

Beneath his cocked hat, John Fisk stood by the gangway smiling at Jon's approach.

"Haraden," Fisk called, clasping Jon's hand. "Good. You're here. The General Court commissioned the *Tyrannicide* today under a letter of marque. In addition to you as First Lieutenant, Joseph Stockman will be Second Lieutenant and Warrant Officer Benjamin Moses will be our bos'n. Our Sailing Master, Benjamin Lovett, is a man of some experience in the coastal routes we'll be navigating."

"A good beginning," remarked Jon, returning Fisk's smile, for he knew the men and counted them friends. "Have you a need for cabin boys? I can recommend one, Johnny Deadman, a distant cousin of Hannah's."

"Of course. By the time the crew is all here, we'll have many. Some wealthy Salem families are sending their boys to us to learn the sea, and others from poorer families hope to become seamen, even officers. And I've assigned one to myself and one to the surgeon."

Jon was glad he could help the lad, who had come to see him only that morning. "I'll send Johnny along when I return."

"Meantime," said Fisk, "British ships hit Gloucester last week, raiders off Cape Ann, likely from Halifax. We're to cruise from Massachusetts to New Hampshire, chasing down British merchantmen."

"I await with impatience our sailing," said Jon. He climbed the gangway beside Fisk, running a hand along the sloop's oak rail, noting the ship's six-pounders polished for battle. The sea's pull stirred him, a balm to the grief that had clung to him like a damp fog since Hannah's passing. "She's a fine sloop, Captain," said Jon, recognizing

Fisk's new position. "Seventy-five crew, then?"

"Aye," Fisk replied, "which is why it's taking some time for them to arrive."

Jon nodded, scanning the deck where a few crewmen hauled ropes and others tested a cannon for range.

"Word is," said Fisk, "your service in the militia was so outstanding they raised you to a First Lieutenant after a month. Cabot wanted you for my ship and so did I."

"Or he desperately needed a first officer," said Jon with a chuckle.

Fisk laughed. "Come, let me show you your meager cabin."

Jon followed Fisk down the companionway leading to the stern of the ship, the narrow steps creaking beneath their boots. From somewhere forward came the rhythmic thud of a caulker's mallet, the rattle of block and tackle, and the low murmur of men at work, sounds that spoke of a vessel on the brink of action. The scent of fresh pine, tar, and oiled wood mingled with the sharp tang of the sea, a heady reminder of the life ahead.

Fisk stopped before two adjoining doors set opposite the captain's quarters. "This one's yours," Fisk said, pressing his hand against the door on the right. "Not much space, but enough for a man who spends most of his time on deck."

Jon pushed the door open and stepped inside to the earthy small of fresh oak. Sunlight from the single porthole dappled the boards and framed the blue water beyond.

The cabin was small but tidy, bare wooden walls, a shelf bed with a rough-spun blanket folded on top, drawers beneath for stowing clothes. A low shelf held a copy of *The Naval Discipline*.

Having been on merchant ships, Jon had not expected a larger cabin. Meeting Fisk's inquiring gaze, he said, "Fits a man who's ready for a fight."

"Aye," Fisk agreed. "And we've a grand fight ahead, for we go against the most powerful navy in the world."

"But our cause is grander still," Jon said. "'Tis liberty itself. Every mile of sea we command is a mile the British navy cannot."

"Come," said Fisk, "I'll show you the captain's quarters next door. It's got a bit more elbow room. Our meetings will take place there."

Fisk pushed open the captain's door, revealing a cabin bright with afternoon light spilling through four stern windows, the glass thick and slightly wavy. In the center of the space that spanned the width of the ship's stern, was a table and chairs for six. A broad desk was bolted to the deck on one side of the cabin, its surface neat save for a chart of the New England coast and a brass-bound compass. A sea chest sat beneath the stern windows, and a bunk was built into the starboard wall, its dark blue blanket tucked with military precision. A rack of small arms—pistols, a cutlass, and a hanger, its curved blade good for slashing, hung within easy reach.

Jon took in the commanding view aft where the ship's wake would churn white against the blue when underway. Beyond the harbor's sunlit waters, Jon pictured the unbroken horizon and the restless sea. A flicker of the old fire stirred within him. "A fine place from which to keep the king's ships on the run."

Fisk's mouth quirked into a smile. "That's the aim. We've precious few ships in the Massachusetts service, but if we use them well, we'll make the British feel the pinch from Halifax to Portsmouth and remind them the sea is not theirs to keep."

Jon smiled, content to be serving with John Fisk.

Some minutes later, Jon bid Fisk a good day and descended the gangway to return home, Fisk shouted after him from the rail, "If you've a dark green wool coat, plan to wear it. Green and white are the new colors for naval officers in the Massachusetts Navy, as prescribed by the Council. Let them see our colors before they feel our guns."

Haraden house, Salem, late June 1776

EUNICE KNELT BEFORE her trunk, lifting out clothes and books as the late afternoon sun made the sprig wallpaper glow. From the sideboard came the faint scent of lavender, drifting from stalks in a pewter pitcher. A welcome kindness from Martha she hadn't expected.

Next to the lamp on the chest of drawers lay her mother's Kashmir shawl, neatly folded, a gift that tethered her to home. The spiraling red and orange patterns seemed to hold warmth in their threads, enough to brighten the drabbest gown and chase away a lonely night.

The door to the girls' sleeping room stood open so that Eunice could hear Polly's cry should she wake. The wet nurse had left a short time ago and the child slept.

Eunice hummed a hymn, as she lifted her Bible from the trunk, worn from years of use. When Thomas had died, the hymns helped to remind her God had not forsaken her.

Jonathan Haraden gazed from the silver-framed portrait on the shelf, his eyes somehow more alive in the portrait than when she'd last seen them shadowed by loss. Perhaps she would offer to put the portrait in the girls' sleeping room. Meantime, she would pray his new position as an officer on the *Tyrannicide* helped him recover. Surely a position of such great importance would distract him from his grief.

She was just finishing emptying her trunk when a creak announced Hannah in the doorway, her golden hair catching the candlelight, her pretty face drawn into a wary frown. "Mama sang better," she said after a moment. "Her songs kept Polly content."

Eunice paused, setting down a folded gown. "I'd love to hear your mama's songs, Hannah. Maybe you'll teach me one?" Her voice carried hope for friendship.

Hannah's frown deepened, but she stepped closer. "She liked lavender," she murmured, glancing at the flowers. "She said it smelled like summer." Her voice wavered, a crack in her guard.

"I think so, too." Then remembering the small portrait, she said, "Hannah, would you like your papa's portrait in your room? We can move it there if you like."

She nodded, her gaze darting to the small painting of her father.

"Then we shall do it," said Eunice, smiling at Hannah.

Polly began to stir, emitting a grunt. Eunice rose and

reached for the small portrait. "Let's check on your sister." She offered her hand. Hannah didn't take it but followed with light footsteps.

In the girls' sleeping room, Eunice set the small silver frame with its portrait on the chest under the window and then went to the cradle. Polly smiled up at her reaching with her small arms. Martha bustled past the doorway carrying a stack of linens and stopped, her mob cap askew. "You've a knack for calmin' that one."

Eunice's cheeks heated. "Thank you, Martha." She lifted Polly out of the cradle and checked her cotton clout. "She needs changing."

"Here," said Martha, handing her a cotton square from the stack she carried, "a fresh one. Do you know how to change it?"

"As it happens," said Eunice, "I do. From changing my older sister's babies."

Martha put the linens in a hall cupboard, then joined Eunice to watch her place Polly on the bed and change her. "You're fittin' in well, Mrs. Mason. Keep it up and you just might keep this house from fallin' apart." Her crinkled smile showed trust, a bond forming over shared care for the girls. "Here, give me the soiled one and I'll put it with the others to be rinsed and washed."

Eunice handed the clout to Martha and carried Polly downstairs. Hannah trailed behind her. "Shall we read a story to Polly while Martha prepares supper?"

"Mama told me a story about a man named Jonah who was swallowed by a giant fish."

Eunice smiled, imagining the scene. "That's a good story. There are many good stories in the Bible. Would you like me to tell you another?"

For the next hour, Eunice told Hannah the story of the shepherd boy, David, how he killed a lion and a bear that threatened his sheep and how he honored God in slaying a giant. She had many questions and Eunice took care to answer every one.

"How old was David when he killed Goliath?" Hannah asked, leaning forward.

"A good question, Hannah. The Bible doesn't tell us exactly. Both King Saul and David's older brothers called him a 'boy'. He was the youngest of eight brothers. He might have been only twelve or in his early teens."

After puzzling over that for a moment, she asked, "Why did he take up five stones when he only needed one to kill Goliath?"

"Ah," Eunice said with a smile, "that's something my father told me when I was your age. Goliath had four brothers, all giants like him."

As the smells of supper filled the parlor, the front door opened, and Mr. Haraden stepped inside. He appeared a different man than when he had left, the shadows in his eyes eased, the set of his shoulders lighter than when she'd first met him.

Hannah ran to him and he lifted her into his arms. "How's my girl?"

"I am good, Papa. Polly, too." He kissed Hannah on the cheek and set her down.

"Evening, Mrs. Mason. I see you have Polly well content. Have you settled in?"

"I have, thank you. How did you find your new ship?"

For the first time since she'd met him, Eunice saw a

glimmer of excitement in his eyes. "She's a beauty, a fine sloop with polished decks and new guns just waiting to be fired. With a name like the *Tyrannicide*, we'll make sure the British tyrants think twice before they sail our waters."

Eunice laughed. "Indeed."

Martha came into the parlor. "Evenin', sir. Supper's ready as soon as you are."

"I'll be down in a bit," he said, turning to ascend the stairs.

Martha nudged Eunice. "He's got that look again, off to fight the British, this time on the sea."

Eunice smiled, as she lifted Polly and carried her into the kitchen. Walking beside Eunice, Hannah said proudly, "My papa's going to sea."

"Yes, he is," Eunice replied, meeting her gaze. "Our country needs him and others like him. The fight for liberty will not be easily won."

JONATHAN SPENT THE next week on the *Tyrannicide*, getting to know the crew, directing the stowing of supplies, drilling the men on the fourteen cannon and poring over coastal charts with Captain Fisk. The weather held fair, as July's sun made the work almost pleasant.

Midweek, Johnny Deadman came aboard and quickly found his place among the other cabin boys. Jon often caught sight of the boy's mop of blond curls darting from belowdecks to quarterdeck on some errand for the captain or cook.

Jon watched Bosun Moses aloft in the rigging, the man's hands sure as he checked the lines. "How's it looking, Moses?" Jon called.

"Sound as a church bell's cord, sir," Moses replied, securing a knot. "Taut for gales off Cape Ann!"

A blur of blond shot past. Johnny Deadman again, a powder sack clutched under one arm. "Not so fast, Johnny!" Jon barked. The boy slowed, throwing him a sheepish glance. Running on a wet deck was asking for trouble, and a lad with dreams of becoming an officer needed the habit of discipline. There were a dozen such boys aboard, most barely into their teens. The captain had said many would leave after the first cruise. However long young Deadman stayed, Jon meant to keep an eye on him.

Jon wore the new uniform colors prescribed by the Massachusetts Council, a dark green coat to which he added a buff waistcoat, breeches, and a white cravat. Fisk approached, his own coat a crisp green, clearly fresh from the tailor.

"Lieutenant Stockman, secure those casks!" Fisk called.

Stockman, shorter than Jon but carrying himself smartly, echoed, "Aye, aye, Captain." "Move sharp, lads!" he urged, as men rolled barrels of salt pork across the deck, then directed the stowing of fresh cod, beef, grog, and hardtack. Amid the bustle, a sailor hefted a small cask clearly marked *Coffee*. Jon's eye lingered on it. The barrel was a well-made piece, its staves tight and true. Years ago, as an apprentice in the Cabots' cooperage, he'd learned to judge a cask's worth at a glance. The sight of it, and the promise of coffee at sea, brought a smile to his face.

"When you've finished," Fisk told Stockman, "see to the rum, then join Haraden and me in my cabin."

At the helm, Warrant Officer John Bray looked up from his tally. "Salt pork, salted cod, fresh cod, and beef, a month's worth, Captain, if we eat the fresh stuff first." He sealed a pork barrel and added, "I'll get this to the cook."

"Good work, Bray," Fisk said.

Turning to Jon, he added, "Haraden, you should meet our chaplain, John Marsh, and our cook, John Reed. They came aboard this morning and have gone belowdecks. Benjamin Lovett, our sailing master, will be along later, as well as Henry Malcom, the surgeon."

Belowdecks, Jon found Chaplain Marsh in a cabin even smaller than his own. A dignified clergyman with dark hair, he wore the black suit typical of clergy at sea. A small sea chest served as table and storage; a well-used Bible rested on top beside the man's spectacles. The chaplain's pale skin hinted at more time spent indoors than out.

"Salem-born," Marsh said when Jon asked what brought him to sea. "Ships have been my neighbors all my life. I wanted to serve the cause. This was the natural choice."

"I was in the militia," Jon said. "But the sea's in my blood, so when the position was offered, I took it. I recently lost my wife to a fever...the sea is my refuge now."

"Children?"

"Two daughters. A governess and staff keep them safe. My wife and I also lost three sons, all very young."

Marsh rested a hand on Jon's shoulder. "Then I will pray for you, Lieutenant, that God eases your burden and comforts you in your loss."

Jon nodded, the simple promise comforting him.

From there, he headed to the galley where the sound of pots and pans clanging together drew him. Cook John Reed bent over an open sack, taking stock. Sunlight from a porthole caught the man's dark red hair. Around him, small barrels lined one wall, and a cast-iron stove dominated the space. He had yet to don an apron and wore only loose-fitting breeches, a light tan shirt and a blue waistcoat left unbuttoned.

"Does the galley suit?" Jon asked after introducing himself.

"Aye," Reed said. "It's smaller than I've had, but new and clean. I've served the Cabots and Captain Fisk on their merchantmen for years, mostly sailing to the West Indies. This is my first time in the Massachusetts Navy."

Jon nodded. "It's the first time for all of us since the navy's new and the war's just begun in earnest. The captain clearly asked for you, so I'll be expecting good cooking."

Reed grinned. "You'll have it. And when the fresh meat's gone, I make a fine Cheshire Pork Pie from salt pork. I brought pippins and onions aboard for it."

"Sounds like a feast worth waiting for."

Jon went next to the captain's cabin where he and Stockman joined Fisk over a chart of the New England coast. The captain traced the coastline with one finger, marking shoals and the latest British sightings. While they were discussing the latter, Sailing Master Benjamin Lovett stepped inside. "Captain, do you want me in on this?"

"Yes, Lovett," said Fisk. "You can give my lieutenants a better sense of the hazards we'll face along the coast."

Introductions were made, and the older sailing master leaned over the chart, his weathered hands moving with the ease of long habit as he spoke of hidden rocks, fickle tides and sudden squalls. The room filled with the salt-and-tar scent clinging to his coat. His quiet authority drew their attention.

When he'd finished, Fisk gave a satisfied nod. "If we're at full strength by day's end, gentlemen, and all is in readiness, we sail tomorrow."

IN THE HARADEN parlor, Eunice stood in the doorway, rocking Polly in her arms, hoping the baby would finally settle. Silas sat cross-legged by the hearth, his callused fingers working a length of rope. Hannah perched on a small stool beside him, her eyes fixed on the looping and twisting of the strands. The hearth was laid for a fire, but the pleasant evening didn't require one.

Jon was at the wharf again, drilling the crew on the cannon. His talk at supper lately had been all charts, sightings of British ships, and Captain Fisk, sure signs they'd sail soon.

"This here's a sailor's knot, Lass," Silas said, his voice roughened by years of salt air. "Saved me off Jamaica when a storm near tore our ship apart. Loop it like so, strong as your papa's will." His grin softened his weathered face.

Hannah took the rope, brows knitting as she copied the twist. "Did Mama know knots?"

Silas chuckled, helping her with the rope. "Your mama? She'd have tied a prettier knot than me, but her gift

27

was stitchin' and embroidery. Twern't no one like her for such." He guided Hannah's small hands, the rope slipping at first. Hannah's brow furrowed, but she looped it, her fingers steady.

Martha bustled in, her apron smudged from kitchen work, her hazel eyes glinting as she scanned the parlor. "Knots won't bake bread, Silas! Hannah can help me in the kitchen."

"Her papa's going to sea," Silas countered, "and she means to tie him a proper knot before he leaves."

"Ah, well, that's all right then," said the cook. Her crinkled grin belied her grumble, her love for Hannah shining through. Martha headed back to the kitchen mumbling about biscuits in the oven.

Hannah's lips twitched, but her voice trembled when she asked, "Will Papa be safe?"

Silas leaned in, lowering his tone. "Your papa's a fine sailor. On the *Tyrannicide* with Captain Fisk, he'll only get better." He patted her shoulder. "There. Solid as a church rope."

Eunice stepped forward to tuck the now sleeping Polly into her cradle. "A fine knot, Hannah. Your papa will be proud."

Hannah's eyes flickered, a small smile on her lips.

The front door opened and Jon stepped in, his eyes betraying a weariness. Eunice was glad to recognize fatigue and not grief.

"Evening, Mrs. Mason," he said to Eunice. She nodded in reply.

Hannah jumped up and held her work to him. "Papa! See my knot!"

Jon took the knot in his hand and turned it over, nodding. "Good work, Hannah. Silas, you'll make a bos'n's mate of her yet."

"Aye, sir. She has the makin's."

Martha glided into the parlor carrying a plate of fresh-baked biscuits, the scent of the treats making Eunice's mouth water.

Hannah stepped to the plate and took one. "Cracknels!"

Jon shifted his gaze to Eunice. "Cracknels are Hannah's favorite."

Eunice was familiar with the baked treat made with flour, butter, sugar and caraway seeds. As a child, they had been one of her favorite treats, too.

Martha offered her one and she took it, taking a bite. "They are very good, Martha."

The cook smiled and offered Jon some. "Sailors don't eat air, sir. Fill your belly with a few of these fresh from the oven. 'Twill be some time afore supper's ready."

He thanked her and took one from the plate. Heading upstairs, he said over his shoulder, "I'll be down in a bit. I've some papers to read and my chest to pack. We sail tomorrow!"

Martha set the plate of biscuits on the table and shared a look with Silas. "You will take the master to his ship?"

"Aye, we'll need a cart for the chest."

Hannah began to look teary-eyed. Eunice took a seat in a chair facing the child. "Just think, Hannah, by the time your papa returns from his first cruise, Polly may be walking."

Hannah gazed at her younger sister sleeping in her

cradle. "I'll help her learn like big sisters do."

"Won't your papa be proud!" exclaimed Eunice.

Martha arched a brow at Silas. "Meantime, Silas Turner, the child would do better to take up sewin' or cookin' than ropework."

Silas shook his head, a half-smile tugging at his mouth. "You don't mean that, Martha, my sweet."

"None of your nonsense, now," said Martha, turning toward the kitchen. "You talk more than you work."

"Only when the company's worth it," he said with a look that made Martha's cheeks redden.

Eunice winked at Hannah, thinking her charge enjoyed the banter between the old seaman and the cook as much as she did. It had become clear to Eunice that Silas had a fondness for Martha, and the cook tolerated his teasing with only mild protests.

"We are in the very midst of a revolution the most
complete, unexpected and remarkable of any in
the history of nations."

– John Adams 1776

CHAPTER 3

Off the Massachusetts coast, 12 July 1776

FOUR DAYS OUT from Salem, the *Tyrannicide* sliced
through gray swells under a heavy sky, her pine tree flag
snapping in the wind. Spray leapt from her bow, scattering
cold salt water over the quarterdeck where Jon stood,
spyglass trained on the sea ahead.

A pale fleck danced at the horizon. "Sir," he said to
Captain Fisk standing beside him, "a sail."

A heartbeat later came the lookout's shout from the
fighting top. "Sail ho! Dead ahead!"

Shading his eyes, Fisk asked, "What is it?"

The fleck swelled into the sharp lines of a schooner.
Jon steadied the glass. "Eight carriage guns…twelve

swivels. A schooner flying a British ensign. Could be a packet bound for New York. We've the guns to take her."

Fisk took the glass, studied her, and handed it back. "Aye. Let's close in and test her mettle. Packets carry messages, sometimes important ones." Lifting the speaking trumpet from its hook, he shouted, "Beat to quarters!"

The fife sounded and the drum rolled. The ship came alive. Barefoot powder boys dashed to the magazine deep within the ship's hull, as gunners ran out the six-pounders. The smell of salt and tar was overtaken by the sharper tang of slow matches burning.

Jon spotted Johnny Deadman, his face serious beneath his blond locks as he cradled a powder sack for a sweating gunner. His fellow cabin boy, Bobby Grover, passed round shot to the crewman at the next gun.

"Load and prime the cannon!" Jon bellowed.

"Aye!" echoed Stockman from amidships. "Move sharp, lads!"

Bosun Benjamin Moses called up to a tar clinging to the ratlines, "Shorten that sail and make her snug!"

The schooner's bow swung, her swivels flashing. The hiss and whine of shot were followed by splinters exploding from the *Tyrannicide*'s starboard rail. A ball smashed into the galley stores. Staves burst in a spray of oak and coffee beans.

For an instant, through the smoke and chaos, the familiar scent took Jon's mind home, the deep, earthy fragrance of fresh beans as he'd known them in the Cabots' cooperage, stacked in the cool dim light of the storehouse. His hands remembered the ring of the hammer setting hoops.

Then the memory was gone, swept away by the next broadside. "Fire!" roared Fisk.

Seven of the *Tyrannicide*'s six-pounders thundered in unison, the deck trembling beneath Jon's boots. Smoke billowed, choking, as iron smashed into the British schooner's hull.

She fired back. The roar of the broadside split the air, and for Jon the world slowed. The schooner rolled and dipped with deliberate grace, the arcs of smoke curling like lazy ribbons. A cannonball spun end over end through the haze, its black iron gleaming in the sunlight. He noted its path without flinching, his hands steady on the rail. While others shouted and ducked, he found himself unfazed as he measured angles, gauging their next move. In that instant, Jon understood. This was where he was meant to be.

"Hard to starboard!" Fisk ordered. Sailing Master Benjamin Lovett spun the wheel, and the *Tyrannicide* swung to rake the schooner's stern.

"Target her rigging, lads!" Jon called. "Slow her down!"

Round shot tore through the British sails, rigging cascading down in tangles. Jon could now read her name in the swirl of smoke...*Dispatch*. Fitting, he thought grimly, for a packet ship running for New York.

For an hour and a half, the ships traded hammering fire. The *Tyrannicide* shuddered from hits. One man lay dead, ten others wounded. Surgeon Malcom, black brows drawn tight beneath his cocked hat, shouted for men to carry the injured to the orlop deck, where his mates would be working in the cramped, reeking heat.

At last, the *Dispatch*'s guns fell silent and she struck her colors. Cheers erupted from the *Tyrannicide*'s crew. Johnny and Bobby clapped each other on the back, grinning through powder-smudged faces. The captain's cabin boy, Joshua Trask, came to join them in celebration.

"Well done, Haraden," Fisk said, clapping Jon's shoulder. His grin was quick but his brown eyes were hard. "Let's board her."

They crossed over in a small boat with a few armed crewmen to the boarding ladder the captured ship tossed down, the tarred hemp black against the splintered planking.

Jon climbed first, Fisk behind him. The *Dispatch*'s deck was a wreckage of torn lines and shattered spars, the acrid reek of powder thick in the air. Blood smeared the scuppers where bodies had been dragged aside.

The first lieutenant, face blackened with smoke, stepped forward and surrendered his sword, the steel dull with salt spray.

"Your commander?" Fisk asked.

"Captain Gutteridge is dead, sir. The bos'n as well."

"And his papers?" Jon asked.

"Overboard, before we struck. Those were our orders." His voice was firm, but there was raw bitterness in his eyes.

A quick tally showed eight carriage guns, twelve swivels, twenty small arms, sixteen pistols, twenty cutlasses, powder, and shot, everything in good order despite the fight. In addition to the captain and the bos'n who'd been killed, seven crewmen on the *Dispatch* were wounded.

"Return to the *Tyrannicide*," Fisk ordered Jon. "Set a prize crew on her and assess our damage. I'll join you shortly."

Jon appointed Lieutenant Stockman as prize master. He, in turn, selected several crewmembers to go with him. "Take a gunner," said Jon. "You'll be sailing the *Dispatch* into Salem."

"Yes, sir."

Once Stockman and the prize crew were aboard the *Dispatch*, Jon was joined by Fisk on the *Tyrannicide*. "The damage report, Jon?"

"One crewmember dead and ten wounded being tended by the surgeon. The ship has shattered spars, torn sails, a damaged topmast and a hole in the gunwale. I recommend we return to Salem."

The captain gazed around him. "I agree. Still, not bad for our first prize. And we can take the weapons we found aboard the schooner and her cargo of flour and rum. Let Lieutenant Stockman know he's to follow us."

That evening, Joshua Trask, the captain's cabin boy, delivered cod-and-beef stew to the captain's cabin where Fisk dined with Jon, Chaplain Marsh and Surgeon Malcom.

"What is the state of the crew?" asked Fisk.

"The wounded will recover," Malcom reported.

Marsh inclined his head. "I'll conduct services for our dead, and for Captain Gutteridge and the *Dispatch*'s bos'n, if the surviving officers wish it."

"Very good, Chaplain," said the captain. "We can offer."

Salem Harbor, 16 July 1776

THE *TYRANNICIDE* ROUNDED Marblehead Neck under shortened sail, her pine tree flag lifting in the light morning wind. Ahead lay Salem's wharves bristling with masts and rigging. From the quarterdeck, Jon saw gulls wheeling, dockhands rolling casks, and the fishwives' stalls glittering with the morning catch.

The peal of the bells from the Old North Church rolled across the water, not the slow toll for a funeral, but a quick, jubilant clamoring.

"They've heard," Captain Fisk murmured, a wry smile tugging at his mouth. "Word of the *Dispatch*'s capture has run ahead of us."

Jon thought it strange. They'd made all speed from far out in the Atlantic where they'd met the *Dispatch*, yet somehow news had beaten them home. Still, in a harbor town, word could travel on the wind.

The captured schooner, under Lieutenant Stockman's command, had followed them in, her patched rig drawing stares and pointed fingers from the crowd. Murmurs swelled into cheers, hats raised and waved.

As the *Tyrannicide* eased alongside Derby Wharf where the state's ships docked, lines were tossed ashore and caught by waiting dockhands. The crowd pressed close to the edge of the planks, waving hats and shawls, the hum of voices rising to a roar.

Jon followed Fisk down the gangplank into the crush, the smell of tar, salt, and drying nets mingling with the warm scents of bread and molasses from the market. Someone clapped Jon on the back. Another called out,

"Well done, lads!"

"Haraden!" A familiar voice cut through the noise. Jon turned to see Silas, grinning. "Have you heard the news, sir? We're free men now, right as a fair wind!"

"What's that?" Jon asked, though the glint in Silas' eyes and the shouts all around hinted at the answer.

Silas thrust a folded sheet of the *American Gazette* into Jon's hands. The bold heading leapt out: *In Congress, July 4, 1776*. Beneath it ran the words of the *Declaration*, printed in tight columns.

"They read it aloud not an hour ago in Town House Square," Silas said. "Straight from Philadelphia! No more petitions, sir. We've declared our independence!"

Jon's eyes traveled over the page as the breeze tugged at its edges. Men he had fought beside, men he had buried, seemed to stand with him in that moment. The words struck like the crack of a broadside. *...that these united Colonies are, and of Right ought to be, Free and Independent States.* He felt the familiar salt sting at the corners of his eyes, though whether from wind or pride, he could not say.

"Mr. Haraden!" The call was lighter, warm. Eunice Mason came through the crowd, her bonnet ribbons fluttering, her eyes alight.

Hannah was gripping her right hand. "Papa!" she shouted, waving.

The governess stopped just short of him, smiling openly. "We saw your ship from the upper windows. Martha says the whole town's speaking of your victory, only days after you sailed!"

Jon bent to hug his daughter.

"We prayed for you, Papa!"

He smiled at Hannah, then at Eunice. Behind them stood Silas with a pleased expression. "Well, your prayers were answered. We took a British packet bound for New York. She'll serve the cause better here than in British hands."

Silas glanced toward the *Dispatch* riding at anchor giving her the quick survey of a sailor measuring a ship's worth. Then he looked back to Jon. "Aye, sir, and she'll fly better colors for us than she ever did for King George."

"Just think," said Mrs. Mason, "you brought her in on the very day we learned our country is free. Two victories, Lieutenant."

"One for Salem, perhaps," Jon said quietly. "The other belongs to us all."

"That's the ship you captured?" asked Hannah, pointing to the damaged schooner.

"Aye," said Jon. "Like the *Tyrannicide*, she's a bit worse for the battle."

"Is that why you're here?" asked Mrs. Mason.

"Yes, we must make repairs before our next cruise." The words had barely left his mouth when, further up the wharf, Captain Fisk's voice rang out, "Haraden! Report!"

Jon folded the newspaper with care and tucked it into his coat. "Until later, Mrs. Mason, Hannah, Silas."

The governess nodded, her smile lingering.

Hannah waved. "Till later, Papa!"

Past the cheering townsfolk, beyond the smell of tar, salt, and the fish market's drying nets, Town House Square lay up the hill. Jon tried to imagine that morning when a voice rang out over the cobbles, reading the

Declaration of Independence to the gathered citizens of Salem. And now, with the prize ship safely anchored and the war still ahead, Jon felt, for the first time, the truth of it. They were no longer British subjects, but a free people with their own country.

THE SCENT OF roasting chicken met Eunice as she came down the stairs and went into the parlor. Hannah was perched on a stool beside Silas, who sat on the hearth rug, showing her a new knot she had yet to try.

"A reef knot this time, Miss Hannah," he said, the rope moving deftly through his callused hands. "Strong as they come. Holds when the wind howls and comes free when you ask it."

Martha appeared in the doorway, her cheeks dusted with flour. "Strong knots don't put food on the table, Silas Turner."

Silas grinned without looking up. "Aye, but they might keep the table from driftin' off in a gale." Eunice failed to stifle a chuckle as she caught an appreciative tilt of Silas' head toward the kitchen. "That chicken you're cookin' smells mighty good, Martha."

Eunice shook her head, smiling despite herself. This back-and-forth had become part of the household's music. She glanced toward the stairs. She had heard Mr. Haraden come in and go up to change out of his sea-stained coat. Eunice hoped he returned before Martha's chicken cooled.

Minutes later, he descended the stairs as if summoned. Hannah was on him at once. "Papa! Silas showed me a new knot."

"Then you'll have to show me after supper," Jon said, giving her a brief hug before offering a nod to Eunice. "I'm starving." Then to Eunice, "Shall we?"

In the dining room, Martha brought in the roast chicken on a large platter, the golden skin gleaming in the candlelight. "She's a fat hen cooked to perfection if I do say so myself." Turning to reach for two bowls, she placed them on the table, adding with quiet pride, "The peas and carrots are from my garden, and there's potatoes, too."

"All looks wonderful, Martha," said Eunice as she took her place across from Hannah. Mr. Haraden sat at the head of the table and proceeded to carve the bird with an ease that spoke of long practice. His demeanor had changed since his last meal at this table, a change she'd first noticed on the wharf when the *Tyrannicide* arrived. There was a steadiness about him now, as though he was at ease with himself and his chosen path.

Partway through the meal, the wet nurse slipped in with Polly, drowsy and smelling of warm milk. She laid the baby gently in Jon's arms. He looked down at his youngest daughter, his expression softening, and Eunice felt something ease in her own chest. He brushed his hand over the tufts of blonde hair on Polly's head before kissing her cheek and handing her back with a quiet word of thanks.

The wet nurse placed the sated baby in her cradle and bid the family a good evening.

Martha came in to see how the meal was going. Hands on hips, she said, "Well, what's the verdict?"

"Everything is delicious, Martha," said Eunice.

"I fed Silas some from a second chicken," said Martha,

"and he seemed to like it."

"Silas would like anything you cooked," said Mr. Haraden, "but in truth, the meal is superb. You've outdone yourself."

Martha smiled. Her love for the family and pride in what she could do for them was there in her eyes. She returned to the kitchen and brought back the Indian pudding. Eunice found the earthy smell of cornmeal mixed with molasses, cinnamon and ginger to be comforting. "That looks tasty," she told Martha, who set the large dish on the table.

"It does, indeed," said Jon, dishing out some for his daughter.

Hannah leaned forward eagerly. "Papa, tell us what you're fixing on the *Tyrannicide* to sail again. Silas told me some but I want you to tell me."

Jon set down his spoon and licked his lips. "A sprung plank near the bow, new spars and rigging aloft, and a topmast for the main. Beyond that, there's a hole in the hull near the gunwale and the entire deck needs to be cleaned. We'll be in port for several days."

Eunice nodded, thinking of the list against the backdrop of the war. "Enough time for Hannah to learn another knot," she said with amusement.

Jon smiled faintly. "One I will be happy to see," he said to his daughter. "And more meals like this one before we're off again."

When the dishes were cleared, Eunice lingered a moment, candlelight glancing off the silver. Through the clatter from the kitchen and the sound of Hannah chattering to Martha, her thoughts returned to the look in

Jon's eyes, that quiet confidence she had not seen before. Whatever had happened at sea had tempered, not hardened him. She knew the shape of grief well enough to see when something stronger had taken root alongside it, and she found herself silently speaking her gratitude to God.

She asked him about the crew and was delighted to hear of the cabin boys. "So many!"

"Aye, yet they all seem to be well-occupied. There's much to do with seventy-five crew and officers. I was able to help a lad, Johnny Deadman, the son of one of my wife's distant relatives gain one of the cabin boy positions."

Eunice could see he was pleased. "It must have felt good to help him," she said.

"It surely did, and if he does well, he'll have a life at sea if he wants one."

When they moved back to the parlor after supper, Martha was already there with her knitting, spectacles perched low on her nose. Silas lounged in the corner chair, drinking coffee while stretching one leg gingerly before him. He had told Eunice the old injury made itself known when the weather changed.

"You missed a fine puddin', Silas," Martha said without looking up. "Not that you deserve any, sittin' idle while others work, but I left some for you in the kitchen."

Silas grinned at her over the top of his mug. "Idle? I've been hard at it all evenin', keepin' your seat warm for you. It's not my fault you chose another chair."

"Hmph. I'll thank you not to flatten it."

Hannah giggled, and even Mr. Haraden's mouth

twitched at the corner as he looked up from his well-thumbed copy of *The Practical Navigator*, a book Eunice had seen left on the small table near his chair.

"The pudding is quite good, Silas," Eunice encouraged. "You might want to try it."

"I just might." Silas leaned forward, resting his forearms on his knees. "I hear you've a sprung plank, sir. Best let me watch the shipwrights, to make sure they're not skimpin' on the oakum."

"Watch them?" Martha snorted. "More like get in their way and talk them half to death."

"Aye," Silas said, utterly unoffended, "but I'll do it with style. Can't have the *Tyrannicide* lookin' shabby in port."

"No," said Mr. Haraden with a smile, "we can't have that."

Inwardly, Eunice smiled, too, noting the fondness under their bickering. In a house that had known too much loss, such scraps of humor felt to her like a kind of ballast, keeping them steady for whatever lay ahead.

THE NEXT MORNING Eunice rose early, the light from the summer sun spilling across the floorboards before the church bell struck six. By the time she and Hannah left for the harbor with Silas, Mr. Haraden had departed for the *Tyrannicide*, Martha was busy in the kitchen, and Polly was in the wet nurse's care.

They arrived to find the tide high and the wharves alive with shouts, hammering, and the cry of gulls overhead.

The *Tyrannicide* still lay alongside Derby Wharf, her pine tree flag stirring in the light breeze, her sails furled. Men swarmed her deck and rigging, voices overlapping as they hauled lines and lowered spars. The topmast had already been removed. The smell of fresh-cut timber mixed with tar and the sharper scent of oakum filled the air.

As they drew closer, Eunice's eyes fixed on a ragged hole above the waterline near the gunwale, the planking bent inward and splintered like broken stakes, as if something had punched through from the sea. Sunlight glinted off damp wood inside the gap. She felt an involuntary shiver, thinking of shot slamming into the ship while Captain Fisk and Lieutenant Haraden stood aboard.

"That'll be patched today," Silas said at her elbow, leaning on his cane. "A six-pounder did that, near took the gun crew with it I expect. Lucky shot for the king's man, but not lucky enough. She'll be sealed like a ship's rum jar before the tide's out."

Hannah's hand tightened in Eunice's. "Was Papa there when it happened?"

"Aye, Miss Hannah," Silas said, "but your papa's quicker than splinters, and twice as hard to knock down. 'Sides, he was likely on the quarterdeck."

From where Eunice stood, she could see Mr. Haraden near the bow, coat off, sleeves rolled, speaking with a shipwright whose face was browned like old leather. He gestured toward the forward planking, the movement decisive. The shipwright nodded once, then turned to bellow an order.

"That's the sprung plank he spoke of," Silas added.

"Takes a man who knows his ship to spot it before she lets you know herself, usually in the middle of a blow."

Mr. Haraden caught sight of them then and came down the gangplank, the smell of pine tar clinging to him as he approached. "Up early?" he asked, a smile touching his mouth.

"We thought we'd see the work beginning," Eunice said. "And perhaps walk to market after."

"You'll find it busy," Jon said, glancing toward the cluster of ships unloading cargo farther down.

From behind her, Silas asked, "Has the prize court convened yet?"

"Soon," said Mr. Haraden. "Langdon will want every detail of the *Dispatch's* capture."

Eunice inclined her head. "Will you be testifying?"

"Perhaps. The captain has already written a report of the capture. Our first priority is to get the *Tyrannicide* ready to sail."

Silas said, "Martha told me should you come home with tar on your trousers, sir, you'll answer to her."

"I imagine I will," he said, looking at his trousers blackened in places with soot. Eunice saw a glimmer of amusement in his eyes before he turned back toward the *Tyrannicide*.

"Will you be home for supper, Papa?" Hannah inquired.

"I will. You can tell Martha I look forward to another great meal. Meantime, the ship's carpenter is waiting, and I must not delay him if we're to go to sea soon. The war will not pause for us." He gave them a brief nod as he turned back toward the gangplank.

Eunice and Hannah left Derby Wharf and followed Silas toward the market square. It was no formal hall, but a patchwork of stalls and carts set out along the open street near the Custom House, with the smell of the docks mingling with wood smoke from cookfires and the tang of freshly cut herbs.

Women in homespun gowns bargained with fishermen in tarred jackets, their hands still smelling of the sea. A boy darted past with a basket of crabs, the shells clacking together like castanets. Beside the fishmongers, a farmer she recognized from Danvers had laid out baskets of green peas, carrots with their feathery tops, and heads of cabbage pale as candlewax. "Morning," Eunice said to him.

"Mrs. Mason," he replied, dipping his hat.

Hannah's eyes grew wide at the sight of a fisherman lifting a huge silver cod from his tub, the scales flashing like coins in the sun. "For the kitchen?" Hannah asked, looking up at Eunice.

Eunice smiled. "For Martha." She handed the man a shilling, dear enough, but worth it for so large and fresh a catch. He wrapped the fish in clean linen and set it in her basket atop a loaf of rye bread from a nearby baker's stall.

Silas lingered near a merchant selling small kegs of molasses, running his hand over the smooth staves as if judging the workmanship. "You keep your barrels tight and your door hinges tighter," he told the merchant with a wink, "or you'll be patchin' kegs and cleaning molasses off the street before winter's through."

Hannah watched the two men, then turned to Eunice. "Papa knows barrels. Silas, too."

Silas glanced at Eunice. "Martha would put some of this to good use."

Eunice nodded. "For the gingerbread she's been wanting to make." She passed over a few coins to the merchant for a small keg of molasses. The merchant's helper hoisted it into the basket beside the cod. The mingled scents of sea-brine, fresh bread, and the dark sweetness of molasses rose to meet her.

"Martha will be happy," said Hannah.

"Here," said Silas. "That basket's heavy by now. I'll carry it."

"You're a true gentleman," said Eunice, handing him the now full basket.

As they turned for home, the church bell began its slow toll for the hour. The sound carried above the gulls' cries, a reminder that the day of prayer and fasting called for by the House of Representatives was approaching. Would Mr. Haraden be at sea then? She tightened her hand on Hannah's, thinking of the *Tyrannicide* riding the ocean's swells toward danger. Somewhere beyond that horizon, war was waiting. She wondered if the sea felt as wide to him as it did to those left ashore.

"Courage, then, my countrymen, our contest is not only whether we ourselves shall be free, but whether there shall be left to mankind an asylum on earth for civil and religious liberty."

– Samuel Adams 1776

CHAPTER 4

Haraden house, Salem, 31 July 1776

THE DUCK HAD been stewing since early afternoon, the rich scent of claret wine, herbs, and bone broth filling the kitchen and drifting into the dining room and beyond.

The wonderful smells had drawn Eunice to inquire of the cook. "Shall I call Mr. Haraden and Hannah to supper?"

"Aye, 'tis time if they want it hot. His last meal before sailin' ought to be one he'll remember."

"What about Polly?" asked Eunice. The baby was with the wet nurse and due to return.

"She'll be here any moment. Only a month until the

wee lass is weaned. I've already found my old receipts for gruel and pottage." Martha's eyes twinkled. "Truth be told, if she's like Hannah, the child will likely prefer gingerbread."

"Anyone would," said Eunice, going back to the parlor to announce, "Martha says supper is ready."

"Good," said Mr. Haraden, closing his book and rising from his chair. "The smells coming from there have been tormenting me since she started cooking."

Hannah looked up from the knot Silas was showing her.

"You go, Lass," Silas said. "We'll finish it after supper."

Filing into the dining room, Mr. Haraden took his place at the head of the table. Hannah and Eunice sat in their usual places across from one another.

With a flourish, Martha brought in the stewed duck, the skin browned to a deep mahogany and the meat so tender it threatened to part from the bone. Following the duck, the cook set down a bowl of mashed potatoes with a glossy gravy thickened from the pan drippings, and a platter of asparagus fresh from the garden, still bright and green from its brief boiling.

"Mind you don't get that gravy on my tablecloth," Martha teased, arching a brow at Hannah as she handed Mr. Haraden the serving ladle. "It's the last clean one 'til Monday wash."

"We'll all be careful," said Mr. Haraden with a wink at his eldest daughter.

Martha returned to the kitchen as Eunice poured Mr. Haraden and herself glasses of claret, and Hannah watered cider. Mr. Haraden lifted a plate and ladled out portions.

Finally, he served himself.

The first mouthful of duck melted against Eunice's tongue, savory with wine and herbs, underpinned by the richness of the broth. The potatoes were buttery smooth, the gravy deep with the essence of the roasting pan. "This food is wonderful, Martha," Eunice said loud enough for the cook to hear in the kitchen.

Martha reappeared, hands planted on her hips, a confident tilt to her chin. "And I'll warrant you'll not taste better in Boston or the West Indies, so mind you remember it, sir, when the ship's cook serves you salt pork."

Mr. Haraden's mouth quirked. "I expect I'll be dreaming of your duck when walking the deck at night."

Hannah giggled into her cup, glancing between them as if she'd just witnessed a private contest of wits.

Eunice smiled into her claret, struck by the quiet ease between them, the rhythm of a household already formed around her presence in ways she had never anticipated. "Are all the repairs completed on the *Tyrannicide*?" she asked.

"Aye," said Mr. Haraden, "and the crew's been returning over the week."

Hannah's eyes lit. "What about the cabin boys? Mrs. Mason said some are near my age."

"Most of the lads signed for ninety days. I expect many have renewed. The *Tyrannicide* is a good place for them to learn."

Eunice set down her fork. "While you are at sea, Hannah and I plan to go with my mother to East Church for the day of prayer and fasting on the fifth. We'll pray for your safe return."

"I'll say a prayer, too," Hannah said.

Eunice smiled at her charge. "I think God would like that very much."

When the duck was gone and plates cleared, Martha returned with a plate of dark, moist gingerbread, the crust still faintly crisp from the oven. The warm scents of ginger and spice curled into the room.

"The molasses you brought from market is baked right in," she told Eunice and Hannah with pride.

Mr. Haraden's smile deepened as he took a bite. "If this is how you see me off, I'll be counting the days until I'm back."

The summer evening brought a soft light through the windows as they adjourned to the parlor where Mr. Haraden poured them a glass of sherry. Outside, the waterfront waited for the next tide.

Hannah resumed her lesson in knots with Silas, who sat opposite, a length of rope coiled in his hands.

"Now," he said, "where were we? Ah. Half hitch, snug it tight. A loose knot's no better than a hole in your shoe."

Hannah's tongue peeked from the corner of her mouth as she worked. "Like this?"

"Near enough to hold a cow, or your papa's ship, if you keep at it," Silas chuckled.

From the doorway, Martha called, "Mind you tie that knot tight, Hannah. Your papa's bound to need every line holdin' fast."

Silas gave a grunt of approval. "A knot worth trustin' is a knot worth takin' your time on."

Hannah's fingers moved more carefully over the rope. "Then I'll make one Papa can trust."

Mr. Haraden leaned forward, setting down his glass. "Mind your tuck there, Hannah," he said, pointing. "If the line slips, you'll lose the whole knot." His tone was mild, but his eyes sharp, as Eunice imagined they would be on deck.

Silas gave a grunt of approval. "Aye, that's a captain speakin'."

Martha's mouth curved in a small, satisfied smile as she vanished back toward the kitchen, leaving the scent of gingerbread in her wake.

From the corner of the parlor, Eunice shared a glance with Mr. Haraden. They had just witnessed an old sailor passing down his craft to a girl who, in her way, was as much part of the *Tyrannicide*'s crew as any man aboard.

On the Tyrannicide at sea, 5 August 1776

MORNING SUNLIGHT GLINTED off the *Tyrannicide*'s damp rigging, still wet from the sea spray. Jon watched the waters around the ship, calm as glass. From the fo'c'sle came the muted rasp of holystones, the brittle sandstone used to scrub the deck, mingled with the creak of blocks hoisting and adjusting canvas.

Johnny Deadman, barefoot and quick as a cat, picked his way toward the quarterdeck with a steaming tin mug. "Your coffee, sir," he said, holding it out with a grin. "Captain says he'll be up in a minute."

Jon took the mug, warm in his hands, and inhaled the bitter steam. "You'll make a sailor yet, Johnny, if you don't spill it."

"Not a drop, sir," Johnny declared, swiping his sleeve across his nose.

As the *Tyrannicide* cruised between Cape Sable and Nantucket off the Massachusetts coast, the early morning passed uneventfully with routine sail trimming, the occasional course correction, and a distant school of porpoises breaking the surface like skipping stones.

From the foretop, the lookout's voice rang sharp across the water.

"Sail ho!"

Jon's head snapped up. "Where away?"

"Two points off the larboard bow, sir. Brig-rigged!"

The *Tyrannicide* came alive, Jon shouting orders. Men swarmed aloft to loosen canvas, the helmsman brought her around, and the deck tilted underfoot as the wind filled the sails.

Within the hour, the brig lay dead ahead. Through his glass, Jon spotted her crew scattering as the *Tyrannicide* ran out her guns. Two warning shots and a burst of boarding pikes later, the British brig *St. John* was theirs, her cargo of flour, rum and naval stores a welcome prize.

Captain Fisk had come to the quarterdeck and, upon his order, Jon sent Lieutenant Stockman aboard the *St. John* with a prize crew.

As the boarding party reached the *St. John*, the lookout's cry came again. Another sail, this time a trim schooner, the *Three Brothers*. From what Jon could see through his spyglass, the schooner was straining under every stitch of canvas to escape. "This one will not yield easily," he said to Fisk.

"I'll let you take her," said Fisk. "Good practice."

Jon watched as the schooner ran hard before the wind, every sail straining. "Fire the first bow chaser!" he ordered.

The schooner answered the *Tyrannicide*'s first bow gun with a swivel blast that shattered the sloop's rail. Splinters flew like darts. Men ducked, and one tar cried out clutching his cheek.

"Run out the starboard battery!" Jon bellowed. "Give her the next one amidships!"

The *Tyrannicide*'s deck thundered with the recoil of her guns. The schooner lurched, wood flying from her bulwark, but she swung to return fire.

For twenty minutes the two ships traded shots, smoke and flame writhing in the breeze, the sea alive with round shot skipping across its surface. Twice the *Tyrannicide*'s rigging shivered under hits aloft. A halyard parted with a snap and a yard came down with a crash, narrowly missing the gun crew below.

Still, Jon ordered the crew to press closer to the British ship. With the breeze freshening in their favor, the *Tyrannicide* ranged up across her stern and loosed a raking broadside. That settled her. The schooner's colors dropped to the deck in surrender.

Jon wiped sweat and powder grit from his brow, then sent Benjamin Moses with a prize crew to take her in.

"Good capture," said Fisk with a grin.

But the day was not yet done. By mid-afternoon, another merchantman loomed, a fat catch. She struck her colors without a shot, and Jon ordered John Bray forward with a third prize crew.

The prize had barely hove to when the cry from the

foretop came sharp and thin against the wind. "Frigate to windward!"

Jon swung round. A great hull bore down, sails taut, gunports bristling black. The Royal Navy had arrived.

"Abandon the prize!" Jon shouted, the order echoed at once by Fisk. Bray and his men pulled back in haste, the merchantman left wallowing.

The frigate's bow chasers opened fire, balls howling overhead. One smashed into the quarter, showering the deck with splinters. A gunner fell screaming, his leg mangled, while another shot tore through the shrouds, blocks and rigging crashing down. For a breathless instant the mainmast trembled, but held.

"All hands to stations!" Jon roared. "Stand by to wear ship!"

The *Tyrannicide* leapt as her sails filled, the helm hard over. Gun crews ducked as the enemy's fire raked the water, geysers of spray leaping high. Each boom of the frigate's guns seemed nearer, each impact shuddering through the *Tyrannicide*'s planks.

"Bear away for the shoals!" Fisk snapped.

Jon's jaw clenched. They were running for their lives, and all depended on reaching shallower water where the frigate dared not follow. The enemy closed, minute by minute, the thunder of her bow chasers like a storm breaking on their heels.

Another crash aft, followed by smoke, blood, the cry of a wounded seaman. Still the *Tyrannicide* flew on.

At last, the sound of the frigate's guns thinned, the shots falling short. With one final boom, the Royal Navy ship fell away, unwilling to hazard the shoals.

Jon drew a ragged breath, scanning the deck. Blood on the planks, scars in the timbers. But her mast still stood. Two prizes safe, headed for Salem, one lost, and the *Tyrannicide* herself alive to fight another day.

On the quarterdeck Fisk exhaled, his voice rough. "That was a narrow scrape."

Jon's eyes stayed on the horizon, the salt wind whipping his face. "Narrower than I care to see again, sir."

Salem, Massachusetts, 5 August 1776

THE BELLS OF the East Church tolled slow and solemn, their iron voices rolling over the rooftops toward the harbor. Eunice walked with her mother and Hannah through the summer heat, their steps quiet on the worn brick of the path to the church's door.

Inside, the air was still and heavy with the mingled scents of pine pews, beeswax, and the faint scent of salt carried in on the breeze. Light spilled through the tall windows, falling across the congregation in pale stripes. The air held the mingled scents of summer dust and the waterfront a few streets away.

Eunice sat near her mother, Hannah between them, her small hands folded solemnly in her lap. Above the pulpit, the high, white-painted sounding board caught Reverend Diman's voice and sent it ringing through the congregation, as he read from the proclamation calling for a day of prayer and fasting.

"We are gathered," he intoned, "to humble ourselves before the Lord, to seek His mercy on our new country, our new state, and to ask Him to preserve this land and those who fight for her liberty…"

Her father's voice was grave, speaking of the dangers at sea, the hardships endured, and the need for divine protection over "our brave mariners, who hazard all in the cause of liberty."

Somewhere beyond the horizon, Mr. Haraden was under sail, perhaps in pursuit, perhaps being pursued. Without warning, a shiver prickled at the base of Eunice's neck, as if a shadow had passed over her spirit. She gripped Hannah's hand a little tighter. "We must pray for your papa."

Hannah bowed her head, her lips moving with a prayer, her brow furrowed in earnest concentration. Eunice glanced down at her young charge and felt a swell of pride. But even as she bowed her own head to pray, her thoughts wandered to the sea. Her father's words were meant for all sailors, yet in her mind they wrapped themselves around one man's name. She tried to push away the flicker of unease, the image of canvas straining before the wind, of gun smoke drifting over dark water, but it settled in her like a shadow.

She prayed all the harder, for his safety, asking God to bring his ship home.

When the congregation rose to sing, the voices were strong and sure, yet in Eunice's mind they were undercut by the echo of distant thunder, or was it the boom of a ship's broadside imagined across the miles?

As they left the church, a gull's cry pierced the stillness, faint but clear. Eunice saw the bird wheel inland, fighting the wind as if fleeing some unseen storm.

In the shallows off the coast, 6 August 1776

JON'S COAT WAS streaked with soot, his hands blackened where the gun crews' smoke had found him. His eyes smarted, and the faint burn of powder hung on his clothes, a reminder that they'd been too close to the British guns.

The *Tyrannicide* had clung to the safety of the shallows until the frigate was long gone, her deeper draft keeping her from the chase. Only then did Captain Fisk order the sails eased and the wounded tended.

They were bruised and splinter-cut, but no lives had been lost. Her mast still stood, though a shot had torn through the quarter and left the deck scarred. Jon felt the ache in his jaw ease a little. They had escaped, but only just.

By the time they made their slow turn homeward, the two captured prizes, the *St. John* and *Three Brothers*, were long gone ahead, bound for Salem. Their arrival would spread the news of the *Tyrannicide's* victories through the streets, sending spirits soaring and purses ringing in anticipation of the prize court's ruling.

What Salem would not know, not until the *Tyrannicide* limped in days later under patched canvas, was the rest of the story: how a third prize had been in their grasp, and how the pursuit of a British frigate had forced them to cut her loose and run for their lives.

Salem Harbor, mid-August 1776

EUNICE STOOD AMONG the knot of townsfolk gathered on Derby Wharf, the summer air thick with the mingled scents of tar, seaweed, and the salt of low tide. The water glittered under a high sun as she shaded her eyes searching the harbor until a ripple of excitement ran through the crowd.

"There she is!" someone cried, pointing.

Out beyond the anchorage, a single-masted sloop crept in under patched canvas, her lines still proud but her rigging streaked with soot. Even from shore, Eunice could see the scars, a jagged splintering at her quarter, smoke-dark smudges along her rail.

The *Tyrannicide*.

As she drew nearer, the crew came into view, lean, salt-stained men moving with the weary precision of those who had faced the enemy at sea. And there, at the rail, was Jonathan Haraden. Whole, thank God, but his coat was streaked with soot and salt, the cuffs frayed where powder burns had scorched the cloth.

The wind lifted strands of his sun-streaked brown hair from its queue, and for a moment, as they drifted free, he looked straight toward shore, toward her, though she knew he could not possibly pick her out among the press of onlookers.

A flood of relief washed through her, chasing the tight knot that had lived in her chest since the bells rang on the day of prayer. Yet the sight of him, so near, marked by the smoke and fire of battle, yet unscathed, left her throat dry. This was the cost of the victories Salem had already been cheering for days. This was what her seamen risked for liberty.

The London Coffeehouse, 15 Central Street, Salem, mid-September 1776

JON STEPPED FROM the mild afternoon into the London Coffeehouse, thick with pipe smoke and the mingled scents of coffee, rum, and brine. A favorite haunt of merchants and seamen, the coffeehouse was also the meeting place of the Salem chapter of the Sons of Liberty.

Doors stood propped open to the street. Light slanted across tables crowded with charts, broadsides and mugs. His gaze caught on a Boston broadside tacked to the wall lamenting British victories in New York. The lines told of General Howe's rout on Long Island and Washington's evacuation of the city. A sober defeat.

Turning from the broadside, he scanned the crowd, spotting Fisk, Stockman and Benjamin Moses sitting at a corner table with mugs and pewter cups scattered before them. Fisk waved Jon over. "You're just in time, Haraden, to hear my argument for converting our sloop to a brigantine."

Jon took the empty chair. A cup of coffee slid to his hand. "This should be interesting," he said, as he took a drink of the dark, bitter brew.

"With a brigantine rig, square on the foremast, fore and aft on the main," said Fisk, rapping his knuckles on the wood, "she'll carry more canvas and give us more combinations of sail. For a West Indies run, that square sail is worth gold. She'll handle better off the wind, ride steadier in a seaway, and the pull will be shared between both masts instead of all the strain on one."

Stockman frowned into his cup. "More sail aloft means more work aloft. And square sails require different skills. We'll need extra topmen to make and shorten canvas. Seventy-five hands are stretched thin as it is once prize crews are off."

Moses leaned in, eyes bright. "Just a few sharp lads who can climb fast are all that is required. She'll be swifter and more easily maneuvered as a brigantine. She'll hold her course, even in rough seas, so the gunners can stay at their pieces. And with square canvas to drive her, we choose the range, not the king's cruisers."

Jon ran a thumb along the rim of his cup. "Two masts make her quicker to heave to and better to claw off a lee shore. Close-hauled she won't outpoint a fine schooner, but with the wind behind her, she'll all but run away from the slower ships. In the trade winds, that speed is what counts. The West Indies won't feel half so far once she's re-rigged." He glanced up. "And the next frigate that sights us may think twice about the chase."

A chair scraped nearby. Elias Hasket Derby, broad-shouldered, auburn-haired, in a brown coat, turned toward them. "You speak sense, Captain Fisk, and you, Lieutenant Haraden. A brigantine brings her prizes home safer. More sail to run when the king's cruisers prowl, and space enough in her hold for what she seizes, which is important to us merchants."

Across from him, William Gray, younger and keen-eyed, lifted his chin. "Each lawful capture fattens Salem's purse and starves the enemy. Make the change quickly so both commerce and Congress can profit."

"Not commerce enough if New York's lost," someone muttered at a neighboring table, and a hush fell.

Samuel Ropes, nineteen, a bundle of papers under his arm, hovered at the edge of their circle. "Beg pardon, sirs. Dispatch out of Boston says Howe's troops landed at Kips Bay. General Washington quit the city and fell back to Harlem Heights. They say our men gave a smart account of themselves there, but the line won't hold forever."

Derby gave the youth a patient look. "Your father sends you to listen, does he, Lad?"

Samuel colored but kept his chin up. "Our business Page & Ropes would rather be early than surprised, sir."

A ripple of laughter, kindly enough, went round the table.

Fisk raised his cup. "Let New York fall if it must. At sea, we'll make them pay. A brigantine *Tyrannicide* will do her part, I promise you that. We'll fetch cargo that will bring a smile to General Washington's face."

Moses and Stockman lifted their cups. Jon followed, though his thoughts had already slipped beyond the smoke and talk to a stripped hull that would soon wear two masts, and to a quiet parlor where he'd left a little girl bent over her letters with a governess whose quiet strength graced his home.

SEPTEMBER LIGHT SLANTED pale and thin through the parlor windows, pooling on the table where Eunice sat with Hannah bent over her copybook. The fire on the hearth crackled softly, taking the edge off the chill that seeped in from the waterfront as the afternoon length-ened.

Polly sat on a blanket on the floor, playing with an old pot and wooden spoon, her blue eyes alight with the noise she was making.

Hannah traced her letters, her tongue caught between her teeth in concentration. Eight years old as of the first of the month, she wore the blue ribbon Eunice had given her for her birthday, tied in her golden hair. The ribbon had slipped loose as she leaned forward, brushing against her cheek until she tucked it back with an impatient hand. She wore her mother's locket still, and the two tokens, ribbon and locket, seemed to tether her between past and present.

The room was quiet save for Polly's cheerful banging and the faint scratch of Hannah's quill. Outside, the wind off the water carried the distant creak of rigging and the call of gulls, but here, in the parlor, there was only the fragile rhythm of a household that had found its balance again.

"Make the loop higher," Eunice said, her hand guiding Hannah's quill over the tall stroke of the h. "There, now try it again without me."

Hannah carefully shaped the letter, then dipped the quill before scratching the next word. Beside her lay a slate with ciphering problems, a worn Bible, and a dog-eared primer from their earlier lessons.

"Here," said Eunice. "Take a look at this. It's a note your papa wrote to Martha. He has beautiful script, don't you think? See how his capital A curls like a wave, and how the tall strokes lean just so?" Eunice tapped the page with her finger. "He writes as steady as he sails, never wandering from the line. You could not want a more perfect model."

Hannah studied her father's handwriting and sighed. "Even his numbers are perfect."

Eunice laughed softly. "And so will yours be. Now, let's try a different subject." Eunice had discovered the girl had a quick mind and did best when the lessons moved often from one subject to another. "Read me the verse you copied yesterday," Eunice prompted, and Hannah obeyed, her small voice sounding out the words from the Gospel of Matthew.

The front door opened and closed with a thump, admitting a gust of salt air and the scent of coffee. Mr. Haraden stepped inside, brushing his coat. Strands of his hair had pulled free of his queue to lay on his shoulder.

"Any news?" asked Eunice.

"It's been decided. The *Tyrannicide*'s to become a brigantine with two masts and more sail."

Hannah's eyes widened. "Two masts! Then she'll be twice as fast?"

Mr. Haraden shared a look with Eunice at his daughter's words, then crouched beside Hannah, smiling at the earnestness in her face. "Not twice as fast, sweetheart. But steadier, stronger. She'll carry more canvas and hold her course better. A ship with two legs walks steadier than one."

She nodded, then grinned holding up her writing. "Look, Papa, I can write your name."

As Mr. Haraden bent over Hannah's copybook, he

smiled. "Well done. Stay at it, and you'll be keeping my logbook before long."

"Your handwriting is so beautiful," said Eunice to Mr. Haraden, "I think a page or two from your logbook would greatly assist Hannah's lessons. I only had your note to Martha regarding the household to use as an example."

"Well, I thank you for the compliment," said Hannah's father. "Old Cabot insisted all who worked at the cooperage kept perfect letters. I'll see if I can dig up some examples of my writing for you. It will give Hannah a model to practice when I'm away on a long voyage. Fisk is thinking of the West Indies once the *Tyrannicide* is out of the shipyard."

As he continued to engage with Hannah, Eunice watched them, her gaze warm though shadowed with the knowledge of what a "long voyage" meant. The Haraden home, with its crackling fire, shared meals and humor, seemed a fragile defense against the world waiting beyond the harbor. A world at war. Yet like the even strokes in his handwriting, she let herself believe their home was a strong enough bulwark against the tide of war.

"We fight not to enslave, but to set a country free, and to make room upon the earth for honest men to live in."
– Thomas Paine 1777

CHAPTER 5

Becket's Yard, Salem, late October 1776

THE AUTUMN WIND off the harbor carried the smell of salt as Jon strode the length of Becket's Yard. Autumn leaves skittered orange and gold across the ground. All around him, shipwrights called to one another, their mallets thudding, saws rasping, the rhythm of labor woven with the creak of timbers.

Before him, the *Tyrannicide* stood proud in her berth, her new rig rising against the October sky. What had once been a swift sloop now bristled with the taller masts of a brigantine, her rigging taut, sails neatly furled. She looked like a creature transformed, lean and purposeful, waiting only for the sea.

Captain Fisk approached, wiping pitch from his hands with a rag. "She'll run steadier now," he said with a nod toward the ship. "More sail to set in fair weather, and better balance when the winds turn foul. She'll hold her course, none of that constant coaxing at the helm to keep her steady."

Jon studied her a long moment, pride stirring. "A fine change, Captain." And then with a grin, he added, "I don't suppose my cabin has somehow grown larger in the process."

Fisk's mouth twitched in the barest ghost of a smile. "Cabin's as snug as ever, Lieutenant. But she'll serve you well enough."

Jon chuckled, the sound more frequent of late. "A brigantine it is, then, with the same officer cabins, but with more canvas, more fight. Let the redcoats beware."

Fisk reached in his coat and drew out a folded broadside, the *Essex Gazette*, its creases worn and ink blurred. "Speaking of redcoats, have you seen this news just in from New York?" He handed Jon the paper. "Washington's been driven from the Heights. Fort Washington's lost with men deserting. Yet he still keeps them marching."

Jon scanned the sheet, the clamor of the yard dulling as he read. His jaw set hard. "Then we'll play our part at sea. If the land war falters, with God leading us the sea will answer."

"We're needed more now, since most of General Benedict Arnold's fleet was captured or destroyed by General Carleton at Valcour Bay between the New York mainland and Valcour Island."

Jon shook his head at the additional news. "So, we are losing both on land and on water." Yet even so, the sight of the *Tyrannicide*, re-rigged and ready, lent him a surge of resolve.

In a week's time, she would put out to sea, bound for the West Indies. The thought steadied Jon. Yet it also caused him a pang of regret, for it meant leaving his daughters behind, and for how long he could not say.

Haraden house, Salem, late October 1776

CANDLELIGHT GLOWED WARM against the cream-colored walls as the household gathered for supper, and Mr. Haraden prayed over the meal. Eunice admired his faith and shared his desire for his daughters to grow to be women of God.

The prayer ended, and Eunice breathed in the fragrance of stew thick with turnips and carrots, and the fresh-baked loaf Martha set down with a flourish. Polly, in her high chair, banged a wooden spoon against the tray, laughing with delight as if she ruled the table.

"She's a year old now and a clever child," Martha declared, spooning a bit of gruel into a small bowl. "She takes to her porridge like a sailor to rum."

Hannah giggled, reaching to help feed her sister, her hair ribbon slipping to her shoulder. Martha quickly shooed her hand away. "Mind your ribbon, Child, or it'll end up in the gruel."

Hannah sat back, smoothing the blue ribbon back into place with exaggerated care. "I only wanted to help."

"Martha," said Eunice, "I think it's fine if Hannah helps Polly. It is what her mother would have wanted, don't you agree?"

"Oh, very well," said Martha.

Hannah smiled at Eunice. They were beginning to form a bond, one Eunice hoped would heal a hurting child.

Mr. Haraden's gaze was fixed on his two daughters, their golden heads so alike. "You are correct, Mrs. Mason. Their mother would have approved. She told Hannah to care for her sister and she is doing so." Then turning to Hannah, he said, "You are helping, sweetheart. Polly will always know her sister is watching over her."

Eunice glanced across the table, her gaze approving as Hannah resumed helping to feed Polly. "The girls thrive, Mr. Haraden," she said softly. "That's no small blessing."

As Martha set the rest of the bowls on the table, Silas limped in from the harbor, his coat still smelling of the wharves, his expression grave. He leaned his hands on a chair back and said, "News is grim. General Washington's men are in retreat. Some say the cause is near lost."

A silence fell over the table. Hannah's hand crept to her locket as if to shield her heart.

"Lost, is it?" said Martha. "Well, someone best tell the redcoats, because they don't seem to know they've won. And I'll not waste good flour bakin' bread for quitters."

Jon set his spoon down. "The cause isn't lost. General Washington has taken losses to be sure, but he will find his ground again, and we'll do our part at sea."

Eunice met Mr. Haraden's gaze, and in it she saw the quiet strength that answered the fear in the room. Soon enough he would be gone again, the sea calling him to duty, and they would miss him sorely.

Hannah's voice broke the silence. "How long will you be gone, Papa?"

"Longer than before, sweetheart. With fair winds, it's four or five weeks to the West Indies. And we shall be there for a while hunting British merchantmen. But I will think of you and Polly every day."

"And we will pray for you," said Eunice.

THE DAYS THAT followed passed in a quiet rhythm of preparation. Repairs were checked, stores loaded, and the *Tyrannicide* readied for sea. Jon kept the hours at home close, letting himself be drawn into small moments: Polly's laughter at Martha's jingling keys, Hannah reciting her catechism at Eunice's side, the glow of candles softening the cream-painted walls each evening. Those he tried to hold against the tide already tugging at him, treasures to be recalled in his long days at sea.

By the twenty-eighth, the house carried a hush of unspoken knowledge. His sea chest stood at the door, ready. When Jon rose at dawn on the twenty-ninth, the harbor air was sharp with salt and wood smoke, the gulls crying overhead. The *Tyrannicide* tugged at her moorings like a horse eager for the course.

He kissed his daughters, lingered at the door, sharing a smile with Eunice a heartbeat longer than he meant, and then was gone, the sea calling him to duty.

On the Tyrannicide, off the Carolinas, early November 1776

THE RASP OF holystones carried across the deck at dawn, the men scrubbing in steady rhythm as seawater sloshed from buckets. It was the ordinary sound of a ship at sea, until the sky drew Jon's eyes.

The eastern horizon was bruising, a low bank of clouds thickening with an odd, greenish cast. The wind had a weight to it now, heavy and damp.

"Belay that scrubbing!" Jon's voice cut sharp. "Hands aloft! Reef topsail! Lash everything that moves. Gale coming on!"

The stones were quickly set aside as men scrambled to their stations. Bare feet slapped the wet deck, canvas cracked overhead, and the ordered calm of the morning turned to the taut urgency of preparation. Guns were double-lashed, hatches battened down, and in the rigging the topmen clung like gulls, hauling in sail before the squall could tear it loose.

Even the cabin boys threw themselves into the work. Johnny Deadman darted between the gun crews, snatching at loose gear before it could roll, his thin frame moving quicker than men twice his size. His fellow cabin boy, Bobby Grover, hauled at a line alongside the seamen, his face tight with effort. Jon's eyes caught them both, and for a moment pride steadied his chest. With the oncoming storm, every soul aboard was proving his worth.

Captain Fisk came up to the quarterdeck, the wind tugging at his coat. He gave one measuring glance at the sky, then nodded once, brisk and certain. "Good eye, Lieutenant. Keep her snugged down tight. We'll ride it out. Send a hand to see the lashings doubled on the longboat. We'll not lose her."

"Aye, sir," Jon answered, already signaling the order. He felt the crew respond, steady hands working faster, confidence flowing from the quarterdeck down through every station.

The first hard gust hit moments later, shrieking through the rigging. The *Tyrannicide* heeled, but she was ready, secured, braced, her crew at their posts.

By late afternoon, the gale was in full fury. Seas mounted higher than a house, gray-green walls that threatened to swallow the brigantine whole. Spray slashed across the deck in icy sheets, and the men's shouts were snatched away by the wind.

Jon clung to the weather rail, his voice raw from giving orders. "Ease her off! Keep her bow quarter to it. Steady!" The helmsman wrestled the wheel, knuckles white.

Fisk moved beside Jon, calm as ever, his voice pitched low, steadying. "You've the feel of her, Haraden. Don't fight the sea, ride her through."

Jon's hand tightened on the weather rail, knuckles white, though his voice rang firm above the storm. "She's sound, and so are her hands. The sea may try us, but it won't have us." The words were as much for the crew as for himself, and he saw heads lift along the deck, shoulders squaring against the gale.

As the storm raged, spars groaned, ropes strained, but the brigantine held. They had stripped her canvas to bare poles. Still she flew, driven by the screaming wind.

Midnight found Jon on his feet still, every muscle

aching, salt caked in his hair and on his coat. A sea broke across the ship's waist, sweeping two men off their feet, but hands caught them, hauled them gasping back. One man's arm was broken, another cut by a flying block, the injured sent to the orlop deck.

Fisk's lantern swung in the blackness, casting a thin light. "Hold fast, lads. Dawn'll break before long, and this devil will blow itself out." His words, quiet but certain, carried more weight than the gale itself.

When the first light came, it revealed a sea trans-formed. The storm was spent, the horizon clean, and above stretched a sky as brilliant and blue as hammered glass. The *Tyrannicide* rose and fell on long, even swells, her timbers groaning but unbroken.

The men stood at the rail, hollow-eyed, salt-streaked, and grinning. One began to whistle, another laughed outright. Relief rolled through the deck like a fresh wind.

Jon drew a deep breath, his lungs full of the salt-clean air. The ship smelled of tar and wet wood, but also of life, of endurance. His gaze strayed forward where the masts stood tall, ropes taut, the brigantine whole despite the night's fury.

"God's mercy," muttered one seaman, kissing the wooden rail. Jon nodded as he thanked God for delivering them from the storm. His eyes on the horizon, he asked himself, with all that behind them, what might lay ahead?

Beside him, Fisk stretched his back with a wince. "Well, Mr. Haraden," he said, a ghost of humor in his voice, "she's proved herself a brigantine already. Not many ships take a blow like that their first week rigged."

Jon managed a tired smile. "She's sound, Captain. And

thanks to Providence, so are we."

"Now to see if Cook has been able to fix us something hot to eat," said Fisk. "I'm famished and I imagine the crew is tired of hardtack." Giving a curt nod to the deck, he shouted, "Mr. Stockman, you've the watch. Set the warrant officers to secure the lashings, pump her dry, and see the men know they'll have a hot meal. Join me in my cabin once the deck's settled."

"Aye, sir," Stockman replied, already turning to the warrant officers with clipped orders.

Jon followed Fisk down the companionway, his shoulders leaden, the salt crust in his hair and on his coat itching his skin. The air below reeked of wet wood and tar, but as he walked toward the forecastle a warmer scent struck him from the direction of the galley. "I'll just check on the cook's progress, sir," said Jon. At Fisk's nod, Jon ducked into the galley.

"Burgoo, sir," Reed said without looking up, his ladle stirring steadily. The pot hissed, thick with salt beef, biscuit crumbs, and what barley Reed had salvaged. "Give me a half-hour and the officers and men'll have it hot in their bellies."

Jon nodded. "The crew will need it. The sea near broke them last night."

In the captain's cabin, sunlight poured through the stern windows, falling bright across the table. Fisk removed his coat, urging Jon to do so as well, then eased himself into a chair with a grunt, poured two measures of watered rum, and pushed one toward Jon.

"To the goodness of Providence, and to a sound ship," Fisk said.

Jon lifted his glass, his hand trembling from exhaustion. "To Providence," he echoed. The rum burned, then spread its warmth through him. For the first time since the gale struck, his breath came easy.

Fisk leaned back. "You handled her well, Haraden. A man shows his mettle in a blow."

Jon met his captain's eyes. "She's a good ship. And her men trust her. That's what carried us through."

"Our crew trusts you, Haraden. 'Tis obvious." Fisk's tone was quiet, almost offhand, but the words landed heavier than praise of his seamanship.

"Thank you, sir."

A knock at the door broke the moment. The captain's cabin boy, Joshua Trask, entered and began laying out pewter bowls, setting a small wheel of cheese and a dried apple pie beside them, the captain's stores, kept aside for such moments.

Stockman arrived soon after, salt still crusting his coat, hair plastered to his brow. "Deck secured, sir. Pumps are working, lashings tight, and the men know they'll have hot food within the hour."

"Well enough," Fisk said. "Lose your coat and sit, Joe. You've earned it as much as we have."

Stockman hesitated only a moment before taking off his coat and dropping into a chair, fatigue etched deep in his face.

Joshua delivered the burgoo shortly thereafter and poured each man a measure of rum with a boy's earnest care, glancing nervously to Fisk for approval.

Fisk nodded at Joshua as Jon reached for the ladle, filling their bowls, the steam rising rich with beef and biscuit. It was hot and well-seasoned. After the long night, it tasted near to a feast. For a time, the only sound was the scrape of spoons and the creak of the timbers. Weariness pulled at all of them, but with warm food in their bellies the storm seemed less a terror survived than a trial endured.

Fisk finally set down his spoon, eyeing Jon over the rim of his rum. "Storm's behind us. Next test will be the enemy. But I think the *Tyrannicide*'s ready."

Jon answered with a smile, his shoulders loosening. "So do I, sir. And so are her men."

As the meal ended, Fisk pushed back his chair. "Get a few hours of sleep, gentlemen, and then see to the men. After supper, join me in my cabin. We'll lay out our course into the Indies."

Jon and Stockman nodded, exhaustion weighing heavier now that the worst was past. Above deck, the sun climbed higher, gold on the blue sea, and the *Tyrannicide*'s crew worked in weary shifts—pumping, patching, resetting canvas—while their officers finally allowed themselves rest.

By nightfall the ship was steadier, her decks cleared, the crew fed and in good spirits. The storm seemed already like a dark memory left astern.

In the captain's cabin, the lantern swayed with each roll, throwing gold light across the worn chart of the Leeward Islands spread over the table where Fisk had gathered Jon and Stockman again, compass, dividers, and a pewter mug sliding a fraction with each lift of the sea.

Fisk tapped the chart with a blunt finger. "There lies St. Eustatius, the 'Golden Rock'. The Dutch call her neutral, but every mast in the Caribbean knows better. They're supplying Washington's men as steady as the tide. Powder, shot, muskets, saltpeter. And they'll pay good coin for flour and naval stores we capture from the British."

Stockman frowned, his dark brows drawn together, his arms folded. "It's a risk. The Crown calls it smuggling and piracy. We bring a prize into a Dutch port, and the British may claim we've broken faith."

Fisk gave a dry smile. "The Crown calls all we do piracy, Joe. Let them howl. If the Dutch keep their doors open, we gain. If they shut them, better to know now than to learn it when our holds are full and our throats bare of water."

Jon traced the lines of latitude with his thumb, considering. "It's close enough to our course. And if the harbor's thick with flags, as you suggest, sir, it will be difficult to single out one American brigantine among that press. A short stay, then off again with fresh water, rum, and whatever coin they'll give us for our prize's cargo."

Fisk leaned back in his chair, the timbers creaking. "Aye. We'll not linger. Just long enough to test the Golden Rock's welcome, and to remind the men what we fight for. Every cask rolled ashore there is another musket bound north to General Washington. That's worth the risk."

Jon caught Stockman's skeptical look, then met Fisk's eyes, nodding once.

"Very well," said Fisk. "We'll try her harbor with our first prize. If the war falters in New York, then it must be carried on the sea. And the sea runs through St. Eustatius."

The lantern swung again, throwing shadows across the chart. For a moment, Jon thought of Salem, of his daughters' golden heads bent together, of Eunice's quiet voice guiding Hannah's quill. Then he set the thought aside. Ahead lay prizes to be had, the island they called the Golden Rock, and the test of Dutch neutrality.

Off the Leeward Islands, December 1776

THE LOOKOUT'S CRY cracked the quiet. *"Sail ho!"* A snow, brig-rigged, and wallowing heavy with cargo, lay off the starboard, running north under British colors. The crew clustered at the guns, their excitement thinly veiled under the shouts of command.

Jon's voice rang clear across the deck. "Steady her. Keep the windward advantage!" He stood with his hand tight on the rail, eyes fixed on the fleeing vessel. He could taste the moment: the first test since their refit at Salem.

The *Ann* tried to claw away, but with her new brigantine rig the *Tyrannicide* overhauled her swiftly. A warning shot from the bow-chaser sent splinters flying off the snow's quarterdeck. The British captain wavered, his colors still up, until Fisk cupped his hands and shouted across the narrowing water. "Strike your colors, or we'll rake you fore and aft!"

The tension snapped as the red ensign sagged down the mast. A cheer burst from *Tyrannicide*'s men, relief and triumph in one. Jon felt the thrill in his blood.

The *Ann*'s captain, red-faced and bitter, surrendered

his papers and his sword. Cheers rolled across the *Tyrannicide*'s deck. Jon sent Lieutenant Stockman and a prize crew aboard, their grins broad. "We'll sail with you to St. Eustatius," he said.

St. Eustatius in the Dutch Antilles, December 1776

THE LITTLE VOLCANIC island rose out of the sea like a fortress, at its crown the Quill. Its skirts were dotted with red-roofed houses and Dutch warehouses stacked high with goods. Jon stood next to Fisk at the rail eyeing the sight before him.

"The harbor is a forest of masts," said the captain. "French, Spanish, Dutch, American, even the occasional British merchant likely lying low under false papers. When I was merely a merchantman, I often saw this harbor. Two hundred ships can fit in her roadstead."

As the *Tyrannicide* eased into the anchorage beyond the harbor under truce of Dutch neutrality, Jon felt every eye aboard drinking in the sight. Longboats darted across the glittering water and merchants shouted before anchors were even down. Rum, sugar, muskets, powder, every-thing the colonies lacked, the island seemed to pour forth in abundance. Here, the war was commerce.

Dutch customs men, stiff in their blue coats, received Fisk and Jon at the quay as they climbed from their longboat. Dutch clerks fussed over seals and signatures, but Jon caught their eyes following more closely the coin than the ink. Silver spoke louder here than Britain's protests.

Stockman joined Jon on the quay and handed him a leather packet marked with the seal of the Crown. "Found these on our prize."

Jon passed the packet to Captain Fisk. "Sir, the second lieutenant has made a find, papers from London. These documents may serve General Washington better than coin."

Fisk nodded. "Indeed."

By afternoon, the captured *Ann's* cargo of flour and naval stores was stacked in a counting house, and Fisk signed receipts with the flourish of a man doing God's work. In return, casks of rum and sugar rolled down to the water's edge, and quiet parcels of powder were whispered into their hands.

Jon walked the crowded quay, where sailors from half a dozen nations jostled, tavern doors swung wide, and tongues in Dutch, French, and English mingled. He saw the eagerness in his men's faces, felt it in his own chest: proof that their fight stretched far beyond Massachusetts. Every barrel shifted here was another musket for Washington's line, another shipload denied the Crown.

As dusk fell, he and Fisk stood together watching the bustle. Fisk's voice was low. "Remember this, Mr. Haraden. The war isn't only fought with powder and shot. It's fought in warehouses, on ledgers, in every hand that takes a coin for liberty's cause. The Golden Rock feeds Washington as surely as we do."

Jon nodded, the bustle of the quay echoing in his mind, barrels rolling, taverns alive in a dozen tongues.

In Fisk's cabin later that evening, over the chart of the Leewards, one of the Dutch factors, plump and red-faced from the heat, let slip an important tale. Dabbing at his brow with a kerchief, his pride evident, he said, "Ach, it was but last month, ya. An American brig-of-war, the *Andrew Doria*, anchored here under your new flag. Fort Oranje gave her eleven guns, and the salute was answered shot for shot. The first time your colors were honored by any power in Europe or the Indies. The English—" he spread his hands with relish—"they are still gnashing their teeth over it."

Jon felt the words strike like a hammer blow. "A salute," he murmured, picturing the Continental Union flag flying against the Caribbean sky. "Then the world has seen us for what we are. Not rebels, but a new nation."

Fisk's gaze lingered on the Dutchman, then shifted to Jon, quiet approval in his eyes. "Every musket and barrel of powder slipped ashore here since has carried that salute with it. Remember that when you look at these Dutch warehouses, Mr. Haraden. They're the arsenal of liberty."

The factor shrugged, as though it were nothing but good business.

In that moment, Jon realized more fully the importance of trade to the war. He pictured American ships carrying goods into European ports as well as cannon into battle. Surely American captains could do both. The Revolution did live in ledgers as much as in broadsides. The sea was his battlefield, but here in this crowded harbor he saw the breadth of the struggle. He saw the future.

Watching the lamps flicker on the quay, he thought of the endless barrels of sugar, rum, and powder piled high on St. Eustatius. Yet far to the north, British blockades were already choking New England's harbors, cutting off the delivery of goods. How long before shortages reached Salem's markets?

His thoughts turned homeward, to Hannah bent over her copybook, to Polly pounding her spoon in her high chair, to Eunice's quiet strength keeping the household on an even keel, and to Martha with her garden and Silas at her side.

"The harder the conflict, the more glorious
the triumph."
– Thomas Paine 1776

CHAPTER 6

Salem Market, January 1777

MARTHA PULLED THE hood of her cloak up to protect
her ears against the bite of the wind. The snow lay hard-
packed along the streets, but the market square still
thronged with people, a murmur of anxious voices rising
from under woolen hoods and shawls. Prices had climbed
again, flour fetching twice its worth, sugar scarce as gold,
and molasses gone before noon. Wives muttered of
hunger and of merchants grown fat while soldiers froze
and starved.

Martha's grip tightened on the empty basket she carried. If the war was to be won, the hearths of Salem must
be kept burning, and food at the ready for hungry people.
She would not see her neighbors cheated into want.

Near Needham's Bakery, a knot of women pressed forward, their voices rising.

"How am I to keep my children fed," one cried, "when every penny buys only half a loaf?"

Another called, "Fair price or no price, Patriots can't be allowed to starve while the cause marches on!"

Martha stood among the women, her arms folded, her chin lifted. "You've bread enough in your bins, Mr. Needham," she accused, her voice ringing. "Raise your price again and you'll answer to every wife in Salem!"

The baker came from his shop to snap back, "Mind yourself, Woman! I'll not be robbed by fishwives and cooks!" He shoved at Martha's shoulder.

A hand caught her before she stumbled. Silas, strong as ever despite his limp, moved between them, his voice low but firm, his eyes narrowed on the baker. "Easy, Needham. Best watch your tongue. No man prospers long spitin' hungry neighbors."

Martha's cheeks burned, but she tossed her head. "Aye, Needham, best mind yourself, or you'll be eatin' your own loaves for supper." Laughter broke out among the women, though their eyes stayed hard on the baker.

The baker, seeing the faces ranged against him, muttered and dropped his price by a shilling.

Silas gave Martha a look both reproving and admiring as he took her arm. "Next time," he muttered, "give a body warnin' before you take on half the town."

Martha sniffed. "Next time, Silas, I expect you to be at my side, not trailin' after."

The parlor fire glowed against the gathering dark when Martha swept into the house, Silas behind her. Her cheeks were still flushed from the cold and the quarrel. She set her basket down on the parlor table with a thump, harder than she meant, and muttered something under her breath about "graspin' bakers."

Mrs. Mason, who had been mending by the hearth while the girls played, looked up. "Martha? What's happened?"

Silas stamped the snow from his boots as he hung up his cloak. He gave a grunt. "Your Martha near led a riot at Needham's stall. Had half the wives of Salem ready to storm his bins."

Martha entered the parlor, unrepentant. "He thought to raise the price again, but I told him plain, keep on, and he's soon be eatin' his own bread. That cooled him fast enough. Why, I'll teach every woman in Salem to bake better bread than his."

Mrs. Mason pressed a hand to her mouth. "Martha! You didn't!"

"Aye, she did," said Silas. "Took the man's head off. Would've been a riot if she'd gone on longer." Silas shot her a sidelong look, half-admiration, half-exasperation. "I'll say this: the man dropped his price soon enough."

Martha pulled off her cloak with a huff. "What's happened is robbery paradin' as trade."

Silas shed his jacket and lowered himself onto a stool with a groan. "I've heard talk on the wharves, talk of similar scenes in Boston, Portsmouth, even farther south. And it's not just bread, but coffee, tea, sugar, and flour. Anythin' folk can't do without. Women won't see their children starve while merchants line their pockets. It's not the first time, won't be the last."

Mrs. Mason, a serious expression on her face, said, "Part of this must be caused by the British blockade of our ports."

"Aye," said Silas, "and the Continental Army takin' large amounts of flour has created local shortages."

Martha sniffed, though her chin was high. "And some merchants use that as an excuse to raise prices. They shouldn't. If the men are away fightin', it falls to us to keep the hearth and feed the children. Patriots can't be expected to starve while we pray for victory."

Mrs. Mason set her needlework aside, her voice gentle. "I only pray you'll be careful, Martha. Words in anger can cut as deep as any blade."

Martha softened a fraction, though she would not admit it. "Well, if the menfolk won't keep bakers honest, someone has to."

Hannah looked up at Martha, "I think you won."

Silas chuckled, shaking his head. "Won this bout, maybe. But if I'm to keep her out of the gaol, I'll need eyes in the back of my head."

A smile tugged at Martha's lips. "Nonsense. Salem's better for a sharp tongue now and then."

From the corner of the room, little Polly crawled to a chair and lifted herself up. Hannah, watching with bright eyes, smiled at the progress her little sister was making. Martha caught it. "Soon the child will be walkin'."

On the Tyrannicide off the Leeward Islands in the Caribbean, January 1777

THE TRADE WINDS filled the *Tyrannicide*'s canvas, driving her north along the edge of the Leeward Islands, the sea rolling blue and steady beneath her. Jon stood at the rail, the memory of St. Eustatius still vivid, the bustle of the quay, the Dutch factor's tale of the salute to American independence, the casks of sugar and powder shifting from hand to hand.

The lookout's cry broke the morning calm. "Sail ho! Off the larboard bow, a brig, deep laden!"

Jon's heart leapt. He snapped his glass open and steadied himself against the roll. A broad-shouldered vessel lay ahead, brig-rigged, her wake sluggish under her heavy cargo. British colors streamed at her gaff. "The *Henry and Ann*," Jon muttered, his spyglass snapping shut. "Bound north for New York, I'll wager, fat with provisions."

Fisk gave a curt nod, and his orders rang across the deck. "Hands to stations! Run out the guns, and trim her sharp. We'll close the gap."

The men moved with eagerness sharpened by their recent victory. Sailors vaulted into the rigging, the braces creaked as canvas was trimmed, and the brigantine leaned into the wind. Jon felt the thrill course through him. The *Tyrannicide* was no longer a sloop running for her life but a hunter in full stride.

The British brig tried to bear away, but she was slow, heavy with stowed goods. Within the hour, the *Tyrannicide* gained the advantage, standing upwind. Swinging downwind, she crossed astern of the British ship, lining up to rake her vulnerable quarter. The bow-chaser barked flame and smoke. Shot smashed through the *Henry and Ann*'s bulwark, sending splinters spinning.

Still she ran, stubborn, her crew answering with a single stern-chaser that splashed wide. Jon's jaw set. "With your permission, sir, I would take action to see she is ours."

"All yours," said Fisk.

Jon called from the quarterdeck, "Mr. Moses, give her a broadside she won't mistake."

The port guns thundered, the deck shuddering beneath their feet. A round tore through the brig's mizzen, sending rigging slithering down in a tangle. Her flight was broken. Jon imagined the British captain's shoulders sag. A moment later, the red ensign dipped, fluttered, and dropped.

"Colors struck!" came the cry.

A cheer erupted from *Tyrannicide*'s men, raw and triumphant. Jon allowed himself a tight smile. "Boarding party away," he ordered. Senior warrant officer Benjamin Moses led the prize crew, their boat splashing down and pulling hard toward the wounded brig.

When the British master was brought across, he grimaced with fury and defeat. Handing Fisk his sword with stiff formality, he said bitterly, "Brig *Henry and Ann*, laden with flour, pork, and oats for His Majesty's troops in New York."

Fisk passed the sword to Jon. "Mr. Haraden, see to it, if you will, and send her into St. Eustatius." Jon felt the sword's weight in his hand, the war now measured not in glory but in bushels and barrels. Washington's men were starved for want of such cargo. Here, in the tropics, the Revolution's lifeblood had been found.

Jon set the blade aside. "Your ship will serve a better cause now," he said evenly.

By afternoon, the *Henry and Ann* was under prize crew command and on her way to the Golden Rock, her holds deep with foodstuffs that could keep an army on its feet. Jon watched the British ship heading downwind under the hand of the prize crew. The British captain stood rigid at her stern, forced to look back at the ship that had mastered him. After a moment, Jon turned to Fisk.

"What becomes of them in the Dutch port, sir? The prisoners?"

Fisk's eyes followed the departing brig. "In a neutral port like St. Eustatius, they'll be paroled ashore under Dutch oversight, their word given not to take up arms until exchanged. They won't like it, watching their cargo sold and carted off to feed Washington's men, but they'll have no choice."

Jon frowned. "Paroled? You mean they are free to walk, so long as they swear an oath?"

"Aye," Fisk said, his voice flat. "It's honor that binds them. They'll be shipped off soon enough on some Dutch or Spanish vessel and sent back to their own ports. But until then, they're no threat to us."

Jon's gaze narrowed on the emptying horizon. "Strange, isn't it? We parole their men, treat them fair. Yet ours rot in the hulks off New York, starving in the dark. Some never see daylight again. Others waste away in English prisons."

"Aye," Fisk said quietly. "That's the difference between us and them. We fight hard, but we fight as men, not butchers." He let out a long breath and clapped Jon's shoulder. "Best remember it, Haraden. Our honor is as much a weapon as our guns."

Jon nodded, his jaw tight. The words settled heavy, not as an officer's lesson but as a truth he felt to the bone. If war must be fought, then let it be fought with honor, not cruelty. He thought of his daughters and of Eunice Mason's calm hand guiding their learning. What kind of world would they inherit if men waged war like beasts? Better a nation that tempered its steel with mercy. That was a cause worth keeping faith with.

The lookout's cry came at midmorning: "Sail ho, off the lee bow!"

Jon's glass snapped open. A snow, brig-rigged with two masts, wallowed heavy in the water, her sails full but her pace sluggish. "She's burdened," Jon muttered. "Heavy with stores, by the look of her."

"She's 140 tons," said Fisk, "but a merchantman, unprepared for a fight." He gave the order, and the *Tyrannicide* bore down under a press of canvas. Within the hour, she overhauled the stranger. A warning shot from the bow-chaser cracked the air. The British master, with no chance against the brigantine's speed and guns, lowered his colors without firing a shot.

Jon's satisfaction was tempered by the ordinariness of it, not a fight, but a surrender. Still, when the papers revealed her to be the *John*, laden with naval stores, dried fish, and salt, he felt a pulse of grim pleasure. "Washington's men would march a month on what's in the *John*'s hold," he said. Stockman was sent over with a prize crew, and the *Tyrannicide* swung back to her course, still hungry for more.

The next prize presented more of a test. She was sighted late in the afternoon, a trim brig under full sail, the *Three Friends*. Running before the wind, she tried to escape.

"Hands to stations!" Fisk commanded, but his eyes found Jon. "She's yours to bring down, Lieutenant."

Jon's pulse quickened. He leaned toward the helmsman. "Hold her close-hauled! We'll take her to windward." Canvas boomed as the *Tyrannicide* turned, straining to cut the fleeing brig off from her run.

The chase stretched long. Twice the *Three Friends* fired her stern-chasers, round shot plunging into the sea astern. The *Tyrannicide*'s bow-gun barked in answer, splintering the brig's quarterdeck rail. Still she fled.

"Bring us across her bow," Jon called. The brigantine's guns thundered as they raked her from stem to stern. Rigging tumbled, the British crew scrambled, and the master's nerve broke. The red ensign dipped, fluttered, and came down.

A roar went up from the *Tyrannicide*'s deck, not just in victory, but vindication. The brigantine had shown her teeth. Her refit was justified. Jon stood straight at the quarterdeck rail, salt-stiffened hair whipping free of his queue, feeling the men's eyes on him.

Beside him, Fisk said, "They will follow you anywhere now."

When the *Three Friends*' master was brought over and surrendered his sword to Fisk, the *Tyrannicide*'s captain handed it to Jon. The papers showed her hold deep with flour and salt pork, bound north for New York's garrison. Jon thought of Washington's starving men and tightened his grip on the hilt. "These provisions will serve a better army," he said evenly.

St. Eustatius, Dutch Antilles

BY WEEK'S END, the *Tyrannicide* shepherded her newest prizes, the *John* and the *Three Friends*, into St. Eustatius to join the *Henry and Ann*. Their masts added to the crowded forest already filling the anchorage, while the *Ann*, taken earlier, had long since been sold, her cargo of flour and naval stores turned into coin and powder.

On deck, Jon watched the bustle ashore: Dutch clerks tallying, longshoremen rolling barrels, and prisoners led away under guard. "Why sell the *Ann* outright, Captain, and not the others?" he asked quietly.

Fisk's gaze followed the lighters moving cargo between the quay and the prize ship *John*, riding at anchor. "The *Ann* was nearest hand, and her cargo easiest to shift into Dutch warehouses for coin. But the *John*, the *Three Friends* and the *Henry and Ann* carry more than we can sell, much flour, pork, salt. Those must go north, to Salem and to Congress. Powder and muskets we can fetch here, aye, but bread for Washington's men will be worth more than silver."

Jon nodded slowly, seeing it now, the strategy behind what looked like mere barter. "So these three sail for home with us, our prize crews aboard. They'll bring Salem more than profit. They'll feed her soldiers."

"Aye," Fisk said, his tone flat with certainty. "The Revolution doesn't stand on coin alone. It stands on stomachs filled and muskets loaded. Let the Dutch count their silver. We'll count bushels and barrels."

By evening, the *John's* holds were rebalanced with casks of sugar and kegs of powder slipped aboard under the guise of trade. The *Three Friends* and the *Henry and Ann* were provisioned the same. Her captured flour and pork were kept intact, joined by crates of muskets, lead, and flints.

Onshore, British prisoners from the prizes were paroled under Dutch watch, their faces bitter as they watched their cargoes turned to American use. Jon thought of New York's prison hulks where Americans wasted and died, and the contrast gnawed at him. *We treat theirs as men. They starve ours like dogs.*

That night, Fisk gathered his officers in a rented room above a tavern overlooking the crowded quay. The air was thick with pipe smoke, the sound of a dozen tongues rising from below. A table was set with roasted fish, plantains, sugared cakes, and Dutch gin. Even the cabin boys were allowed in. Wide-eyed, Joshua Trask nearly spilled half the bottle as he tried to pour the gin with both hands.

"To the *Tyrannicide*," Fisk said, raising his glass. "She's proved herself in every test—whether storm or battle."

"To Salem," said Stockman, his face gaunt but alight. "May she find her tables the fuller for what we've seized."

Jon lifted his cup high. "To the crew, who have stood every trial with courage, and to the prizes we send north. Let them feed Washington's men as surely as we've fought for them."

A cheer went up, the men's voices shaking the rafters.

At last, the laughter ebbed and the plates lay bare, only crumbs of sugared cake and the dregs of gin remaining. Stockman was already dozing in his chair, and the cabin boys leaned heavy-eyed against the wall, their bravado spent.

Fisk pushed back his chair, the legs scraping against the floorboards, and looked around the table. "We've tested her canvas, her men, and her officers," he said, his tone gentler than Jon had ever heard it. "Now comes the greater test, bringing these prizes home. It's no small thing, gentlemen. These holds carry more than cargo. They carry hope."

Jon felt the words settle on him. He glanced out the window once more, past the oil lamps flickering on the quay to the black sweep of the bay. The prize ships rode at anchor, black silhouettes against the starlight, heavy with food and powder that might mean survival for Washington's ragged army.

Rising, he bid Fisk good night and stepped into the warm Caribbean air, the scent of spice and tar lingering on the breeze. Somewhere down the quay a fiddler struck up a tune. For a moment Jon stood still, breathing in the tropical air, so unlike the sharp salt wind of Salem. The sea had tested them with storm and battle, and tomorrow it would test them again on the long voyage north. But tonight there had been laughter, and loyalty, and the sense that their small brigantine was part of something vast.

He turned back toward the inn, the sound of his crew's voices still carrying faintly through the shutters, and thought of Salem and his daughters. He would bring them home more than stories. He would bring them bread.

Haraden house, Salem, late January 1777

THE FIRE BURNED low in the hearth, shadows stretching long across the parlor as Eunice entered, carrying a sleepy Polly. She laid Polly on a blanket in front of the fire, lit fresh candles against the gathering dark, and drew her shawl close before taking her place by the fire, her knitting in her lap.

Hannah came in and took up her doll, though her fidgeting soon betrayed her boredom.

Setting her knitting aside, Eunice said gently, "Come, Hannah, show me how well you know your catechism."

Hannah left her doll and came close with a small, worn book. She straightened her back and asked, almost solemnly, "What is the chief end of man?" Then, with a small, triumphant smile: "To glorify God, and to enjoy Him forever."

Martha entered just then, sniffing. "Forever's a long time, Miss Hannah. But you can start now."

Eunice hid a smile. "Hannah, do you enjoy knowing God and His angels watch over you, even now?"

"I like knowing He watches over me, Papa and Polly, too," she said.

Glancing at Martha, Eunice said, "These lessons are strengthening her faith and preparing her to one day teach her own children."

Hannah fingered her mother's locket, her lifeline. "Papa would want me to know my catechism," she whispered.

"Yes," Eunice agreed, her voice softening. "Your papa is at sea, keeping faith, trusting God to bring him home. And you are keeping faith here." After a pause she asked gently, "Hannah, does your locket hold miniatures of your parents?"

Hesitating, Hannah nodded.

"May I see them?"

At Eunice's gentle urging, she opened it and offered the chain. Inside, a young fair-haired woman smiled from one side, and Jonathan Haraden's dark blue eyes gazed out from the other.

"These are your parents," Eunice said softly. "So young, and your mother so fair. No wonder you and Polly shine with golden hair."

A tear slipped down Hannah's cheek as Eunice returned the locket and drew her close. "Oh, Hannah, how blessed you are to have had them both for a time. And now you still have your papa."

"And you?" Hannah asked, pulling back to look at Eunice.

Eunice held her gaze. "Yes, you have me, too. God willing, I'll be here with you until you have little ones of your own, and longer, if you'll have me."

Hannah rested her head on Eunice's shoulder and soon started to doze. Martha said, "Best get the child to her bed. Come along, Lass."

Hannah gave Eunice's hand a squeeze before following Martha upstairs.

"I'll stay until Polly sleeps," said Eunice, rocking the cradle.

When Martha returned, she gave Eunice a long look. "You know, Mrs. Mason, for Hannah to hand you that locket...well, that's her heart you were holdin'. She doesn't trust just anyone with it."

Eunice blinked. She felt the truth of Martha's words settle deep, heavier than she expected. "She holds my heart, as well."

"Aye," Martha said, a wry smile tugging at her mouth, "That child wouldn't hand her mother's memory to just anyone. Best not to forget it."

Eunice glanced toward the cradle where Polly had fallen asleep. "I never will."

As the house grew quiet, Eunice felt the truth of it sink deep. This was no longer only Jonathan Haraden's family. It was hers now, too, bound not by blood but by trust, and by a love that had already taken root between herself and the children. Hannah's small hand in hers, Polly's sleepy weight against her shoulder, these were not tokens of duty, but of belonging.

"Freedom is not a gift bestowed upon us by other men, but a right that belongs to us by the laws of God."

– Benjamin Franklin 1774

CHAPTER 7

Salem Harbor, February 1777

JON STOOD ON the quarterdeck with Fisk as the *Tyrannicide* came beating up through the ice-stippled waters of Salem Harbor, taking long angled runs and then tacking back, clawing her way upwind. Jon gazed upward to see her canvas stiff with frost, her lines creaking as though weary from the long haul north. Behind her, the *John*, the *Three Friends*, and the *Henry and Ann* followed, their prize crews guiding them toward the familiar wharves. Smoke rose from the town's chimneys, carried thin and gray in the winter air. Along the wharf, a crowd had gathered despite the cold.

On the quarterdeck beside him, Fisk let out a low

breath, the ghost of a smile crossing his weathered face. "No one can argue with our success. Look at them, staring at the three prizes we've brought in. And they've yet to hear of the *Ann* we sold at the Golden Rock. We'll save that story for later, when they've caught their breath."

Jon's gaze swept the wharf. Merchants craned for the manifests, townsfolk hungry for news, wives and children waving mittened hands. His own eyes found Hannah first, her golden hair flying free of her hood, bright even in the gray morning. He'd been gone mere months, but already she had grown taller. Her hand lifted high catching his eye. Beside her stood Eunice Mason, smiling broadly beneath her hooded cloak. Behind them was Silas, his shoulders hunched against the cold.

"Bring her to, Mr. Stockman," Fisk ordered. "Let's show Salem what she's worth."

The anchors splashed down, sails furled stiffly against their yards, and a cheer rose from the crowd, muffled but strong in the frozen air. Lines were cast ashore, and the brigantine settled against Derby Wharf with a groan of timbers.

Jon stepped down at last onto the wharf's planks. Hannah ran to him, her hair streaming behind her. He swept her up, the chill forgotten in the warmth of her arms.

"Papa, you came back!" she whispered fiercely, as though daring the sea to prove her wrong.

"Of course I did, sweetheart."

Their governess met his eyes, her expression bright with something unspoken. She inclined her head, almost formally, though her gaze lingered. In the morning light with her cheeks red from the cold, her brown eyes sparkled.

"Welcome home, sir!" she exclaimed.

Jon inclined his head in thanks, feeling the warmth of her words despite the chill.

Silas stepped forward, dipping his head. "Well done, sir. Brought back half the Indies, by the look of it. Salem'll eat well now. Martha's home by the hearth with Polly. She'll have a feast waitin' once you've done with these wharf folk. And I'll wager the Board of War'll be smilin' wider still, for I reckon you've more than pork and flour in them holds."

Jon gave Silas a nod. "Aye, we've a few things for General Washington."

Behind them, dockhands and merchants surged to meet the prize crews, tallying barrels and crates. The Board of War's clerk stood ready with his ledger, quill scratching furiously, his grin broadening as he heard the tally of pork, flour, powder, muskets and rum. To the clerk, it was numbers on a page, for he must account for the cargo before any could be sold. To Salem, it meant bread on the table and hope for the cause.

Jon let his eyes roam over the town he had left in autumn. It seemed smaller now, quieter, after the bustling quays of the Caribbean. Yet it was here his heart returned, here his daughters waited, here faith and duty balanced the call of the sea.

Fisk came down the gangway, his boots sounding on the planks. He clasped Jon's shoulder. "Mr. Haraden, see to the prize masters' reports and make certain the Board's clerk has the manifests. Mind the cargo tallies and the men's welfare. When that's done, you've leave to take supper with your family. Report back in the morning, and we'll confer on orders."

Jon inclined his head. "Aye, Captain." Turning to Silas, he said, "I'll be home as soon as I've finished here."

Haraden house, Salem

THE SCENT OF roast cod, winter carrots, and Martha's brown bread met Jon the instant he crossed the threshold. Under his arm he carried a small parcel wrapped in sailcloth that contained molasses, sugar, and coffee brought from St. Eustatius, a gift for the household. Behind him the night air gusted in, sharp with the bite of snow. The warmth of the hearth, the familiar creak of the old floorboards under his boots, struck him like a wave. The day had been both exhausting and exhilarating, and he relished the safe harbor of home.

Martha met him at the door with Hannah at her side, beaming up at him. "Supper's ready, sir, whenever you are."

"I'm eager to taste your cooking, Martha, but need to change out of these salt-soaked clothes. I'll be down in a minute."

"Do hurry, Papa," said Hannah, tugging his hand.

Mrs. Mason, with Polly in her arms, peeked her head into the parlor. "Good evening, sir."

Jon returned her greeting with a nod and took the stairs two at a time.

When he returned, face and hands scrubbed and a

clean shirt beneath his waistcoat, he took his place at the head of the oak table. Frost feathered the windowpanes, blurring the snowdrifts outside into pale shapes, as if the world beyond were held at bay. Inside, the candles burned steady against the drafts, their glow warming the pewter dishes and the steam rising from serving bowls. In the hearth, a fire burned steadily.

Hannah sat on his right, bright with expectation. Mrs. Mason had strapped Polly into her high chair on his left and took her place next to his youngest. The little one was already reaching for a chunk of bread, smearing more of it across her cheeks than into her mouth. Mrs. Mason gently wiped her face with a kerchief, only for Polly to swat her hand and giggle.

Jon bowed his head. He thanked God for the Savior, the *Tyrannicide*'s safe return, for their successful captures, and for the food spread before them this evening.

Martha, bustling in, set down a great platter of roast cod with onions, carrots and parsnips, steam rising into the warm room. "Eat your fill," she told Jon, her chin high. "Let's see if you can do justice to my kitchen now."

Jon laughed softly, shaking his head. "This is a feast, one I've not tasted since I was last at home." He caught Mrs. Mason's glance, warm and approving, and for a moment the ache of his absence eased.

"Tell us about the ships you captured!" Hannah insisted, eyes shining. "Were there awful battles?"

Jon set down his fork. "Very well," he said, noticing Silas leaning into the room from the kitchen doorway, "but first there was a storm unlike any we'd known."

"A storm?" Mrs. Mason leaned forward. Hannah's eyes

grew wide.

"Aye. Off Bermuda, the wind blew so fierce it tore canvas from the yards and near carried away our bowsprit. For a day and a night, the crew pumped without ceasing, and the waves rose higher than the *Tyrannicide*'s masts. More than once I thought we'd founder." He paused, meeting Hannah's gaze. "But God was merciful, and when morning came and the seas calmed, the men cheered as if we'd won a battle."

"And what about the British ships you captured?" Hannah prompted, as Martha came in to gather empty plates.

"We took four fat prizes, merchantmen carrying flour and powder among other things bound for British troops."

"But there were only three ships behind the *Tyrannicide* when you sailed into Salem," Hannah protested. "What happened to the other one?"

"Good eye, sweetheart. The first ship we captured was a snow, the *Ann*, bound for Jamaica with a cargo of flour and lumber. We sold her in St. Eustatius for needed coin. She also carried dispatches bearing the seal of the Crown. I put those in Captain Fisk's hands for General Washington. All the captured ships carried cargo. We made harbor at St. Eustatius, where the Dutch are glad enough to trade with Americans. That is where I bought this." From the floor, he lifted the small parcel of sugar, molasses, and coffee onto the table. "Martha can use the sweets for her puddings, if she likes. And I will be glad enough to drink the coffee."

"Hmph," said Martha, though her eyes softened when she looked at Jon's gifts. "We'll see what use your gifts can be put to."

"It was thoughtful of you to remember the household," said Mrs. Mason. She coaxed a spoonful of mashed parsnip toward Polly, who promptly pushed it back out with her tongue, smearing her gown. "And what is next for you and the *Tyrannicide*?"

"I expect the Board of War will have new orders soon enough. I may know more tomorrow when I meet with Captain Fisk."

When all the platters had been cleared, Martha returned from the kitchen with a steaming apple pie, its crust golden and sugared, the scent filling the room with a sweetness that cut through the winter air.

"Apple pie!" Hannah clapped her hands.

Polly reached across her tray, squealing, and Mrs. Mason quickly cut a small piece into tiny morsels for her. The child ate the soft apple filling with sticky delight, smearing it across her cheeks and the high chair table. "I believe Polly loves the pie, Martha," said Mrs. Mason.

Jon chuckled. "A feast indeed, Martha. You've outdone yourself."

The corners of the cook's mouth twitched. "A sailor home from sea deserves more than fish and bread."

It was then, over pie and candlelight, that Jon leaned back in his chair and, turning to Mrs. Mason, said, "I've been thinking it might be time to invite my cousin Andrew Haraden and his wife Lydia from Gloucester. He's outfitting ships and doing quite well. He and Lydia are raising six daughters. And just to make it lively, one is named Hannah, though they call her Joanna, and their youngest is called Polly." He smiled at his own girls in turn. "I'll send them an invitation to come to Salem. When duty calls me back to sea, their household can join ours, and Andrew and Lydia can have my chamber while they are with us. You'll all be kin in truth then."

"That branch of the Haradens is a stout crew," said Silas, ambling in from the doorway with a glint in his eye. "Andrew's father, now there was a shipwright with tar enough in his veins to wrestle his sloop, the *Squirrel*, right out of pirate hands. Sent those sea wolves off yelpin', he did. A real hero, and no mistake." He chuckled, his whiskers twitching. "So, if the Gloucester cousins come, mind you, this house will be brimful of Haraden salt."

Hannah's eyes shone. "More cousins!"

"Aye, more cousins," Jon said with a laugh. "And more laughter in this house."

For a moment, he let himself believe it would last, the glow of hearth and candles, Polly's delighted chatter, the women's steady presence about him, the snow muffling the world beyond their walls. The sea would call soon enough, and he would eagerly go, but tonight he was only Jonathan Haraden: father, cousin, son of Salem.

Derby Wharf, Salem

THE TIDE LAPPED against the pilings, gray water flecked with ice, as Jon strode the length of Derby Wharf. His breath rose in white clouds, whipped away by the northeast wind that rattled every loose line and set the *Tyrannicide*'s rigging humming like a harp. Snow crusted the planks, crunching under his boots. On either side, stacks of barrel staves, crates of salt fish, and casks of flour bound for the Indies stood rimed in frost, while hogsheads of molasses newly landed from the islands steamed faintly in the cold air.

Merchants in greatcoats stamped their feet for warmth, while apprentices carried ledgers close against the cold.

Gulls wheeled overhead, their cries sharp against the creak of tackle and the steady hammer of shipwrights at work. The smell of tar and oakum mingled with brine was pungent and familiar. The *Tyrannicide* was moored snugly, her sails furled in neat bands, her deck alive with movement. Cauldrons of bubbling tar steamed in the frigid air as men caulked seams split in the storm and battles, while others bent fresh canvas to spars.

Captain Fisk stood near the gangway, a folded paper in hand, conferring with the carpenter. At Jon's approach he looked up, his ruddy face bright against the wind.

"Haraden, you've the look of a man ready for orders."

Jon returned the smile. "That I am, sir. Tell me what the Board of War has decreed for us."

Fisk held up the sheet, its edges fluttering. "No new orders yet. But there's news you'll like better than any commission." He tapped the paper. "You wanted a bigger cabin. Well, you're going to get one."

Jon raised a brow. "A bigger cabin, sir?"

"As of the twentieth," Fisk said, his voice carrying pride as well as certainty, "you are made Captain of the *Tyrannicide*. I'm to be given command of the *Massachusetts*, another brigantine, and a fine one. You'll have Israel Thorndike of Beverly, late of the schooner *Warren*, as your First Lieutenant. A good man. Benjamin Moses of Salem will be your Second. Aye, I know you respect him. Benjamin Lovett of Beverly is Master, and Thomas Hunt Master's Mate."

For a moment, Jon simply stared at him, the hammering and gull cries dimming into silence. *Captain.* The word struck him like a broadside. More than he had dared expect, more than he had sought. He drew a breath.

"This...this is your doing," Jon said at last, his voice low but firm. "Without your support, John, such a commission would never have come my way."

Fisk's eyes twinkled. "Nonsense. You've earned it with your skill and your courage. The men respect you, and so do I. The Board merely had the sense to make it official."

Jon clasped Fisk's hand. "Even so, you have my thanks. I'll not forget it."

Fisk gripped Jon's shoulder, then gestured toward the brigantine, her masts stark against the winter sky. "Then go, Captain Haraden. See to your ship. She's yours now, and I suspect we'll be sailing together for a time."

"Nothing would please me more," Jon said, turning to the *Tyrannicide.* His gaze lingered on the stern where the name stretched proud across blue scrollwork, the four stern windows beneath gleaming like watchful eyes. He had seen her before many times, of course, but now it was different. Painted stars framed a small shield in red, white, and blue, a bold emblem of defiance aimed squarely at the British Crown. Against the gray chop of the harbor and the snow-piled wharves, her ochre hull and bright trim shone like a banner of resistance. She was no ordinary brigantine, but a fighting ship christened for rebellion itself. In her lines he felt the pull of the sea and the cause, as if both had been waiting for him all along.

And now she was his.

THE DOOR CREAKED against the winter draft as Mr. Haraden stepped inside, brushing snow from his shoulders. Eunice looked up to see a raw flush on his cheeks, and something else besides, a brightness in his eyes that was not merely from the cold. Something that was not there when he'd left for the harbor that morning.

She rose from her chair by the hearth where Polly had been playing with a new doll. Hannah sat at the oak table with her primer, lips moving soundlessly as she worked her way through a psalm verse. Both girls looked up, their father's presence filling the room before he had spoken a word.

He hung his cocked hat and cloak on its peg and let his gaze travel over them, steady and intent, as if he had carried them all with him down Derby Wharf. "News," he said simply, his voice low but charged.

Martha stilled at the settle and turned, her hands planted firm on her hips. "Out with it, then, afore the stew goes cold," she said, a glint of humor in her eyes.

Silas leaned in from the passage, his gray brows lifted in expectation.

Eunice held her hands together, willing her heart to slow. Whatever he had to say, she knew it would shape the household as surely as the tide shaped the stones of the harbor.

"The *Tyrannicide* is now mine to command," Jonathan

said. For a long minute, silence hung in the air before they understood. "Henceforth, it's Captain Haraden!"

Hannah gasped and half-rose from her seat, her blue eyes alight. "Captain, Papa? Truly?"

"Truly, my brave girl." His smile was proud, the lines at the corners of his eyes deepening.

Eunice's hand rose to her heart. "Congratulations, sir," she said, smiling. "You deserve to take command."

Martha gave a short, approving nod, though her voice was brisk. "About time, if you ask me. The Board of War could scarce do better."

Silas chuckled from the doorway. "Aye, the old girl's got a captain worthy of her timber."

In Eunice's mind the word captain kept repeating, unsettling her. She saw at once what it meant: longer absences at sea, greater exposure in a battle and the children clinging to her and to Martha when storms of fear came ashore. And yet, she could not deny the way his bearing filled the room, as if he had stepped into the place Providence had marked for him from the beginning. And she realized this was always his destiny. Hers was to keep faith at home and help shape his daughters as they grew. Eunice glanced toward Hannah and at Polly nestled in her father's arms. In that moment, she felt both the weight and the honor of it, as if Providence had bound their paths together in different but equal callings.

Polly, though not aware of the gravity of the situation nor the honor bestowed upon her father, still realized something was afoot. She smiled at her papa, hugging his neck. He pressed his face to her curls as though to seal the moment. "Aye, sweet one," he murmured, "your papa's a captain now."

Eunice watched him, her heart stirring strangely. The house had lost so much with his wife's passing, yet after nearly a year, tonight it seemed to gain something new, a sense of purpose as bright as the winter stars outside. She prayed silently that God would keep him safe upon the ocean as he sailed forth to face the enemy.

Derby Wharf, Salem, March 1777

THE HARBOR TEEMED with life as the townsfolk gathered along Derby Wharf. Eunice stood a little apart with Hannah and Polly, Martha and Silas flanking her like steadfast sentries, her gaze fixed on the ship that would soon carry Captain Haraden across the sea.

Children darted between the legs of sailors and merchants, craning for a glimpse of the two brigantines at anchor. Hawkers cried out, "Hot chestnuts and ginger cakes!" Their voices carried over the slap of rigging against masts. The crowd pressed close, for all Salem knew this morning marked more than a departure, it was a declaration. Two state ships, the *Tyrannicide* and the *Massachusetts*, would sail together to strike the enemy across the ocean.

The *Tyrannicide* drew many eyes: her ochre hull gleamed against the gray chop of the water, her blue stern scrollwork and painted stars catching the weak spring sunlight. The townsfolk pointed at her proudly, whispering her new captain's name.

Captain Haraden stood on the wharf, not far away, his

sea cloak drawn tight against the March wind, returning greetings with nods and brief words, and conferring with his new first lieutenant, Israel Thorndike, to whom Eunice had only just been introduced. The first officer was tall and broad-shouldered, young but with an alertness about him that marked him as more than a seaman. A year ago, Captain Haraden had been a first lieutenant. Today, he bore the full weight of command. Eunice and his whole family were very proud of him.

John Fisk, brisk and booming beside the new captain, barked last-minute orders to his own officers aboard the *Massachusetts* before turning to clap Captain Haraden's shoulder. "The tide waits for no man. Let's show His Majesty what two Salem brigantines can do. As soon as the good reverend blesses our ships, we'll be off."

Johnny Deadman came running down the gangplank to Captain Haraden's side. "Your cabin is all in order sir," he said breathlessly. "Your chest is in place and your instruments and books are set where you told me you like them."

Captain Haraden placed his hand on the boy's shoulder. "Good lad, Johnny."

Hannah tugged at her bonnet, breathless with excitement, while Polly wriggled in Eunice's arms, more interested in the bustle than the ships. Eunice's parents had joined them. Her father, Reverend James Diman, grave in his black preaching robe, stood nearby, a dark figure against the gray harbor. Beside him, the face of her mother, Mary Diman, softened with concern. They had come to see the ships off and to pray for their successful return.

Eunice's mother bent close to Eunice, her voice low but insistent. "You have done well with Captain Haraden's children and household," she said gently, "but at twenty-five you are still young. In time, should you wish it, you might think of marrying again."

Eunice adjusted Polly in her arms. "This is where God has me, Mother. This is where I belong. They need me." She kept her eyes on Captain Haraden, knowing her answer was true, whatever her future might hold.

"Very well," said her mother. Her glance flicked toward Captain Haraden. "There will be suitors enough when you are ready."

When all was prepared, Eunice's father stepped forward, his black preaching robe blown back by the raw March wind. He lifted his voice above the harbor noise, and the crowd hushed as he prayed aloud, commending the ships and their crews to God's keeping, asking for courage, for wisdom, and for triumph over the foe. His words rolled out strong and certain, the same cadence Eunice remembered from her youth.

Captain Haraden crossed the short distance to his family, bending to press a kiss to Hannah's brow before turning to Polly in Eunice's arms. He kissed the little girl's cheek, and in doing so, his head came so near to Eunice's that she caught the clean salt scent of the sea still clinging to him. For an instant her breath quickened, then she took hold of herself, dismissing the feeling as swiftly as it came. "Mind your lessons, my girl," he said to Hannah, his voice calm as his eyes softened. "Do all Mrs. Mason asks of you."

"I will, Papa," Hannah whispered fiercely. "Bring us

back a prize!"

He chuckled. "I will certainly try." Then he turned to Eunice, Martha and Silas. The din of the harbor faded, and there was only his quiet gaze meeting hers. "The house is in good hands," he told them. His gaze rested on each in turn before settling on Eunice. "I'll not worry while I'm at sea. Not while you hold those I love."

"You have our prayers," Eunice answered, her tone calm, though she felt her heart clench.

Martha sniffed and muttered, "Best be bringin' back more than prayers."

Silas gave a gruff chuckle, lifting a hand in salute.

The sailors cheered when Captain Haraden strode up the gangplank, and the bos'n's whistle trilled. Lines were cast off, canvas climbed the masts, and with the captain's orders, the *Tyrannicide* eased from her berth.

The brigantines stood out together, bowsprits cutting eastward, sails swelling white against the pale sky. From the deck, Captain Haraden lifted his hand in farewell. The crowd's cheer rose as they waved.

On the wharf, Hannah raised her voice high and clear. "God keep you, Papa!"

"Yes, good captain," Eunice whispered, "God keep you."

"I wish to have no connection with any ship that does not sail fast; for I intend to go in harm's way."
– John Paul Jones

CHAPTER 8

The middle of the Atlantic Ocean, April 1777

THE ATLANTIC HEAVED in long blue swells, the two Salem brigantines riding them with steady grace. The *Tyrannicide* and the *Massachusetts* had been out scarcely a fortnight when, on the morning of the 8th of April, the lookout's cry carried down from the foremast. "Sail ho! Off the larboard bow!"

Jon raised his glass, the April wind whipping his hair as he steadied himself on the *Tyrannicide*'s quarterdeck. The stranger loomed on the gray horizon, sails straining eastward, a bluff-bowed bark, deep in the water with cargo. Her canvas strained under a freshening breeze, bound westward. No colors flew from her mast.

He lowered the glass, jaw tightening. "What ship runs

without colors in these waters?"

Israel Thorndike, his new first lieutenant, shaded his eyes. "Could be a neutral, Captain. Or she's British and waiting to see if we dare press her."

Jon's gaze flicked to the *Massachusetts* a cable's length away, her sails taut as she kept station. "Let's press her." Through his glass, Jon studied the vessel. On her taffrail gleamed the name *Lonsdale*, though she showed no port of registry. "Name sounds English, and she's five hundred tons, if she's an ounce," he said, lowering the glass. "She's no coaster. That's an ocean trader, ripe for plucking." Jon lowered his glass and turned to his first lieutenant. "Mr. Thorndike, signal the *Massachusetts*. We'll wear Dutch colors."

"Aye, sir."

A seaman sprang to the halyards. Moments later, the *Tyrannicide*'s Dutch tricolor climbed her peak. Across the water, the *Massachusetts* answered with the same, her own Appeal to Heaven and Continental Union flag hauled down and replaced. To the *Lonsdale*'s watch, two harmless traders now bore down upon her.

He lifted his speaking trumpet. "Mr. Lovett, bring us down across her wake. Clear away the starboard guns."

Fisk, aboard the *Massachusetts*, hailed across the chop. "Shall we try her, Haraden?"

Jon gave a short nod. Both Salem ships broke from their line, adjusting sail to cut across the bark's course. To all eyes they wore the tricolors of Holland, safe passage for merchantmen, or so the *Lonsdale*'s master might believe.

The hours dragged as the Americans closed. Finally, the bark hoisted her own flag: a red ensign. A British merchantman.

"She shows her teeth," Thorndike muttered at Haraden's elbow.

"Aye. And we'll see how sharp they are."

At pistol-shot range, Haraden gave the order, "Strike the Dutch flag!" The Dutch flag snapped down, and in its place soared two banners of the United States: the Continental Union flag and the Appeal to Heaven pine tree flag, streaming proud in the April wind.

The bark's deck erupted with shouts. A gun boomed from her larboard side, the shot falling short.

"Mr. Moses," Haraden called, "run out the starboard battery."

The *Tyrannicide*'s guns heaved against their tackles. Her crew stood tense at the batteries, matches poised, handspikes braced. Powder boys clutched their bags, eyes wide.

Jon lifted his trumpet, his voice carrying above the wind. "Stand by! …Fire as your guns bear!"

Through the smoke, Thorndike shouted, "Fire!" And his order was relayed down the line.

The broadside thundered, the ship staggering as flame and smoke leapt from her flanks. Round shot smashed into the *Lonsdale*'s hull and rigging. Splinters flew like hail, and her foretopmast shivered but held. She answered with a ragged volley, iron balls shrieking overhead and spouting spray from the sea.

From windward a lookout aboard the *Massachusetts* pointed, bellowing across the water. Fisk hoisted a private signal and cupped his hands to shout, "Strange sail to weather! Bearing down!"

"At your discretion!" Jon answered through the trumpet. "Learn her nature and rejoin!"

The *Massachusetts* put her helm up and shouldered off under a press of canvas, slewing away on a slanting course. In moments she was a tumble of wake and white cloth, leaving the *Tyrannicide* to grapple the bark alone.

For three hours they hammered at one another, close-hauled in the rolling Atlantic. Twice the *Lonsdale* tried to sheer off, but the *Tyrannicide* clung to her flank, gunners working like furies under Moses and Lovett. The bark's planking was split and scarred; her sails hung in tatters.

A moment passed and the red ensign that had flown so stubbornly wavered, then came down.

Thorndike, powder-smudged and exultant at Jon's side, shouted, "Colors struck, Captain!"

A cheer split the *Tyrannicide*'s deck. Cabin boys whooped, and the marines in their green coats thumped their muskets in triumph.

"Steady, lads," Jon called, his voice firm over the din. "Mr. Thorndike, detail men for the prize crew and see them armed and ready. Mr. Sibley will take command as prize master and take her into Boston."

Thorndike gave a sharp salute and went at once, calling men to the boats.

Jon took one last look at the battered bark as lines were passed across. Her deck was littered with splintered spars and wounded men, their surgeon already moving among them.

A little before sunset the *Massachusetts* came foaming back into company, her topsails drawing handsomely. Fisk cupped his hands to hail the *Tyrannicide*. "A Frenchman flying the Bourbon flag. No harm done. I see you've got the bark!"

"We have," Jon called back. "Sibley will take her into Boston with a prize crew."

Fisk tipped his hat. "Godspeed to them, and to you, Captain."

As the *Tyrannicide* and *Massachusetts* bore away on their new course, Jon looked back to see the *Lonsdale* wallowing under shortened sail, now flying American colors above her scarred hull. He allowed himself a tight smile. One more blow struck for liberty, and the first prize of his command.

TWO WEEKS LATER, Jon came on deck to join his first lieutenant and accept his morning coffee from Johnny. Taking a sip of the hot brew, Jon gazed out at the Atlantic, rolling gray and restless, whitecaps whipping under a stiff westerly. The *Tyrannicide* and *Massachusetts* kept close company, their canvas straining eastward toward the stormy Bay of Biscay off the west coast of France.

"Convoy to windward!" The lookout's cry snapped every head up.

From the quarterdeck, Jon handed his mug to Johnny and swung his glass, bracing against the pitch. Far off, sails glimmered against the horizon, a line of ships, nine or ten at least, crowded together under escort.

Fisk hailed across the chop from the *Massachusetts*: "British convoy! Bound west, by the look of her!"

Jon's jaw tightened. "For New York, if my guess is right. See there, two men-of-war with them. One of sixty, another of fourteen guns." He lowered the glass. "Too rich for us to swallow whole."

But even as he said it, one vessel lagged, hanging astern of the convoy, struggling to keep pace.

Thorndike's eyes flashed, as he pointed. "Captain, a straggler."

Jon raised the glass again. The brig wallowed clumsily, sails straining, her escort already drawing away with the fleet. "Aye, the *Favorite*, and no one turning back for her." He shouted to Fisk on the *Massachusetts*, "That one's ours!" And to the *Tyrannicide*'s crew, he ordered, "Hoist away!"

The two brigantines bore down under every stitch of canvas. As they closed, the lone brig hoisted the red ensign. Jon raised his glass, catching sight of figures scrambling on her deck and muskets glinting in the sun. "She carries troops."

Within musket shot of the brig, Jon's voice cut through the wind: "Strike your colors and heave to!"

A sputter of musketry cracked from the brig in reply, balls whining overhead into the sea.

"Answer them!" Jon barked. The *Tyrannicide*'s marines leveled their muskets, the volley thundering in return. Fisk's *Massachusetts* swung alongside to cover the other flank, her guns run out, her marines firing as one.

For a heartbeat the British brig held on, stubborn against the twin predators closing on her. Then her red ensign fluttered down. A ragged cheer burst from the *Tyrannicide*'s deck.

Thorndike grinned. "She yields, Captain!"

"Pass the word to Fisk. He'll furnish the prize crew,"

Jon ordered. "We'll take a few of the soldiers from the *Favorite*." Flags broke from the *Tyrannicide*'s halyards, signaling across the water. From the *Massachusetts*, boats were lowered at once, prize master and armed sailors pulling for the captured brig.

Jon soon discovered the troops the brig carried were Hessians, sixty-odd soldiers in green coats with red facings, tall boots, and scowling faces beneath black cocked hats. "Chasseurs in full kit," said Jon to Thorndike. "Light infantry from Germany hired as auxiliaries by the British, and known as expert marksmen." The chasseurs who were ferried across to the *Tyrannicide* under guard, bore sullen expressions. Their cartridge boxes and sabers were taken, their mutters in guttural German punctuated with black looks.

The *Tyrannicide* received a handful—officers and men enough for questioning—while the bulk of the Germans remained aboard the *Favorite* under Fisk's guard. One spat into the sea as his comrades scowled beneath their cocked hats.

Benjamin Moses watched grimly as weapons clattered into piles. "Better in the holds of our ships than in the hands of the British army."

Jon looked on, his face hard, though a spark of satisfaction burned behind his eyes. "Aye. Washington will know how to put such a windfall to use."

Fisk's voice carried from his own quarterdeck as he hailed across the water, "Well taken, Haraden! That'll nettle the Crown more than a dozen merchant brigs."

Jon nodded as the convoy, sails swelling, vanished westward over the horizon, but their straggler, the transport *Favorite*, now stood captured, her Hessian passengers sullen captives of the Massachusetts' Navy.

Off the coast of Cape Clear, Ireland, late April 1777

THE *TYRANNICIDE* WAS two days off the coast of Ireland under a gray sky when Jon heard the lookout's hail shouted down the mast, "Sail ho! Off the larboard bow!"

Jon lifted his glass, sighting the two-masted snow *Sally* driving hard before the wind. "She's no fishing craft," he said to his first lieutenant. "Deep laden, bound westward." The *Massachusetts* held close company off their quarter, Fisk already lifting his spyglass to his eye.

As the brigantines bore down, the snow broke out her colors, the red ensign snapping bright against the gloom. Jon's mouth, set in a hard line. "British, and trying for Quebec if I judge her course."

"Orders, Captain?" Thorndike asked.

"Run out the guns."

The two American ships fanned to either side, hemming the stranger in. Faced with a double broadside, the snow fired one defiant shot, the ball skipping wide. The reply from the *Tyrannicide* and *Massachusetts* was thunder and iron. Splinters flew from the snow's bulwarks. Within minutes her red ensign fluttered down.

Jon lowered his glass, satisfaction burning in his chest. "Mr. Moses, stand ready to board her."

When the prize crew returned with her manifest, the truth of their catch stirred a cheer from stem to stern. Three to four thousand blankets, bales of cloth, and other goods bound for the British army in Quebec would now provide comfort for Patriot soldiers. Benjamin Moses himself brought the papers to Jon, his grin boyish despite the powder stains on his coat.

"Blankets, Captain. Enough to warm half of Washington's camp."

Jon's eyes narrowed on the bundled cargo. "Then we've struck a true blow. No man fights well when he freezes. See that she's secured, Mr. Thorndike, and let Master Benjamin Lovett lead the prize crew taking her into Boston."

Three days later, on the last day of April, fortune smiled again. East of Cape Clear, Jon's lookout sighted another sail wallowing heavy with cargo. This one hoisted no flag until the Americans pressed close. Then the red ensign flew stubbornly from her peak.

Jon gave a sharp nod. "Another Briton. Let's take her."

The *Massachusetts* led the chase, her bow churning white foam. The *Tyrannicide* pressed hard to starboard. The ship was the brig *Trespassy*, and she could not outpace them. A shot across her bows brought her up sharp.

She yielded with scarcely a fight, and when boarded, proved to be 160 tons, her hold packed deep with salt, flour and goods for Newfoundland. A poor prize compared to the *Sally*, but a prize nonetheless.

Fisk's booming voice carried across the sea as the vessels hove to. "Another safe for Boston, Haraden! The Board of War will be pleased!"

Jon permitted himself a rare smile. Two stout prizes in a week, and the Atlantic still wide before them. The men cheered, dreaming already of shares and silver.

But Jon's gaze turned eastward, where the horizon loomed uncertain. He knew well enough the British would not long leave such depredations unanswered.

Haraden house, late April 1777

WHILE CAPTAIN HARADEN was far away at sea, Eunice anticipated visitors, for the Gloucester Haradens had sent word they were on their way. One morning, as she was busy in the parlor with Hannah's lessons, the clatter of wheels on the cobbled street and the high chatter of girls' voices broke the still air.

Hannah raced to the windows. "Cousins!"

Eunice went to the door and opened it to see the Haraden cousins from Gloucester stepping down from the chaise. Andrew Haraden, tall and broad-shouldered, with brown hair queued at his neck, offered his hand to his wife, Lydia, a handsome woman with dark hair, while around them clustered their daughters, six in all, a flock of dark-haired sparrows eager to scatter into the dooryard.

"Mercy on us," Martha exclaimed, drying her hands on her apron as she came to the door. "The Haraden girls have grown like weeds! And don't tell me they eat like weeds, too, or I'll be in my grave by Michaelmas."

"Line up, girls," said Lydia Haraden briskly, "so that I may properly present you." At once the six Haraden children formed a line, beginning with the tallest.

Eunice stepped forward. "Good day and welcome! I am Mrs. Mason, the girls' governess."

From behind his wife, Andrew lifted a toddler from

the chaise. "Jonathan explained all in his letter, Mrs. Mason. We were glad of his invitation, and gladder still to hear how you're tending Hannah and Polly. We've two by those names ourselves, though our Hannah is called Joanna most days." He nodded toward Martha. "'Lo, Martha, how are you?"

"Fine now," said Martha with a sniff. "We'll see how fine when I've eight young ones underfoot and a table to stretch to fit them all."

Andrew chuckled and began the introductions. "This is Joanna. She's nineteen. Then," he said gesturing, "come Lydia and Betsey, who are fourteen and twelve. Peggy is ten, Jane four, and this squirming creature is our Polly."

Little Polly wriggled, reaching for the ground. Martha stepped forward to take her. "Here, I'll see to her. She can keep our Polly company. Silas is mindin her in the parlor." With that, Martha disappeared inside with the child.

The house filled at once with the stir of kin: cloaks hung on pegs, chatter at the hearth, Martha bustling to set extra places for the meal with the help of the older Haraden girls.

In the parlor, Silas chuckled at the din as Eunice invited Andrew and Lydia to sit. She gathered the younger girls close to help shed their wrappings, feeling the air brighten with family warmth despite the spring chill.

Andrew clasped Silas' hand firmly. "It seemed the right time to come." And handing him an envelope, he said, "Give this to Martha. It's for expenses, increased for our coming."

Silas nodded. "Will do, sir."

Lydia's glance found Eunice. "We shall pray for Jonathan together," she said gently.

Martha bustled in again, never one to hold her tongue. "Prayers, aye, but there's news already in town. They say the captain's taken a bark called the *Lonsdale*, a snow *Sally*, brimmin' with blankets, and another ship stuffed with Hessians who'll never trouble our shores."

The words set the room astir at once. Hannah's eyes went wide, and she clutched Eunice's hand. "Is it true, Mrs. Mason? Has Papa truly taken ships?"

Eunice's heart swelled at the eagerness in the girl's face. "So the newsmen say," she answered steadily. "Your papa is doing his duty, and God has blessed his hands."

Silas gave a grunt. "Aye. If half the talk is true, the Crown will rue the day they let Captain Haraden slip out of Salem Harbor."

Martha returned with glasses of wine for the travelers and watered cider and cracknels for the girls, which were gratefully accepted.

"Jonathan told us in his letter you are the daughter of Reverend Diman," said Andrew.

"I am," Eunice replied, watching the two Pollys on the carpet side by side, as alike in mischief as in name.

"How fortunate he was to find you," Lydia said. "A virtuous young widow for his daughters."

"Aye," Martha added. "God was smilin' on the captain."

The chatter rose, cousins darting, the two other women speaking of children, war, and needed prayer. Eunice stood amidst it all, for a moment feeling the house alive as it had been not since the funeral a year ago. Yet the laughter, so bright, only sharpened her longing. She prayed silently that Captain Haraden might live to walk again among such noise and warmth, and that his daughters might keep his memory alive until he returned.

When the din in the parlor eased, Eunice said, "Martha will need more of everything with such a merry garrison. If the older girls will come with me, we can fetch what's wanted from the market."

"Bless you," Martha replied, her relief plain. "Bring a sack of good flour, two cheeses, clams for chowder, onions, a side of salt pork if the price is fair, some nice cod, and winter apples if any keep yet, and whatever greens you can find. Oh, and molasses if the merchant's cask hasn't run dry."

Andrew, shrugging into his coat, tipped his hat. "I'll step to the London Coffeehouse and see who's in from sea. Might have more news of Cousin Jonathan."

"Go," Lydia told him, smiling. "We'll be quite well here."

Eunice gathered Hannah, the older Joanna from Gloucester, Lydia, and Betsey, leaving Peggy to mind the little ones, as they set off down the street, bonnets bobbing in a row. Silas went with them, his stride steady at the rear, a quiet guardian.

When Joanna hoisted the flour sack to her hip, Silas gave a grunt of approval and plucked it from her arms, slinging it over his shoulder as though it weighed no more than kindling. At the fishmonger's stall he eyed the cod and muttered, "Robbery, but better robbed than hungry," which made the girls laugh.

The market square smelled of salt and smoke: fishmongers calling haddock and cod, a farmer's cart with tired cabbages, and a woman selling eggs dearer than last week. The girls made a game of Martha's list: Lydia haggling shrewdly for cheese, Betsey testing onions for soundness, Joanna lifting baskets with a practiced arm.

Now and again a townsman touched his hat to them. "You've added to your charges, Mrs. Mason," one said.

"I have," she replied. "Cousins from Gloucester."

He stopped to add, "News says the *Tyrannicide* and *Massachusetts* have captured a snow, the *Sally*, with 4,000 blankets aboard!"

Hannah looked up at Eunice. "Is that the ship Papa captured?"

"Yes," said Eunice. "One that carried blankets much needed for General Washington's army. I think your father is exactly where Providence means him to be, capturing every enemy ship that comes across his path."

Hannah stayed close to Eunice's skirts, shy among the taller cousins, until the eldest of the Gloucester brood, Joanna, bent to her with an easy smile. "We share a name, little cousin, though they call me Joanna most days. That makes us a pair."

Salem's Hannah brightened. "And you've a Polly, too!"

Betsey laughed and linked arms with her sister, Lydia. "Two Pollys. Martha will have to label their cups."

"One has dark hair and one fair, but they may be better known by their mischief," said Lydia, eyes dancing.

Back at the house, the older girls lugged sacks to the pantry and then joined Eunice in the parlor. Silas had already returned by another way and now sat in his accustomed chair by the hearth, pipe in hand and a block of pine in his lap. His knife moved in slow, easy strokes, whittling shavings that curled to a bowl on the floor while the younger girls played at his feet. "This house hasn't seen such a muster of skirts in years," he said dryly, though the corners of his mouth twitched. "If the captain were here, he'd think he'd walked into a regiment."

THE LAUGHTER THAT followed carried into the kitchen, where Martha set the dough to kneading with Mrs. Haraden. She had known the Gloucester Haradens since the early days of the captain's marriage to Hannah Deadman and always enjoyed their company.

"You keep a fine kitchen," Lydia said, working the dough with a sure, rhythmic push as she gazed around at the neat cupboards and pots and pans.

"I keep it movin'," Martha said, though pride warmed her tone. "And with eight girls under one roof, I'll keep it marchin'. 'Twas good I baked pies this mornin'."

Lydia chuckled. "The girls love pies."

For a time they worked in companionable noise, the thud of kneading, the hiss from the kettle, the two young Pollys babbling in the next room as Mrs. Mason warned them away from the fireplace tools. Lydia glanced toward the parlor where Eunice's voice rose gentle and sure, organizing all into order, as she offered to read the girls a story.

"She has a way," Lydia said softly. "Mrs. Mason. The children look to her and grow calmer. A pretty woman, too, handsome in the best sense."

Martha's mouth twitched. "Aye. Pretty won't count if

there's no backbone behind it. But our Mrs. Mason has both."

"I do not mean to play the matchmaker," Lydia went on, eyes on the dough she was kneading, "Jonathan's path is mostly at sea now, and the girls are young. But a house can't stand long without a mistress who loves it. Might Providence have such a thing in mind, do you think?"

Martha dusted the loaf with flour and set it to rise. Looking off into the distance, she said, "If Providence means to knit such things, He'll do it in His time. Till then, the captain and the governess seem ignorant of how well suited they are. The captain's girls have all they need: a governess with sense, a father who is doing his part for the cause, a kitchen that feeds them, a church to worship in, and kin close by."

Lydia smiled. "Then we shall be content with that."

"Content, and busy," Martha said, reaching for a pie tin. "Hand me those apples, Lydia. With a dozen to feed, I'd best make another pie."

"The greatest man is he…who is calmest in storms, and whose reliance on truth, on virtue, on God, is the most unfaltering."
– Seneca

CHAPTER 9

Bay of Biscay, May 1777

THE *TYRANNICIDE* WAS lighter of crew than Jon liked. Success had cost him dearly. Every prize taken had meant sending off officers and hands to sail her into port, and now his brigantine sailed lean, her decks crowded with goods but her watches thin. Even the cabin boys had stepped into duties beyond their years. Johnny Deadman, Bobby Grover and Joshua Trask were fetching coffee to the quarterdeck, powdering cartridges in the magazine, and scrubbing decks, all with the wiry energy of the young.

The *Massachusetts* held close off their larboard quarter as dawn light spilled across a restless Atlantic. Jon had his glass trained on a sail to windward, a single ship running eastward, ripe for the chase. Then the lookout's cry split the air. "Three sail bearing down!"

Jon swung his glass and his stomach clenched. Warships, unmistakable, hulls dark and bristling with guns, their sails straining in the morning breeze. A squadron. Not three, but nine, looming larger with every heartbeat.

"The Royal Navy," Thorndike breathed beside him.

Jon's jaw hardened. "Aye. And with us square in their sights."

With the *Massachusetts* close enough to hear, Fisk hailed across the water, "What's our play, Haraden?"

Jon's answer was crisp, grim. "We run!"

The two brigantines surged ahead together, bows driving into the swells, their masts straining under every inch of canvas. Side by side they fled, chased by the gray wall of the squadron. For hours the *Massachusetts* clung to the *Tyrannicide*'s wake, Fisk's voice sometimes faintly heard over the wind as he bellowed orders to his own crew.

The *Tyrannicide*'s timbers creaked as she strained eastward, but the great British men-of-war pressed closer, their guns glinting like hungry teeth.

Hours passed in a blur of canvas adjustments, shouted orders, and the heave of the Atlantic. By evening the chase had scattered. A single British frigate pressed hardest on their heels, her long guns already booming across the water. Jon caught sight of Fisk's brig luffing away to the north, hauling to the wind in a desperate bid to shake pursuit.

"The *Massachusetts* is breaking off," Thorndike cried.

Jon's heart clenched, but he thrust down the fear. "He must do what he can. We'll do the same."

"We're too heavy, Captain," Thorndike said, voice taut. "She'll not outpace them carrying all this."

Jon's decision was instant. "Lighten the ship. Guns first."

A gasp rippled across the deck, but the order flew. Crews ran to the batteries, heaving cannon from carriages, tumbling them overboard one by one. "Better we lose our guns than our lives," he muttered under his breath.

The brigantine shuddered as iron splashed into the sea, her broadside gone. Jon ordered the stores overboard next, casks, spare timber, anything not nailed fast.

Johnny Deadman clung to a rail, wide-eyed, then darted to help heave a water cask toward the gunport. Jon caught his eye, gave a sharp nod. Even the boys were doing their part.

Freed of her burden, the *Tyrannicide* lifted on the swell, riding lighter, faster. The sea foamed white at her bow. The gap widened, inch by inch, the roar of British guns fading astern. By nightfall, the *Massachusetts* was lost to sight, swallowed by the heaving dark. Astern, the enemy's lanterns dwindled, their chase abandoned.

Jon leaned on the taffrail, chest heaving, hands raw from the day's work. The ship was stripped, her teeth gone, her belly empty, but she was free. Ahead, faint and welcome, the lights of Bilbao, Spain shimmered through the night haze.

Safety at last.

Bilbao, Spain, early June 1777

BILBAO'S HARBOR CRADLED the weary *Tyrannicide*, her masts stark against the green hills that rose steep from the water. The quays bustled with Basque fishermen mending nets, women carrying baskets of oranges and onions, and stevedores shouting in Spanish as they rolled wine casks down to waiting ships. The air was thick with tar, salt, and the smell of smoked sardines.

Here, among friendly strangers, the American brigantine found refuge. Local shipwrights helped her crew patch sails and caulk seams, while fresh cannon were hauled aboard from the foundries upriver. Chaplain Marsh led the men in a prayer service on the deck, giving thanks for deliverance and Providence's continued favor.

Once repairs were made and the ship provisioned, Jon wasted no time venturing out to sea. On the 6th of June. the *Tyrannicide* fell in with the British merchantman *Chalkley*, her hold stuffed with goods. The merchant captain quickly struck his colors, and Jon sent her back to port under a prize crew.

Not a week later they snapped up the *Eagle*, another British prize, this one heavy with cargo. Johnny Deadman nearly burst with pride, crowing to anyone who would listen, "Captain Haraden doesn't miss his mark, not once!"

Jon allowed the boy his boasting. In truth, each capture stoked his own fierce satisfaction. He had slipped the jaws of the British squadron, and he was not done yet.

But as the *Tyrannicide* rocked gently in Bilbao's harbor, her new guns secure and her crew refreshed, Jon felt the pull of home stronger than the sea wind. The prizes were already consigned to the merchants' agents ashore, their cargoes to be sold for the profit of state and crew. Now his duty was to carry his own ship, lean, fast, and ready, safely back across the ocean to Massachusetts.

Nantes, France, 21 May 1777

JOHN FISK SAT in his cabin on the *Massachusetts*, quill in hand, careful not to smudge the ink as the ship's motion jostled his hand. He paused, staring out the stern windows at the Loire, crowded with masts and French merchants bustling on the wharves.

He'd reached a safe harbor, but there was no word of Captain Haraden. He had put off his report to the Board of War as long as he could. Now, he wrote steadily, though his hand tightened on the page.

> *I regret I do not have the pleasure of advising you the* Tyrannicide *is here with me. On the seventeenth at nine in the morning we gave chase to a ship standing to the eastward and came up fast. At three we got within two miles of the ship, then saw three sail in the N.E. bearing down to us, and then the whole squadron appeared. One of said sail hoisted English colors. I bore away and made sail from them; the ship gave me chase. Captain Haraden bore away also, chased by another ship. The ship came up with us fast. At nine at night, I hauled my wind; Captain Haraden bore away before the wind. At half after nine, I lost sight of Captain Haraden and soon after, lost sight of the ship. At ten, I saw three flashes of guns, which I suppose the ship fired at Cap-*

*tain Haraden. I am afraid the ship took him, as I have
not heard nor seen anything of him since.*

Setting down the quill, he pressed his brow with ink-stained fingers. Rumors had already reached Nantes that the mighty *Foudroyant*, a Royal Navy ship of the line, had been seen patrolling the coast. Fisk almost fancied he could hear her guns in memory, echoing across the Bay of Biscay, thunder that had not yet spent itself.

He shook the thought away, blotted the page, and sealed the letter. A French clerk waited discreetly at the cabin door to see it delivered to the packet bound across the Atlantic. Soon the words would make their own perilous voyage, and in Salem they would fall like shot through the heart: Captain Haraden lost, the *Tyrannicide* taken.

Salem, early June 1777

THE NEWS CAME first in murmurs at the wharves, carried ashore from a coaster out of France. By evening it was on every tongue: the *Tyrannicide* had been chased by a British squadron off the Bay of Biscay, and Captain Haraden was lost. Some swore a ship of the line had taken him, the dreaded *Foudroyant* with her towering guns.

By morning, the talk reached the market at Essex and Central Streets. Martha heard it from the fishmonger, who shook his head as he wrapped her cod. "They say your captain's gone, Martha. Taken, or worse."

She snapped her head up. "No. Jonathan Haraden's

too sharp for them, you'll see. He's bested worse odds."

But the fishmonger only sighed, and Martha's voice faltered as the denial turned to dread. She came back to the house with her basket heavy, her step heavier still.

Mrs. Mason was in the parlor with Hannah and Polly and the Gloucester Haraden girls. Martha blurted the rumor before she could stop herself.

Hannah froze, eyes wide as saucers. "Papa? Taken?"

Mrs. Mason was on her knees in a moment, in front of the child's chair, drawing her close. "Hush, love. We do not know the truth yet. Rumors run faster than fact. Your father is cleverer than most men afloat. If there is a way clear, he will find it. God will guide him."

"She has the right of it," said Martha, wanting to encourage the child.

The next day was Sunday. The pew was full. Andrew and Lydia Haraden sat close with their brood, their faces solemn. Martha in her best cap, lips pressed tight, sat next to Silas.

Hannah clutched Mrs. Mason's hand and her locket in the other. Polly leaned into the governess.

The reverend's voice carried from the pulpit: prayers for the sick, for the soldiers in the field, and for those at sea, "especially Captain Jonathan Haraden, master of the *Tyrannicide*, and his men, whose fate we know not but commend to the keeping of Almighty God."

"Amen," Silas rumbled, his seaman's growl breaking the silence, and the congregation echoed him, a low murmur of assent.

Mrs. Mason bowed her head and Martha bowed hers, too. Around them, the children fidgeted in silence. Martha prayed as hard as she ever had, that the captain lived, that Providence watched over him, that the whispers of capture would prove only shadows.

When the hymn rose—"O God, our help in ages past"—the Haraden pews sang with the rest, voices thin but resolute, clinging to the promise that God's hand still guided those on the seas.

Marblehead Harbor, 23 July 1777

THE *MASSACHUSETTS* CAME to anchor off Marblehead on a clear summer morning, her sails worn thin from weeks of hard weather. Captain John Fisk stood at the rail, watching the town stir along its narrow streets and crowded wharves. Here was home, though not quite. Salem was where his hearth lay, but Marblehead was where the ship belonged.

"Strike the colors and furl her neat," he told his men. "We'll make her tidy before the yardmen set eyes on her."

The brigantine had come in lean, her crew thinned by prize crews sent off, her timbers sorely in need of a carpenter's care. John wasted no time once they dropped anchor. He dispatched a runner to Boston with his official report for the Board of War. Clerks and shipyard hands came aboard to tally goods, and he gave orders to strip out tired cordage, mend spars, and bring in provisions for the next cruise.

Pausing on the quarterdeck, his gaze lingered toward the northwest, where Salem lay only three miles distant. Duty first, always. But when the *Massachusetts* was squared away, he meant to ride to Salem at once. Word had reached him in France and must be carried: Captain Haraden was not captured or worse, as rumor had it, but safe at Bilbao, his brig refitted and prizes in tow.

The wharf was crowded with townsfolk craning for a glimpse of the *Massachusetts'* captain and crew. A boat was lowered, and John came ashore, shoulders stooped with weariness, his coat salt-stained from the Atlantic. Yet there was a brightness in his eyes that belied his grave manner.

The people pressed in around him, voices clamoring:

"Captain Fisk! What of Haraden?"

"Is the *Tyrannicide* taken?"

"Speak, sir," said another, "we've heard the worst!"

John lifted a hand for quiet. "Friends," he said, his voice hoarse but clear, "when last I parted from Captain Haraden, I feared him lost. The British squadron had us both in chase, and when I saw flashes of their guns, I thought him taken."

A groan rippled through the crowd. Heads bowed, women clutched children tighter. But John's tone shifted, rising firm above the murmurs.

"Yet before I quitted France, a schooner out of Bilbao brought tidings. Haraden was safe! The *Tyrannicide* ran the gauntlet, threw her guns and stores overboard to lighten the ship, and so made Bilbao Harbor. He is free and sound, with prizes of his own to boast."

The wharf erupted, cries of joy, hats flung aloft, neighbors clasping hands in sudden relief. "Alive! Haraden lives!" the call rang, carried into the town.

John's face eased into a weary smile. "I'll not tarry. Salem must hear this. Captain Haraden's children have waited long enough for the truth."

He stepped into a waiting chaise bound for Salem. The crowd parted with cheers and blessings, following him with their eyes until the road turned inland.

Salem, later that day

EUNICE WAS WITH Hannah in the parlor when the knock came. She rose and opened the door to find John Fisk himself on the step, sunburned and his hair lighter with the sun, but with a spark in his eyes.

"Captain Fisk!" she exclaimed, stepping aside at once. "Come in. Have you news?"

Martha came from the kitchen wiping her hands on her apron. "I can see from your face what news you carry is not bad."

Eunice gestured the captain to a chair. "Please sit."

Hannah stared, wide-eyed, at the familiar seaman. Polly looked up from the hearth rug where she had been playing.

"I've come from Marblehead," Fisk said, lowering himself wearily into the chair, his cocked hat in his hand. "And with news I think you'll welcome."

Hannah's voice burst out before Eunice could hush her. "Is it Papa? Have you seen him?"

"I have not seen him, Child," Fisk said gently. "But I have word. You may put aside your fears. A schooner out of Spain brought the report to Nantes where I had put in. Captain Haraden made Bilbao safe. He threw his guns and stores overboard to outsail a British squadron, and he's alive and well." Then with a chuckle, he added, "Took two prizes since, bold as ever."

Eunice felt Hannah's grip tighten on her hand, then loosen in sudden relief. Her own spirit was awash in joy for the news. "He is saved! God be praised, our prayers are answered."

Martha's eyes shone as she gave a sharp nod. "Aye, God heard us plain enough."

Fisk went on, his tone firm. "The *Massachusetts* is laid up for refit in Marblehead. Captain Haraden, God willing, will follow me home in due time. When he does, he'll come into Boston, for his brigantine will need more than a patch and a spar. But until then, you may know he lives, and he fights still."

"You'll be stayin' for supper and no questions," Martha told Captain Fisk as she hurried off to the kitchen. "Wait till Silas hears this!"

In the stillness that followed, Hannah pressed close to Eunice, her eyes bright with hope. Polly clambered to her sister and stood. Eunice, her heart steady for the first time since the fearful news, resolved to write to the Gloucester cousins that very night. They must hear that Captain Haraden lived, and that Salem's prayers had been answered.

Boston Harbor, 30 August 1777

JOHNNY DEADMAN APPEARED at the cabin door, holding a steaming cup with both hands. "Coffee, Captain. Strong as you like it."

Jon accepted the mug with a grateful smile, the boy's eagerness softening the morning's weight. Outside the stern windows, Boston's spires had just crept into view, pale against the haze. The *Tyrannicide* moved stiffly through the anchorage, her sails weathered, her timbers aching for care, but she was home. Fresh cannon gleamed at her ports, gifts of Bilbao, yet the long crossing and endless strain had left her needing more than new guns.

Setting the coffee aside, Jon bent to his writing table, quill scratching across the page:

My dear Mrs. Mason,

By God's mercy we are safely arrived in Boston this morning. The Tyrannicide is sore spent by our cruising but still afloat, and I long to see Salem again. I thank you for seeing to the welfare of my daughters. Tell Hannah and Polly their father lives and thinks of them each hour. I shall come as soon as the Board of War releases me from my duties here.

Jonathan Haraden.

He sanded and folded the page, sealing it fast. Johnny would carry it ashore to a post rider bound for Salem before the day was out.

A knock at the cabin door brought a clerk from the Board of War, papers under his arm, his face grave. "Captain Haraden," he said, "the Board bids me welcome you home. And there is much you'll wish to know, some news is good, some not."

Jon gestured him in, and they sat with the harbor breeze fluttering the dispatches. One by one the clerk gave the tidings. "Congress has resolved a new flag for the United States: thirteen stars in a blue field, thirteen stripes red and white."

Inwardly, Jon smiled. "America's banner for us to fight under at last."

"On the 5th of July, Fort Ticonderoga was abandoned. A bitter blow."

Jon's jaw tightened.

"Earlier this month at Oriskany, New York, the field was made bloody with stubborn fighting, but our militia stood their ground."

Jon shook his head. "Is there no good news for Washington?"

"Aye," the clerk's voice lifted with pride. "You'll like this one. On the sixteenth, at Bennington, our New England boys gave General Burgoyne's detachment a drubbing. Captured cannon, prisoners, the works. A true victory."

Jon exhaled slowly, the words settling in. "So, the tide runs both ways."

"It does," the clerk said, meeting his gaze. "And General Washington holds firm. His fortitude keeps the army whole when little else does. That is the truth of it."

Jon nodded. "He is a great leader."

The clerk placed a folded *Boston Gazette* on the table. "Here, Captain. Best read the rest yourself."

Left alone, Jon laid a hand on the paper but let his eyes wander instead to the open window. Shipwrights were boarding the *Tyrannicide* to measure her wounds. She would need months of repair. But Salem lay a day's ride away, and in Salem were two daughters who had believed him lost.

His heart was already gone from the harbor, racing ahead up the road.

Salem, early September 1777

THE LAST OF the daylight slanted across Charter Street when Jon knocked at his door. It swung wide, and he heard Martha mutter about late callers, as she wiped her hands on her apron. Then she looked up and blinked. "Captain Haraden!"

Jon knew what a sight he made, his dark blue coat road-dusted, his hair sun-bleached and salt-tangled, his shoulders weary from months at sea. "Why, Martha, you don't look half so pleased as I'd hoped."

"Pleased? Aye, and vexed besides. You've near put us in mournin' with your silence. Best come in before I scold you proper."

From the stairs came a cry. "Papa!" Hannah flew down and flung herself into his arms.

He hugged her tight, his voice rough. "Hello, sweetheart. Grown taller, I see."

Mrs. Mason followed, hand to her breast at the sight of him. "Oh, my! It is you. How wonderful!" She steadied herself, then stepped forward. "Your letter came, sir. It was thoughtfulness itself to write the moment you reached Boston."

He bowed his head slightly, eyes warm. "I owed you that much." With a glance at Martha, he added, "Too long have you borne rumor and silence in my stead."

With tears in her eyes, Martha shooed him inside. "No standin' on the step like a stranger. Supper's near ready, and more than enough to feed one more."

Jon laughed, the sound joyous in his own ears. "God bless you all," he said as he set down his satchel and came into the parlor.

"Would you like a glass of wine or cider, sir?" asked Mrs. Mason.

"Claret if you please. The carriage from Boston was dusty, and I had enough captures to keep us well stocked." He went into the parlor and sank into his chair. Mrs. Mason handed him a glass of claret with a smile.

"I see you're keeping Hannah, and I presume Polly, fat and rosy as apples, Martha."

"The child's napping," said Mrs. Mason. "You won't recognize her, Captain. She's walking now."

"I helped," said Hannah proudly.

"You did, indeed," said the governess.

Just then, Silas came in from the yard, shoulders dusted with flour. "Been helpin' a neighbor grind corn." He stopped short, blinking, then strode forward with hand outstretched. "Captain! By God, you've slipped the king's jaws again."

Jon clasped his hand firmly. "Not for the first time, and I pray not the last. I see you've kept the hearth stout, and that's worth as much as any broadside."

"Aye," Silas said, pride thick in his voice. "But it's no hearth without the master. Welcome home."

When supper was laid, they all filed into the dining room, Mrs. Mason bringing Polly from her nap. Seeing Jon, the child reached for him, "Pa-pa."

"She's nearly two now," said Mrs. Mason, handing the young child to him. Jon wrapped his arms around his youngest, her warm body a comfort to his soul. He kissed her forehead and handed her back to Mrs. Mason, who slipped Polly into her high chair.

The table was filled with light and noise as dishes were set down. Roasted fowl, turnips, vegetables from Martha's garden and brown bread. "A feast!" exclaimed Jon.

"There's apple pie, too," said Martha. "Just set it to coolin' this mornin'."

Jon sat at the head of the table, Hannah on one side and Mrs. Mason and Polly on the other, the girls' chatter tumbling over each other.

Mrs. Mason poured him another glass of wine. "We had your cousins from Gloucester with us in June," she told him, smiling at the memory. "Six daughters filled the house from hearth to stair, every bedchamber filled. Hannah here found herself with another Hannah, though they call her Joanna. The two are fast friends, and we had two Pollys besides."

Jon could not resist a smile at the thought. "Then you've had a regular garrison of girls in my absence. I almost pity you, Mrs. Mason."

"She bore it better than I did," Martha snorted, though affection softened her tone. "But it kept the house lively, and that was no bad thing."

The meal was a chorus of voices, Hannah telling of her lessons, Polly showing the doll the Gloucester cousins had left behind, Martha breaking in to correct details with her sharp tongue.

Silas came in at the end of the meal to gruffly supply

the latest town gossip. Jon listened, soaking in every word, his gaze often straying to Eunice, whose quiet composure seemed to anchor the household as surely as ballast steadies a ship. *How fortunate are we to have her.*

When the candles burned low, Jon leaned back, contentment flowing through him. For one evening, the sea was far away, the guns silent, and he was only a father at his table, home among his own. The sea had its compass, but this house had Martha, Silas and Eunice, hearth and heart together, and they kept its course as sure as any star.

"Tyranny, like hell, is not easily conquered."
– Thomas Paine 1776

CHAPTER 10

Salem, autumn 1777

THE LEAVES TURNED and dropped in Salem, and for the first time in many months Jonathan Haraden watched them fall from his own threshold. His days ashore passed in a rhythm he had nearly forgotten: mornings spent walking Charter Street with Hannah clutching his hand, evenings at the hearth where Polly's laughter tumbled like bells. The salt of the sea still clung to him, but the aroma of Martha's fresh bread and the sound of Silas splitting kindling in the yard became their own kind of ballast.

He rode often to Boston, summoned by the Board of War. There, in rooms crowded with ledgers and quills, he gave account of the *Tyrannicide*'s escape and her captures. Clerks pressed him with questions, and he left each session weary, longing for open air. But duty held: the brigantine was ordered into Charlestown yard for another refit, and Jon oversaw her repairs with a captain's eye for detail.

Once, leaving the Board, Jon asked after Captain Fisk. A fellow officer only shrugged. "He's gone into trade, I hear. Salem ships make their profit in many ways, not only at the gun's mouth."

Jon felt a pang of surprise, then respect. Fisk had served his turn, and if peace was his harbor, who could gainsay him? Still, Jon knew his own course was not so easily altered.

In Salem, the house on Charter Street was a hive of activity. Hannah pestered him with questions about Spain and Bilbao, tracing her finger across a worn chart he had brought home. Polly tottered across the floor, waving her rag doll and crowing at her own small triumphs. Mrs. Mason, ever calm, kept the household in trim: lessons at the table, games of hopscotch on the sidewalk, and Bible stories in the afternoon. Jon often found his gaze drawn to the governess, the quiet anchor amid the storm of voices.

As always, Martha reigned in the kitchen, while Silas tended to the heavier chores, their teasing conversations a constant source of entertainment.

One evening in late October, a courier from Boston brought Jon's new orders. Jon read them by candlelight while Mrs. Mason took Hannah and Polly up to bed. The *Tyrannicide*, newly fitted, was to sail in company with Captain Simeon Sampson's brigantine, the *Hazard*. Their course: the coasts of Spain and Portugal, thence southward toward Madeira, and home again by the Indies.

He folded the dispatch slowly, the flame glinting in his eyes. Another cruise, another gauntlet. Mrs. Mason came down the stairs to join him in front of the fire blazing in the hearth. "I'll not be alone this time," he said quietly. "Captain Simeon Sampson will sail with me to Spain, Portugal and the Indies."

"Do you know him?"

"By name and reputation. A Plymouth man, he had the brigantine *Independence* before she was lost near Halifax. He held his ground so fiercely even his captors in the Royal Navy honored him. Now he has the *Hazard*, and I'll be glad to see her alongside me rather than another squadron at my stern."

Mrs. Mason inclined her head, her gaze softening. "Then we will pray for two ships, not one."

Jon smiled. "I rely on those prayers of yours."

Outside, the autumn wind stirred through the branches. In the morning, a carpet of gold and red leaves would grace the ground. Soon enough it would be the sea's voice in his ears again, but for this season he was home, and 'twas a harbor he cherished more than any in Spain or Portugal, kept safe by the prayers and care of those who tended it.

Boston Harbor, November 1777

THE *TYRANNICIDE* LAY taut and trim at Charlestown yard, her new cordage humming faintly in the cold wind. Along her deck, familiar figures went briskly about their tasks. Israel Thorndike, first lieutenant, paced the quarterdeck, sharp-eyed as ever. Benjamin Moses checked a tally of powder with John Bray, who had traded his purser's pen for a lieutenant's sword. At the main hatch, Sailing Master Benjamin Lovett barked to the riggers while John Reed, the redheaded cook, squabbled with a stevedore about the quality of the beef casks.

Two boys scuttled between them: Bobby Grover with a coil of line nearly bigger than himself, and Billy Andrews, fresh-joined in October, all elbows and eagerness, carrying a basket of hardtack to the galley. "Mind the steps, Lad!" Reed growled, though there was pride in his voice.

Johnny Deadman had left the ship at the end of August. Jon had been sad to see him go but the lad had a vision for his future and determination enough to see it through.

From the quarterdeck, Jon took in the scene, pleased with what he saw. Lean though they were, these were his men, steady hands that had seen him through Biscay and back. Now, refitted and provisioned, they were ready for another adventure for liberty's sake.

Alongside, the *Hazard* made ready as well, Captain Simeon Sampson towering by her gangway. Sampson's keen gaze swept the *Tyrannicide* before settling on Jon. He came striding across the planks. The two captains clasped hands firmly.

"Trim ship," Sampson said with a nod toward Jon's deck. "Let's see if she keeps it so after a month at sea."

Jon gave a wry smile. "We'll keep her as neat as the *Hazard*, or better." Both men had come through trials and Jon knew he wasn't the only one eager to rejoin the fight.

A spark of competition flashed in Sampson's eyes, tempered with respect. "Then may we both come home heavy with prizes."

On the wharf, Silas lifted Polly to his shoulder so she could see over the bustle. Beside them stood nine-year-old Hannah and Mrs. Mason pointing out the ships to her charge. When Jon came down the gangway for a last word, Hannah reached for him at once.

"Papa, will you be back by Christmas?"

He bent to her height, his weathered hands smoothing her cap. "I cannot say for certain, sweetheart. More likely, it will be spring."

Mrs. Mason's brown eyes shone with sincerity, her voice calm. "God go with you, Captain. All will be kept in good order here."

Jon's eyes softened, lingering a beat too long on hers. "I never doubt it, Mrs. Mason."

Martha appeared from behind with a basket, thrusting it into his hands. "Bread, cheese, and a pie. Don't let those boys eat it all the first day."

Jon laughed. "Then I'd best share it before Reed hides it in the galley."

Just before Jon mounted the gangway, Chaplain John Marsh stepped forward from the quarterdeck rail, his Bible tucked under one arm. He lifted his voice above the harbor noise. "May the Lord watch between us while we are absent one from another. May His hand steady our helm, His mercy preserve us in storm and battle, and His Providence return us safe to these shores again."

The crew stilled, some bowing their heads, others lifting eyes to the gray November sky. Even the *Hazard*'s men paused, hats in hand.

Jon inclined his head, voice low but firm. "Amen."

The bos'n's whistle shrilled from above. Time. Jon clasped Silas' hand, kissed Hannah's brow, and touched Polly's nose before giving Mrs. Mason a final nod. Then he turned and mounted the gangway.

From the deck he raised his hat. A cheer went up from both brigantines, sails swelling as the lines were cast free. Slowly, the *Tyrannicide* and the *Hazard* stood out together, white canvas leaning into the November wind.

On the wharf, Hannah's voice carried faintly, "God keep you, Papa!"

Jon turned his face eastward, the sea's wide road opening before him, and alongside, for the first time, a new partner to share the dangers.

Falmouth, Massachusetts, December 1777

THE WIND HAD blown cruel for days, cold spray turning to ice along the *Tyrannicide*'s rigging. Jon stood braced at the quarterdeck rail, every line of his face drawn tight with frustration. The brigantine would not answer her helm. No matter how Thorndike fought her wheel, she fell off or clawed into the wind, a stubborn beast with her rigging untrimmed.

"She's lost her grip, Captain," Thorndike called from the quarterdeck rail, his voice raised above the wind. He had one hand braced on the binnacle, eyes fixed forward.

At the wheel, the helmsman wrestled the spokes. "She's gripin' again, sir!" he shouted.

"Ease her! Keep her steady!" Lieutenant Moses bellowed, snapping orders, his body leaned against the gale as he tried to coax obedience from the stubborn brigantine.

John Bray, his hair plastered by spray, bent over the logbook, scribbling furiously. "Marking the drift, Captain. She's throwing her head up five points with every gust."

Jon strode to the quarterdeck rail, jaw tight as he felt the brigantine shudder beneath his boots. "Enough. Bring her in." To Thorndike, he said, "Signal the *Hazard* we're putting into Falmouth to refit before we lose the whole voyage to her temper."

A shout went forward, and the crew sprang to braces, the deck alive with running feet and creaking lines. Slowly, the ship turned her head toward the shelter of Falmouth Harbor, the *Hazard* holding off to windward and watching.

The decision weighed like a stone. To limp into port was galling, but better a humbled ship than a crippled one adrift in the turbulent Bay of Biscay. Jon kept his eyes on the town's gray wharves drawing near. He knew the risk of delay, but better to seize a harbor now than founder on the sea with a ship that would not mind her helm.

By evening they slipped into Falmouth Harbor, the little town huddled against winter winds, lanterns pricking the dark. The brig came alongside the wharf with a weary groan of timbers. Jon gave the order to make her fast, then remained a moment, his hand flat on the rail.

Falmouth still bore its scars. Two years past, Captain Henry Mowat had stood offshore with a squadron under orders from Vice Admiral Samuel Graves to "lay waste, burn, and destroy such seaport towns as are accessible to His Majesty's ships." Falmouth had been the first lesson. The town had burned from end to end, its people scattered, its wharves charred stumps against the tide. It would take many years for the town to recover, but Jon could see a few new houses climbed the slope, clapboard still raw and pale. The smell of fresh-sawn timber mingled with the salt air. A town dealt a death blow by the British, yet it would rise from its ashes beneath the very eyes of the Crown.

He gazed at the town once more, as though to share the kinship of survivors, and then turned to the work of seeing his ship made sound. A few townsfolk gathered, curious at the battered brig and her crew. Shipwrights were sent for, their hammers ringing before the night was out. Jon made his report to the Board of War in a brief letter, the quill biting deep.

> I have lost the brig's grip, and am obliged to put in-
> to Falmouth to refit.

The crew were granted shore leave in watches, but the lure of taverns proved too strong. Four men deserted within a night, their sea chests gone with them. Jon received the news grim-faced the next morning, standing on the frosty wharf.

"Four fewer hands when we sail," Lieutenant Thorn-dike said quietly.

Jon's eyes narrowed on the gray line of sea beyond the harbor mouth. "Then we'll sail with fewer. Better short-handed than broken."

As the men bent to their lines, Jon's voice carried clear across the deck. "We sail leaner, but we sail truer. The hands who stood fast in Falmouth will find this captain does not forget it. Tonight you'll have an extra ration of rum, for loyalty deserves its measure."

A cheer went up, rough voices ringing in the winter air, and the canvas cracked aloft like a promise renewed.

Repairs pressed on quickly, new cordage spliced, rigging reset, sails patched against the winter gales. By week's end, the *Tyrannicide* stood ready again, leaner but sound. Sampson's *Hazard* hovered just offshore, her signal flags urging them on.

As the anchor was weighed, Jon cast one last look at Falmouth's clustered houses. "You've patched our bones, but the sea waits," he murmured. Then, louder, to his men: "Set canvas! We'll show them the *Tyrannicide*'s just begun."

The ship answered better now, her helm steady under the mate's hands. Ahead lay the hunt once more.

In the North Atlantic off Nova Scotia, 13 December 1777

THE LOOKOUT'S CRY split the December gloom. "Sail ho! Brig to windward!"

On the quarterdeck, Jon raised his spyglass and turned to the rail, peering into the pewter sky. The Atlantic swelled under them, long gray rollers capped with spindrift. The *Tyrannicide*'s decks, slick with brine, heaved beneath their boots as she pitched into the seas.

Through the glass the brig showed herself plainly, two masts, square-rigged, laboring south from Halifax, her hull riding low with cargo. On her stern the name *Alexander*.

"She's heavy-laden," Jon said to his first lieutenant. "Doubtless bound for the Indies." He lowered the glass.

"Helm, bear away two points. Mr. Lovett, see the sails trimmed."

The brigantine answered eagerly. Canvas bellied, rigging thrummed, and the ship leapt ahead. Off the starboard quarter, the *Hazard* bore down hard, Captain Sampson angling to take the weather gage, upwind of the enemy ship. Between the two brigantines, the *Alexander* had nowhere to run.

Spray stung the men at the braces as they hauled to Jon's quick, firm orders. For an hour, the chase held, the distance narrowing with each tack and surge.

At last the brig came within range. Jon ordered Lieutenant Thorndike to give the signal. The *Tyrannicide*'s bow chaser boomed, the ball splashing close across the *Alexander*'s bow, close enough to carry its meaning.

The *Hazard* closed to windward, her broadside ready. Hemmed in, the stranger rounded up and struck her colors at once. Cheers broke from the *Tyrannicide*'s deck, men slapping one another's backs. Jon only nodded once, sharp and spare.

Jon summoned his officers, weighing the balance of his crew before naming a prize master. Down four men, Jon needed Sampson to share in the prize crew. He raised the speaking trumpet to his mouth. "*Hazard* ahoy! Captain Sampson!"

The answering call came faintly across the wind. "Aye, Captain Haraden!"

"We're short four hands. Can you spare two for the prize crew?"

"Aye, Cooper and Flint. They'll see her safe to Boston."

Jon lowered the trumpet. "My thanks. I'll note the share accordingly."

"Lower away a boat," Jon ordered. "Lieutenant Moses, take three hands. Mr. Carpenter, you'll go with him. Make haste."

By mid-afternoon the report was in hand: the brig *Alexander*, 130 tons, laden with fish, oil, lumber, and staves, cleared for the Indies. A handsome capture.

Charts and arms were transferred, sea bags slung across, while the *Alexander's* master stood glum by the rail, watching Americans command his deck.

As the sun dipped toward the sea, the prize parted ways. The *Alexander* turned toward Boston flying her captors' colors, while the *Tyrannicide* and the *Hazard* resumed their patrol together.

The men cheered again, already calculating shares in their heads. Jon let them have their moment. For him, the sea still promised more.

In the North Atlantic, 22 December 1777

NIGHT HAD FALLEN early, as it always did in December. In his great cabin, the lanterns swung with the ship's slow roll, their yellow glow mingling with the pale wash of moonlight through the stern windows. Jon bent over his desk, quill in hand, the salt-stained logbook open before him.

Mrs. Mason had complimented his handwriting, but in truth, he wrote not for flourish, but for order. There had been too many prizes to hold in memory alone. The pages of his logbook bore neat lines, the brief facts of each victory: the ship's name, her tonnage, her master, her cargo, her destination. All reduced to a few sentences, though each prize meant a moment of triumph at sea, another cheer from his men, another blow against the British.

Afternoon, 22 December 1777

At four o'clock we took the schooner Good Intent, Captain William Dashpar, from Newfoundland bound for Dominica, her hold filled with fish and hoops. Prize crew sent aboard and ordered her for Boston.

Morning, 23 December 1777

At nine o'clock we captured the brig Polly, Captain Walter Stevens, from St. John's, Newfoundland, bound for Barbados, with a cargo of fish, oil, wood, and flour. Prize crew ordered for Boston.

Afternoon, 23 December 1777

At three o'clock, after a short chase, we took the snow Swift of Bristol, bound for New York with a cargo of flour. A valuable prize. The prize crew ordered for Boston.

The record was plain, as was his satisfaction. In scarcely more than a week, the *Tyrannicide* and her consort *Hazard* had taken one ship after another. The value of these captures would spread well beyond the quarterdeck: shares to his men, profits for Salem's merchants, revenue for Massachusetts and stores for General Washington. For his own household, it meant a measure of security, something he had promised Mrs. Mason and Martha when he first went to sea.

Pausing a moment, listening to the creak of timbers and the rush of the sea against the hull, he thought about the captures recorded. Tonight, he inked only three, but they spoke volumes: evidence of a young country's naval strength, and of the *Tyrannicide*'s growing legend.

He set aside his quill, flexing his cramped fingers. Their orders had spoken grandly of Portugal and Spain, of showing the flag in Europe before pressing onward to the Indies. On paper, it sounded bold, a voyage across the Atlantic to foreign ports, there to harry British trade at Europe's very doorstep.

But the sea had its own logic, and he was not a man to argue with it. Conferring with Sampson, his fellow captain agreed. Every vessel they had taken since November had been Indies-bound: brigs heavy with fish, schooners with oil and lumber, snows deep in flour. Why chase Iberian shores when the lifeblood of Britain's empire flowed southward, straight into their path? The best way to hurt England and make her feel the war was through the pocketbooks of her merchants and the seizure of her merchant ships.

It was here, in the western ocean, that fortunes were made or lost. It was here they could strike at the heart of British trade. The fish and flour of Newfoundland fed the sugar islands, and the sugar islands fed the coffers of London. To strike those arteries was to wound the empire more surely than any gesture at Lisbon. There would be time enough to venture to Europe's shores. For now, Providence had led him here, and here was where he could do the most good.

Jon dipped his quill again. If his commissioners in Boston wished to see Iberia on the horizon, so be it. For his part, he was content enough with the Indies' trade swelling his logbook, and with the wealth it promised for his men, for the cause, and the family waiting for him in Salem.

…it is very certain that half the army is almost
naked, in a great measure bare-footed."
– Johann de Kalb, Valley Forge, Christmas
Day 1777

CHAPTER 11

Salem, Massachusetts, 22 December 1777

SNOW FELL THICK and steady that Monday afternoon as Eunice heard sleigh bells jingle down the street. Hannah pressed her face to the frosted window. "They're here!" she cried, racing for the door.

The Gloucester Haradens tumbled in at last, Andrew and Lydia, stamping snow from their boots, their brood of six girls following close behind in cloaks dusted white. Laughter and chatter filled the entry as Silas shouldered in their baggage and hurried the wet cloaks upstairs to hang on pegs in their bedchambers.

"Welcome, welcome!" Eunice called, drawing Lydia into a warm embrace. The Gloucester cousins hurried to

165

the hearth, holding out mittened hands to the blaze, while the adults let the heat sink into their bones.

"By the smells coming from the kitchen," remarked Lydia, "Your Martha has outdone herself."

Martha came into the parlor wiping her hands on her apron, beaming at the praise. "Aye, I've been cookin'. And there's hot spiced wine on the stove and cider for the girls."

In the parlor, Hannah danced with her cousins, and games were quickly arranged with laughter spilling through the house.

The adults retreated to the dining room, where a fire burned in the small hearth. Martha brought in a pot from the stove, the aroma of spices in the heated red wine wafting in the air. Eunice served the spiced claret, as they traded stories of the Gloucester girls and Hannah and Polly.

"Snow and children, both leave a mess," said Martha, "but since they are here, includin' our Hannah and Polly, best to warm yourselves by the hearth fire in the parlor, and I'll see you're well fed before the day is out."

Lydia exchanged a smile with Eunice. Andrew Haraden leaned closer. "And Jonathan?" he asked Eunice. "Have you word?"

Eunice smiled, producing a folded letter. "Only last week. He writes that the *Tyrannicide* has captured ship after ship loaded with cargo bound for the Indies. Providence has favored them and they do well." Pride lit her face, though her eyes flicked briefly to the empty chair at the head of the table where the captain always sat.

Silas came into the dining room. "With all that snow

outside, I wager the girls would be glad to raise a snow-man before supper."

"I think mine would love that," said Lydia.

"Any excuse," said Andrew.

"Hannah, too," said Eunice. "And I can watch the two Pollys."

That afternoon, the yard rang with laughter as the cousins rolled great balls of snow across the lawn. Their mittens were soaked, their cheeks red, but together they built a snowman tall enough to guard the front gate, with sticks for his arm, a carrot Martha donated for his nose, and a hat borrowed from Silas perched on his head.

Christmas arrived on Thursday as the smell of roasting turkey and the sweet tang of apples and spice wafted through the air. The two families gathered at the table. In Captain Haraden's absence, Andrew carved the turkey, its savory scent mingling with plain pudding and mince pies cooling on the sideboard. Children chattered, and toasts were raised, to health, to the men who would not see their families at Christmas for sake of the greater cause. It was a day filled with laughter and warmth as they celebrated the Savior's birth.

By week's end, the snow had stopped and the sun glistened on melting icicles hanging from roofs. On Sunday morning the two families bundled into heavy cloaks and mittens. Martha waved the older girls toward the door with a snort. "Off with you, then. I'll keep the two little Pollys here by the fire. It's near their nap besides. No sense draggin' babes out to freeze and fidget through a sermon."

"Thank you, Martha," said Lydia.

"Yes," agreed Eunice.

Snow crunched underfoot and their breath rose white into the still air as they trudged together to the East Church where Eunice's father, Reverend Diman, would be preaching.

As they entered, Eunice's parents greeted them. "Greetings, Daughter," said her father, "and to all those with you."

"What a lovely bevy of young women," remarked Eunice's mother, Mary Diman. "All Haradens, I trust?"

Lydia Haraden laughed. "Yes, all Haradens."

"They are cousins from Gloucester," Eunice explained, "come to join us for Christmas."

Inside the church, they took their places in the family pew. Candles flickered against frosted panes as the congregation filed in, wishing each other a blessed day.

A woman with a lovely voice sang "Come, Thou Almighty King" after which the congregation joined in to sing together "Joy to the World".

When the music ended, Reverend Diman mounted the pulpit, his black robe with white preaching bands reminding all of his ordination. "We gather to praise God for His goodness and to rejoice at the Savior's birth." He then prayed and all heads bowed. When the prayer ended, he said, "My friends, while we rejoice at Christ's birth, yet we must not forget those who suffer even now for our liberty." He pulled a paper from his black robe, his face grave. "A messenger has brought word from Pennsylvania that General Washington's army at Valley Forge is in want of food, clothing, and blankets. Near half the camp is sick or dying, and snow lies deep upon them."

Gasps and murmurs ran through the congregation. Eunice had heard nothing and suspected others knew little of what conditions the Continental Army was enduring in snow-covered Valley Forge.

Eunice's father read slowly, his voice carrying through the hushed church. "Our soldiers are without shoes, without stockings, without blankets. Many are sick, many more half-naked, yet they hold the line for liberty. For three days, a heavy snow has fallen. Unless some great and capital change suddenly takes place, this army must inevitably starve, dissolve, or disperse. Thousands of our horses are perishing for want of forage. I cannot describe the distress it brings me to see brave men so poorly provided for and noble beasts failing for want of food, when they deserve everything a grateful country can give."

Diman lowered the page, his gaze sweeping the pews. "Friends, these are the conditions at Valley Forge. Let us not only thank God for our Savior's birth, but pray for our commander and his suffering army, that Providence will sustain them through this trial. And, let us send what aid we can."

Hannah's small hand tightened on Eunice's sleeve. "What if Papa is cold like them?"

Eunice bent close, her voice steady though her heart ached. "Didn't your father's letter speak of his well-being? He is safe, and God has blessed his work. Now, we must also pray for our soldiers."

Reverend Diman lifted his hands. "Let us pray for our commander-in-chief, for our soldiers at Valley Forge, and for this cause of liberty in which we are all joined."

The families bowed their heads. In that hush, warmed by faith though chilled by winter, the people of Salem felt themselves bound to those ragged men in Pennsylvania, and to the perilous promise of independence.

As they were leaving the church, Eunice said to her mother. "We will contribute clothing and blankets for our soldiers and bring those to the church."

"Bless you, my dear," her mother said as she gave her a last hug.

Boston Harbor, early May 1778

EASTER HAD COME and gone as the *Tyrannicide* limped into Boston, her rigging frayed, her sails patched, her decks heavy with silence. Word spread quickly along the wharves that Captain Haraden had returned. But when she warped into her berth, onlookers saw hammocks strung on deck and pale faces peering from the forecastle. She looked more like a hospital ship than a brig of war.

Jon stood at the quarterdeck rail, his own body aching with fever. Of a crew once proud and able, near fifty were on the surgeon's list, some with agues, others spotted with the marks of smallpox. He had buried three at sea, committed to the deep with prayers hastily spoken by Chaplain Marsh. Others he had left behind in Martinique hospitals, too weak to rise when the brigantine sailed.

He forced himself below to the great cabin, to scratch out the letter he dreaded writing. The quill shook in his hand as he bent over the log-stained desk.

Gentlemen, I have been very unfortunate ever since

I left home. My people have been sick more or less every day of the whole cruise. I was obliged to leave several in Martinique, some with fevers, others with the smallpox. And to crown all my misfortunes, the day we sailed from Martinique, I had a man taken down with smallpox, which obliged me to inoculate thirty others who had not had the disorder.

The words blurred for a moment as his head swam. He dipped the quill again, pressing on.

I have buried three. Near fifty are sick still. In a gale, I was parted from Captain Sampson. In our weak condition we could not stand against any armed vessel. By God's grace, we captured a snow from Bristol laden with flour, though her master threw his papers overboard before we boarded.

He signed his name with effort, then added the plea that weighed most heavily:

I beg you to write me what I shall do with the sick that I have on board, whether I shall land them that have the smallpox on Rainsford Island, or leave them at Marblehead, as most belong there. I also beg you to send me money, for I must buy fresh provisions for the sick, and I myself am unwell.

Jon set aside the quill, his hand cramped, the ink spattered. Outside the stern windows, Boston Harbor glittered in spring light. But inside the cabin, the air smelled of fever and fear. He prayed the Board would send word quickly, before more names joined the list of the dead.

Boston Harbor, June 1778

THE BOARD OF War chamber was close with heat, the tall windows open to the summer air. Jon sat stiff-backed before the member of the board. At the secretary's desk the clerk read aloud the letter just received.

> *The agents at St. Pierre protest the great sums advanced in refitting the Tyrannicide and the Hazard. They find fault especially in regard to rations. Henceforth, such requisitions will not be complied with.*

Rations. Jon's hands clenched behind his back. He thought of the sick men he had left in Martinique's hospitals, of the three already consigned to the sea's grave, of those he had inoculated against smallpox on the open deck, fever hollowing their faces. He remembered writing for funds while barely able to hold the quill upright. And the Board's concern was the cost of bread and beef?

The clerk droned on, finishing with a thin smile: "The Board expresses surprise the commander applied for rations at all. In the future, no such requisitions will be granted."

Jon pushed back from the desk, the secretary's quill splattering ink across the margin. His voice cut the silence. "They've no notion what it takes to keep a crew alive. I ate what the men ate. The so-called 'extra' was the strength that kept me standing on my feet when I could scarce draw breath. If you want commanders half-starved at their guns, say so plain." He rose, jaw tight, and fixed the Board with a hard gaze. "But if this be your answer, you will have to find yourselves another commander. I resign my commission."

A stir rippled through the chamber. The secretary's quill scratched furiously, noting every word, but Jon did not linger to explain. He had said what needed saying.

Outside in the yard, his officers Thorndike, Moses, and Lovett waited. Back aboard ship, he told them plain what had transpired.

Benjamin Moses shifted uneasily. "They think you extravagant, Captain. Triple rations for yourself, double for us. They'll never see it for what it was."

Jon looked around the table at their faces, drawn but loyal. Lieutenant Thorndike spoke for them all. "We've served honorably. We've risked everything. Yet now we're treated like schoolboys."

Jon tapped the Board's letter against the table, then laid it aside. "Gentlemen, I have resigned my commission. With reluctance, aye, but I will not command under such misarrangements. The *Tyrannicide* will sail again, but not under my command. We are mariners, not beggars. If Massachusetts wants her brigantine, she must find another man to sail her."

For a long moment, there was only the scrape of chairs, the creak of timbers in the quiet cabin. Then Thorndike said what all of them felt. "Where you go, Captain, we go." Every head nodded in turn.

Jon felt resolve harden in him like iron. He had served the Commonwealth faithfully. Now he would serve in his own way, freer, bolder, and with better reward for his men. Privateering was the course ahead.

Salem, early summer 1778

THE LETTER CAME in Jon's own elegant hand, though the script wavered at points as if written through fatigue. Eunice broke the seal at the parlor window while Hannah read her lesson nearby, and Polly played with her new doll on the hearth rug.

> *My dear Mrs. Mason,*
>
> *I have been very unfortunate since last I sailed. That is not to say we didn't have many captures. But my crew has been sick more or less every day of the whole cruise. Some I was obliged to leave in Martinique's hospitals, some I had to inoculate against the smallpox, and some I buried at sea.*
>
> *Near fifty were on the doctor's list when we limped into Boston. In such a state I could not hope to stand against any armed vessel. Providence spared us, and I give thanks, but I confess I am worn to the quick. The Board of War has taken issue with our expenses, which has displeased both me and my officers.*
>
> *I have much to tell you, and God willing I shall be home soon, though not in the Tyrannicide.*
>
> *Yours in esteem,*
> *Jon Haraden*

Eunice read the letter twice over, her eyes lingering on the places where the ink had blotted, as if his hand shook from fever. She could almost see his dark blue eyes, clouded with sickness and grief for the men he had lost. She had grown accustomed to his calm assurance, the strong presence that anchored his household even when he was away at sea. Without him, the house felt less secure.

"Is it from Papa?" Hannah asked, pressing close. She was nearly ten now, old enough to read her father's hand for herself.

"Yes, dear." Eunice folded the paper quickly. "He writes that he is safe and will be home soon."

Little Polly walked across the floor to lay her doll in Eunice's lap, the child's blonde curls now falling to her shoulders, her steps sure at three. Eunice caught her up, pressing her cheek against the child's curls.

She prayed silently for the captain's return, and wondered at his words. *Not in the Tyrannicide.* If not in his ship, then what had happened? What had driven him to come home by horse, or perhaps by carriage, and what tales of misfortune weighed upon him?

Setting Polly down, the child skipped off to see her sister. Leaving the girls, Eunice went to the kitchen where Martha was baking bread.

"Who was the letter from, then?" she asked, one eyebrow arched.

"Captain Haraden," Eunice answered quietly. "He writes that he is coming home...but not sailing the *Tyrannicide.*"

Martha gave a snort. "Trust the Massachusetts Navy to wear out a brig and a man both. Best he comes home on wheels. At least they won't sink under him."

Eunice could not resist the small smile, though the words in the letter still pressed heavily on her heart.

Haraden house, Salem, summer 1778

LATE IN THE afternoon a carriage rolled up Charter Street, wheels jolting on the cobblestones. Eunice heard the clatter and hurried to the doorway, Hannah at her side, Polly toddling close behind.

The carriage door swung open and Jon stepped down first. He was thinner than when she'd last seen him, his face worn from fever and grief, yet his bearing was unshaken. He bent to kiss Hannah on the forehead and swept Polly into his arms, then turned to give Eunice a weary smile.

Behind him came a broad-shouldered young man, nearly as tall as the captain, an officer by his dress. Two seamen followed, hefting sea chests. Gesturing to the officer, the captain said, "Mrs. Mason, this is Lieutenant Israel Thorndike of Beverly. He served with distinction aboard the *Tyrannicide* and will be my lieutenant when next I sail."

Thorndike bowed politely, his dark eyes bright with youthful confidence. "An honor, Ma'am. The captain has spoken of his household often."

From the kitchen, Martha appeared with flour still on her hands. She gave a sniff. "Another officer, is it? Best you've a stouter constitution than the poor souls the captain's had to deal with. I've no patience for men who sicken at sea."

Jon chuckled faintly. "Aye, many were sick on my last cruise, including me, Martha." Eunice watched him, thinking the house was already a happier place for his return. "Thorndike will do fine," he added. "He's stout as any man I've known."

The London Coffeehouse, Salem, summer 1778

THE COFFEEHOUSE WAS thick with pipe smoke and the hum of talk, as merchants and seamen gathered around small tables where news of the war mingled with shipping lists and wagers on the next convoy from the Indies. Light streamed in through the tall windows flooding the large room.

When Jon and Israel Thorndike stepped through the door, the room fell to a murmur. Jon heard the whispers on every tongue: the captain who had struck blow after blow at British trade had resigned his commission in disgust with Boston's Board of War.

George Williams rose and waved him over to a table where he sat with John Fisk and Elias Hasket Derby. Jon crossed the room to join them, Thorndike at his side.

Williams clasped Jon's hand. "Take a seat, Haraden." Then he waved the server over. "Two more coffees if you will." When they were seated, Williams said, "Boston may carp over accounts, Haraden, but Salem knows her own. You've brought in more prizes than any brig they've yet commissioned. If the Board of War will not keep you, then we will."

Jon introduced the men to Thorndike. "Israel served as my First Officer and did a fine job. I invited him to Salem for the interim."

Fisk leaned forward to shake Thorndike's hand. "Haraden and I sailed together for some while," he said, smiling. Then to Jon, "Privateering is no easy venture, Haraden. But you have the name and the skill to draw a crew. And the returns—well, with the right ship and the right man, they may be beyond reckoning. We believe you are that man."

Derby leaned forward, his voice carrying over the murmur of voices and scrape of chairs. "The Board tied you down with quills and complaints. Salem's merchants will free your hands. Now that France has entered the war on the side of America, we've an ally we can count on and many investors are building letter of marque ships for privateering." He tapped the table for emphasis. "There's a ship nearly fitted here in Salem, the *General Pickering*, a two-masted brig, one hundred eighty tons, sixteen guns, and berths for at least fifty men. She's named for Timothy Pickering. You know him, of course. A Salem man, who sat in the General Court and served at Boston. He now rises fast in the Continental Army. A sound name for a sound ship and one to stir pride in Salem."

Jon inclined his head. "Aye, I know him. Salem will take pride in a ship that carries his name, a name that will make her feared on the sea."

"Williams and Fisk will stand bond, along with me," said Derby. "With your name as commander, she'll not lack for crew nor for backers."

The two men Derby named nodded.

From the side, Thorndike spoke up, his voice firm. "And she'll not lack for officers. It will be my honor to stand by the captain, as I did aboard the *Tyrannicide*."

Jon smiled at his former first officer. "As would be my desire, Israel."

A rumble of assent went around the table. Other shipmasters and merchants who sat nearby raised their cups, men eager to see the *Pickering* under Jon's command.

Jon looked from face to face, taking in Williams' open confidence, Fisk's careful nod, Derby's sharp conviction, and Thorndike's loyalty bright in his eyes. He thought of his officers who had left the *Tyrannicide* with him, refusing to serve another. The leaders of Salem were offering not only a ship, but a fresh beginning, one he was eager to accept.

He lifted his cup. "Then 'tis settled. If Boston will not have me, Salem shall. We can do more than disrupt British trade, we can carry goods to Europe, bringing profit to you. It has long been my thought to do both. With your bonds and God's favor, the *Pickering* will sail: for this town, for liberty, and for every prize we can wrest from the king's commerce."

The coffeehouse erupted in cheers, cups raised high. Salem had claimed her captain anew.

"Our cause is noble; it is the cause of mankind!"
– George Washington 1779

CHAPTER 12

Haraden house, Salem, summer 1778

THAT EVENING JON brought Israel Thorndike home for supper and to stay as his guest until he must leave for his home in Beverly. The merchants had given Jon a new course, but 'twas here, on Charter Street, that the weight of it settled, his children, his household, and the governess who kept them steady in his absence.

Martha had set the supper table with roast fowl, root vegetables, and fresh bread, the air faintly sweet with the scent of cool cider. Hannah chattered merrily as she sat beside Thorndike, her eyes shining with admiration.

"You sailed with Papa, didn't you?" she asked, leaning toward him. "Did you fire the great guns?"

Thorndike laughed good-naturedly. "Aye, I did, or rather, I passed your father's orders to the gunners."

Hannah's sigh of delight made Jon chuckle, seeing her gaze linger on the young lieutenant with girlish awe.

Across the table, Mrs. Mason cut a slice of bread and buttered it for Polly. The governess joined the conversation lightly, offering Thorndike a dish of vegetables, answering his polite questions about Salem and the household. Her gown was a plain olive green with a gold-colored bodice. The candlelight caught in her brown hair, the strands touched with summer's sun, and deepened the warmth of her brown eyes. She was not adorned, not dressed to dazzle, yet there was a quiet grace in her that drew a man's gaze more surely than finery.

Thorndike glanced in her direction more than once, which Jon could not help but notice. Though the governess did nothing to encourage him, Thorndike was clearly enamored.

They talked of the new ship, the *Pickering*. "She's not large," said Thorndike, "but she'll carry enough guns to do the job."

"Aye," said Jon. "And enough room in her hold for plenty of cargo both ways. Tomorrow we should go see her."

"I would like that," said Thorndike.

"Might Hannah and I accompany you, Captain?" asked Mrs. Mason.

"Oh, yes!" said Hannah. "I want to see your new ship, Papa."

Jon nodded. "Very well, we shall all go together."

When the meal was done, and the governess took the girls into the parlor, Martha bustled about clearing the platters, while Jon and Thorndike lingered at the table over a glass of claret.

Lowering his voice, the young lieutenant said, "Captain, if I may speak plain…Mrs. Mason is an extraordinary woman. Capable, gracious and beautiful, besides. You are fortunate to have her as governess for your daughters."

Jon's brow lifted slightly. His eyes followed Thorndike's glance in the direction of the parlor and, for the first time, he saw the governess through Thorndike's eyes, an attractive young woman in her prime, nearer Thorndike's age than his own, pretty in her simplicity and entirely at ease in his household. He had never considered other men of marriageable age might look upon her in such a way.

"Why, yes," said Jon. "I have always thought her so. A preacher's daughter, a young widow, both steady and wise, she does very well with my girls." A curious pang stirred in him. Pride, yes, for she added much to his home and the children were safe in her hands. But something else stirred besides, something he could not yet name.

Salem Waterfront, the next day, summer 1778

THE HARBOR LAY bright beneath a clear summer sky, the air salted with tar and tide. Ships rocked gently at their moorings, their rigging etched against the blue waters. Reaching the Derby Wharf the *General Pickering* stood out at once, a trim brig of 180 tons, two masts square-rigged, her timbers fresh, her rigging taut, her gunports promising.

Jon walked ahead with Thorndike, pointing out the line of her hull, the cut of her sails, while behind them

Mrs. Mason and Hannah followed. Looking back, Jon saw Hannah skipping to keep pace, craning her neck at the maze of rigging.

"She looks fierce," Hannah said in wonder as she gazed at the gunports. "Does she bite like a sea monster?"

Thorndike laughed, turning toward her. "Only when your father says the word. Otherwise she swims as gentle as a dolphin in calm seas."

Mrs. Mason's laugh followed, warm, unguarded, carried on the sea breeze. Jon turned at the sound. She stood a pace behind, strands of her hair lifted by the wind, her eyes alight as she smiled at Thorndike's jest. Something in Thorndike's ready charm pricked him. He was too quick, too attentive for Jon's liking.

Jon's gaze lingered a moment longer. She had asked to come, after all. Perhaps it was right she should be here, to see the ship that would carry so much of their fortunes. Certainly Hannah should see the vessel that would carry her father across the sea. And yet, the ease with which the governess laughed at another man's words unsettled him.

"Come along," Jon called more sharply than intended. "Let us go aboard."

Thorndike offered his hand to Mrs. Mason as she stepped onto the gangplank. Jon noted it, his jaw tightening, though she accepted with perfect composure, neither flustered nor coy. Still, when she stood beside him on the deck, her eyes went wide at the sweep of the quarterdeck, the dark mouths of the guns, the scent of powder and tar, the creak of timbers beneath their feet.

"It is a fine ship," she said softly. "And now Hannah and I can imagine you here."

Jon straightened to his full height, pride settling on his shoulders. "Aye. And with her, we shall show the king's men what Salem can do. And more, we'll carry cargo to Europe and goods back to Salem to the profit of all concerned."

Thorndike grinned, running a hand along the nearest carronade. "She'll be the making of us, Captain. Mark me."

Jon's eyes went again to Mrs. Mason, her hair bright where the sun caught it, her hand resting lightly on Hannah's shoulder. The child beamed, her awe plain. But Jon found his own gaze drawn not to the guns, nor to the rigging, but to the governess who stood so easily among them, laughing a moment ago, now watching him with that calm assurance, and suddenly he was the one unsteady on his own deck.

"Where do you sleep, Papa?"

"This way," said Jon as he led them below to the great cabin aft. Light from the stern windows poured over the broad table where charts would be spread, a hanging lamp swaying above. The air smelled of oak and beeswax polish, new timbers not yet worn by the sea.

"This will be my quarters," Jon said, resting a hand on the table. "Here I'll keep the ship's log, confer with my officers, plan our course."

Hannah ran to the windows, pressing her small hands to the glass. "You can see the whole harbor, Papa!"

Mrs. Mason stepped in more slowly, her eyes tracing the paneled bulkheads, the neat lockers, the captain's berth curtained in dark blue cloth. "It feels...ordered," she said at last. "As though even the sea might be tamed, if only within these bulkheads."

Jon looked at her, struck. Few landsmen noticed what a cabin meant to a captain, not comfort, but command. That she understood, even dimly, unsettled him more than Thorndike's laughter ever could.

His pride in the *Pickering* swelled, yet his gaze lingered on her longer than it should have, and he noticed a stray curl of her brown hair that had been touched by the sun and her eyes warm and sure. For an instant, it was not the guns nor the timbers that claimed his attention, only the governess.

Haraden house, Salem, late September 1778

THE PARLOR FIRE glowed warmly, the evening air still holding autumn's edge. A table had been laid with wine and cold meats, bread and cheese, and Martha's spiced cakes. Around it gathered Jon's officers, invited for a gathering before their sailing in a few days' time: Israel Thorndike, John Carnes, Robert Cowan, William Prosser, and the bos'n, Robert Bowan. Their new chaplain, David McClure, a solid Patriot and sober presence, sat among them as well. Voices were low as they spoke of crew lists and supplies.

Jon had excused himself to go upstairs for a brief change of attire. The talk quieted when he returned. He had set aside the plain green coat of the Massachusetts Navy. Now he wore a long dark blue coat trimmed in gold braid, a gold waistcoat bright beneath it, his white stock tied crisp at the throat. The hilt of his sword caught the lamplight as he rested a hand on it.

Thorndike rose, giving a low whistle. "You've traded the Board of War's coat for something grand, Captain. Salem will scarce know you."

Jon's mouth quirked as he came to stand before the men. "Aye, I've done with their mismanagement. I sail now as a privateer captain of Salem, beholden to my owners, my officers and crew, and to God. When I go after an enemy ship, I'll not do it in rags. Let them see me in my finest. Let them know exactly who they face."

Martha came in at that moment with another tray of spice cakes, eyeing Jon's coat. "Well then, Captain, you finally look as fine as the stories make you out. Let's hope the braid holds up as stout as you do."

His officers chuckled at her words.

Thorndike lifted his glass. "I believe your appearance will put the fear in them, sir."

Moses laughed, reaching for a glass of wine. "Or make them think you've robbed a general's wardrobe."

"Better that than to be thought ragged," Jon said dryly, drawing his coat back to rest his hand more firmly on his sword. "Intimidation wins battles before the first broadside. I mean to give them no doubt whose guns are bearing down. Mark my words, they will know the *Pickering* is to be feared on the high seas."

Carnes leaned forward, nodding with approval. "The French dress their captains in lace and braid, and it serves them well. I'd wager the sight of you on the quarterdeck will give more pause than any broadside."

"Then let's be sure the ship sails as fine as her captain," Thorndike said with a grin, raising his glass high.

The other officers followed, glasses lifted. "To the *Pickering* and her captain!"

McClure's voice was firm as he added, "And may Providence grant her victory."

From the doorway, Mrs. Mason stood with Hannah beside her, the child's eyes shining. Polly clung to her skirts, yawning, but even she gazed round-eyed at her father in his new finery. "You cut a fine figure, Captain," the governess said as she stepped forward to offer more wine to their guests.

Her compliment meant more than his officers' good-natured chiding. "Why, thank you, Mrs. Mason."

Derby Wharf, Salem, late September 1778

THE MORNING SUN struck the waters of Salem Harbor, turning the ripples to gold. Along Derby Wharf, men bustled with casks and crates, voices raised above the cries of gulls wheeling overhead. The *Pickering* lay at her berth, fresh timbers gleaming, rigging taut, her guns run out and black against the bright sky.

Jon stood on the wharf with Thorndike and Carnes beside him, overseeing the last of the provisions. Bosun Bowan shouted orders as barrels of salt beef and fresh water were rolled aboard. Sailcloth, powder, and ball followed, checked against the purser's list. Around them the crew gathered, some seasoned seamen with weathered faces, others young and eager, gripping their sea bags with nervous pride. Jon had selected each man for his skill, experience and worth.

Merchants stood off to one side, George Williams, John Fisk, and Derby himself, their hands clasped behind their backs, eyes fixed on their investment. Derby's nod was curt but satisfied. "She'll do, Captain. And may she bring Salem profit as well as honor."

Jon inclined his head. "She will. You have my word."

A little way off, Mrs. Mason stood with Hannah and Polly. Martha and Silas had come, too. Hannah's face shone with pride, as she clutched her governess' hand tightly. Polly, restless, leaned against Martha, watching the fevered activity with wide eyes.

Thorndike noticed them first and nudged Jon lightly. Jon crossed to where they stood, the gold braid on his dark blue coat catching the morning light. Hannah rushed into his arms, and he bent to kiss Polly's fair curls before straightening to meet the governess' steady gaze.

"You'll keep them well," he said quietly.

"As always, Captain," she replied, her voice composed though her eyes softened. "God go with you. Write when you can. The girls look forward to your letters."

"And you, Mrs. Mason? Do you also look forward to my letters?"

A blush came to her cheeks. "Of course."

Martha said with a sniff just loud enough for him to hear, "Mind you bring yourself back with the ship, Captain. We've no use for a fine brig without her master."

"I shall," said Jon with a smile for his housekeeper.

Silas touched his hat. "We'll keep the house and hearth in order till you return, sir."

Jon gave a brief nod, then turned back toward the ship. Already the crew were mustering, lining the deck as

Thorndike called them to order. Jon mounted the gangplank, his step firm.

On the wharf, Hannah waved furiously, and Polly tried to copy her. Mrs. Mason stood still, watching as the lines were cast off and the *Pickering* drifted from her berth, sails loosed to the wind. She raised a single hand and he thought he heard her say, "Godspeed."

The brig gathered way, her bow turning toward the open sea. From the quarterdeck, Jon raised his hat in salute, to his daughters, to the governess who cared for them, to Martha and Silas, to Salem itself. The wind filled the canvas, the gulls cried overhead, and the *Pickering* slipped past the headland into the waiting ocean.

THE *PICKERING* WAS no sooner at sea than she proved herself swift and willing. Her crew, a mix of Salem and Beverly men and eager lads drawn by the promise of prizes, were working well together. Jon drove her hard across the Atlantic, her holds heavy with American goods—fish, flour, lumber—bound for French ports.

Outward, he sailed as near to a blockade runner as a man could be, slipping through the teeth of British patrols with the boldness of a smuggler. On the homeward leg, she would show another face, her guns speaking when opportunity offered. A brig or schooner here, a merchantman there, not enough to fill a newspaper, but enough to line purses and prove her mettle.

One raw December morning off the Banks, Thorndike leaned beside him on the quarterdeck, coat collar turned up against the wind. "She'll do, Captain. Quick in the chase, steady in the blow. The *Pickering*'s a lucky ship."

Jon's eyes swept the horizon. "Not luck, Mr. Thorn-dike. Discipline and Providence. And France. Their fleets keep the Royal Navy looking over its shoulder. Britain must fight in every sea now, not just one."

There was little time in Salem, but they managed brief returns between voyages. A night or two under his own roof was welcome. From his letters, Hannah had questions, which he answered, delighted at her interest. Polly would fall asleep in his arms before the candle guttered.

One such night, with the girls abed, Mrs. Mason sat across from him by the hearth, mending Hannah's gown. The firelight caught the gold strands in her brown hair as she looked down at her work.

"Tell me true, Captain," she said softly, looking up, "is the ship and your new freedom as a privateer all you wished them to be?"

Jon watched the flames a moment before answering. "Aye. She gives me command without interference, profit for my men, and profit for Salem. But 'tis not freedom entirely. The sea never grants that. Nor does the war. France fights with us now, God be thanked, yet the British strike still. You tell me Savannah has fallen. Aye and they will not stop there. We do our part at sea, but it will be a long fight."

Her needle paused, her brown eyes meeting his. "Then may Providence grant you more than the next chase, Captain. May God grant you victory on the sea and safe home again."

For Jon, it was a year of consistent profit, though without the great triumphs he hoped would eventually come. But in Salem, his reputation grew. Townsfolk whispered of Captain Haraden, no longer a man bound to Boston's Board of War but the master of his own ship, one who could slip through blockades and return with prize money in his purse. It was satisfying to be free of the Board's petty dealings but not enough for Jon. He looked for the greater triumphs that still lay ahead.

The London Coffeehouse, Salem, February 1779

THE WINTER HAD been hard, the harbor bound in ice for weeks, but by February the merchants were gathered again at the London Coffeehouse, where the talk ran to ships, convoys, and France's fleets abroad. Jon entered with Thorndike at his side, stamping the frost from his boots. Williams, Fisk, and Derby beckoned him to their table. Coffee was soon delivered.

"You've kept the *Pickering* busy," Derby said, his sharp eyes taking measure, "for which we are grateful. But now I understand you want to re-rig her as a ship. Another mast, more canvas, and more men, all of which require more money. Why should we?"

Jon set down his cup as his gaze swept the three men. He was prepared for the question. "The *Pickering* must be more than a brig if we are to do what we have set out to do. She sails fast, aye, but with two masts her reach is limited. Step a third mast, rig her as a ship, and she will run before the wind like no other privateer out of Massachusetts. We'll not only hunt prizes but carry goods to Europe and back. A ship's rig will give us speed, endurance, and the look of a predator. At a distance we may be mistaken for a naval frigate. The enemy will think twice before standing to fight."

Thorndike leaned forward. "The captain speaks true. I've seen what she can do as a brig. With a third mast, she'll run down anything afloat."

Fisk's brows drew together. "We trust your judgment, Jon, and yours, Israel. If you say a third mast is necessary for the long runs to Europe and for success against British vessels, well, I won't oppose it."

Williams took a drink of his coffee, and set down his cup. "It would give her presence. A ship-rigged *Pickering* would be spoken of not only in Salem, but in every port in Europe. That alone is worth the expense."

Jon's gaze swept the three men. "Gentlemen, this is not just for Salem's merchants, though you will see your profits. Every British ship we seize starves their army and feeds ours. Last winter, Washington's men froze at Valley Forge. This winter, their lot is somewhat improved in New Jersey, but shortages of food, clothing, and gunpowder remain. The Continental Navy is too small to do all America needs done. But we privateers can deliver. Ship-rigged, with the skilled crew she carries, the *Pickering* will be feared wherever she sails."

Derby tapped his cane against the floor, thinking. At last, he gave a short nod. "Very well. You have convinced us. We'll see her altered. But make the cost worth it, Captain. Every pound we spend must come back in prizes."

Jon inclined his head. "You have my word, gentlemen. The *Pickering* will earn her keep."

Haraden house, Salem

WHEN JON RETURNED to Charter Street that evening, his daughters scrambled to meet him, Hannah with her eager questions and news of her day and Polly climbing into his lap, her small voice saying, "Papa."

Mrs. Mason looked up from her sewing where she sat by the fire, her brown eyes shining as she listened to him speak of the merchants' agreement.

"They have agreed to rig her as a ship," Jon told her, pride warming his voice. "Three masts, square-rigged. She will look every inch the hunter she is."

"I'm so glad you prevailed upon them," said the governess.

Thorndike, who had walked back with him, bent to stir the fire. "And Salem folks will stare at her as though she were a frigate. A ship for a captain of your renown, sir." His glance shifted toward the governess, and his smile softened. "Would you not like to see her, Mrs. Mason, when her new mast is stepped?"

She returned the smile politely, smoothing Hannah's hair where the child leaned against her. "If Captain Haraden permits, Hannah and I would both like to see her."

"Oh, yes, Papa! I want to see your ship's new mast."

Jon caught the exchange between his first officer and the governess, a flicker of something stirring in him, pride in her interest, and a trace of possessiveness at Thorndike's easy gallantry.

At that moment, Martha came in from the kitchen with a tray of bread and cheese. She set it down with a thump. "So, the merchants will part with their coin after all? About time. A fine ship needs feedin' same as a family. 'Tis good you include the lieutenant in our suppers, Captain, so I can see if he eats as heartily as he talks."

Thorndike laughed, bowing slightly in her direction. "I'm honored, Ma'am. You are an excellent cook."

Jon hid a smile. Martha's tongue could be sharp, but in her way, she had welcomed his officer into the household.

Salem Waterfront & Derby Wharf, May 1779

THE SPRING AIR smelled of tar and salt, mingled with the sharp bite of oak being sawn for spars. The *Pickering* stood high in her berth, scaffolding up around her as shipwrights swarmed the deck. The new third mast had just been stepped, its fresh timbers pale against the weathered hull, riggers perched like gulls along the yards. Salem folks lined the wharf, pointing and whispering that Haraden's brig had become a ship.

Thorndike leaned close as Jon inspected the work. "She's becoming all you promised, sir. With your leave, I should go to Beverly for a few days. My father has business that needs me. I'll be back before the drills begin."

Jon clasped his shoulder. "Go then, Israel. The ship will wait, but she won't drill herself. Be back in time to teach the new hands their work. We should be at sea by sometime in September."

Meanwhile, Jon was restless with much to do. There were carpenters and gunners still to be hired, as well as additional seamen. The posters had just gone up around Salem seeking new recruits, and his lieutenants Carnes and Cowan were meeting men at the taverns. But Jon would make the final choices himself. In the midst of this, Jon found time for his family.

A day later, he proposed a walk to the harbor with Hannah and her governess. His eldest daughter clapped her hands in delight. Polly would stay home, but he promised her a trip to see the ship when the work was done. Together the three of them walked down Charter Street toward the wharves, Hannah skipping ahead.

On the wharf, the crew working alongside the shipwrights waved at him. "Good day, Captain! She's coming along."

Turning to his companions, Jon said, "I would take you both aboard but, as you can see, the deck's a bit messy just now. When the work is finished, you can come back to see her from the deck."

Even the wharf was cluttered with boards and supplies. The governess' skirts brushed a stack of lumber as she attempted to navigate her way. Jon steadied her arm past coils of rope and casks being rolled aboard. She stood beside him, watching his ship grow into its new form, as much a part of his world as any of his officers.

"The changes suit her," she said softly, her gaze following the new mast. "She looks stronger, as though she has grown with you, Captain. The two of you seem well matched."

Jon's throat tightened, though he only said, "She'll be ready for the wider seas by summer's end."

"What flag will she fly?" Mrs. Mason asked, glancing

toward the stern.

"The Stars and Stripes when it suits. But a captain must sometimes borrow another flag—a ruse of war, nothing more."

"Oh, that's right," she said, a smile coming to her lovely face. "I had forgotten that sometimes it is necessary to sail in disguise."

Hannah stood wide-eyed next to the gangplank watching as a sail was hoisted. "Papa, will she ever be finished?"

Jon and the governess shared a laugh. "Yes, but not as soon as I might like."

Further, we are by Pliny told
This serpent is extremely cold;
So cold that, put it in the fire,
'Twill make the very flames expire.

– *Description of a Salamander*, Jonathan Swift 1705

CHAPTER 13

Salem, Massachusetts, May 1779

ON SUNDAY, AFTER church service, Jon asked if Mrs. Mason and his daughters would walk with him. Knowing their destination, he had arranged with Mrs. Diman to provide him a bouquet of flowers, which he claimed as they left the church.

Mary Diman handed him the posy of lilacs and daisies. "They are fresh from my garden, a lovely thought on your part, Captain."

He thanked her and they moved on. When they turned not toward home but toward the Old Burying Point Cemetery, Hannah, holding her young sister's hand, asked, "Where are we going, Papa?"

Lifting Polly into his arms, he said, "To visit your mother's grave. It has been three years, and I thought you would like to pay your respects."

Hannah's fingers worried her mother's locket at her throat. "I would like that."

"That is very considerate of you, Captain," said Mrs. Mason. "We have sometimes visited the graveyard, but to have you with them will mean much."

When they reached the graveyard, Jon handed the flowers to Hannah and set Polly on her feet. "Perhaps you and Polly might place them on the grave?" At the Haraden stone marker that read Hannah Deadman Haraden, Hannah handed some of the flowers to Polly and the two laid them on the grass. "For Mama," Hannah said solemnly, looking up at her father.

Polly mimicked her sister as she placed her flowers, "For Mama."

Jon bowed his head, the words of prayer caught in his chest. He had not lingered here often since that first terrible year. Now, standing with his daughters beside him and the governess who had become so much a part of their lives on his other side, he felt the old grief soften. "Rest well, Hannah. Your children are safe this side of Heaven. All is well on this shore."

Beside him, Mrs. Mason's voice was gentle. "She is with God in Heaven, Captain. And He has spared you for more years, perhaps in His grace for many more."

Jon turned then, studying her face, the warmth of her eyes, the quiet strength in her bearing. She, too, had lost, and yet she had endured. In her presence, his household had thrived. In her presence, he had thrived.

They walked back in silence, Hannah skipping ahead again, this time with Polly laughing with her.

"It just occurred to me," he said, "that Polly has only ever known you as mother."

"True, and she and Hannah are my only children."

He smiled at her reply. "They could love you no more if they were your own."

Martha met them at the door, wiping flour from her hands. "There's cracknels and cider for you two," she said to the girls. "See you don't spill!"

The girls raced ahead. "I'll watch them," said Mrs. Mason, as she followed the girls inside.

Jon paused on the step, and Martha gave him a sharp look. "Captain, if you're wise, you'll not let the good Lord's second chance for a virtuous woman pass you by."

Jon managed a small, wry smile. "Martha, you meddle too much."

"Aye," she sniffed, "and I'm usually right."

Salem Waterfront, early September 1779

BY SUMMER'S END, the *Pickering* rose anew, a ship fit for the high seas. Where once her two masts had marked her as a brig, now three square-rigged masts rose above her deck, taut and ready. Her new mast and rigging gave her a prouder stance. Salem folks along Derby Wharf paused to marvel. Some said she looked as fine as a frigate. Others remarked that Captain Haraden had made her into the equal of any British privateer afloat.

Jon heard their remarks as he stood on the wharf with Thorndike, watching the men finish bending canvas to the yards. The drills had gone well through August, new hands finding their places under the sharp eyes of his officers. Carnes and Cowan drilled the gun crews, but with the shortage of gunpowder, they didn't use live fire.

"She's ready, sir," Thorndike said with quiet pride. "A ship now in truth, and a crew fit to follow wherever you lead."

Jon let his gaze rest on the proud sweep of her lines, the Stars and Stripes fluttering at her stern. "Aye. She's all I asked of her. Now the sea will judge if she's worthy, if we are."

From a little way back, Mrs. Mason had come down with Hannah and Polly to see the final preparations. Hannah pointed eagerly, naming off guns and sails as though she were part of the crew herself, while Polly clutched her doll, more interested in the bustle of sailors and the shouts of mates.

Jon's eyes lingered on the governess for a moment as her gaze followed the ship. She had walked beside him through grief and now through renewal, and he felt both the weight of command and the lightness of a man on the threshold of something larger than the sea alone.

Within the week, the *Pickering* would put out to sea, bound for the capes of Delaware, where rumor said British convoys gathered thick. The year ahead promised danger, but also the triumphs Jon had long sought.

Haraden house, Salem, that evening

THE HOUSE ON Charter Street felt unusually still, as though it, too, sensed Captain Haraden's departure was near. Supper had been simple, Martha saying little as she cleared the dishes. Now, in the parlor, Eunice sat with a book in her lap, though her eyes seldom focused on the pages.

Hannah nestled at her father's side, chattering over her book, a story about a cabin boy, and asking endless questions about ships and faraway ports. Polly clambered into his lap with her doll, eyelids drooping as she pressed her cheek against his coat. Watching them together stirred a familiar ache in Eunice, pride mingled with quiet dread. They adored him so, and she knew too well how soon his chair by the hearth would stand empty again.

When at last the girls were coaxed upstairs, their laughter fading along the stairwell, the room seemed to hush. Captain Haraden remained by the fire, his face shadowed by thought. Eunice sat opposite, listening to the pop and crackle of the logs. For a time neither spoke.

It was she who broke the silence, her voice low. "They will miss you, Captain. Hannah understands more now, and Polly...she knows only that she wakes and you are not there. You gave them the summer and that was a fine gift."

His eyes turned toward the staircase. "Aye. It weighs on me each time I sail. But the sea is where I must do my part. The war won't wait for a father's comfort."

The firelight caught in his dark blue eyes, and Eunice understood the emotion behind his words. She set aside her book. "No. But it waits for men of courage. And they will remember, when they are grown, what kind of man their father was. All of Salem will remember."

For a heartbeat his gaze held hers, and something in her chest tightened. He said quietly, "And they will remember the woman who cared for them when he was gone."

Her breath caught. She could find no reply before Martha bustled in with a tray. "Best not to sit broodin', Captain. There's fresh bread for the mornin', and your sea chest still wants packin' unless you mean to sail with it half-empty."

Jon smiled faintly at the interruption, yet his eyes lingered on Eunice as he rose. She lowered her gaze to her hands, but in her heart she carried the look he had given her. Tomorrow the sea would take him, but tonight she would remember the warmth of the hearth, the softness in his voice, and the thought—perhaps dangerous, certainly unspoken—that she had become more to him than the governess of his daughters.

Salem Harbor, late September 1779

FROM THE DECK of the *Pickering*, Jon gazed at the wharf where many townsfolk had gathered to wish them Godspeed. Hannah and Polly waved furiously, Mrs. Mason between them, holding Polly's hand. Nearby, Martha smiled and Silas lifted his hat. Jon raised his own hat in return, before striding to the quarterdeck.

Thorndike came to his shoulder, eyes on the sails

filling above them. "She answers the wind smartly, Captain."

At his elbow, Bobby Grover piped up, eager as ever. "Shall I bring you coffee, sir? Cook says it's hot."

Jon allowed himself the faintest smile. "Aye, Bobby. Coffee, and then the work begins."

Lines were cast off, sails unfurled, and the *Pickering* gathered way, gliding past the headland into the wide Atlantic.

By sunrise the next day, Salem was far astern. Ahead lay the Delaware Capes, the cruising grounds of British privateers, Jon's hunting ground.

Cape Henlopen, 1 October, 1779

THE *PICKERING* STOOD off the Delaware Capes under a light wind, her sails just drawing. Thorndike, glass to his eye, looked to windward just as the lookout shouted, "Sail ho!"

"Two sail, Captain," said Thorndike. "They've marked us. Shall we beat to quarters and chase them down?"

Jon shook his head, calm as ever. He had something else in mind. Raising his own glass, he made out a cutter and a smaller sloop. "Not yet. They'll not stand if they know what we are. Patience wins more than speed, Mr. Thorndike. We must appear heavy, dull, a merchantman ripe for the plucking."

Thorndike frowned but held his peace.

Jon's voice carried across the deck. "Bos'n! Stream the drogues astern. Ease her way."

"Aye, sir!" Bowan bellowed. The crew hove the heavy canvas bags overboard, and the *Pickering* sagged against her canvas, wallowing as though deep-laden with cargo. The deck tilted sluggishly with the false drag, the rigging creaking overhead. Men shifted uneasily, whispering.

"Hold your nerve, lads," Jon said evenly. "We'll not chase them; they'll chase us."

Sure enough, the strangers crowded on sail, bowsprits knifing the water, spray flying as they bore down. By sundown they were close enough to see the *Pickering*'s ports and guns, only then realizing she was no merchant-man. Panic flickered. The cutter and her consort clawed for escape with canvas spilling and booms swinging wide.

As night thickened, Jon raised his night glass, watching the two split, one north, the other south. "They've scented us," Thorndike muttered.

"Cut free the drogues!" Jon snapped. "Hands to braces! Bring her about smartly."

Axes bit through rope, and the ship leapt forward, freed of her burden. Canvas cracked taut, the deck shuddering as she surged across the wind. At nine bells, the larger vessel hove about. Jon cupped his hands and hailed her, but no answer came.

"Run out the starboard battery!" Thorndike barked. "Mr. Carnes, see the men to their guns! Master Gunner, light your matches!"

The crews heaved the cannon outboard, iron wheels grinding on the planks. Slow matches glowed in the gathering dark, their sulfurous reek mixing with the salt air.

"Fire!" Jon commanded.

The broadside split the night with a roar like thunder. Smoke billowed, choking and acrid, sparks drifting. The cutter staggered under the blast, but her rigging held and she drove on, lanterns swinging wildly in her shrouds.

"They've more stubbornness than wit," Thorndike growled, wiping powder grit from his cheek.

Jon's jaw tightened. "Then tack across her bow. Give her another broadside."

The helm creaked, yards groaning as the *Pickering* came about. "Stand fast!" Thorndike called, his voice cutting through the din. The gunners braced, and the second volley ripped out, flame and iron flashing in the blackness.

This time, Jon's hail was answered through the smoke. "From New York!"

Jon's reply rang iron-hard. "Then strike your colors!"

Almost at once lanterns dipped, sails shivered, and the cutter's flag came down. Fourteen guns, thirty-eight men, and she was theirs without another shot fired.

When the cutter struck, the men gave a ragged cheer. Jon lowered his glass long enough to see the smaller sloop's stern vanishing into the dark.

Thorndike muttered, "She's clean and fast, Captain. No catching her now."

Jon's expression did not change. "Let her run. We've work enough with the prize in hand." Leaning on the rail, he met the eyes of his first officer. "Remember this, Mr. Thorndike. Providence sometimes favors nerve and guile."

Off Sandy Hook, New Jersey, 13 October 1779

THE WIND CARRIED the bite of powder even before the first gun fired. Off Sandy Hook, three British privateers bore down on the *Pickering*: the *Hope* with fourteen guns, the brig *Pomona* with twelve, and the cutter *Royal George* with another dozen. Together they mounted more metal than the *Pickering*, and Jon could see by their faces his crew knew it.

At Jon's side on the quarterdeck, Lieutenant Thorndike snapped his glass shut. "All three are standing for us, sir. They mean to crush us outright."

Jon kept his voice calm, almost cool. "Then we'll not waste shot." Turning to Mr. Carnes, he said, "Beat to quarters!" and to Mr. Bowan, he shouted, "Run out the long guns. Powder division, open your tubs."

The shrill of the fife cut across the deck, drums rattling in answer. Bare feet slapped the planks as men rushed to stations. Gun tackles groaned, wheels squealed as the nine-pounders were heaved outboard. The bos'n's mates passed the word. "Silence there! Hands to your stations!"

The bite of powder drifted up from the hatch, stinging Jon's nose as the cartridges came on deck. Jon raised his hand and the hustle stilled. He swept his gaze along the deck, every man's eyes on him. "We've danced with worse. Hold your fire till I give the word. Let them think us timid. When they are in close, we'll strike."

The enemy closed, white water curling from their bows. Smoke drifted from their forward chasers, balls whistling overhead to thud into the sea. One struck the bulwark near the quarterdeck with a crash that sprayed splinters past Jon in a burst sharp as knives. He did not flinch. "Steady, lads. The closer they come, the harder we'll bite."

The ship *Hope* ranged up on the larboard quarter, her gunports yawning black. "Now, Mr. Thorndike. Give her the larboard battery."

"Fire!" Thorndike bellowed to the larboard gunners.

The *Pickering* leapt in smoke and thunder. Flame spat from eight guns, the crash reverberating through her very bones. The blast scorched the air, smoke stinging Jon's eyes and burning in his throat. Through the haze, he glimpsed British rigging part and spars tumble, men's shouts carrying faint over the roar.

"Reload smartly!" Carnes cried. The ships' boys dashed with round shot and cartridges, gunners swabbed and rammed. Jon watched, pleased the rhythm held despite the chaos.

The brig *Pomona* pressed close on the starboard side, her broadside hammering the *Pickering*'s hull. Splinters slashed the air. A man cried out, clutching his arm. Blood slicked the planks where he fell, cabin boys leaping over him with cartridges clutched to their chests. Two hands lifted him, bearing him to the surgeon belowdecks.

"Starboard battery, fire!" Jon's order cut through the chaos. The reply was instant: another roar, another sheet of flame and iron tearing into the *Pomona* until her foretopmast crashed down in a snarl of rigging.

Now the cutter *Royal George* tried her luck, darting close, spitting iron. Jon's jaw tightened. "Bring her under our bow. Mr. Carnes, give her the chase gun."

The bow-gun thundered, smashing into the cutter's

deck. She sheered off, her colors drooping.

For half an hour the sea boiled in smoke and flame. When at last the echoes faded, all three enemy vessels lay struck, their colors down. The *Pickering*'s deck was scorched and black with powder, her planks littered with spent wads and tangled rigging, smoke still burning Jon's eyes. But beyond the haze he saw his men grinning, wild with disbelief, their triumph written plain.

And from amidships, Bobby Grover beamed up at his captain.

Thorndike, face streaked with soot, laughed aloud. "Three to one and not a man here thought it possible. Captain, the men will never forget this day."

Later, when the deck was cleared, the wounded tended, and the prize crews aboard the captured vessels and headed for Salem, Jon supped with his officers in the great cabin. He had invited the chaplain, David McClure, to join them and give God their thanks. The cook proudly served salt beef, ship's biscuit softened in broth, and a pie of salt pork and onions, to which Jon added a bottle of Madeira.

McClure bowed his head, his voice steady though the cabin rocked with the sea. "We thank Thee, Lord, who brought us through fire and smoke this day. Grant us mercy for the wounded, justice for our foes, and safe return for all. You have been ever kind to us. Lastly, we thank you for this meal."

"Amen," said Jon before pouring the Madeira. Their conversation was low, exhaustion dulling the edge of victory as they ate.

It was Bobby Grover, the cabin boy, who slipped in with a jug of water, cheeks still smeared with soot. He hesitated, then blurted, "Beg pardon, Captain, but I thought you should know. The men are calling you the Salamander."

Jon looked up sharply. "The what?"

Bobby shuffled his feet. "The Salamander, sir. They say you thrive in fire, like the creature of old, where any other man would burn. You stood like the guns themselves, cool as ever, while the whole sea was aflame around you."

The officers chuckled, Thorndike grinning as he lifted his glass. "A fitting name, Captain. And mark my words, one that will carry."

Jon studied the boy, then the faces around the table. At last a smile tugged his mouth. "If the crew must give me a name, let it be for their own pride, not mine. But see to it, Bobby. Tell them a salamander endures the fire because God is with him and his men fight with courage. Without God, we could not prevail. And without them, I'm nothing but another mariner."

Bobby's eyes shone. "Aye, Captain. I'll tell them."

Thorndike raised his glass higher. "To the Salamander and to the *Pickering*!"

The other officers raised their glasses in response. "To the Salamander!"

Glasses clinked. Outside, the sea rolled on, carrying the name forward into Jon's future.

The West Indies, November 1779

IT WAS A GOOD time to be in the Caribbean. The

weather was warm and balmy and not oppressively hot. Jon stood on the quarterdeck drinking his morning coffee as the *Pickering* rolled in a long swell. Canvas sagged in the light air, the sea as blue as molten glass.

He was just handing back his mug to Bobby when the lookout's hail carried down to him. Jon raised his glass to see a stout ship on the horizon, square-rigged, flying the red ensign bright against the clear blue sky.

"Royal Mail," Thorndike muttered, narrowing his eyes. "They'll be armed. They always are. And fat with bullion"

Jon's mouth curved faintly. "All the better. A prize worth the fight and gold for the cause."

"Beat to quarters!" Jon commanded.

Thorndike's voice rang out at once, carrying the order down the deck. "Beat to quarters! Hands to stations!" The drummer rattled his sticks, the fife shrilled, and bare feet slapped the planks as men leapt to their guns.

The first exchange was savage. Iron screamed overhead, splinters flying as balls smashed through bulwarks. The deck quivered under the blast of the enemy's broadside. "So, she wants a fight," Jon said, smiling.

The *Pickering* answered with her own thunder, fire belching from the gunports, acrid smoke choking the air until it seemed the world itself was aflame.

Hours dragged. Both ships broke off, crews heaving at pumps, men hauling lines and spars. Jon wiped powder grit from his brow, sweat stinging his eyes. The *Pickering*'s rigging hung in tatters, yet he gave no thought of yielding. He was just getting started.

"Captain," Carnes said hoarsely, "powder's near gone. Barely enough for a single broadside."

Jon looked across the swells at the Royal Mail ship, her rigging ragged but her flag still flying. His voice stayed calm. "Then one shot is all we need. But first, we must make her ready."

The crew worked like demons to patch sails and reload what little powder remained. By dawn they were ready. Jon ordered the *Pickering* brought close, her bowsprit looming almost over the enemy's deck. "Her captain can see my blue coat," said Jon, "but we can get closer still." When the distance closed to pistol range, Jon stepped forward, his voice carrying like iron over the smoke.

"Strike your colors, or I'll rake you stem to stern!"

For a moment there was silence, then the red flag fluttered down.

A ragged cheer burst from the *Pickering*'s decks. Men laughed, shouted, embraced.

Thorndike, his face streaked with soot, barked a laugh. "By God, sir, they've struck! And you had but one shot left in the locker."

At the rail, Bobby Grover's voice came in a hushed whisper, eyes wide with awe. "That's why they call you the Salamander, Captain. Fire and smoke don't touch you."

Jon set his hand to the rail, his gaze on the fallen British flag drifting down the enemy's mast. "No, Lad. The fire touches us all. But we prevail because Providence is with us and we endure together. Never forget that."

The boy's eyes shone as though lit from within, and Jon felt the sight settle in his mind. Whatever he said, the name would cling. In Salem, at sea, in every port that whispered the tale, he would forever be the Salamander.

"To do good and be good is the whole duty of a man in a few words."

– Abigail Adams 1796

CHAPTER 14

Salem Harbor, December 1779

JON STOOD ON the quarterdeck, his greatcoat buttoned to the throat, the high collar turned up against the bite of winter, and his hat snug on his head as the *Pickering* sailed into Salem's harbor, her canvas stiff in the cold air, her hull streaked with the scars of battle. The afternoon sky hung low and gray over the harbor rimmed with snow from a recent storm. Their five captured prizes crowded Salem's wharves, patched sails hanging limp, rigging creaking in the icy breeze.

As they eased toward Derby Wharf under shortened sail, the roar of the crowd reached Jon's ears. Townsfolk rushed forward, hats waving and voices raised in shouts that carried across the water. Jon drew in the salt and wood smoke air, sharp as a blade, and felt the harbor's energy surge into his bones.

The prizes already alongside were being stripped of their cargo. Barrels of sugar and casks of rum rolled across the wharf, bolts of cloth and chests of goods heaved onto sledges waiting in the snow. Men shouted, tallying, merchants craned for a closer look, children darted between barrels to peer at the bounty. The sight of Salem feasting on his victories filled Jon with a quiet pride.

Thorndike was at his side, calling crisp orders. "Hands to clew up the sails! Stand by with the lines!" Bos'n Robert Bowan bellowed them along, his voice carrying over the deck, while Bobby Grover darted across the deck, relaying word from quarterdeck to forecastle, grinning with the pride of a boy who had lived through fire and brought home victory.

The ship came alongside with a creak of timbers and slap of water nearly drowned out by the cheers ashore. Jon saw merchants pressing forward: George Williams with his hands raised in triumph, John Fisk already speaking to Elias Derby, who stood tall, his cane planted firmly, eyes gleaming.

As the gangplank thumped into place, Elias Derby stepped forward, raising his voice above the din. "We saved a spot for the *Pickering*, Captain, though we had to move vessels around to make room for all your prizes!"

Jon tipped his hat, his smile genuine. "Next time, I'll try to bring fewer, if only to spare your wharfingers the trouble."

The jest drew another burst of laughter and applause from the crowd, the sound carrying over the frozen harbor.

"The Royal Mail hides bullion in her hold," he said to Derby. "Might want your clerks to take special care overseeing the unloading of that one."

Jon's gaze searched the crowd until he saw them at the front of the press: Martha with her cloak tight around her, Silas lifting his hat high, and beside them Mrs. Mason with Hannah and little Polly clutched close.

Hannah waved furiously, her face shining. Polly bounced with glee. Though he could not hear their words, he knew his daughters shouted "Papa!" The governess' eyes met his and for a moment the crowd dimmed. He lifted his hat in salute, not just to the town, not just to his patrons, but to his family, the hearth waiting at Charter Street, the life that anchored him for a time before the sea called him back.

With that warming his heart, he strode down the gangplank, the roar of Salem around him, the sting of snow in the air, and victory in his step.

EUNICE WATCHED AS Captain Haraden stepped down from the *Pickering* with the sea still clinging to him, his greatcoat buttoned high, a short cape draped over his shoulders, brass buttons winking in the pale afternoon light. The crowd roared its welcome, but Eunice scarcely heard. Her breath caught as she watched him descend, a warrior returned, not only with his ship but with five more taken from the enemy.

How different he seemed from the man who had left them in September, his shoulders broader somehow, his bearing steadier, as though victory itself had entered his bones. She told herself it was pride, nothing more, but her heart did not listen.

Silas eased his way forward through the throng, his cart rattling over the frozen planks. "Room there, mates! Let's clear a bit of way for the captain's chest!" he called in his seaman's burr, waving his arms like a deck officer. Two sailors followed, Jon's sea chest slung between them. With a grunt and a heave, they set it into the cart.

The captain bent to kiss Hannah's hair and ruffled Polly's curls before lifting the younger one into his arms, his eyes warm on them both before meeting hers. For an instant, Eunice forgot the cold entirely.

"I'll not keep you waiting long," he told them. "The harbor master will have me sign in the *Pickering* and the prizes, and then I'll come straight home."

Martha gave a knowing sniff, her cloak wrapped tight. "Then don't dawdle, Captain. There's a fire on the hearth, a fat roast chicken in the oven, and the girls will not sleep until you've had your supper."

The captain laughed, the sound low and full, and lifted his hat in salute to them all. Setting Polly down, he said, "Then I'll make haste. Keep the fire burning for me."

Eunice took Polly's mittened hand, her pulse unsteady. Around them the crowd still cheered, but in her heart she carried the quiet promise of his words, and the knowledge that tonight he would be home again, at least for a time.

The walk back up Charter Street was slow in the winter dusk, snow crunching underfoot, the cart wheels creaking where the frost had stiffened the axles. Hannah skipped at her side, chattering about Papa's victories, while Polly sang nonsense songs to her doll. By the time they reached the house, smoke curled from the chimney and the windows glowed with firelight.

Inside, the warmth embraced them, scented with roasting fowl, fresh bread, and Martha's winter herbs. Silas hauled the sea chest to its corner with a grunt, and Martha shooed the girls to wash their hands before supper.

Eunice moved quietly among them, every beat of her heart was marked by the thought of the man who would soon walk through that door. The captain, yes, and Salem's hero, but also the father of the children she had come to love as her own, and the man whose presence anchored her days. She caught herself smoothing her gown, brushing a curl back into place. The gesture startled her, but she did not stop. Tonight, she thought, would be the first true night of homecoming.

A half-hour later, the latch lifted, and the door swung wide, a gust of frosty air curling in before the fire's warmth claimed it. Captain Haraden stepped inside, frost still clinging to his coat. The girls rushed to him at once, Hannah with a book to show him, Polly with her doll, both clamoring for his lap. He laughed as he shed his cape and greatcoat and hung them on a peg, then kneeled to gather them close.

Minutes passed and then Martha called them to the dining room where a fire burned in the small hearth, banishing the chill from the air. Carrying in the chicken, golden-skinned and steaming, she set it on the table with a flourish. "There now. Enough of the sea. The bird will want carvin', Captain."

Jon sat at the head of the table, his daughters at either side, his smile softening as he glanced toward Eunice sitting next to Polly. Taking the carving knife in hand, he said quietly, "I'll carve, aye. It's good to sit at my own table again, among those I care for most."

Eunice bowed her head as he spoke the blessing, her hands folded in her lap. When she raised her eyes, she caught his gaze lingering on her across the candles, warm, and unguarded. Her breath caught, and her heart gave a startled leap.

Tonight was not only a homecoming for him. It felt like a beginning, though she dared not speak it yet, not even to herself.

Eunice's voice was quiet across the table. "You must tell us where you've been. We hear so many rumors in Salem, and Silas brings us stories from the harbor, but I would rather have the truth from you."

The captain's expression softened. "It was warmer in the Caribbean, I'll say that much. The sea was bright as glass, though it burned hotter in the fighting. The Royal Mail ship there thought to make sport of us. She learned different. And off Sandy Hook, three of them came against us at once, but the *Pickering* sent them all limping to Salem behind us."

Hannah's eyes went wide. "Did you fire all the cannon, Papa?"

Jon chuckled, handing her a portion of chicken. "Every last one, sweetheart, and when we had but a single shot left, we made it do. That's all it took."

Martha clucked her tongue as she set fresh bread on the table. "A wonder you're here to tell it."

At that moment, Silas came in from the kitchen, cap in his hands, his weathered face grinning. "The whole harbor's ablaze with talk, Captain. Five prizes tied up, and your name on every tongue. They say no Salem man has ever done the like."

Jon shook his head, though his eyes gleamed. "Then let them say so, Silas. The crew made it possible. They work well together."

Silas gave a satisfied sniff, tugging at his cap. "Aye, sir. But still. I hear they're callin' you the Salamander, their captain who is impervious to fire." His grin widened before he ducked back toward the kitchen, leaving the words hanging in the air.

"The Salamander?" asked Eunice.

"Aye. The crew gave me that name when we took three ships at one time with flames shooting across the deck."

"'Tis a fitting nickname, Captain," said Eunice, "and it says much about your men's affection for you."

He appeared to ignore the compliment but she detected his pleasure at the term. Glancing at his daughters, he asked, "How have my girls been?"

Eunice smiled at Hannah as she leaned close to her father. "The girls have been well, Captain. Hannah keeps her copybook neat, and she's beginning her embroidery in earnest. Her manners are impeccable. Polly knows nearly all her letters now and will read in another year."

Polly beamed. "I read 'cat', Papa!"

The captain's laugh rumbled, and he leaned over to kiss the top of her curls. "Then you've bested half the ship's crew already, little one." His gaze shifted back to

Eunice, gratitude plain though unspoken. "You've done much for them."

Her cheeks warmed at his words. "They are eager pupils," she said, lowering her eyes to her plate.

The candles flickered, the fire glowed, and the talk flowed on, of lessons and neighbors, of the girls' antics and the house kept in his absence. And beneath it all, a quieter thread ran, unspoken but felt in every glance across the table: this was more than a hero's return. It was the weaving together of a home.

When the last of the chicken had been carved and the platters picked over, Martha shooed the girls to the kitchen to wash their sticky fingers. Silas followed with an armful of dishes, humming under his breath about Salem's "Salamander".

The captain leaned back in his chair with a sigh, the glow of cider in his cheeks. "I'd forgotten how fine a meal ashore can taste. Martha, you've spoiled me."

She sniffed, but the corner of her mouth twitched. "See you don't forget it again too soon, Captain." With that, she disappeared after the others.

Eunice rose quietly. "Shall we adjourn to the parlor for a glass of claret?"

"A fine idea," he said.

In the parlor, she poured them each a glass of wine, then gathered her needlework and took a seat by the hearth opposite him.

He shed his boots and stretched his legs toward the blaze. For a while they listened to the steady fire, the faint clatter of dishes in the kitchen, and the voices of the girls talking to Silas as the house settled into its evening rhythm.

"It's a different kind of battle here," he said at last, staring into the flames. "Not guns or sails, but lessons and hearths and little shoes left in the hall. I wonder sometimes which asks the greater courage."

Eunice folded her hands in her lap, her needlework forgotten. "You have both kinds of courage, Captain. You fight at sea for our country, and here you fight to be a good father. Your daughters will remember both."

His gaze lifted, meeting hers across the firelight. "And they'll remember the woman who cared for them when I was at sea."

Heat rose in her face. It had nothing to do with the fire. She bent her head over her sewing, though she could feel the weight of his regard. "They've cared for me, too, in ways I cannot fully explain."

From the dining room came a burst of girlish laughter, followed by Martha's scolding tone as she herded them toward the parlor. "Best move to the hearth fire before you wear Silas out with your chatter."

Hannah and Polly tumbled in, cheeks flushed, their energy spilling into the room like sunlight through a window.

The captain set down his glass, his gaze softening as he looked at his daughters. "That's home," he said softly.

For Eunice, it was more than home. It was the continuation of a beginning.

The London Coffeehouse, Salem, winter 1779

THE LONDON COFFEEHOUSE stood close to the harbor. So, as Jon entered with Thorndike, he expected to see merchants, sailors, and ship captains. He was not disappointed. Every table in the large common room was occupied, the air thick with tobacco smoke and the smell of coffee and rum punch. The scrape of chairs and clatter of tankards blended into a babble of men hungry for news. Steam rose from cups of coffee, mingling with the haze from pipes.

As Jon stepped inside, the noise swelled into cheers. Men rose to clap him on the back, tankards lifted, voices calling his new name. "The Salamander! Here's the Salamander!"

At his side, Thorndike grinned broadly, brushing snow from his cloak as he clapped Jon's shoulder. "Aye, cheer him, lads. I stood at his side when three British wolves thought to bring us down, and never once did he flinch. His crew has named him the Salamander, and 'tis a name well earned."

George Williams waved them over with Fisk and Derby already on their feet. "Captain Haraden," Derby said, his sharp eyes alight as he offered his hand. "Five prizes in four months, and boldest of all, three at once. All Salem is celebrating."

Jon shook their hands. "You know Lieutenant Thorndike, of course."

The men nodded and invited them to sit.

Williams added with a grin, "The ships came in heavy with goods, and the town is already counting the profit."

"And the bullion," Derby put in, tapping his cane. The others nodded gravely. "General Washington will be glad to see the gold."

Jon inclined his head, his voice measured. "Providence favored us, and much credit belongs to the men. They fought like lions."

Thorndike leaned forward, his tone quieter now, less for the crowd than for Jon. "Aye, I'll agree with you about Providence. But as for the men, it was your hand at the helm, sir. Courage alone doesn't win a fight. You made them believe, and that's what carried them through."

Jon met his first officer's gaze briefly, saying nothing, though the corner of his mouth tightened with something near to gratitude.

"Aye," said Fisk, "and the sea itself will remember. Even John Paul Jones, with his *Bonhomme Richard,* could ask for no greater."

At that, the talk shifted to the battle at Flamborough Head, the tale already flying across the Atlantic of John Paul Jones' courage under fire. "It occurred just after you sailed," Fisk said. "Jones' battered ship locked to the *Serapis,* refusing to strike though his decks were awash in blood."

"Finally, with both ships in tatters," said Fisk, his eyes gleaming, "and the *Bonhomme Richard* about to sink, the British captain yielded."

"'Twas a good thing," said Derby. "Jones had to order his crew to move to his prize."

"Tenacity like that," declared Williams, "reminds me of the stories going around about you, Haraden. You and Jones are cut from the same cloth."

Jon said nothing, only let the hot coffee steady him, but he was honored by the comparison. Jones had fought beneath England's gaze and won great notoriety, but both of them fought for America—and for liberty. "I'll not claim Jones' fame, but we share the same sea, the same enemy, and the same duty."

Fisk leaned closer, lowering his voice. "Yet not all news of the war is so bright. Count d'Estaing failed to recover Savannah. The south remains in the king's grip."

"And Washington?" Jon asked.

Williams' face sobered. "Camped at Morristown. Worse than Valley Forge, they say. Snow deeper than a man's waist, scarcely food or clothing enough. A third of his men are unfit for duty. While we count our prizes, they freeze."

The cheer dulled at that truth. For a moment, only the scrape of chairs and the muffled cough of a sailor carried.

Fisk broke the silence. "Washington had his soldiers build a log house city for shelter. The location between New York and Philadelphia provides a good supply of water and wood."

Williams nodded. "'Tis said he is inoculating the army to combat the threat of smallpox."

"A wise thing to do," said Jon.

"There is some brighter news," said Derby. "Lafayette has returned to France to plead our cause. He promises he will not rest until more ships and soldiers are sent. If his voice carries in Versailles, as we believe it does, France may yet turn the tide."

"Amen to that," muttered Fisk.

Thorndike lifted his cup. "Then let us pray Providence

grants him success, as it has granted us a captain who keeps America's flag flying."

Jon set down his tankard, his voice low but firm. "We'll give all we can, gentlemen. Salem will not be found wanting."

Derby's smile was keen. "Salem grows fat on such voyages, and you do well, too, Captain and Lieutenant."

"While the *Pickering* is being refit," Williams said, "take some time with your families. Spring will be here soon enough."

"Thank you," said Jon. "My family will welcome the time."

Derby leaned forward, a pensive look on his face. "In the spring, I've a mind to have you transport a shipment of sugar for Bilboa. The sugar is from Martinique and piled high in my stores. Bilbao hungers for it, and I want the *Pickering* to take it there under your command."

Jon inclined his head. "Then it shall be done. A full hold of sugar, and on the way home we'll see what prizes the seas offer. Salem and the cause will profit twice over, feeding America's coffers and bleeding the king's purse."

Derby returned him a satisfied smile.

Outside, the winter wind howled down Central Street, but inside the coffeehouse, camaraderie and Patriot resolve reigned, the name Salamander on every tongue.

Haraden house, Salem, Christmas Eve 1779

SNOW LAY BANKED along Charter Street, the ruts of cartwheels frozen hard, yet lantern light winked from windows as the Haraden kin from Gloucester arrived to celebrate the Savior's birth. Their laughter carried ahead of them, boots crunching, cloaks flung back as they stamped off the cold. Eunice welcomed them in, the house filling at once, as Martha pressed steaming mugs of spiced cider into chilled hands.

Captain Haraden introduced Lieutenant Thorndike with quiet pride, "My first officer," and Eunice caught the approving nods from Andrew Haraden and his wife, Lydia. It pleased her to see the captain and his officer recognized in his kin's eyes.

Eunice helped the girls slip off their woolen cloaks while the captain relieved Andrew Haraden of his hat and hung the heavier garments on pegs near the door. The brass buttons on the captain's own blue coat gleamed in the firelight as he clasped Andrew's hand. His voice carried warmly. "Where is your eldest daughter?"

"Joanna is with her new husband in Gloucester," Lydia said, a broad smile softening her face. "John Langford. They married in November."

"Good heavens," said Captain Haraden, "how old is she now?"

"Twenty-one," replied Lydia.

"Time moves on," said the captain, dipping his head gravely. "I trust it is a good match?"

"A very good one," said Lydia. "John is a fine young man."

"So, it's only the five youngest with us," Andrew added, flicking his dark locks from his forehead.

The two little Pollys, both four, danced in circles, their piping voices calling "Merry Christmas!" while the older girls crowded round to greet Hannah, all laughing together.

Silas joined them. "Should you not have heard, we celebrate more than Christmas." Lifting his mug high, his weathered voice carried above the din. "To Captain Haraden and his victories, may the Salamander keep the fire burnin' in Salem's hearths and endure the fire on the *Pickering*'s decks!"

The Gloucester Haradens looked puzzled at the strange title until Silas, full of relish, explained how the *Pickering*'s crew had christened their captain after his battles in smoke and flame. The congratulations that followed appeared to Eunice to leave Captain Haraden faintly abashed, though his smile lingered when his gaze found her, causing her cheeks to warm.

That night the two families walked together to East Church, the cold stinging their faces, their breath rising in clouds. Reverend Diman in his black robe with white bands welcomed them at the door. Inside, the press of bodies soon warmed the pews. Candles flickered in the drafts, and shadows leapt on the whitewashed walls as the congregation lifted its voice to sing the carol "While Shepherds Watched Their Flocks by Night".

Eunice's heart stirred at the fervent sound, the children's treble voices weaving with the deeper tones of sailors and townsfolk. Beside her, the captain bowed his head, his daughters nestled close, the hush of reverence binding them all.

Reverend Diman's words rang out, his message a call to endure in time of war and a reminder of joy in Christ's birth. Finally, he prayed for Washington's army at

Morristown, "hungry, cold, yet faithful". He gave thanks, too, for Salem's mariners who had brought victories home. Eunice felt the weight of the words, yet also the hope, and knew she would carry the sound of that prayer in her heart.

Back at Charter Street, supper was laid with plenty of noise. Martha brought out steaming bowls of clam chowder with hot bread and butter, followed by a raisin pudding. The warmth of the food was welcome after the bitter cold of the night air.

Thorndike sat near, cheerful as ever, though Eunice more than once caught his glance straying toward her. She kept her composure, yet she sensed Captain Haraden noticed it too, the brief tightening of his jaw before he forced his attention back to the laughter of his cousins.

Later, when the girls had gone upstairs with their Gloucester cousins and the house grew quiet, the adults sat before the fire in the parlor. After some discussion of the past year and the places the two Haradens had been, Thorndike turned to the captain. "With your leave, sir, while the ship is refit, I'll be spending some weeks in Beverly. There's a young woman there, Mercy Trask. I met her last time in port, and I mean to court her."

The captain's brows lifted. "Mercy Trask? Sister to young Joshua, one of our cabin boys?"

"Aye. She's a good sort, and I'll not deny, I've hopes she'll have me." His smile was boyish, shy even.

"She'll have you," Eunice said gently. "A rising officer in Salem's service? Of course she will."

The captain clasped Thorndike's shoulder with approval. "Then you'd best see to it, Israel. A man should not put off such things forever."

Thorndike grinned, raising his glass. "Not forever, no."

The fire burned lower, the house settling to quiet. Eunice lingered only a little longer with the three men and Lydia before she rose, smoothing her skirts. "Well, gentlemen and Lydia, I leave you to your wine. Until tomorrow."

As she climbed the stairs, the soft rumble of their voices drifted after her, but her thoughts lingered on the captain, the way he had looked at her in the candlelight at Thorndike's words, and the way her own heart had answered.

"Remember all Men would be tyrants if they could. If particular care and attention is not paid to the Ladies we are determined to foment a Rebellion, and will not hold ourselves bound by any Laws in which we have no voice, or Representation."
– Abigail Adams 1776

CHAPTER 15

Haraden house, Salem, Christmas Day 1779

MORNING DAWNED CLEAR and sharp, the snow along Charter Street glittering under a pale winter sun. Frost feathered the windows when Jon came down the stairs, the smell of salt pork and johnnycakes rising from the kitchen. In the parlor, his cousins from Gloucester sipped coffee near the fire, while children darted about in their stockings.

A small fire burned in the dining room hearth as Martha called them to breakfast. With Silas assisting, she set steaming platters on the long table, an extender added to accommodate twelve. The cook's cheeks glowed from the stove. "Sit yourselves, all of you. 'Tis Christmas mornin', and you'll not leave my table hungry."

Eggs, fried pork, johnnycakes with maple syrup, and crocks of cider warmed with nutmeg filled the board. Jon took his place at one head, Andrew at the other. Eunice sat along the side, passing syrup and bread to the little ones.

As chatter rose, Andrew leaned toward Jon and passed an envelope to him. "For the extra expenses."

Jon passed it back. "The Almighty has blessed me. You have my thanks, but it is not necessary."

Andrew nodded. "I am glad you prosper, Cousin. When next will you sail?"

Jon wiped his hands. "Come spring, if the shipyard does its part. Derby has in mind a sugar run to Bilboa. And if the seas give us prizes, so much the better."

Andrew lifted his brows. "Spain? That's a far reach. And dangerous seas between."

Jon's mouth curved faintly. "Danger is the sea's native tongue. Better we speak it than shy from it."

Andrew chuckled, shaking his head. "You speak more like a legend than a sailor."

Jon waved the comment off, though his eyes gleamed. "Fame's a fickle wind, Cousin. Best we trim our sails to Providence and not pride."

Andrew raised his mug. "Aye, and may that wind hold."

After breakfast, the younger Haradens clamored for the yard. "Snowballs! A snowman!" cried the two Pollys together, and soon cloaks and mittens were flying on. Jon followed them out, his greatcoat collar turned high against the cold.

The yard rang with shrieks as snowballs flew. Hannah's strong arm sent several square at her father, while little Polly darted about like a sprite. Andrew's older daughters pelted their cousins, their voices ringing with mirth.

Thorndike joined in, laughing, scooping a double handful and hurling it at Jon. The ball burst across his shoulder in a scatter of white shards. Jon grinned, stooped, and returned fire with an aim that sent Thorndike staggering back.

"Papa's the best shot!" Hannah crowed, clapping mittened hands.

From the porch, Eunice laughed, her hood fallen back, hair dusted with snow. When Jon lobbed a ball toward her skirts, she gasped, then scooped her own handful and flung it true. It struck him square, and the children shrieked in delight. Soon her mittens and cloak were powdered white, her laughter mingling with theirs, and Jon's breath caught at the sight, though he turned quickly back to the melee.

By afternoon, the house glowed with candles and the scent of roast goose. Martha had tended the birds since Michaelmas, and now their skins gleamed gold on the platters, juices hissing as Jon carved. Lydia and Eunice set out apple, mince, and pumpkin pies with loaves of bread. Platters of steaming goose went round, glasses raised in toasts to family, to Salem, to victories past and to come. For a time, the war seemed far away.

Jon lifted his glass toward Martha as she swept in with another dish. "A toast to our cook. Martha, you've outdone yourself. Goose fit for an admiral, and better company to share it with."

When the feast was done, they gathered in the parlor. Silas heaved a log onto the fire so it leapt high. The girls sang carols, then begged riddles of their uncle and aunt, who obliged with roaring laughter. Thorndike played draughts with Andrew, while Lydia and Martha set the younger children to forfeits.

Soon the girls crowded near Silas, clamoring for a story. With a wink, he drew a coil of line from his pocket and perched on a stool. "First, a lesson," he said, fingers moving nimbly. "A proper knot can save a ship, or a sailor's life."

Hannah copied his motions carefully. "Like this?" she asked, holding up a neat bowline.

"Aye, well enough for a young mate," Silas said, grinning.

Polly tried next, but her line snarled in her curls. Laughter erupted as Silas freed her. "That's the mermaid's knot, rare and dangerous, but harmless ashore."

"Now a tale!" the girls begged.

Silas leaned closer to the firelight. "Once, off Cape Ann, I saw a monster rise from the deep. Scales like iron, eyes like lanterns, teeth the size of anchors. It followed us three leagues before it dove, leavin' foam enough to swamp a yawl."

The children squealed, half-thrilled, half-terrified. Just then, Martha bustled in with a tray of spiced nuts and steaming mugs. "Silas Turner, you'll give them nightmares!" she scolded. "Best you tell them of dolphins chasin' the ship instead."

The room rang with laughter. Jon, stretched in his chair with cider warm in hand, added, "Best they hear both the wonders and the terrors. That's the sea, after all."

As evening deepened, one by one the children drooped. Lydia and Betsey shepherded the younger ones upstairs until only the fire's glow and the murmur of adult voices remained.

Andrew turned to Jon. "There's talk enough comparing you to John Paul Jones. It makes us proud, Cousin."

Thorndike said quietly, "I saw him stand fast against three ships at once. Seamanship like that deserves every word."

Martha, pausing in the doorway, gave a brisk nod. "And every woman here prayed you home. Victories may belong to the sea, but waitin' belongs to us."

Lydia smiled, glancing at Eunice. "And you've kept the captain's daughters thriving, Mrs. Mason. No small victory there."

Eunice's cheeks warmed at the praise. Jon met her eyes across the firelight, gratitude plain though unspoken.

The talk drifted to neighbors, to the shipyard, to Derby's plans for spring. Jon stretched his boots toward the blaze, letting the moment settle. The sea would call him soon enough, but tonight he was only a man among kin, his daughters safe in their beds, and across the hearth sat the quiet figure of the governess who had become more than he dared name.

For that Christmas night, it was enough.

Haraden house, Salem, February 1780

THE GLOUCESTER HARADENS had returned to their home the month before, and Jon missed the chatter of so many daughters and the conversations he often had with Andrew.

By February, snow still clung in dirty heaps along Charter Street, though the day's thaw had left the cobbles slick. By evening, frost hardened again, and the lamps along the street shone in halos of ice. Inside the Haraden house, however, warmth and noise reigned.

The girls had spread themselves across the parlor rug: Hannah arranging her embroidery threads in neat rows while Polly and her doll staged a pitched battle with wooden soldiers Silas had carved for her. Laughter spilled in bursts as Polly toppled her army with a sweep of her hand.

Martha hurried in, calling all to the dining room where she had set steaming bowls of beef stew with root vegetables, the scent of the stew and fresh bread filling the air. "Mind yourselves, now! The table's set, and I'll not have the victuals grow cold."

Jon rose from his chair by the hearth where a fire blazed and crossed to lift Polly into his arms, grinning as she squealed, "Papa! My soldiers fell!"

"They'll stand again," he told her, kissing her cheek before carrying her into the dining room and setting her on a pillow in her chair, for she no longer needed the high chair. "As long as their captain is brave."

As the family gathered at the table, a knock came at the front door. Mrs. Mason went to open it. Returning, her face alight, she said, "It's Mr. Thorndike just arrived in Salem!"

Jon welcomed his first mate, though he frowned at the governess' enthusiasm for her admirer. "Sit and have some stew, Israel."

Israel Thorndike stepped in, brushing snow from his blue coat, his cheeks ruddy from the cold. He looked a little sheepish, but his eyes shone with a warmth Jon hadn't seen before. Bowing lightly to Mrs. Mason, then to Martha, he clasped Jon's hand. "Forgive me, Captain. My 'few weeks' in Beverly stretched longer. But a man weds only once, and I've just done it."

The room stilled. Jon's daughters looked at him as though waiting for him to explain what this meant.

Mrs. Mason broke the silence with a smile. "Married? How wonderful! And to whom?"

Thorndike took a seat, Martha bustling to set another place before him. His grin widened. "To Mercy Trask, sister of young Joshua. We wed in January. She's a jewel, Captain. I'd have brought her tonight, but she's with her people still and searching for a home for us in Beverly."

Silas stepped in from the kitchen, a slice of bread in his hand, and gave a low whistle. "So that's what kept you, Lieutenant. I thought you'd fallen into a snowbank and couldn't dig yourself out."

Laughter rippled around the table. Martha wagged her spoon at Thorndike. "Then we'll expect her here soon enough, to see if she can keep you properly fed."

"Aye," Thorndike said with mock solemnity. "Mercy manages me well already, and she can cook, Martha."

The meal went on with good cheer. Hannah pressed

Thorndike with questions about his bride, while Polly solemnly announced that she would marry Papa when she grew up, earning laughter from all, even Mrs. Mason, though Jon saw her eyes soften when he leaned down to kiss his younger daughter's curls.

After supper they gathered in the parlor again. Martha brought in a dish of candied nuts and mugs of heated cider spiced with cinnamon. At Hannah's urging, Silas spun a yarn about a ship that had once seen dolphins chasing its wake all the way to the Azores. His hands sketched arcs in the firelight. "Leapin', shinin' like silver coins in the moonlight. The men swore it meant good fortune."

"And did it?" asked Hannah.

"Aye," Silas said with a wink. "They made port in Spain heavy with treasure and not a man lost."

At that, Jon and Thorndike exchanged a look. Soon enough, Spain would be their own port.

The girls begged for a song, so Mrs. Mason led them in *Rejoice, the Lord is King,* their young voices rising with enthusiasm. Jon and Thorndike joined in, their deeper tones rounding out the hymn, and even Silas rumbled along on the chorus.

Jon leaned back in his chair, watching the scene: his kin gathered, his daughters safe, Mrs. Mason's hand gently stroking Polly's hair. Across the hearth, the governess looked up, her eyes meeting his for a brief moment. Something unspoken passed between them, fragile, yet warming as surely as the fire.

When the song ended, Thorndike said, "I'll be at the shipyard tomorrow, Captain."

"You must stay with us until we sail, Israel," Jon replied. "Mercy would expect it, and we like having you. Your room upstairs has been kept ready in anticipation of your arrival. Rest easy tonight, and tomorrow we'll see the *Pickering* and think of masts and rigging again."

As the house settled, Martha gathered the mugs and Silas tended the fire. The children's laughter faded upstairs as Thorndike shepherded them off. Soon only Jon and the governess lingered in the parlor, the fire reduced to coals.

Jon stretched his long legs before him, the silence companionable. "It seems quieter than it should," he said at last.

Mrs. Mason smoothed Polly's abandoned doll across her lap, her fingers lingering on the fabric. "That's what happens when the children sleep. The house holds its breath."

He turned his head, studying her in the lamplight, the curve of her cheek, the strength in her posture, the presence that steadied his very home. "You've given them more than lessons," he said quietly. "You've given them love and joy."

Her gaze met his, her voice low. "And they, and you, have given me a place I thought I'd lost forever."

Jon felt the words strike deeper than any broadside. He should have looked away, but he could not. For one heartbeat too long he let himself imagine what could not be spoken aloud, at least not now.

At last he rose, slowly, and took up the taper. "Best we see the house to rest," he said, though his voice was huskier than he intended.

The governess rose, too, smoothing her gown. She paused at the open door, her eyes lifting once more to his.

"Good night, Captain."

"Good night, Mrs. Mason."

He waited until her footsteps faded above, then bent to bank the fire. The last glow winked beneath the ash, steady and enduring, like the memory of her brown eyes that would follow him over the sea.

Salem Shipyard, the next morning

FROST RIMED THE rigging of ships along the harbor, but the sun shone bright in a clear blue sky. The timbers of the *Pickering* rang with the blows of caulkers' mallets as Jon and Thorndike stepped onto the frozen planks of the shipyard. Their breath smoked in the morning air, the smell of tar and oak shavings sharp in their lungs.

Thorndike rubbed his hands together briskly. "A night by the hearth almost makes a man forget how bitter our winter mornings can be."

Jon's eyes were on his ship. The new rigging gleamed with fresh tar, the seams of her planks tight with pitch, the great yards braced square. "Better we remember that the sea won't go easy on a ship that's been coddled. She must be sound from keel to truck."

"Aye, you're right, Captain."

A gang of shipwrights passed with spar timbers on their shoulders, nodding respectfully as they went. One lingered to report, "Caulking's near finished, Captain. Next we'll scrape her bottom clean and pay it with tallow, new standing rigging to set up, sails near done in the loft, gun carriages wanting fresh trucks, and the pumps overhauled before you dare the Atlantic. All told, she'll be fit for sea in April."

Jon gave a curt nod, though his jaw tightened. A month and more to wait. Still, there was no hurrying such work. "See it done, then." He strode up the gangplank and laid a gloved hand on the rail, noting the familiar grain, as though reassuring himself she still breathed. "She'll ride low with Derby's sugar, but she'll carry. And she'll fight if she must."

He stood a moment, watching the shipwrights busy aloft and below, the shipyard clattering with hammers, saws, and the creak of timbers. The sea tugged at him, as it always did, but at least the delay meant he would be in Salem for Easter.

Thorndike leaned beside him, his grin quick. "Captain, if she'll not be ready till April, do you suppose I might spend March in Beverly? Mercy would thank you for it."

Jon glanced at him, his stern mouth easing a fraction. "You've a wife now, Israel. You'd best learn she'll expect all the time you can give her. Go when the work allows, but be back when I call. Spain will not wait."

"Aye, Captain," Thorndike said, satisfaction plain on his face.

Jon allowed himself the smallest smile, then turned toward the wharf, boots crunching on the frost-rimed planks. "Come, Lieutenant. The shipwrights have their work, and we might as well find what tidings the world has for us. The coffeehouse will tell us what news the war brings."

The coffeehouse on Central Street was thick with tobacco smoke and talk when Jon and his first officer pushed in from the cold. Men looked up from their tables, calling greetings as they doffed their hats. Word of the *Pickering*'s prizes still lingered, but now the air was hungry for news from farther afield.

At the back, Elias Derby sat with George Williams, their cups steaming. Derby's sharp gaze fixed on Jon at once, while Williams' expression warmed into a smile. "Captain. I hear from the yard your ship won't be ready till April?"

Jon inclined his head, settling his gloves on the table. "Aye. Caulking's near done, but new rigging, sails and even carpenters are taking more time. She'll not be fit to sail before then. It seems I'll be home for Easter this year."

"A rare gift for your family," Williams said, his voice easy, before leaning closer. "But you'll not lack for work once she's ready. The war presses on."

Derby's finger tapped his cup. "You and Mr. Thorndike came for news, I think?"

"Aye," Jon said. "The yard rings with mallets, but a man wants to hear what stirs beyond Salem."

Derby lifted his cup. "Some of it brighter than months past. We are hopeful Lafayette will meet with success. If God wills it, he'll soon bring back ships and gold."

Thorndike leaned forward, eyes bright. "If he brings French ships, Captain, your next prizes may sail under their very guns."

"A pleasant thought," Jon said.

Williams nodded. "Franklin stays in Paris, bargaining for more loans. The French know America bleeds, but they also see our ships take prize after prize. Trade keeps their hopes in us alive, and Franklin keeps commissioning privateers."

"And in the north?" Jon asked.

Williams' smile faded. "Washington's army still lies at Morristown. Snow waist deep, soldiers starving. Yet he holds them together somehow. He's begging food and forage from New Jersey farmers, and so far they answer. That alone is a miracle."

Derby's voice cut in, brisk as ever. "But mark this: if the south falls, the king will claim half the continent. I hear whispers of Charleston next. We'll need more victories at sea to keep the tide from turning."

Jon felt every eye on him, merchants and captains alike. He set down his cup, his voice firm. "Then we'll do our part. If Spain hungers for sugar, Salem will deliver it. And between here and Bilbao, we'll strike what blows we can. Not only for trade, but for America, and for liberty."

A murmur of approval passed around the table, and even Derby's sharp eyes softened. Williams gave a slow nod, practical as ever, while Thorndike looked fit to sail that very night.

Outside, the wind howled down Central Street, but inside the coffeehouse the air seemed warmer, as if Salem's pulse beat in that room.

Derby Wharf, Salem, March 1780

BY LATE MARCH, the *Pickering* had been moved from the shipyard to Derby Wharf. Her hull, freshly caulked and pitched, gleamed dark against the water. Alongside her, barrels and hogsheads were being hoisted aboard, the air sharp with the smell of molasses and raw sugar. Kegs of powder, casks of salted beef, and crates of hardtack stood ready on the planks, guarded by Derby's clerks with their tally books in hand. The ship's crew, some fresh from Beverly and Gloucester, drifted back to her decks with their sea chests, voices lifted in shanties that carried down the wharf.

Jon stood with Thorndike near the gangway, his eye running over the bustle with quiet satisfaction. "She rides lower already," he said. "By the time Derby's sugar is stowed, she'll sit deep in the water. But she'll carry it."

Thorndike grinned. "And with Spain's gold at the end of it, Derby will be thinking it was well worth the wait. And the men'll like it, too. Word of prize shares keeps them eager."

At that moment, Elias Derby approached, his manner brisk, his cane tapping on the planks in brisk rhythm. "Haraden, there's news from Boston, confirmed this time. A French fleet of forty vessels is assembling at Brest under General Rochambeau. Six thousand sailors, marines and officers and more than five thousand soldiers."

A murmur of excitement swept along the wharf as others heard his words. Sailors leaned on their coils of rope, merchants paused over their ledgers, the very air seemed to catch.

"Can it be true?" Thorndike asked, his voice carrying his wonder at the news.

Derby nod was curt. "The reports are strong enough that I'll not dismiss them. God willing, those ships will sail by summer and America will fight with the strength of the French navy."

Jon's chest tightened at the thought. French soldiers

landing on American soil, fighting at Washington's side. For months, the news from Morristown had been grim, and darker still from the south. But if Rochambeau came, then Providence had indeed answered their prayers.

George Williams joined them to hear the last of Derby's report. "Mark me, Haraden, if that fleet crosses the Atlantic, the war changes. Until then, we must keep the sea lanes bleeding red with captured ships. Spain will have sugar, and Salem will have prizes."

Derby's sharp gaze flicked back to Jon. "And the *Pickering* will be at the fore of it."

Jon inclined his head to them both. "She's near ready. We'll give Washington what help we can."

Two days later, on Easter Sunday, Jon gathered with others in the East Church. The air inside was chill despite the crush of bodies. Candles guttered in the draft. Reverend Diman spoke of endurance in hardship, of Christ's resurrection as the blessed hope, the pledge that death had been defeated, and despair would never have the final word. He prayed openly for Washington's army at Morristown, and thanked God for the expected aid from France.

Jon bowed his head, Hannah pressed close on one side, Polly on the other. Beside them, Mrs. Mason prayed. When the prayer ended, the hymn began, "Christ the Lord Is Risen Today", their voices strong despite the cold.

Jon held his daughters close and let the hymn rise in worship to God. For this Easter morning he was home, anchored in the blessings of hearth and family. Yet he knew the sea waited, and soon enough the *Pickering* would carry him far from Salem's shores once more. Silently, he asked God to go before him.

Derby Wharf, Salem, April 1780

THE MORNING AIR was sharp with salt and the smell of pitch as Jon gazed up at the blue sky above the harbor. Gulls wheeled overhead as the *Pickering* lay heavy against the wharf. Her gunwales rode low, barrels of sugar stacked in her hold until she looked more merchantman than privateer. Jon smiled at the thought. He was content to be both, and her sixteen guns stood ready, black mouths peering from their ports, a promise she was no common trader.

On the planks, clerks with tally books checked off kegs of powder, casks of beef, and bundles of canvas as they were swung aboard. Barrels of shot clinked as they rolled, muskets in their racks clattered on sailors' shoulders, and a stack of boarding pikes gleamed like a hedge of iron. Sailors tramped past with sea chests and their own pistols and cutlasses belted on, voices raised in rough shanties that mingled with the creak of tackle and the slap of waves against the piles.

Jon stood with Thorndike at the foot of the gangway beside Elias Derby and George Williams. He and his first officer wore their officers' dress, dark blue coats with brass buttons, buff breeches, and buckled shoes, their hair queued beneath cocked hats. The two merchants were sober in brown, their white stockings neat.

"As you see, gentlemen, the *Pickering* carries a full load," Jon said, a smile coming to his lips. "Your sugar."

"Your ship is both sword and plowshare, Captain," Derby replied, his cane tapping the planks. "I've every confidence you will see she serves us well."

Williams clapped Jon's shoulder with quiet warmth. "And see she brings you home again. Salem has had glory enough from your last cruise, but your daughters will settle for nothing less than your safe return."

Jon inclined his head gravely. "If that is to be, gentlemen, then I ask your prayers."

Down the wharf, Martha stood with Silas and the girls, Hannah's hand clasped tight in her governess', Polly bouncing in Mrs. Mason's other hand. Hannah waved furiously, calling, "Papa!" Polly echoed her in a piping voice.

Jon excused himself and strode to them, kneeling to gather both daughters into his arms. "Mind your letters, Polly," he said gently, "and you, Hannah, keep to your sewing and your cooking." His smile masked the ache beneath. His daughters did not ask when he might return. Raised in a ship captain's house, they knew he could not promise a date. He could not even promise he would return at all.

Jon kissed each girl, then rose. Martha tugged her shawl close. "Don't forget, Captain, thanks to your provision, there's food enough in the pantry for when you return, and mind, the girls will want you at the table again."

Silas raised his hat, his weathered face steady. "The Lord guard you, Captain. We'll keep the hearth warm and your family safe till you're home again."

Jon's throat tightened. He looked to Mrs. Mason then, her eyes warm as she held fast to his daughters. In that moment he knew she was very much a part of his family now. For an instant, the noise of the wharf dimmed.

As Jon rose, a tug at his sleeve made him turn. Bobby Grover stood there, cap in hand, his brown locks blowing in the wind, his grin wide. "Captain, all's ready in your cabin, your sea chest's stowed and your logbook set out. I'm ready to serve you again, running every errand quick as a shot."

Jon ruffled the boy's hair, pride in his tone. "You've already proved yourself, Bobby. Stand fast, and you'll do more than errands before long. While you're here, meet my daughters. Turning to his girls he said, "Hannah will be twelve this year—your age—and Polly will be five."

Bobby doffed his hat to Hannah and smiled at Polly, who looked up at the boy in wonder.

From the *Pickering*'s deck came Thorndike's sharp call: "Hands aboard! Loose the lines!"

The gangway thudded as men hurried up, Bobby among them, quick as a sprite. Jon lingered only a moment longer, lifting his hat to Mrs. Mason, the girls, and to Martha and Silas, then he followed.

Lines were cast off, sails sheeted home with a snap of canvas, and slowly, heavily, the *Pickering* eased from the wharf. The crowd that had come to see them off raised a cheer, hats waving, voices carrying across the water.

Jon took his place on the quarterdeck, the familiar roll beneath his boots, and watched Salem's rooftops fall astern. The cheer of the crowd faded, gulls shrieked above and the sharpness of tar gave way to the clean salt of open sea. Home, hearth, and harbor slipped away. Ahead lay the wide Atlantic and whatever trials God set before them.

"The harder the conflict, the greater the honor."
– George Washington 1776

CHAPTER 16

Bay of Biscay, 29 May 1780

WEEKS OF STEADY sailing carried the *Pickering* across the Atlantic, her holds heavy with Derby's sugar and her crew falling into the hard rhythm of sea life. By late May, the long swells of the Bay of Biscay were beginning to heave beneath her. The weather had been fickle with sudden squalls, then blinding bursts of sun.

That morning, Bobby had just brought Jon coffee when a cry from the main-top lookout split the air. "Sail to windward!"

Handing Bobby his coffee, Jon raised his glass, salt crusting at its rim. A cutter, broad in the beam, running fast, her sides bristling with twenty guns was bearing down like a hawk swooping upon its prey.

Thorndike's boots sounded on the deck beside him.

"She's armed heavier than we are, sir. Shall we run?"

Jon lowered the glass. "No. She's chosen her fight. Ready the guns. We'll show her the *Pickering* was built for more than sugar."

Bobby scrambled down from the quarterdeck, Jon's mug in hand. He would want to be part of the action to follow.

Orders cracked across the deck. Gun crews threw open the ports; black muzzles thrust out, priming horns at the ready. Powder boys dashed with cartridges, Bobby among them, his face alight with eagerness.

The sea narrowed between hunter and hunted. The cutter fired first, a crashing broadside, iron screaming across the water. A ball punched through the *Pickering*'s bulwark, splinters flying. Men ducked instinctively, then steadied as Jon's voice cut clear. "Stand fast! Fire as she bears!"

The *Pickering*'s guns answered, smoke roiling out, the deck shuddering with the recoil. Through the drifting haze Jon saw the cutter stagger under the blows, her jib fluttering ragged, her rigging cut. And then he made a discovery: the *Pickering*'s sugar-laden weight kept her low in the water, every shot biting into the enemy's hull near the waterline. The cutter, riding higher, hurled much of her fire too far aloft, splintering spars and sails but leaving the ship's heart whole. The very burden that made them slow had given them teeth.

For nearly two hours they traded thunder. Shot tore sails, splintered rails, and sent iron clanging across the decks. Twice the *Pickering* shuddered under solid hits, but her timbers held. Jon moved on the quarterdeck with calm authority, spyglass in hand, shouting orders through the smoke. "Shift your aim lower! Break her waterline! Steady, lads, give her Salem's fire!"

Thorndike's voice rose with his. "Run out the guns! Give her another!"

The cutter pressed hard, circling to rake, but the *Pickering* answered at every turn, her smaller frame nimble where the cutter lumbered. At last a shot struck true and the cutter's main topmast splintered, crashing in a tangle of sail and cordage. A cheer broke from the *Pickering*'s deck as the cutter fell off, bearing away to leeward.

Jon held his glass a moment longer, watching her dwindling hull. Part of him longed to chase and finish it, but the sugar below, Derby's fortune and Salem's stake, bound him to his course. To linger was to risk losing all.

"Secure the guns and the wounded," Jon ordered. Only then did he allow himself a slow nod.

Bobby appeared at his elbow, powder-stained and grinning through smoke. "We showed her, Captain! Sent her running!"

Jon allowed himself the ghost of a smile. "Aye, Bobby. The first trial of this cruise, and she's stood it well."

The cheer still echoed across the deck, but Jon's thoughts were already ahead, into the wide Bay of Biscay and the greater tests yet to come.

"If I might, sir," Bobby asked, his eyes bright, "why didn't we try and take her?"

Jon looked down at the boy, then back at the sugar-laden ship under his feet. "Because we sail for Bilbao with Salem's fortune in our hold," he said evenly. "Our guns must guard it. To chase her would risk all, and I'll not gamble the town's stake for pride." Jon's gaze lingered on the cutter limping away, her topmast down. The prize-hunter in him longed to give chase, but he clenched his jaw. *Not here, not now.* "Bilbao lies ahead. If I find a prize near that safe harbor, we'll take her then."

Bobby's grin softened into something more thoughtful. "So we fight when we must, but not always."

Jon rested a hand briefly on the boy's shoulder. "Aye, Lad. And that's the harder duty of command."

Offshore of Bilboa in the Bay of Biscay, 1 June 1780

THE BAY OF Biscay lay restless under a rising moon, long swells shouldering the *Pickering* as she pressed south, her holds groaning with Derby's sugar. She looked every inch a trader, but her gunports told another tale: sixteen black mouths ready if pressed.

Near dusk, the lookout's hail broke the monotony. "Sail ahead! To leeward!"

Jon raised his night glass. In the fading light he made her out: a wide beam, sails well set, bristling with twenty-two guns. A privateer, no mistaking.

Thorndike's jaw tightened. "She's got more guns that the *Pickering*, sir. Could be she's hunting."

Jon lowered the glass. "Aye. That's the *Golden Eagle*. She thinks she's the hawk, and we're the pigeon. We'll see."

As the sky darkened, he ordered lanterns doused and the *Pickering*'s sails trimmed just enough to feign weariness. From the enemy's deck, the *Pickering* would appear a fat merchantman, ripe for the taking. When the *Golden Eagle* bore close, Jon snapped his order. "Wear ship. Bring us under her bow—now!"

The *Pickering* swung sudden as a cat on the prowl, canvas cracking in the night wind. In the moon's pale wash, she loomed broadside on, gunports yawning wide. Jon raised his speaking trumpet, his voice carrying like iron across the water. "Surrender or be sunk!"

A hush seemed to fall between the ships, the sea itself holding its breath. The *Golden Eagle*, expecting an easy prize, had not reckoned on such sudden menace. And, in the dark, her master did not know the real size of the *Pickering*. He peered through the gloom at the *Pickering*'s bristling guns, her bold posture. He faltered. Moments later, her colors came down.

A roar of triumph burst from the *Pickering*'s men. Bobby Grover, powder-stained from the earlier skirmish, danced on the deck. "We've got her, Captain! We've taken her without a shot!"

Jon stayed composed. "Thorndike, take men over. Secure her decks. Lieutenant Carnes will command her as prize."

Thorndike, already gathering men, beckoned Lieutenant Carnes. "Take charge, Mr. Carnes, and see her safe into Bilbao."

Bobby edged forward, cap clutched in his hands. His eyes shone with a mix of nerves and excitement. "Captain, sir, might I go with Mr. Carnes? Just this once? It's a short run to Bilbao, and Joshua Trask can serve you in my stead while I'm on the *Eagle*. He's near as quick as I am."

Jon studied the boy, reading both his eagerness and his

pride. To serve on a prize crew was no small honor for a cabin boy. "You're certain of it, Bobby?"

"Aye, sir," he said, his voice firm despite the flush in his cheeks. "I'd like to say I helped bring her in."

Jon's gaze flicked to Thorndike, who gave a slight shrug, then back to the boy. After a pause, he nodded. "Very well. Go, and mind Lieutenant Carnes. But remember, you carry the *Pickering*'s honor with you."

Bobby's grin broke wide as he dashed to join the boat, calling over his shoulder, "Aye, Captain!"

When the British captain, Robert Scott, was brought aboard the *Pickering* under guard, his face was thunderous. He had submitted to a phantom armament, and the truth of his folly stood plain for him to see. The *Pickering* was smaller, lower, and not half so fierce as she'd seemed in the shadows.

"You tricked me," he spat, his voice thick with humiliation. "By God, I thought you a ship of the line!"

Jon met his fury with calm. "A captain takes his chances at sea, sir. Tonight, chance was mine. If it's any consolation, I will allow you your freedom on parole for return to London, so long as you give your word not to fight again until exchanged for an American."

Scott's face flushed a deeper red, the muscle in his jaw jumping. For a moment he seemed about to lash out again. But the weight of defeat and the offer of parole left him caught between pride and gratitude. His voice came low and bitter. "You shame me twice, sir, once with your trick, and again with your courtesy. I'll give my word, though it galls me."

Thorndike returned from the *Golden Eagle*, reporting

briskly. "Her stores are sound, sir, her guns heavier than ours. She makes a fine prize."

Jon gave a single nod. "Then we set course for Bilbao. Two ships now, not one."

The day darkened early, low clouds scudding in from the Atlantic, a heavy stillness before the night. The *Pickering* and her prize pressed south toward Bilbao and the Spanish coast, a shadow on the horizon.

Near dusk the lookout's hail split the wind. "Sail astern! Large, and gaining fast!"

Jon raised his night glass. Out of the gray loomed a vast hull, rig crowded with canvas, her deck overflowing with guns. Even before Thorndike spoke, Jon knew her. "God help us. That's the *Achilles*."

A murmur spread across the deck as men caught sight of her towering spars, the largest lugger ever fitted. Though a privateer, she looked more like a ship of war. Jon's jaw tightened. Forty-odd cannon against his sixteen, and ten of his best men, including Bobby, were away on the *Eagle*.

"Steady," Jon called, his voice level, though his stomach turned like the sea. "She'll show her hand soon enough."

They did not have long to wait. The *Achilles* bore straight for the *Pickering*'s prize, her bow wave foaming white. Jon stood helpless at the rail, watching as the giant lugger closed on the *Golden Eagle*. The Stars and Stripes snapped in defiance above the deck, and a few shots rang out. But the *Achilles* came swarming, red coats spilling over the rail. In minutes, the American colors were hauled down, the British flag up in their place.

Beside him, Thorndike swore under his breath. "They've taken her back and with our own men aboard."

Jon lowered the glass. His throat tightened. Bobby was there, quick, eager Bobby, who had begged to serve on the *Eagle*. The boy's grin, so bright with pride, flashed in his mind, and now he was in enemy hands. The sight cut deep: his prize gone, his men taken, his cabin boy snatched from him. He felt every eye on him, waiting for orders he could not give. To rush the *Achilles* now was madness. The sugar in his hold, Salem's fortune, weighed like a stone in his chest.

He clenched his jaw, his voice carrying across the deck. "We'll not waste men in the dark. She has the *Eagle* tonight, but come the morning, she'll reckon with the *Pickering*. Mark me, we'll stand and fight."

"Aye, Captain," came the reply from the main deck.

A heavy overcast draped the bay as the sun slid down. The *Achilles* held her distance, looming like a predator biding its hour. Jon turned the deck over to Thorndike and went below.

In his cabin the lantern swung with the swell, casting long shadows over his table. Jon shed his coat and sat, opening his Bible, the pages worn from salt and handling. His eyes fell on Galatians: "Stand fast therefore in the liberty wherewith Christ hath made us free."

He bowed his head, the words forming not for show but for life itself. "Lord," he whispered, "You know Bobby, bold beyond his years, eager to serve. Keep him safe tonight, wherever he lies. Bring him back to me, and let me not fail him, nor these men, nor the cause we serve. Grant me wisdom to stand fast, not in pride, but in Your strength."

For a moment he sat still, the ache of old grief stirring. He thought of the sons he and Hannah had buried in infancy, tiny graves that still lay in Salem's earth. Perhaps that was why he felt the pull so keenly toward his cabin boys and his crew as well. He was a father to them all in some small way. Bobby most of all. To lose him, or any of those entrusted to his command, was unthinkable.

With that, he closed his Bible, blew out the lantern, and lay down on his berth. Sleep took him swiftly, deep and untroubled, while beyond the timbers the sea groaned with the promise of battle.

The gray light of dawn had seeped into the cabin as Thorndike burst in, breathless. "Captain, the *Achilles* is upon us!"

Waking from a deep sleep, Jon swung his legs to the deck, and reached for his coat. He took care with his cravat before setting his hat on his head with the composure of a man summoned to breakfast, not to battle. Seeing Thorndike was nervous, he explained, "I believe in dressing for an engagement such as this."

"Yes, sir," said his first officer.

"Very well," Jon said evenly. "Let us meet her, Mr. Thorndike."

On deck, the men waited, nerves tight as bowstrings. Jon looked them over and saw the fear in their faces and the knowledge of the odds etched clear: one small ship against a monster lugger. Worse still, ten of their best hands and Bobby were aboard the *Golden Eagle*.

He raised his voice so all could hear. "We are few against their many, aye, but we are not alone. There are sixty prisoners below, and some may earn their freedom this day."

The word spread swiftly. In minutes, the hatch was thrown back and men climbed out, blinking in the pale light. Jon offered gold to any who would stand with them. "Today you can fight with Patriots. Today you can earn your freedom." To his surprise, ten stepped forward, among them a boatswain and nine of his fellows. They took their stations, and the crew's strength grew to forty-seven men and boys.

Jon moved among them, laying a hand on shoulders, nodding at powder boys. "Mark me, lads. She is bigger, aye, and mounts more guns, but size does not win a fight. Steadiness and determination do, and with our prayers, Providence guides us. Do not throw away your fire. Marines take particular aim at their white boot tops. Every shot there will bite deep."

The words steadied the men. They nodded, bending to their work, hauling tubs of water into place, checking sponges and handspikes, laying out crowbars and coils of match. The gun deck bristled with readiness.

Ashore, Bilbao stirred to life like a waking giant. From the high hills to the quayside, tens of thousands gathered to watch, the city's bells clanging. Boats crowded the water, daring to get close for a better view. Beside Jon, Thorndike said, "They say a hundred thousand eyes are upon us."

Jon smiled at his first officer. "Then we must provide a sight worth telling." Jon turned to shout to the main deck. "They came for a show; let's give them one." His orders rang in measured cadence, echoing down the low-beamed deck. "Cast off tackles and breechings...seize the breechings...unstop the touch-hole...ram home wad and cartridge...shot the gun-wad...run out the gun...lay down handspikes and crowbars...point your gun—FIRE!"

The *Pickering*'s first broadside thundered, smoke bursting across the waves. The *Achilles* answered, her forty-odd guns shaking the very sea. Shot screamed overhead, splintering spars and tearing canvas, yet the *Pickering*, deep-laden with sugar, rode low. As Jon had observed with the first British ship they'd encountered, nearly every shot of the *Pickering*'s bit into the enemy's hull at the waterline, but the *Achilles'* fire roared high, smashing spars and tearing canvas but leaving the ship's heart untouched.

Jon stood exposed on the quarterdeck, shouting calm orders as if it were no more than a drill. Splinters flew, round shot screamed past his ear, but he never flinched. The fight raged close and brutal. At one blast, a cannonball took off the head of the volunteer bos'n, showering his gun crew in blood. Eight more lay wounded, but the line held.

Still the *Achilles* pressed in, towering over them, while Jon's voice cut through the smoke. "Steady, lads! White boot tops! Fire low and true!"

Aboard the Golden Eagle offshore of Bilboa, Spain

THE FIGHT WORE on, the bay echoing with thunder. From the *Eagle*'s deck, Lieutenant John Carnes could see little save smoke and fire, the *Pickering* half-lost in the haze. Yet he heard enough: the cadence of her broadsides, steady as a drummer's beat, and the answering fury of the *Achilles*.

The British prize master, a hard-faced man Carnes had learned was the *Achilles'* second officer, stalked the deck, every blast making him flinch. At last he rounded on Carnes, his face flushed with anger. "This is madness! Look at her! Your ship is no more than a longboat beside our lugger. She'll be splintered to pieces before the hour is out!"

Carnes clasped his hands behind his back, his voice sure. "You don't know Haraden. He fights like a man possessed, aye, but with his wits about him. He'll stay close, keep low, and force the *Achilles* to waste her fire. If Providence is with us, your lugger will break before he does."

The Englishman swore again and turned away, but Carnes' words rang true even to his own ears. He remembered other fights where Haraden strode across the quarterdeck, calm where any other man would break. The captain's steadiness was a weapon in itself and all the crew knew it.

Amidships, Haraden's cabin boy, Bobby Grover, had not stopped watching. His small hands gripped the rail, knuckles white, eyes fixed on the smoke-wreathed *Pickering*. Every fresh broadside lit his face with fierce pride. "She'll never give way," the boy said fiercely, as if daring the British crew to contradict him. "That's my master out there. He'll beat her, you'll see."

A murmur passed among the enemy sailors, some shaking their heads, others watching more warily. The boy's certainty seemed to unnerve them more than the shot itself. When word of Bobby's boast reached the prize master, the British officer hauled the lad aft.

"Is it true what you've been telling my men?" he demanded.

Bobby lifted his chin. "Aye, sir. Captain Haraden takes everything he goes alongside of. He'll have this ship again before the sun is down."

A ripple of laughter followed, but not all of it was mocking. Some of the British looked unsettled, glancing back toward the haze where flames shot between the two ships.

Carnes stepped forward then. "Best you believe him, sir. I've seen Haraden make good on worse odds than these. Why, once he captured three British ships in a single day. If you think today will be different, you don't know the man."

The *Achilles* officer's jaw tightened, but he gave no reply. John held his gaze a moment longer, then turned back to the fight. The *Pickering* still held her ground, stubborn and unyielding, smoke rising in columns as the broadsides crashed on. Beyond the haze, the roar of the Spanish crowd ashore carried faint across the water, like the sea itself had joined the battle.

In that moment Carnes felt it as keenly as Bobby did. The tide had not turned yet, but Haraden was far from beaten.

Aboard the Pickering offshore of Bilboa, Spain

THE SMOKE LAY heavy, stinging eyes and throats, the

roar of guns rolling across the bay like thunder upon thunder. The *Achilles* loomed close alongside, her decks crowded with men, her sides vomiting fire.

Jon stood firm on the quarterdeck, his voice carrying through the chaos. "Steady, lads! White boot tops, aim low!"

The *Pickering* shuddered under each broadside, timbers groaning, rigging slashed to ribbons. Splinters flew like knives.

Thorndike came running, his face blackened with powder. "Captain, the lockers are near empty! We've shot near all our rounds!"

Jon's jaw clenched. He had seen the enemy's rigging hold, though sails fluttered ragged where shot had found canvas. To break her, he needed more than iron. He thought for only a moment before turning to the master gunner. "We've crowbars in the cargo. Use them and whatever iron you can find. Fire it into her rigging. She'll not stand long with her wings clipped."

Word swept the deck, and men scrambled to load what they had: crowbars from the stores, shards of iron scavenged from the hold, even bent bolts. Rammed home and fired, they screamed aloft with savage force. A cheer went up as iron bars scythed through *Achilles'* rigging, sails tearing loose, ropes parting in a shower of sparks.

"Again!" Jon roared, and the next broadside sent more of the makeshift shot into the enemy's spars. The *Achilles* faltered, her foreyard sagging, a tangle of canvas trailing into the sea.

Still the *Achilles* hammered back, her weight of metal thundering. Yet many of her shots screamed overhead, tearing sky instead of timbers. Jon knew their low profile was saving them, the sugar in the hold, which had seemed a burden, now made her a deadly weapon.

For near three hours the duel had raged, broadside for broadside, until at last Jon saw what he had prayed for: the *Achilles'* helm came over, her bow swinging away. She was breaking off.

A ragged cheer swelled from the *Pickering's* crew, hoarse but fierce. Men leaned from the ports, shouting after the retreating lugger. Jon lifted his glass, watching her dwindling stern, then let it fall with a slow breath. She was hurt, aye, but too swift to be caught now.

He turned to Thorndike, his voice steady though his heart still hammered. "Come about. We'll have the *Eagle* back." *And Bobby.*

As the *Achilles* fell away, the *Eagle's* captain, who had stood silent on the *Pickering* through the carnage, let out a low, grudging breath. "By rights, she should have sunk you. God help me, but no man alive handles a ship like that."

Jon glanced toward the fading *Achilles*, Thorndike at his side. "If this day proves anything, Lieutenant, it is that our cause is no fleeting venture. Britain may have power, but America has heart enough to match it, and Providence goes before us."

The *Pickering* wheeled across the churned water, smoke drifting from her scarred flanks. Soon the prize hove into view again, the Stars and Stripes raised once more as Carnes and the American prize crew cast off their captors.

Jon stepped to the rail as they drew alongside, calling

across the gap, "Mr. Carnes, well held. Bring her in to Bilbao with us. Keep the prisoners safe."

"Aye, aye, sir," returned Lieutenant Carnes.

As the *Eagle* came alongside, Bobby could be seen at her rail, grinning through the grime, cap waving high. His eyes met Jon's across the narrow strip of water, alight with triumph, as if to say without words: *I told them you'd have us back.*

The two ships limped into Bilboa Harbor, battered but unbowed. And though the men were blackened with powder, their clothes torn and their bodies bruised, they lifted their voices in triumph.

Bilbao, Spain 4 June 1780

THE HARBOR BOILED with life. Small boats swarmed about the *Pickering* and the *Golden Eagle* until the sea itself seemed paved with wood. Spaniards shouted and cheered, some dipping oars to keep pace, others waving hats and kerchiefs. Boys scrambled barefoot to the gunwales, shrilling their delight. The air was thick with the scent of powder smoke and salt, but it was laced now with wine, garlic, and roasting meat drifting from the quay.

With a glance at the main hatch, Jon said, "Mr. Thorndike, the prisoners—are they secure below?"

Thorndike gave a brisk nod. "Aye, Captain. Well-guarded, and the men on watch tonight will have their run of Bilbao tomorrow. They've earned it."

"Captain Scott may go with us into Bilboa. I have given him his freedom on parole, and those of his men who fought with us. Once the *Eagle* is sold, those men will have their reward."

Thorndike's brows rose, but he nodded. "As you wish, sir."

Jon glimpsed Joshua Trask lingering at the quarter-deck rail, already bearing the look of a servant grown. When John Fisk took command of the *Massachusetts*, Joshua had insisted on staying with Bobby to serve under Jon. His eyes met Joshua's, and the lad straightened, lifting a hand as though to remind the captain he still stood ready. Jon gave the boy an approving nod. "You did well, Lad."

"Captain," the surgeon said as he came to Jon. "My place is with the wounded for now. Once they are seen to, I'll come ashore."

"You do rightly. They'll know you care. And I will see them tonight."

Turning to gaze over the flotilla of small craft, Jon stood amazed. Beside him, Thorndike said, "By God, you could walk ashore over their boats if you dared."

Jon stared at the sight. "Best we don't try, but I'll not forget this sight while I live."

At anchor, the Spaniards' fervor only deepened. When Jon stepped ashore with Thorndike, Carnes, Cowan, and the others, a roar went up, echoing off the stone houses of Bilbao. Bobby Grover, now off the *Eagle*, ran to Jon. "You did it, sir! I told them on the *Eagle* you would."

Jon rested his hand on the boy's shoulder. "You did well."

A dozen men pressed forward, seized Jon by the arms, and before he could protest, they bore him aloft on their shoulders. Hats flew into the air, women cried blessings, and a chant rose. *"¡Viva el Capitán! ¡Viva!"* He was carried through the narrow streets in triumph, the crowd swelling around him until he was set down at last before a broad-arched tavern whose windows blazed with lamplight.

Inside, the Spaniards had laid a feast, bread crusty from the oven, bowls of olives slick with oil, roasted fish, platters of lamb and pork, pitchers of Rioja wine. Jon's men, still blackened from smoke and salt, were pressed into seats and given brimming cups. Laughter and music swelled, a fiddler striking up while townsfolk clapped the rhythm.

At a heavy oak table near the hearth, Jon sat with Thorndike, Carnes, Cowan and several other officers. Bobby darted in and out like a spark, sometimes perched on a Spaniard's knee to tell the man he was Captain Haraden's cabin boy. Sometimes he dashed back to Joshua to whisper some mischief. Chaplain McClure, who had followed them in, rose to say a prayer of thanks in English and halting Spanish. The townsfolk bowed their heads before the clamor resumed.

The Spaniards would not let the cups of the *Pickering* officers stand empty, and soon Lieutenant Cowan, glass in hand, leaned forward as the Spaniards listened eagerly. Cowan's voice was rough from smoke but carried the weight of awe. "The *Pickering*," he said, shaking his head slowly, "looked like a longboat beside that great lugger. And yet..." He paused, searching the faces before him. "And yet Captain Haraden fought with a determination that seemed superhuman. Shot flew round him like hail, but the captain"—Cowan gestured at Jon, "—he was as calm as though it were but a shower of snowflakes."

A hush fell for a moment, broken only by the murmurs of the Spaniards at Cowan's words. Then the tavern erupted in cheers as they pounded the tables, raising their cups. "¡Viva el Capitán!"

Jon inclined his head, his smile betraying nothing of the storm still quieting inside him. "It was the Pickering's crew who stood fast today. No captain wins a battle alone."

A dark-haired Spanish beauty slipped through the crowd, her eyes flashing, her bodice bright with embroidery. She leaned over Jon's chair, pressing a kiss to his cheek, murmuring in broken English, "Brave Capitán...hero." Her long dark hair brushed his sleeve, her perfume sharp and sweet, and her hand lingered warm upon his shoulder. "I can reward you as others cannot."

For an instant the room seemed to hush, the offer shimmering before him like wine in the cup he held in his hand. But his gaze did not follow her dark eyes. In his mind rose another face, a gentler one, that of Eunice Mason, standing on Salem's wharf with Hannah and Polly, her smile like a harbor light. Jon reached up, gently lifting the Spaniard's hand from his shoulder.

"You honor me, dear señorita," he said, his tone courteous but unyielding. "But my heart is already spoken for."

The woman laughed, unoffended, and whirled away into the press of dancers. Jon watched her go, then set his untouched cup back on the table. His thoughts were already turning homeward, to the woman whose face appeared in his mind.

From across the table Thorndike gave a low chuckle, lifting his glass. "Ah, but I've seen the woman who holds his heart, and she is beyond compare. No señorita in Spain could rival her."

A murmur of agreement passed among the Salem men. Bobby, perched nearby, nudged Joshua with a grin. "Told you the captain's heart was already taken. I could tell."

Jon smiled faintly, saying nothing, but the warmth that stirred in his chest was not owed to wine or cheers.

"It is not in the still calm of life that great characters are formed. The habits of a vigorous mind are formed in contending with difficulties. Great necessities call out great virtues."
– Abigail Adams 1780

CHAPTER 17

The Haraden house, Salem, late August 1780

THE SOUND OF children's voices drifted through the open window with the slight breeze. Hannah and Polly were in the garden with Martha, "helping", or so they said. Eunice sat in the parlor, using the afternoon light to finish her mending, though her thoughts were far out at sea. Every knock at the door quickened her pulse. *Where was Captain Haraden now?* The question was not without significance. Something had happened between them when he was last at home and her heart was now tethered to his.

The front door opened and Silas Turner stamped dust

from his boots as he stepped inside, his face alight with the look of a man bearing tidings. He wore no jacket, the day too hot for that. From his waistcoat he drew a folded newspaper and held it up.

"Letters from Spain have reached Boston," he said, his voice brimming. "*The Independent Chronicle* carried the report. Best you hear it here, 'fore the streets are bawlin' it loud enough for the gulls to carry across the harbor."

From the back of the house came Martha's firm voice: "Girls, take your shoes off in the kitchen, mind you! Then come along."

A moment later she entered the parlor, wiping her hands on her apron, the girls trailing behind her in their stockings. She gave Silas a pointed look. "What news have you? Is there news of the captain?"

"Not in his own hand, no," said Silas, "but about him. Shall I read it?"

Martha frowned. "Of course, read it. Don't dawdle, Silas!"

"It's about Papa, isn't it?" asked Hannah, who had been standing in the doorway with Polly.

"It is, Child," said Martha.

Silas unfolded the sheet and smoothed it against his knee, as his voice took on the careful cadence of printed words. "'By letters just received from Spain, we are informed that Captain Jonathan Haraden in the ship *Pickering*, of sixteen six-pounders and forty-eight men and boys, on his passage from Salem to Bilbao fell in with a British cruiser... and after engagin' her for five glasses obliged her to sheer off, the *Pickering* sufferin' great damages.'"

272

Eunice's mind focused on the word "damages" as she beckoned the restless Polly to her. Pulling the child into her lap, she whispered, "Let's listen."

Silas read on, the tale unfolding of a prize taken, the *Golden Eagle*. "The *Pickering* was makin' the best of her way into Bilboa with the prize when she was pursued by a very large lugger."

Eunice's heart stopped.

Martha gasped softly. "Oh, Lord preserve them."

"What's a lugger?" asked Hannah. Eunice had gone over the ships they frequently saw in Salem's harbor but this was a new term for Hannah.

"That name refers to the sail configuration," said Silas. Looking back at the paper, he added, "This wasn't just any lugger. 'Twas the *Achilles*, the largest ever fitted out from Britain, havin' forty-three guns and one hundred and thirty men. She re-captured the *Eagle* from Captain Haraden."

"What happened then?" asked Martha, her voice impatient.

Eunice held her breath.

Silas' voice carried on, "A most violent contest ensued and continued for nearly three hours. The lugger, larger and stout as she was, should have won the fight, but the *Pickering* won and the *Achilles* was glad to leave them." Silas stopped and smiled. "He sent the brute runnin'!"

"And?" asked Martha.

Silas looked down at the paper. "The *Pickering* pursued the prize and took her again, in sight of their vanquished enemy, and the two sailed into Bilboa."

The room was still when he finished, the only sound

the ticking of the mantel clock.

Eunice set Polly down and rose, crossing to the window. A tear slipped down her cheek as she gazed out toward the harbor beyond the rooftops. Her heart beat with mingled pride and fear. "He has looked into the very jaws of death," she murmured, more to herself than to the others. "And yet God preserves him." Turning to the others, she said, "Our prayers are answered. He lives and triumphs."

Martha wiped her eyes, her voice trembling. "The Lord surely holds him in His hand."

Hannah's voice piped high and clear. "Papa won! When will he be home?"

Eunice gathered her composure with effort. "It may be some months yet, sweetheart. His ship will be needing repairs and his prize must be sold. But we'll keep praying."

The London Coffeehouse, Salem

LATER THAT SAME day, anxious to share the news, Silas made his way to the London Coffeehouse where the captain often met with his merchant sponsors.

The smell of roasted beans and pipe smoke hung heavy in the air as he stepped in. Merchants crowded the tables, voices buzzed with the talk of convoys, prices, and the war. The scrape of quills tallying accounts mingled with the low hum.

Silas shouldered through, the folded paper clutched in his hand. Not seeing the merchants he was looking for in the crowd, he slapped the paper on a table. "Gentlemen!

News out of Spain, hot as pitch and worth your ears. It's our own Captain Haraden, the Salamander!"

Heads turned; cups stilled halfway to lips.

Silas cleared his throat and read aloud, his voice rising with each line: the duel with the British cruiser, the capture of the *Golden Eagle*, and then the great contest with the *Achilles*.

By the time he reached the line, "The lugger, large and stout as she was, was glad to leave them," the room erupted in cheers. Men leapt to their feet, pounding the table, some crying, "Three cheers for Haraden!"

One older shipowner shook his head in wonder. "Forty-three guns against sixteen? I'd not have believed it if it weren't in print."

Another raised his cup high. "Salem breeds no common captains!"

From the corner, a merchant called, "Aye, the Salamander indeed!" and the name was taken up in a chorus.

Silas grinned, savoring the moment. He thought of Mrs. Mason at the window, tears in her eyes though she tried to hide it. And he thought of Hannah and Polly, anxious to see their beloved papa. Slapping the table with the paper, he said, "Mark me, lads, this ain't just a victory at sea. It's proof enough Britain misjudges us yet, but America's sons won't be cowed."

The cheer that answered him shook the rafters, a roar of pride for Salem's own.

Bilbao, Spain, September 1780

THE MORNING SUN spilled over the tiled roofs of Bilbao and onto the crowded quays. There, it caught the banners and kerchiefs waved by the crowd. Bells clanged from church towers, their peals rolling down to the water where the *Pickering* rode at anchor, refitted and provisioned for the long passage west.

Jon stood on the quarterdeck, hat tucked under his arm, watching as carts rattled down the quay bearing the last gifts from the Spanish merchants: fresh fruit, casks of wine, bolts of sailcloth. Their generosity had been near boundless since the battle, their gratitude reflected not only in feasts and parades but in supplies laid aboard at no cost.

Along the quay, another vessel lay with Spanish colors newly hoisted, the *Golden Eagle*, no longer theirs, her timbers and cargo already sold into other hands. Jon's gaze lingered on her only a moment. She had been hard-won, but prizes passed quickly into commerce.

Earlier in the week, he had seen Captain Scott and the few British who had fought beside his men safely paroled, bound home under their word of honor. The rest of the *Achilles'* crew he had left in Spanish custody. Mr. Franklin in Paris would be glad enough of them, for every British prisoner in Europe could be weighed against an American languishing in irons. The thought of giving more of his countrymen a chance at freedom pleased Jon. His charge now was the ship that bore his men and his flag home, well provisioned, with prize money secured, and carrying with her the honor of triumph against the odds.

Thorndike came to his side, eyes scanning the throng. "They'll cheer us till their throats are raw, sir. I've never seen the like. We're heroes here."

Jon returned Thorndike a slight smile. "Heroes fade quickly, Mr. Thorndike. But ships and men, they must endure." He looked again to the quay, where women tossed flowers into the tide. "Let them remember the flag we carried, if nothing else."

From the dock rose a cheer as the lines were cast off. Oars dipped, the ship's boats tugging their charges clear of the shore until the sails could take them. Bobby and Joshua scrambled aloft with the other boys, nimble as cats, their shrill voices mingling with the creak of rigging and the flap of canvas.

Overhead, three white swans took flight as the wind filled the sails. Jon lifted his gaze, taking it as a good omen, and his spirits rose with them. As the *Pickering* leaned into her course, the cheers of Bilbao swelled. *"¡Viva el Capitán! ¡Viva América!"* Hats flew skyward, church bells tolled again, and for a moment the very harbor seemed to shake with it.

Jon lifted his hat in return, bowing once toward the town that had feted him like a king. Yet even as he did, his thoughts turned westward, past the wide Atlantic, past the dangers yet to come, to a quiet house in Salem. That vision steadied him more than all the cheers of Spain.

"Set our course, Mr. Thorndike," he said at last, setting his hat back on. "West for Salem. And whatever prizes God sends us along the way."

Thorndike's grin was wolfish. "Aye, Captain. Salem will not see us return empty."

The sails bellied, the water foamed under the bow, and Bilbao's voices faded into the morning haze.

In the Atlantic, September 1780

THE BAY OF Biscay fell astern, its green headlands fading into haze. Ahead stretched the vast Atlantic, steel blue and glittering in the sun, the endless road back to Salem. The *Pickering*, tight in her rigging and sound from her refit, moved like a hound eager for the chase.

Jon took his place on the quarterdeck with Thorndike at his side, scanning the horizon. On the main deck, the crew's spirits ran high. They had the coin promised them, honor earned, and the scent of more prizes in their noses. Yet when Jon's thoughts turned inward, it was not to silver nor to spoils, but to Eunice Mason's soft brown eyes waiting across the sea, the words he would speak to her.

It was Thorndike who spied the merchantman first. "Captain," he said pointing, "a square-rigged ship, fat in the water and sluggish with cargo."

The lookout confirmed the sighting with a shout. "Sail ho, starboard!" Jon raised his glass and saw the truth at once. English colors, no escort, and no match for a ship as nimble as the *Pickering*.

"Clear for chase," Jon said calmly.

Thorndike echoed the orders and the men sprang to their stations. Sails were trimmed sharp, and the ship surged forward, overtaking the merchantman in hours. A warning shot across the bow was enough; the *Rodney* hove to without a fight, hauling down her colors.

The *Rodney*'s master, pale and tight-lipped, was brought aboard the *Pickering*, his hat clutched under his arm, his brown salt-stained coat damp at the seams. He offered up his papers with a trembling hand. Jon flipped through them without triumph, merely duty, but noted with satisfaction her cargo: tobacco, lumber, rice, fish, sugar, and rum.

"One hundred and twenty tons," he remarked to Thorndike, "and bound for London." To the merchant-man's master, he added, "We'll be seeing you safely into Salem."

The *Pickering*'s crew gave three cheers as Lieutenant Carnes was sent over with a prize crew. Bobby darted after him, wide-eyed at the captured vessel, but Jon's voice checked him. "Not this time, Lad. You've had enough of prizes for now." Bobby flushed but nodded, returning to his station.

The captured captain was lodged in a small aft cabin, under watch of a sentry, treated with civility but kept well away from Jon's papers and charts.

Days later, when the seas lay glassy under a pale sky, another sail rose on the horizon. She proved to be the brigantine *Myrrh*, smaller than the *Rodney* but swifter, her master unwilling to yield. The chase dragged on, canvas straining, as the *Pickering* pressed harder, until Jon ordered a shot. The ball screamed past the brigantine's quarter, splintering spray. Still she ran.

"Another, Mr. Thorndike," Jon said evenly.

This one struck home, shattering her mizzen. The *Myrrh* faltered, her flight ended. Her captain surrendered with bitter grace. Once onboard the *Pickering*, he bowed stiffly before Jon and handed over his sword, muttering darkly, "The sea grows thick with you Salem men. One cannot trade in peace for fear of you."

Jon's eyes flickered with amusement. "The sea is thick with Patriots, good sir, for America means to win this war."

"Your cargo, sir?" asked Thorndike.

The *Myrrh*'s captain shrugged. "Stores for British troops, blankets and tents for the winter."

Thorndike gave a sharp grin, eyeing her sound hull. "She'll fetch a fine price and keep Patriots warm instead."

Jon nodded, though his eyes softened as he watched the prize crew hoist the Stars and Stripes above the *Myrrh*'s mast. "Another step toward home," he said quietly.

It had just turned October and the nights were cool, the myriad of stars sharp as ice, when they came upon the brigantine *Venus*, her hold heavy, her pace slow. She offered a token broadside, but her guns were few and her men apparently not well trained. Within a half-hour she, too, struck her colors.

Jon received her master courteously, then turned the matter over to Thorndike. When the British captain was taken below, Jon turned to his men on deck and shouted loud enough for all to hear. "Three prizes in as many weeks. Providence has favored us again, for which we must all be grateful. But lest we forget how swiftly matters can change, let us see our prizes into Salem."

The men answered with cheers, Bobby loudest among them, and Joshua right beside him, both boys flushed with pride.

Salem Harbor, October 1780

THE AUTUMN WIND carried the scent of wood smoke across Salem Sound as the *Pickering* came on, her sails weathered. Astern, in a stately line, followed the *Rodney*, the *Myrrh*, and the *Venus*, each flying American colors aloft. The sight was enough to set the town astir before the cannon of Winter Island at the mouth of Salem Harbor could give a salute.

By the time Jon brought the ship across the bar, half of Salem crowded the wharves and headlands. Men stood on warehouse roofs, boys scrambled up rigging on other ships, women waved shawls from balconies and windows. A murmur swelled into a cheer that rolled over the harbor like surf.

"God save us, he's brought three!" a man on the dock shouted, cap flying from his hand. "Three in one cruise and already took the *Golden Eagle* and bested the *Achilles*!"

From the quarterdeck, Jon kept his hat tucked beneath his arm, his expression composed, but his heart thudded. He thought of the lads clinging to the shrouds, Bobby and Joshua waving their caps with the other cabin boys, their grins fierce with pride. He thought of his weary men at the guns, blackened by powder, straight-backed and smiling, as the ship carried them home in triumph with more prize money soon to be had. And he thought of Eunice Mason somewhere in that throng.

Thorndike grinned broadly. "All Salem's turned out, Captain. I reckon they've been starved for good news."

"Then let us give them their fill," Jon said.

The *Pickering* fired a single gun, its report echoing off

the warehouses. Cheers answered like thunder. The prizes followed her in, their rigging manned by prize crews who called across to one another, voices sharp with victory.

At Derby Wharf, the crowd surged so thick that sailors had to hold the line to make room for the gangways. A band of local boys struck up "Yankee Doodle" on fifes, the tune shrill and defiant above the roar, while a dozen boys beat their drums until the planks themselves seemed to tremble. Merchants elbowed forward, hats in hand. Jon smiled at the thought of them already weighing cargo in their minds. Wives and sweethearts wept openly, reaching for men not yet ashore.

Jon rested his hand on the rail, his gaze sweeping the chaos with quiet pride. "Salem will eat well this winter," he murmured. Then, more softly still, "And I am home."

THE PRESS OF bodies on the wharf was nearly suffocating, the air thick with wood smoke and salt spray. Eunice held fast to Polly, who tugged and strained to see above the crowd. Martha had Hannah's hand in a firm grip. The thunder of the salute gun still echoed when the fifes took up "Yankee Doodle", high and piercing, answered by the steady tattoo of boys' drums.

"There, Child, do you see?" Martha said, pointing across the harbor. "Your papa's ship, and three more behind her."

Hannah gazed wide-eyed, her face pale with awe, while Polly, wriggling free, clapped her hands.

Eunice shaded her eyes, her breath catching at the sight. The *Pickering* came on proudly, sails patched, her flanks scarred from battle yet defiant. Behind her the prizes flew the American flag, bright against the gray of sea and sky. A murmur rippled through the crowd, swelling into a roar as the ships closed the distance.

"There he is!" Polly cried, pointing at the quarterdeck. The girl had just turned five and was a bundle of energy. Eunice had her hands full most days.

She saw him then, tall and handsome with an air of serene composure. With his hat tucked beneath his arm, he dominated the quarterdeck. Though he appeared composed, she knew how his heart must be pounding. The sight brought a sting to her eyes, though she blinked it away quickly.

When Jon lifted his head toward the throng, his eyes found her across the distance, amid the crush of townsfolk and the thunder of drums, as though no one else existed. Their gazes met and, for a breathless moment, neither looked away.

Martha sniffed sharply beside her, dabbing at her eyes with her apron. "Well, God be praised, he's home again. And richer than ever, I'll warrant."

But Eunice scarcely heard. All the noise and movement of the wharf faded, leaving only the unshaken look of the man on the quarterdeck. Her heart answered it, fierce and sure.

The gangways were laid, sailors straining to keep the press of townsfolk from surging forward too soon. Children scrambled onto barrels for a better view, and merchants jostled to the fore, calling out greetings as if their voices alone might hasten the captain ashore.

Eunice watched as Silas pushed through, his broad

shoulders parting the crowd. He planted himself near the landing place, arms crossed, a grin spreading through his salt-stubbled beard.

As Jon descended the gangway, Silas lifted his voice above the din. "Captain, you've near emptied the Atlantic of British trade and filled Salem with cheer besides! A finer homecomin' I've never seen."

Jon clasped the old sailor's hand warmly before the crowd surged around them. "Thank you, Silas. The sea gave us a hard trial, but Providence brought us through. Salem will eat well this winter."

The roar of welcome rose again, but for Eunice it blurred to nothing as Jon's dark blue eyes found hers once more, closer now, steady as ever.

The Haraden house, Salem, October 1780

ISRAEL THORNDIKE HAD seen many a welcome on wharves, but never one like he witnessed this day. The merchants Elias Derby and George Williams near danced in their boots when they heard the cargoes named— tobacco, rice, lumber, sugar, rum, blankets and stores besides. Their eyes had shone brighter than a prize lantern at midnight.

Three prizes in as many weeks, Thorndike thought as he followed his captain homeward. And every bale and barrel would be worth its weight in gold to this town and to the *Pickering*'s crew.

Now, seated at the dining table in Haraden's house, Thorndike carved into the roast fowl on his plate with the appetite of a man who'd lived too long on salt pork and ship's biscuit. The hearth glowed steadily, warming the room and carrying the scent of wood smoke beneath the fragrance of the roasted meat and fresh bread.

At the other end of the table, the captain sat with his daughters at either elbow, Hannah chattering questions, Polly wriggling for her father's attention. He answered each with the same patience he showed under fire.

"Papa, did the Spanish really carry you through the streets?" Hannah pressed, eyes wide.

"Aye," Haraden said, his mouth quirking. "They shouted loud enough to rattle the tiles from the roofs."

"Did you fire the big guns at the *Achilles*?" Polly asked, bouncing.

Jon smiled, smoothing her hair. "We did, little one. And the *Achilles* fired back, yet by the Lord's mercy, I am still here."

The questions tumbled on, as Israel noticed how well the girls waited their turns, folded their hands as they spoke, even remembered to say "please" and "thank you". The captain looked at them with a touch of pride, then raised his eyes to Eunice Mason.

"You've polished their manners as neatly as their shoes," Haraden said warmly. "I see it in every word."

Color touched the governess' cheeks. "They've been diligent pupils, Captain. Every day we take time from our lessons and sewing to practice deportment."

Not for the first time, Israel thought the captain a fortunate man to have found such a jewel for his daughters' governess. He noticed, too, the way the captain's gaze lingered on her. When she poured their wine, her sleeve brushed his hand. She looked away quickly, but Israel had not missed it, nor the flicker of warmth in the captain's eyes.

Martha entered just then and set down a steaming pudding still damp from its boiling cloth. "That's God's truth," she said with a sniff. "Mrs. Mason's had them readin' and recitin' as smart as any minister's children. Now then, here's plum puddin', with currants enough to sweeten the captain's homecomin'."

The girls clapped, leaning forward eagerly as Martha sliced the pudding into generous portions.

Thorndike chuckled, lifting his glass. "I'll drink to that. And to the captain, who's given Salem such a feast, both in news and in prizes." He ate a spoonful of the pudding, finding it rich, heavy and sweet, then caught himself grinning, belly full and heart lightened by the day. "The town near went mad this afternoon," he said. "I swear, Captain, you could've walked from Derby Wharf to the coffeehouse without your boots touching ground, just hats and shoulders to carry you."

The girls giggled at his words. Jon nodded, a smile coming to his lips. "Salem needed cheer," he said. "If we've given them some, then I'm content."

Martha returned to glance at everyone's plate. Her voice was softer than her words. "You've near filled the town coffers, Captain. That's more than cheer. And I never saw smiles like those on the faces of your crew."

"They were pleased with the results of our cruise," said the captain. Then turning to Mrs. Mason, he asked, "What have you heard of the war? Has Silas brought home any rumors he's been hearing from his friends in the harbor?"

"Actually, yes," the governess replied, looking down at her hands before facing him. "There is one report, though it grieves me to say it. The papers tell us that General Benedict Arnold has betrayed us."

The room stilled.

"What?" Israel exclaimed. "When?"

"Last month," Mrs. Mason answered. "Since August, he was in command at West Point, and conspired to hand the fort to the British."

Haraden shook his head, his disbelief plain. "Why? The man was Washington's trusted general—he won victories for us."

"They say money was a part of it," the governess explained. "He was in debt, and bitter at the army for what he felt was poor treatment. And there is his new wife, Peggy Shippen. Her family are known Loyalists in Philadelphia."

The captain's face was grave. "It will strike Washington like a cannonball. He trusted Arnold, and with reason."

"And throw the general's officers into disarray," added Israel. He sipped his wine, weighing the treachery. But his gaze stayed fixed on his captain. Haraden's expression showed deep thought, yet his eyes strayed often toward Eunice Mason. And though she turned her head to hide it, Israel saw the faint color rise in her cheeks.

Aye, he thought, leaning back in his chair, letting the fire warm his boots and the plum pudding settle in his belly. The captain's heart fights its own battle now, and I'd wager Salem's richest prize for him may not be a ship taken at sea.

"We have this day restored the Sovereign to whom all alone men ought to be obedient. He reigns in Heaven, and with a propitious eye beholds His subjects assuming that freedom of thought, and dignity of self-direction which He bestowed on them. From the rising to the setting sun, may His kingdom come."
– John Adams 1776

CHAPTER 18

The London Coffeehouse, Salem, mid-October 1780

JON HAD COME at the request of George Williams and Elias Derby, who wished to discuss the prize money from the sale of the three ships. The moment he stepped inside, the aroma of strong, bitter coffee hit him, and the low roar of men talking ships, trade, and war. Heads turned, hands reached for him, confirmation the news of the *Pickering*'s return had run through Salem faster than fire in dry pine.

He made his way to the table where Derby and Williams bent over their notes. The merchants rose to greet him warmly, and chairs scraped as others pressed close to listen.

"You are to be congratulated, Captain," Williams said. "For your brilliant command of the *Pickering*. Your crew sings your praises in every tavern on the waterfront."

Jon inclined his head. "I am blessed with a wonderful crew, every man a Patriot."

Williams tapped the papers with his quill. "We thought you would like to know the *Rodney* sold this day for ninety thousand pounds."

Jon's brows rose despite himself. "Ninety thousand!" He let the figure roll in his mind, a fortune beyond most men's imagining. "A fine price for a fine ship."

Derby leaned in. "And bought, I might add, by none other than George here."

Williams gave a modest nod, but the ripple of approval through the crowd spoke louder than words.

Jon sat back and stared at Williams. The man was clearly successful. After all, he owned the *Pickering*, but ninety thousand pounds?

"The *Myrrh*," Derby went on, "fetched twenty-five thousand and thirty. Stores, blankets, tents aplenty. The king's loss will be Washington's gain."

"The brigantine *Venus*," Williams concluded, "sold for twenty-four thousand. Sound hull, good cargo. She went quick."

Slate pencils squeaked, quills scratched. Men leaned back in their chairs, eyes alight as though the coins already lay in their purses.

A smile crossed Williams' face. "With these sales settled, Captain, you and your men will soon see your prize shares. Salem's coffers prosper, aye, but so too shall every hand that served aboard the *Pickering*."

Jon inclined his head. "My men are counting on it."

Derby drummed his fingers on the table. "George and I have been talking about your next cruise, Captain. The Indies, perhaps. Winter seas there are more kindly than the Atlantic. What say you?"

"Aye," Jon said with a nod. "The Caribbean would be a welcome respite for my men."

Williams cast a glance at Derby, then bent to lift a large, cloth-wrapped parcel from beside his chair. "We have something for you, Captain, to memorialize your victory over the *Achilles* and in thanks for the many prizes you have taken."

The room stilled as he drew back the cloth. A heavy silver plate gleamed in the lamplight, its edge wrought with scrollwork. In the center was engraved *Captain Jonathan Haraden of Salem*, and beneath it the words: *From a grateful town and its merchants who extol his courage under fire and his victories at sea for America's independence.*

A murmur of admiration rippled through the merchants. Jon felt the weight of every eye upon him as Williams set the plate before him. For a moment, he could only run his hand lightly over the engraving, struck silent. At last he said, "I thank you, gentlemen. This honor belongs not to me alone, but to every man who stood his post aboard the *Pickering*."

An older merchant sitting nearby fixed his gaze on the silver. "Three prizes and Salem is richer by near one hundred and forty thousand. It is fitting to honor such a man. No wonder London fears Haraden's name."

From the corner, where he sat with his seafaring friends, Silas raised his cup, his voice rough with pride. "Haraden's our Salamander! He's given the British proof we'll not be starved nor cowed."

The cheer that followed rattled cups on the tables.

Jon traced the inscription once more, then covered the plate with the cloth. The cheer still rang in his ears as he bid Williams and Derby a good day and left the coffee-house with Silas at his side. Outside, the afternoon mist had crept in from the harbor, softening the outlines of masts and rooftops. The silver plate weighed heavy under his arm, but heavier still was the thought that the town's gratitude could never match what he most desired.

"Fine gift," Silas said, pulling his coat tighter. "Salem's proud of you, Captain."

"Perhaps," he acknowledged, though his eyes turned eastward, toward the streets that led home. What was silver or renown, compared with the quiet look of Eunice Mason when she met his gaze? And the thought of spending the rest of his days with her that came to his mind. The town might call him their Salamander, but it was she who steadied the fire in him.

The Haraden house, November 1780

THE FIRE ON the parlor hearth burned low, its glow soft upon the walls. Outside, the wind rattled the bare branches against the windows, but within, all was still. Eunice sat with a glass of claret in her hand, the warmth of it spreading through her even as her heart beat with a different heat.

It had been weeks since Captain Haraden's return, weeks of dinners and laughter, of Sundays spent walking home from church with Hannah and Polly skipping between them. Yet tonight, seated alone with him, she felt the weight of every moment they had shared pressing toward some unspoken end.

Jon leaned forward in his chair, his face lit by the shifting glow. His dark blue eyes held hers, unflinching. "Mrs. Mason," he began, his voice quiet but firm, "these weeks at home have been more precious to me than I knew could be granted a man who lives by the sea. You have cared for my daughters with a tenderness and patience that humbles me." For a moment, he seemed to weigh words too dear to spend lightly. Then his gaze lifted to hers, steady and intent. "They have made me see clearly what it has taken me too long to speak. I have admired you since first I saw how my girls looked to you," he went on, his voice thickening. "But admiration is not the word any longer. 'Tis love that fills my heart when I gaze into your lovely face. Too long have I left it unspoken."

Her breath caught. Tears welled and slipped unchecked down her cheeks. She had hoped, prayed, but never let herself believe it might be true. "Love?" she whispered. "I had not believed it could return to me after all that was lost." Her voice broke as she whispered, "And love it is I have for you, Captain."

For a moment neither moved, only the fire filling the silence between them. Jon rose then and came to her, taking her hands gently into his own as he knelt before her. His touch was firm, warm, anchoring her trembling fingers. "And yet here it is, between us."

Eunice searched his face, both afraid and full of hope. "And your daughters? What will they think?"

His answer came with a quiet certainty. "I will speak to them. But as I see it, you are already their mother."

Her tears fell freely then, though her smile broke through them. "And I, their own."

"Then hear me," he said, his voice roughened with feeling. "Will you do me the honor of becoming my wife? When I return from this next cruise, I would have your father marry us. If you will consent, it would be my greatest joy."

"Yes," Eunice breathed, the word breaking with her sob. "Yes, with all my heart."

He bent and kissed her hands, his head bowed as though in prayer. The fire crackled softly, and outside the wind sighed through the eaves. But within the parlor, there was only their joined hands, the promise spoken at last, and the knowledge that no ocean between them could unmake it.

THE NEXT MORNING dawned clear, the air sharp with the bite of late autumn. The red and gold leaves had fallen from the trees but the first snowfall had yet to come. Jon buttoned his coat and called to the girls, who came running, cloaks flapping, eager for the promise of a walk. They made their way along the lane toward the common. What leaves remained were crisp beneath their boots, their breath visible in the chill.

Hannah skipped at her father's side, her hand tucked into his, while Polly darted ahead to chase a crow that strutted along the fence rail. Jon watched them both, his heart full, then drew a steadying breath.

"My dears," he began, his voice gentle, "I've something to ask you." They turned to him with expectant gazes. "You know Mrs. Mason has cared for you these last several years, taught you, guided you, and watched over you. Since you were a baby, Polly."

Hannah looked up as if waiting for more. "And?"

"She makes us practice our curtsies," said Polly, twirling to show hers.

Jon chuckled, then grew more serious. "I hold her in the highest regard. More than regard, in truth. I have come to love her. I have asked her to be my wife, but I would not do so without knowing your hearts. What think you, if she were to become your mother?"

The girls stopped in their tracks. Hannah's eyes widened, thoughtful beyond her years. She had not worn her mother's locket in some while, which he took to mean she was healing. Polly clapped her hands in delight. "Then she'll always stay with us?"

"Yes," said Jon. "She would really be your mother."

Hannah's gaze softened. "She is already like a mother. I should like it very much."

"Me, too!" said Polly.

Jon felt a weight lift from his shoulders. He gathered them both close, his voice thick. "Then it is settled. We will be a family in truth, not just in name."

The girls laughed and squeezed him, their chatter bubbling again as they walked on. Jon looked skyward, whispering thanks for blessings far greater than prizes or silver.

As soon as Jon opened the front door, his daughters rushed into the parlor and Hannah blurted out to Martha and Silas, "Papa is going to marry our governess! Mrs. Mason will be our mother!"

Jon cleared his throat. "Martha, Silas, I was going to tell you but it seems the news cannot wait." With a smile he could not resist, he added, "Mrs. Mason has agreed to be my wife."

Martha's needle froze in mid-stitch, then she sniffed, her eyes suspiciously bright. "Well, it's about time. I saw it in the way you looked at her. The girls will thrive for it."

Just then, Mrs. Mason came down the stairs. "They know," Jon said to her, "and the girls are delighted."

Polly rushed up to her. "What do we call you now?"

Jon spoke for her. "She'll remain Mrs. Mason out of respect until we are wed. Then you can call her Mama if you like. And, of course," he said to Martha and Silas, "if she permits it, you could call her Eunice then."

"Mama would be the happiest name I could ever carry," Eunice said softly. "And, yes, by all means Martha, Silas, call me by my given name."

Silas puffed once, slow and thoughtful. "Captain, this is the bravest course you've set yet. And the right one. Congratulations."

Eunice blushed. Jon took one of her hands in his own, meeting the gaze of the old seaman.

"It gladdens me to have your blessing," he said.

"You've had it all along," Silas replied gruffly. "We were just waitin' for you to find your tongue."

Martha chuckled, rising to stir the fire. "Now sit your-selves down and take a cup. There's a weddin' to think of, even if we must wait until the sea gives the captain back to us again."

Jon glanced at Eunice, her smile lit by the firelight, and thought there was no sea storm fierce enough to drive him from this course now.

Salem, 10 November 1780

THE HARADEN HOUSE stood quiet in the gray dawn, frost silvering the windows, as Jon watched Silas loading Jon's sea chest on the cart. Soon after, they set off for the Derby Wharf, Mrs. Mason and the girls accompanying them.

Once there, his men relieved Silas of the chest, and Jon turned to his daughters, their sad faces lifted to him. He kissed Hannah and Polly, then bent to whisper in their ears, promises of something from the Indies and of his safe return.

Eunice Mason stood a pace apart, her hands folded in front of her. When at last he came to her, he held her gaze as though to fix it in his memory. He touched her hands briefly, all he dared with many watching, and said low, "Keep me in your prayers and may the Good Lord bring me back to you, my bride to be."

She smiled then. "I will be waiting, Captain."

"Godspeed, sir," said Silas with a salute.

Around Jon, the air was sharp with cold. Merchants and seamen bustled about the *Pickering*, canvas straining as the ship readied for sea. Jon waved to his family and Silas, then strode aboard and took his place on the quarterdeck with Lieutenant Thorndike. He saluted Derby and Williams who had come to see him and the ship off.

Bobby hurried up with a steaming cup. "All is ready in your cabin, sir."

"Thank you, Lad."

The wind freshened, snapping the rigging. Jon looked aloft, the call of the open sea stirring in his chest. "West Indies, Mr. Thorndike."

"Aye, Captain," Thorndike turned to the deck and lifted his voice. "Hands to the capstan! Heave away! Loose the topsails aloft!"

The deep thrum of voices rose in chorus as the men bent to the capstan bars. Wood groaned, iron clinked, yards rose, and sails unfurled with a crack swelling white against the pale sky. Lines were cast off, and the *Pickering* eased into the channel.

From the wharf rose a cheer, wives and sweethearts waving. Hannah's and Polly's small hands fluttered like birds. Eunice Mason drew her dark green cloak close, her hand lifted, her face turned to him. That single glimpse would have to sustain him through the long months ahead.

The harbor bells tolled farewell as the ship slid seaward, carrying him once more into war.

Two weeks later, as they sailed south, the *Pickering* fell in with a humble Yankee trading schooner that had been to the West Indies with lumber and was sailing home with the beggarly proceeds of the voyage. As the schooner approached, her captain signaled Jon and put out a boat to come to the ship.

"Whatever he wants," said Thorndike, "he's one of our own."

"Aye, he is," said Thorndike, "and given the poor state of his schooner, her rigging in tatters and her sails ripped, we will do all we can to help him."

The schooner's captain came aboard, hollow-eyed and his clothing bedraggled. Bowing his head to Jon, he introduced himself. "Captain Kendrick of the schooner *Marianne* out of Harwich, Massachusetts on Cape Cod. I'm in desperate need of your help, sir."

Jon offered his hand. "I am Captain Jonathan Haraden of Salem, and this is my First Lieutenant, Israel Thorndike. What happened?"

"There is much to tell," said Kendrick.

"Come," said Jon, "let us retire to my cabin where you can tell us what plight you have suffered." Turning to his Second Lieutenant, Jon said, "Lieutenant Carnes, you have the deck."

"Aye, aye, sir," replied Carnes before ascending to the quarterdeck.

Once seated at Jon's table, Bobby offered Kendrick a cup of steaming coffee, which he gratefully accepted. At first, his words were halting, and then they rushed out like a fountain. "We were overhauled by a British letter of marque schooner, and ill-equipped to resist her many guns. They boarded us and robbed me of my quadrant and compass and our provisions, then stripped the *Marianne* of much of her rigging. With a curse and a kick from her captain, they left us to drift and starve."

Jon's jaw tightened as he shared a look of disdain with Thorndike whose face bore a scowl. "To treat a sailor so," said Jon, "'tis piracy, not war. Worry not, Captain. You have fallen in with honorable Patriots. We will see your schooner re-rigged, your cabin and forecastle provisioned, and I will personally loan you instruments with which to work your passage home."

The man's relief was clear on his face. "I thank God for you, Captain Haraden. You are an answer to our prayers."

At once, Jon ordered Thorndike to send men over and see all he had promised accomplished. "Gladly, sir," said Thorndike.

Back on deck, Jon watched with the schooner's captain as provisions and instruments were rowed to his ship and his rigging came back to life. Kendrick's eyes brimmed as he clasped Jon's hand. "You've given me back my life, Captain."

Jon's reply was curt but kind. "You'll reach your home port safe. I will go in search of the British miscreant who did this thing and I welcome you to accompany me. With Providence guiding us, the British ship will soon face Yankee justice."

"I will gladly go with you," said Kendrick.

The next day fortune favored them, as the *Pickering* fell in with the very letter of marque that had robbed the Yankee trader. Under threat of burning his ship to the water, the British captain struck his colors.

Jon dressed himself in his best and, to add dignity to the occasion, summoned the arrogant, erring British captain to his cabin where Thorndike and Captain

Kendrick waited. With his hands clasped behind his back, Jon told the man coldly, "You have dishonored your profession."

The British captain, who Jon judged to be of an age with him, blustered, attempting to defend his actions. "This is war!"

"Even in war, there is honor," replied Jon. "A sailor does not rob a brother sailor of the means to live. And, for doing so, you will face American justice. On behalf of the *Marianne*, my men will take their reprisal, as is their right. They will leave you afloat, but marked with shame enough to remind you what honor demands of a sailor."

Turning to Thorndike, he said, "Whatever pleases their fancy," said Jon, his eyes never leaving the British captain, "see it done, including kicking and cuffing the offending seamen the length of their deck."

Thorndike smiled. "Aye, Captain. The men will be glad of it."

Jon added, "Tell them to take what you deem fit, but leave her hull afloat. She's not worth sinking."

Thorndike shook his head, grinning. "A hard hand in battle, a steady hand in justice. There's the measure of you, Captain. The Salamander in action."

The British captain stared at Jon. "The Salamander? The one who stood against the *Achilles* at Bilbao?"

"The very same," said Thorndike, a gleam in his eyes.

Jon said nothing, only held the British man's gaze. In his heart he knew that honor was the only ballast to keep a sailor steady in war, and he would carry that weight so long as the sea called him.

When at last the *Marianne* stood ready, Kendrick

clasped Jon's hand once more. "You've given me back my ship, my honor, and my hope."

Jon's reply was simple. "Then take them home, Captain. And remember, a Yankee never sails alone."

Leeward Islands, the Caribbean, January 1781

THE SEAS JUST north of the Leeward Islands heaved under a blazing sun, spray flying as the *Pickering* closed the distance to a king's mail packet, stout-hulled and homeward bound from the Indies. The two ships squared off, and the contest began in earnest.

For four hours they battered each other, broadside for broadside. Thunder rolled across the water, smoke boiled skyward, and the air reeked of brimstone and salt. The *Pickering's* rigging was torn in half in a dozen places, braces shot away, her decks littered with splinters and shattered blocks. Men staggered under the recoil of the guns, sweat streaming down their powder-blackened faces.

Bobby clung to the mizzen shrouds on the quarterdeck, eyes wide at the carnage. "Captain, sir, shall I fetch water for the men?"

"Stand fast, Lad," Jon said sharply, though his tone softened after. "This is no place for you." He nodded to Thorndike. "See him below. The surgeon may find use for his hands."

"Aye, Captain," Thorndike said, waving the boy toward the companionway.

At last, Jon gave the order to sheer off, his eyes stinging from smoke.

Thorndike frowned. "Sir?"

Jon strode the quarterdeck, calm despite the chaos. "Only a pause. Make fast repairs! Double-shot the guns. This ends today."

Thorndike's voice cracked like a whip. "Boarders, stand ready! Topmen, patch those braces!"

Catching the drift of their captain's intention, the men fell to it with a will. Canvas was hastily stitched, jury braces spliced, the decks cleared. Within the hour the *Pickering* came about once more, her scars showing but her spirit undimmed.

Jon cupped his hands and bellowed across the narrow gap between the *Pickering* and the mail packet, his voice carrying clear above the groaning timbers, "You have five minutes to strike your colors, or I'll send you to the bottom!"

The British master stood stiff on his quarterdeck, lips pressed thin. His men wavered behind him, faces gray. Three long minutes passed, heavy as lead. At last the Union Jack fluttered down.

A ragged cheer rose from the *Pickering*'s crew, powder-grimed voices breaking into triumph. Hats waved aloft. Even Thorndike allowed himself a grin.

Jon decided to see for himself what the battle had wrought. Leaving Second Lieutenant John Carnes in command, he went over the side into the longboat with Thorndike at his back.

The packet's deck told the price of victory. Blood ran from the scuppers, pooled dark around fallen men. The stench of powder and iron filled the air.

The packet's captain met him there, face haggard, his coat in tatters. Wordlessly he drew his sword, its edge nicked and stained, and presented it hilt-first.

Jon accepted it with a grave bow, then returned it. "You fought with courage. Keep your blade. You will need it again, if Providence spares you."

On the packet's quarterdeck, slumped in an armchair, sat an old man in fine clothes now stained with blood. His jaw was clenched, one cheek torn through by a musket ball. Yet his grip was firm on the blunderbuss he had fired through the long ordeal.

"The governor, most like," Thorndike murmured.

Jon inclined his head in respect. "Sir, you fought bravely. You shall have treatment for your wound. Our surgeon remains aboard the *Pickering* to tend our wounded, but yours shall have whatever supplies he requires."

The old man's eyes met his, fierce even in pain. He gave a single, stiff nod.

Jon straightened, his voice carrying to friend and foe alike. "See to the wounded, ours and theirs. Let it be known the *Pickering* grants no quarter to dishonor, but mercy to the valiant."

The men moved quickly, binding wounds, carrying the dead below. It was a grim victory, but necessary, one more blow against Britain's might, and another proof that even the king's ships could not sail the Indies without fear of Salem's privateers.

As Jon turned to go, the wounded governor lifted his blunderbuss once more, not in threat but in salute. Jon acknowledged the gesture with a nod, a warrior's respect passing silently between enemies.

THE *PICKERING* HAD scarcely patched her sails from the mail packet fight when fortune placed another sail upon the horizon. At first glance, Jon thought her British. She was trim in her lines, her course set north. But when he raised his glass, he saw the truth: a Boston vessel, long familiar in Salem, now flying British colors.

Thorndike's jaw tightened. "One of ours, sir. Taken and pressed into His Majesty's service."

Jon lowered his glass. "Then we must have her back."

The chase was short. Her British prize crew, unnerved and outnumbered, fired a few token shots, but their hearts were not in it. Within the hour, the Union Jack came down, replaced swiftly by the Stars and Stripes.

When Jon stepped aboard, he was met by the ragged cheers of her original crew, men who had been penned below since their capture. They stumbled into the sunlight, weeping, grasping the hands of *Pickering* sailors, crying out thanks to God and to Jon.

The British lieutenant surrendered his sword with a sour look. "She was ours by right of conquest."

Amused, Jon took the blade, his tone iron. "By theft, not right. She belongs to her home port, and now, her people will have her again."

Thorndike grinned as the men raised their voices in joy. "Salem will bless your name twice over, Captain, once for the prizes, and once for bringing her sons home."

Jon looked to the recaptured crew, and his heart swelled. This was no golden cargo, no prize to line purses, but a victory of another kind, for they had restored brothers-in-arms to freedom, sending them home to families who thought them lost.

He stood at the rail, watching the colors snap in the wind. "Set a course to keep her with us," he ordered. "No man taken from Salem shall be left to rot under another flag if we can help it."

Thorndike tipped his hat against the sun. "Aye, Captain. We can protect her on the journey home, if her master wills it, once we leave the Golden Rock."

Jon nodded, eyes fixed on the horizon where the sea met sky. St. Eustatius and the Dutch free port that welcomed American traders lay ahead, a safe harbor where his damaged ship could procure the repairs she desperately needed.

From the hatchway came a stir, then the gaunt figure of her master was helped on deck, blinking in the sunlight. His coat hung loose, but his bearing was unmistakably that of a master mariner.

Jon stepped forward. "Captain, welcome back to your own deck. I am Jonathan Haraden of Salem."

The man bowed slightly. "Nathaniel Curtis, late master of this vessel out of Boston. Sir, I owe you more than words. I thought never to see the open sky again."

Jon clasped his arm firmly. "Then let me ask, do you wish the *Pickering* to see you safe home? We can keep you under our protection as far as Boston or Salem, if that is your desire. But first, we must put in to St. Eustatius for needed repairs."

Curtis glanced to the horizon, then back at Jon with gratitude. "Aye, Captain. If it be no great burden, I would welcome your escort. My men have seen enough shot and chains. To sail in company with the *Pickering* is to sail under Providence itself."

Jon inclined his head. "Then so it shall be. We'll stand together into safe harbor."

Thorndike, who had listened in silence, gave a satisfied nod. "Boston and Salem both will bless your name for this, Captain. Twice over."

"These are the times that try men's souls."
– Thomas Paine 1776

CHAPTER 19

Oranje Bay, St. Eustatius, early March 1781

FROM THE QUARTERDECK, Jon scanned the bay crowded with masts as the *Pickering* slowly sailed into the anchorage at Oranje Bay. To starboard rode the recaptured Boston ship, Captain Curtis striding her deck with new pride, the Stars and Stripes snapping in the breeze. And behind them, the *Pickering*'s prizes.

Jon's eyes swept the shore. The rows of Dutch warehouses, the taverns and counting houses of the Lower Town were the same. The red-roofed buildings he had seen before still stood on the hills surrounding the port. And, over all, the Dutch flag flew over the fort. This was neutral ground, a safe harbor at last. Repairs and respite lay just ahead. But amidst it all an eerie discomfort gripped his chest. Something was not right.

"I am anxious for the good meal I last had in this port," said Thorndike at his side.

Jon allowed himself a small smile. "Aye, Eustatius has ever been a friend to our cause."

But before his words had finished echoing, the lookout aloft gave a shout that froze the deck. "Sail ho! Fleet to windward! British ensigns, by God!"

Jon snatched the glass from Thorndike. Canvas as far as the eye could see, lines of ships of the line, frigates bristling with guns, their masts like a forest. And at their heart, the flag of Admiral Sir George Rodney.

Thorndike's face went pale. "The British have taken St. Eustatius!"

Jon swung his glass shoreward. Redcoats poured down from the fort above Oranje Bay, muskets flashing in the sun. The Dutch tricolor still flew but St. Eustatius was neutral ground no longer.

"Captain!" Curtis cried hoarsely from his deck. "British ships! We are trapped!"

And trapped they were. Already the men-of-war in the bay were wheeling broadside-on, hemming them in, their gunports open like black, waiting mouths. Astern, more sails filled the channel they had entered, closing the gate. There was nowhere to run.

Jon's hands clenched at the rail, fury hot in his chest. To fight was to see his men slaughtered pointlessly, prizes lost in flame and wreck. He forced the words out, steady and hard. "Better trapped in honor than fleeing like cowards. Mr. Carnes, strike our colors before they rake us with broadsides. We'll not waste lives in a hopeless fight."

A groan went up from the deck. Still, the order was

obeyed. With heavy hearts, the Stars and Stripes fluttered down. Across the water, Curtis' Boston ship struck her flag as well. And behind them, Jon's prize crews lowered the American flag. Silence followed, heavier than the roar of any guns.

The officers and cabin boys clustered around Jon and Thorndike as they came down to the main deck. Within the hour, British boats swarmed them. Officers in scarlet strode aboard, pistols drawn. Jon handed over his sword without bowing his head.

The boarding officer sneered as he accepted it. "To Admiral Rodney," he said, tucking the blade under his arm.

Jon's voice rang clear enough for his men to hear. "Tell him he takes a ship, not her spirit."

Thorndike and the other officers were disarmed beside him. Curtis and his Boston crew were driven from their reclaimed deck at bayonet point. Together, captains and men alike were ferried ashore under guard.

Once ashore, they were herded into the West India Company's weighing house on the Lower Town quay, its thick stone walls swallowing the sunlight. The cavernous hall smelled of dust, rum, and sweat. Great beams loomed overhead, iron scales dangling like gallows. Straw was scattered across the floor for bedding, already fouled by the press of captives. Faces crowded the windows, hollow-eyed men staring out at the bay where their ships lay under foreign flags.

Jon turned to his officers and the cabin boys who crowded together like saplings in a gale, their faces hollow with worry. "Stay close. We'll not be separated if I can help it." He looked to a gaunt man near the far wall. "When did this happen?"

"Only weeks ago," came the weary reply. "They took the Dutch unawares. One lone Dutch frigate couldn't stand against fifteen of Rodney's warships. The garrison was but sixty men, no match for the landing force. Rodney seized near one hundred and fifty ships in the harbor."

"And the Dutch flag?" asked Jon. "A ruse?"

"Aye, the British fly the Dutch flag over St. Eustatius to lure unsuspecting enemy ships. Most were American."

A Dutch voice, raw with anger, added, "The Jews fared worse than the rest of us. Rodney singled them out for harsh treatment. They were beaten and robbed of everything they had, even stripped for cash or precious stones secreted in their clothing. Then he ordered them expelled on one day's notice, without telling their families or giving them access to their homes."

Another said, "They were here in the weighing house for a time before they were deported to St. Kitts, even the ones who were British."

Jon set his jaw. "Rodney picked on people who brought commerce to the island. It's dishonorable to the last. Meantime, we'll endure. We'll not rot here forever."

Bobby, pale but resolute, lifted his chin. "Not while you lead us, Captain."

The words rippled through the room, drawing murmurs of courage from the weary men. Jon rested a hand on the boy's shoulder, his heart set like iron. Whatever came, they would not break.

As the hours wore on, the weighing house stank of

too many bodies crammed into stone walls that trapped the day's heat. Jon sat with his back against a beam, Thorndike beside him, his officers, Captain Curtis and Bobby near at hand. The only light came from a smoking lantern, shadows stretching across the iron scales and thick timbers overhead.

"It's stifling," muttered one sailor, tugging his collar open. "Feels like hell itself."

"And it is only spring," another answered darkly. "Wait till summer. Hot, wet, and crawling with fever. We'll rot in here."

Jon's voice, quiet but firm, cut through the murmurs. "No, we won't. Not if I draw breath. I've seen worse prisons than this in battle, and I tell you men, *Providence* has not brought us this far to abandon us now."

The grumbling eased, though sweat still ran down every face.

The heat did not relent after sundown. The stone walls sweated damp, and the stink of unwashed men clung heavy as tar. Jon lay on the planks with his coat folded beneath his head, staring at the beams lost in shadow. Sleep would not come.

Thorndike leaned close. "Captain?"

"Aye," Jon whispered.

"We can't sit like penned hens waiting for Rodney's pleasure. If we can slip past their guards, take a boat—"

"—and run straight into a fleet of ships of the line?" Curtis' voice came low from the darkness. "It's folly, Mr. Thorndike. They've blocked every boat, every slip."

"Folly or not," Thorndike growled, "better to die trying than to rot in this oven."

Jon exhaled slowly, his mind turning. "You're both right. The fleet pins us in, and the guards watch us close. But Rodney's men will grow careless. The Dutch are no friends to Britain; they may aid us in small ways. We must be ready when the opportunity comes."

Curtis lifted himself on one elbow. "And if it never comes?"

Jon turned his head, eyes hard in the gloom. "Then we make our own."

Bobby's small voice broke the silence from the corner. "You'll find the way, Captain. You always do."

Jon closed his eyes, heart tightening. "Aye, Lad, we'll find it. And when we do, we'll not leave a soul behind."

The murmurs of the prisoners faded into snores and mutters. Still Jon lay awake, watching the darkness, his mind working like a compass, searching for the course that would lead them home. "Lord, go before us," he silently prayed.

Fort Oranje, Governor's House, March 1781

JON WAS MARCHED up the hill under heavy guard, the noon sun hammering the redcoats and polished bayonets around him. His wrists itched where the soldiers had tugged too roughly on the shackles, but he kept his head high, his step firm on the stone steps leading to the Governor's House.

Inside, the air was thick with the smell of ink, sweat, and plunder, tables stacked with seized ledgers, crates half-filled with jewels and sugar loaves awaiting inventory.

Behind a broad desk stood Admiral Sir George Rodney, powdered wig immaculate, his dark blue coat heavy with gold trim and at his neck a cravat of white lace. His sharp blue eyes beneath dark brows fixed on Jon as though weighing him like so much captured cargo.

"Can this be the same Jonathan Haraden who held the mighty *Achilles* at bay off Bilbao?" Rodney's voice was smooth as silk but edged with steel, as he let the words hang. Then he smiled thinly. "And yet you walked straight into my harbor like a lamb to slaughter. Quite a comedown, Captain."

Jon inclined his head, refusing to be baited. "The Dutch flag flew when last I called here, the island's merchants engaged in legitimate trade under the principle of neutrality. It was not foolhardy to trust that neutrality. 'Twas not cowardice but trust betrayed that has seen my ship confiscated."

Rodney sat in his chair and leaned back, steepling his fingers. "Trust, aye. A fine virtue for a preacher, but a poor compass for a privateer. You should have known every port in these waters bends to the strongest fleet. At present, that fleet is mine."

Jon's jaw tightened. "For a season, perhaps. But power shifts with the tide, Admiral. And do not forget the French are now with us, and they have a great navy. You may hold Eustatius today, but you cannot hold the hearts of free men forever."

Rodney's laugh was rich, contemptuous. "Fine words. Yet words do not mend your torn sails or return your prizes. Your gallant *Pickering* will soon ride at anchor in His Majesty's fleet, a toy for stronger hands. As for you…"

He gestured carelessly with his quill. "Rot here, or rot in St. Kitts. It makes little difference to me."

Jon met his gaze. "I'll not be rotting, Admiral. A man who chased off your *Achilles* won't lie idle while Britain strangles the Indies. You'll see me again, free and armed."

Rodney's smirk faltered just a fraction. He rapped the desk. "Take him back. I've no patience for the boasts of beaten men."

The guards seized Jon by the arms and marched him out. He did not resist. But as he stepped into the blinding sun, his thoughts burned hotter still. *Rodney plunders, Rodney gloats, but Rodney has given me one gift. He thinks me finished. And that is his mistake.*

At the weighing house, the guards released Jon's hands from the shackles and shoved him inside. The heat of the day pressed down like a weight of its own. Jon found a seat against the stone wall, his wrists red where the irons had chafed. The stench of unwashed bodies and stagnant water filled the low chamber. Through the single barred window, he caught a glimpse of the harbor.

Thorndike crouched nearby, his face hollow. "What did he say, Captain?"

Jon frowned remembering the conversation. "He mocked me. Spoke of the *Achilles*, then called me a fool for walking into his trap. Said we could rot here or in St. Kitts, he cares not. He takes pride in plunder and calls it victory. The man has no honor."

Curtis, seated a few feet away, gave a weary, bitter laugh. "That's the man for you. Half a merchant, half a butcher. Our fellow prisoners say he's sold half the island already, and the other half's dying of hunger."

"And all arrogance," Jon said. "He'll choke on it one day."

From a dark corner came a hoarse voice, one of Jon's seamen. "He's right, sir. They've taken the stores. We're to get no food but moldy biscuit and foul water. Men are starving."

Jon turned toward him, his tone firm but gentle. "We'll endure. You hear me? We're not beaten yet."

Beside him, Bobby shifted uneasily. "I—I gave my biscuit to Joshua, sir. He's bad sick."

Jon laid his hand on the boy's shoulder. "You did right, Lad. Tonight you'll have half of mine."

Thorndike shook his head. "Captain, you can't—"

"I can," Jon said quietly. "A captain eats last." He leaned his head against the wall, eyes half-closed. He could still hear Rodney's smooth derision, *rot here or rot in St. Kitts*, and felt it coil in his gut. Let Rodney preen over his plunder. The man mistook patience for defeat. Jon would bide his time, learn every stone of this place, every guard's habit, and when the hour came, he would break his chains the same way he had broken the British blockades. In the meantime, he would encourage the men so they did not lose heart.

Outside, the afternoon breeze carried the faint scent of the sea. The guards laughed somewhere up the lane. From time to time a wagon rumbled by, heavy with crates, the spoils of a conquered island.

Curtis drew a slow breath. "The Dutch townsfolk have hearts yet. One of them bribed a guard today to bring me this." He opened his coat to show a papaya and a coarse loaf. "Said more might come if we keep quiet and don't draw notice."

Jon looked at the offerings, then at the men slumped in the shadows. "Divide it. All of it."

A few murmured thanks, the sound rough with exhaustion.

"The Dutch haven't forgotten who filled their warehouses," Curtis added. "They'll risk much to see us fed."

The afternoon turned to evening as heat ebbed from the stone walls. Somewhere near dawn, a man coughed his last. The others said nothing, only bowed their heads.

At length Thorndike spoke, low and urgent. "We can't stay like this, sir. The men will die. What's your mind?"

Jon stared up at the faint light edging through the barred window. "Rodney thinks we'll rot here. He's wrong. There's not a prison yet built that can hold a man with reason to fight. We'll ask the Dutch who are yet free to aid us. America will not forget them for it." He turned his head toward Thorndike and Curtis, eyes hard but alight. "Watch the guards. Count their rounds. Learn which one drinks and which one listens. The Dutch here remember who their friends were before the redcoats came. They may lend us a hand for more than food. When the time's right, we'll take the harbor back one soul at a time."

Thorndike leaned forward. "Captain, I can take a few men to check the soil in this building. Perhaps there is a place to dig unnoticed."

Jon nodded. "Good. See what lies beneath these stones. You have my blessing for the effort."

Bobby looked up, his voice small but certain. "You'll get us home, Captain. I know you will."

Jon managed a smile. "Aye, Lad. We'll see Salem again. By God's grace, we'll see it." Calling his chaplain to him, he said, "Chaplain McClure, pray for us all and call the devout to join you."

McClure's face softened. "I'd be pleased to do that, Captain. I have been praying with the men, but I think a group prayer will be stronger. 'Where two or more are gathered...'"

That night, as the island cooled a little, the wind stirred through the broken shutters, carrying the faint hum of the sea. Despite their situation, hope sparked in Jon, fragile and defiant, like a match struck in a storm. He leaned against the stone, closed his eyes and thought of Eunice, wondering what she would feel when the news of their capture reached Salem.

Salem Market, June 1781

EUNICE WALKED BRISKLY through the crowded market as the summer sun climbed higher, bright on the roofs of Salem and warm upon her shoulders. Hannah kept pace at her side, the wicker basket swinging between them, its bottom lined with linen and green sprigs of mint. The air smelled of the sea and of fresh produce, salt, fish, and ripe berries mingled with the scent of baking bread from the stalls along Essex Street.

"The Gloucester Haradens will think we've laid a feast," said Hannah, her blonde curls escaping from beneath her bonnet.

"I hope so," Eunice replied, smiling faintly. "Martha

wants everything to be perfect for their arrival later today and we've a lot to find if we mean to return before the heat grows unbearable. We must find butter, two roasting fowl, potatoes, some greens and berries for tarts. Then we can go home."

They moved between vendors calling their wares. Hannah found some ripe strawberries. Eunice paused to consider the chickens, purchased two, then bargained for new potatoes. Yet her thoughts were elsewhere, turned toward the south and the long silence from the Indies. Six months now since Jonathan's last letter, his elegant hand promising to return before midsummer to claim his bride.

A shout from the wharf end of the market broke her reverie. A rider had come through the crowd, his horse flecked with foam, calling out news from the harbor. "Packet ship in from Antigua! Word from the Indies! Rodney's fleet has taken the Dutch island of St. Eustatius! Every American vessel in port seized!"

The market stilled. A murmur swept through the people. One man cried, "Do they name the ships?"

The rider unrolled a damp sheet of gazette print. "They do. Merchantmen, brigs, and privateers, among them the *Pickering* of Salem!"

Eunice's hand went to her throat. "No…"

Hannah tugged her sleeve. "What did they say about Papa's ship?"

Eunice swallowed hard. The child was old enough to know. "They say it's been captured."

The thought caused Eunice's knees to nearly give way. A fishwife caught her arm, steadying her. "God's mercy, Miss, it may be rumor yet. The gazettes are full of errors."

But the words rang clearly in her mind. *The Pickering of Salem.*

She managed to whisper, "We must go home." With their basket in hand, Eunice pressed through the crowd, her heart hammering. Beside her, Hannah's face had gone pale. Faces blurred past, the market noise receding into a dull roar, until at last the gate of the Haraden house came into view.

The garden gate banged behind them as she and Hannah hurried up the path. Silas was in the yard splitting kindling. He straightened at once when he saw their faces. "Mrs. Mason? What's amiss?"

She could barely find her breath. Hannah, stricken with worry, clung to Eunice, wide-eyed and silent. "The market," said Eunice. "News from the Indies. Admiral Rodney has taken St. Eustatius." Her voice broke. "They've captured the *Pickering.*"

The basket slipped from her grasp. Strawberries rolled across the flagstones, bright as spilled blood. Silas caught the basket before it fell, his face paling as though the strength had gone out of him. "Lord help us," he said at last. "Are you certain?"

Eunice shook her head, tears blurring everything. "They named her, Silas. They named *his* ship."

The front door opened. Martha appeared on the step, shading her eyes against the glare. "Mrs. Mason? Hannah? What has happened?"

Silas turned toward her. "Word from the Indies. The *Pickering*'s taken by the British."

For a moment, Martha seemed carved from stone.

Then she came swiftly down the steps, her skirts brushing the stone, and took Eunice by the shoulders. "Hush now," she said softly, drawing both her and Hannah close. "We'll not believe every harbor cry till the minister reads the dispatch himself. Come inside, my dears."

Her voice was steady, but Eunice could feel the tremor in her hands. As the door opened, the scent of supper drifted from the kitchen, onions and bread and something stewing. The small, ordinary comforts of life continuing in the face of ruin.

As Martha guided her and Hannah toward the parlor, Eunice glanced back. Silas still stood in the doorway, the basket hugged to his chest, staring toward the harbor where the gulls wheeled above the masts. "God bring him home," he said.

The long summer light still lingered over Salem when the Gloucester Haradens arrived, the carriage rattling to a stop before the house. Though her eyes were still red from crying, Eunice went to the door to meet them.

Lydia Haraden stepped down slowly, her full figure showing the burden of pregnancy, one hand braced on the arm of her daughter, Lydia, now seventeen. Her husband, Andrew, helped their other four daughters down one by one, dark-haired girls all, their lively eyes betraying both curiosity and fatigue.

"Welcome! We are glad you've come."

"And we to be here," Lydia said. "Though I think this child means to be born before the week is out," she added, pressing a hand to her belly. "The ride from Gloucester was longer than I remembered."

"We put lots of pillows in the carriage to make Mama's ride more comfortable," said sixteen-year-old Betsey.

Silas came to help with the baggage, and Eunice noticed he whispered something to Andrew that made his face take on a concerned look.

Inside, the air was warm with the smell of roast fowl and potatoes cooked with onions and spice, and strawberries stewed with sugar. Yet even with all the bustle, the house felt hushed. Eunice had dressed carefully and set the table, but her eyes were swollen from tears. Lydia was the first to notice. "Something has happened."

It was a minute before Eunice could summon an answer. She felt as if the words themselves would make the loss real. At last she said quietly, "Once you are settled in your chambers, we can gather in the parlor and tell you all we know." They had agreed not to speak of St. Eustatius until their guests were seated and calm.

A quarter-hour later, the Gloucester Haradens were gathered in the parlor. The mantel clock ticked with unhurried gravity. Hannah and Polly sat together on the hearth rug, hands clasped, their faces pale in the shifting light. Martha and Silas stood just inside the door.

Her hands folded in her lap, Eunice began. "You know from the captain's letter before he sailed that he and I are to be wed upon his return to Salem."

"Yes," Lydia interrupted, "and we were delighted to hear it."

"His last letter," Eunice continued, "written months ago, spoke of prizes and a happy crew. And then nothing until today. News arrived by packet from Antigua. Admiral Rodney has taken St. Eustatius, and the *Pickering* is named among the captured ships."

Lydia Haraden gasped and covered her mouth.

Betsey stared, dark eyes wide. "Captured? Uncle Jonathan?"

The younger girls, Jane and Polly, said nothing, their lips pressed tight.

"Is he dead?" asked fourteen-year-old Peggy.

"Papa's not dead!" Hannah cried.

"No, darling," Eunice said quickly. "No one said he was dead. He lives. I know in my heart he lives. We must trust God to bring him home."

Silas, who had been standing by the door, moved forward, and produced the crumpled *Gazette*. "This was read aloud at the market," he said, smoothing it with his hands before handing it to Andrew. "It names the *Pickering of Salem, Captain Jonathan Haraden* taken in Oranje Bay. The Dutch island is now under British control."

Andrew studied the page, his mouth set. "Rodney's work. The man's half-admiral, half-pirate. When did he take St. Eustatius?"

"In February," Silas replied. "The captain would have sailed into what he believed was a friendly port, unaware of its capture."

"Rodney will strip that island bare before he quits it," Andrew muttered, his face twisted in anger.

Lydia Haraden laid a hand on her husband's sleeve. "There's no comfort in anger, Andrew. We must pray for Jonathan."

"Aye," said Martha softly. "Why don't you adjourn to the dinin' room where we can do that. You must be hungry after your travel, and supper is ready. Even sorrow needs strength, especially you, Mrs. Haraden, for the sake of the babe."

When they had gathered around the table, Eunice asked Andrew to say the blessing. He bowed his head. "Heavenly Father, we trust You with Jonathan and his men. Bring them home and bless this food to our bodies."

The murmur of *Amen* was soft, uncertain. For a time, there was only the clink of plates and the whisper of the younger children. A log shifted in the hearth with a sigh.

Lydia looked across the table at Eunice, who had not touched her food. "Child, you are pale as milk. Have you eaten at all?"

Eunice shook her head. "I can't. It feels wrong to eat when I don't know if the captain has bread or water. Rodney is said to be cruel."

Lydia reached for Eunice's hand. "He will have both, and more. God has not forgotten him."

Silence settled again, broken only by the faint noises of people eating. Then the youngest Gloucester girl, Polly, looked up from her plate and said softly, "Will Uncle Jonathan come home soon?"

Every adult at the table seemed to draw breath at once. From the doorway to the kitchen, Martha managed a smile. "Aye, sweetin'. He will come home when God wills it. Your uncle is a brave man, and the best captain on the seas. The Lord watches over him."

Andrew Haraden lifted his glass. "With that in mind, I toast my cousin, Captain Jonathan Haraden, and all who serve the cause of liberty upon the sea."

The family murmured assent, their voices thick with feeling as they raised their glasses. Outside, the harbor bells tolled the last light of day, and the wind off the sea carried a chill even in summer. In the evening quiet, the hope of his return bound them together, a fragile, steadfast light against the gathering dark.

Later, when the younger girls had been shown to their beds, the adults gathered again in the parlor. The candles burned low, their flames wavering in the draft. Eunice poured wine for their guests, her hands still trembling.

A knock sounded at the front door. Silas opened it to find Eunice's father, Reverend Diman, hat in hand, his face grave. "Good evening, Silas."

Recognizing the familiar voice, Eunice rose and went to him. "Father."

"I heard the word at the docks," he said quietly. "I thought I should come at once. We'll hold a special service tomorrow at the church, a prayer meeting for Captain Haraden and his men."

Tears welling in her eyes, Eunice could only whisper, "Thank you."

The mantel clock struck nine. Its measured beat filled the silence as if to mark their vigil. Outside, the wind shifted, carrying the faint scent of salt and the promise of a new day.

East Church, Salem, the next morning

THE BELL OF the East Church tolled slowly above the harbor, its sound carrying through the still June air. From every lane and alley came townsfolk, merchants, sailors' wives, apprentices, widows, and children. All drawn by the same anxious news.

Eunice walked with Martha, Hannah and Polly between the gravestones that bordered the path leading to the church door, the scent of salt and lilac on the morning breeze. Silas followed with the Gloucester Haradens, Lydia supported by Andrew's arm, her other hand pressed protectively to her round belly. The younger girls walked solemnly, their dresses bright against the gray of the old stones.

Inside, the church was cool and dim, its tall windows open to the breeze off the harbor. Shafts of sunlight struck the whitewashed walls and fell across the polished pews. The air smelled faintly of wax and pine boards. As the congregation settled, the soft murmur of voices faded until only the restless creak of the pews remained.

Reverend Diman ascended the pulpit steps, his black robe stirring faintly with the draft from the open doors. He laid a hand on the great Bible before him, his voice deep and measured.

"Brethren, we are gathered to pray for those who sail under our nation's flag, and most especially for Captain Jonathan Haraden of Salem and the men of the *Pickering*, now taken prisoner in foreign seas. The Lord has said, 'When thou passeth through the waters, I will be with thee.' Let us take comfort in that promise, for the waters are deep and the night is long, yet He does not forsake His own."

A murmur ran through the pews, soft as the sigh of surf. For a moment Eunice closed her eyes, her fingers tight around Hannah's hand.

When she opened her eyes, she saw the reverend's gaze sweep the congregation. "Let us remember that the fight for liberty is not waged by soldiers and sailors alone. The wives who wait, the mothers who pray, the children who grow older without fathers, they, too, are part of this struggle. Their courage—your courage—upholds the nation as surely as cannon or musket."

He paused. From the pews came a stifled sob. Lydia Haraden dabbed at her eyes.

"So we pray," Eunice's father continued, his voice gaining strength, "that God will guard the *Pickering*'s company; that He will give wisdom to her captain and grant them favor in the eyes of their captors; and that He will bring them home again, not for glory's sake, but that righteousness may be established among the nations."

When the final prayer ended, the congregation rose, the benches creaking like timbers in a ship's hull. The voices joined together in the hymn "Jesus, Lover of My Soul", rising pure and plaintive against the rafters.

Eunice's throat tightened as she sang. She thought of her captain, standing tall on his quarterdeck, his voice steady as he spoke commands, and she prayed that somewhere across the sea he might hear this very hymn carried on the wind.

As the last notes faded, sunlight spilled through the open door, striking her face with its warmth. Martha slipped her arm around her shoulders. "He will come home," she whispered.

Eunice nodded, unable to speak. The bell began again, slow and solemn, its sound mingling with the murmur of the tide, as though the sea itself were joining in the prayer.

"We shall never be abandoned by Heaven if we
act worthy of its aid."
– Samuel Adams 1777

CHAPTER 20

The weighing house, St. Eustatius, late July 1781

THE HEAT HAD settled like a blanket over the bay.
From the barred windows of the weighing house, Jon
watched the harbor shimmering in haze, masts wavering
in the glare, gulls circling lazily above the half-sunken
hulks left by Rodney's plunder. Inside the weighing house,
the air was thick with the smell of salt, sweat, and mildew.
Flies droned over the buckets of brackish water by the
wall.

Jon gazed toward Fort Oranje, where the Union Jack
still hung limp against its pole. Rodney had dropped his
ruse of flying Dutch colors months ago. Thorndike joined
him, wiping sweat from his brow. "The guards are slow
this morning," he murmured. "I think they've heard the

news."

Jon turned. "About Rodney?"

"Aye. Gone back to England, taking half the fleet and all the plunder and gold he could carry."

Jon's eyes narrowed. "Then the devil's tail has quit the island. That's good news, even if he's left us in his wake."

Across the room, Curtis looked up from the scrap of sailcloth he'd been patching into makeshift bedding. "If Rodney's gone, his dogs may grow careless."

Jon nodded. "Careless guards and hungry men. That's a mix that can open doors. Keep your eyes sharp."

He moved through the dim chamber, stepping over the sleeping forms of two wounded seamen. The Dutch prisoners had managed to bring in fruit and dried fish that morning, smuggled through a bribed sentry. A little of the food lay spread on a board in the corner, mangoes shriveled but sweet, a loaf of coarse bread broken into pieces.

Bobby crouched beside them, dividing the food. "It's more than we had last week, sir," he said, his voice thin but hopeful. "The Dutch woman with the red shawl says she'll come again."

"Give her our thanks if you see her," Jon said quietly. "And our promise that we'll pay our debts when we're free."

Jon took a piece of bread, broke it in two, and handed half to Thorndike. "You see how Providence moves? Even now He stirs hearts outside these walls. The Almighty sends us not plenty, but enough. 'Tis like manna in the wilderness."

Thorndike chewed slowly. "Enough to live, perhaps.

But not to wait forever. The men are restless. Curtis and I have spoken about the loose soil behind that back wall. We've been digging a little each night. Soon, we might reach the cistern trench beyond."

Jon glanced toward the far end of the room where a heap of broken crates hid the wall's lower stones. "How long, do you think?"

"Three months, perhaps less if the Dutch help us hide the dirt."

Jon drew a slow breath, then nodded. "We begin in earnest at dusk. Keep the noise down. Tell the men it's work worth their lives and their liberty."

A faint stir passed through the prisoners as Thorndike spread the word. Curtis joined Jon at the window again. "When we get out, what then? The harbor's still thick with guns."

Jon's gaze fixed on the glinting water. "Then we wait for night and for mercy. A Dutch sloop lies moored beyond the point. Her master's kin to one of our benefactors. When the time comes, she'll bear us clear. And there are fishing craft that may come now that the tyrant is gone."

Curtis smiled faintly. "You've thought it through."

"I think of it every hour I draw breath," Jon said. "A man must plot his freedom as he would a course through reefs, a little each tide, until the way is open."

A gust of wind carried in the sound of the surf and, faintly, the toll of a bell from the Upper Town. It mingled with the rasp of a shovel as the men began to dig. They moved slowly, careful and steady. Hope had returned to their hands.

Jon closed his eyes for a moment, feeling the rhythm of the digging beneath his boots. The work of faith, he thought, was not only in prayer and trust but in persistence, one handful of earth at a time.

The weighing house, St. Eustatius, early September 1781

NIGHT CAME EARLY now and the trade winds had stilled. The air inside the weighing house hung heavy as soup, the stone walls slick with dampness. Jon sat near the small barred window, stripping his last scrap of sailcloth into bandages while Bobby fanned a wounded seaman with a broken palm frond.

From the shadows, Thorndike emerged, his shirt streaked with earth. "Captain," he whispered, "we're through the first layer. Only sand now between us and the cistern trench. Another week, maybe less."

Jon looked up, the dim lamplight catching the sharp lines of his face. "How deep?"

"Four feet, perhaps five. We've been careful, taking out the soil in our pockets, hiding it under the broken planks. The guards think we're patching leaks in the wall."

"Good," Jon said softly. "Better to let them think us tame than desperate."

A soft cough came from the corner. Curtis, thinner than ever, had risen from his place among the sleepers. "Tame men don't survive this long. We've lost three already, God rest them. Another week will kill the sickliest if the British keep cutting our rations."

"They'll not die here," Jon said. "We'll move them

first when the tunnel opens. They'll have the night air before any of us."

Bobby looked up from his work, his voice small. "Do you think the Dutch sloop will still be waiting, sir?"

"She will," Jon replied, though even he could not be sure. "Her captain's a man of conscience. He'll not leave before the rainy season ends."

A sudden clatter of boots echoed down the corridor outside. The men froze. A guard's drunken voice slurred, "Up with the lantern, you lazy curs—inspection!"

Thorndike darted to the corner, sweeping the loose earth with his sleeve. Bobby kicked the empty shovel beneath a pallet just as the bolt scraped open. Two redcoats stumbled in, muskets at the ready, the sour smell of rum on their breath.

The taller one squinted at the gloom. "What's that hole in the floor?"

Jon stood calmly, straight-backed and barefoot. "A drain, Sergeant. The rains have swelled the wall cracks. We've been keeping the floor dry."

The guard grunted, swinging the lantern closer. Thorndike held his breath as the light hovered inches from the patch of disturbed stone. Then the other soldier burped, muttered, "Smells like hell in here," and turned away.

The first one sneered. "Enjoy your paradise, Yankees." He slammed the door behind them, the bolt grinding home.

The silence afterward was deafening.

Bobby exhaled shakily. "That was close."

"Too close," Thorndike muttered.

Jon crouched beside the false drain and brushed the dust from the edge. "We'll cover it better. From now on, we dig only after midnight. No talk, no lamplight. One sound could hang us all."

Curtis nodded grimly. "We'll manage."

Jon leaned against the wall, feeling the faint vibration beneath his palm—the pulse of the sea, or the faint echo of shovels still working. He closed his eyes. In his mind, he pictured Salem: the harbor bells, the smell of the market, Eunice's voice reading by firelight.

"We'll see it again," he murmured. "If God grants us three more weeks of darkness, we'll see the dawn at sea."

Thorndike's tired face broke into the ghost of a grin. "Then let's keep digging, Captain. I'd rather drown free than sweat in this tomb another night."

Jon met his eyes, nodded once, and reached for the shovel. "So be it. We finish what we started."

Haraden house, Salem, October 1781

THE EVENING WIND carried the faint smell of wood smoke from the town chimneys and the harbor where masts stood like bare trees against a copper sky, gulls crying over the ebb tide. Eunice sat by the open window with her sewing basket untouched, her eyes turned to the horizon as if she could will a sail into view. From upstairs came the sound of the girls playing. Martha sat beside her, taking a rare break from her kitchen duties. Behind them a fire crackled in the hearth, its warmth welcome on the chilled night.

Footsteps sounded on the path. A moment later Silas came in, hat in hand, his coat still carrying the smoke of the coffeehouse hearth.

"You've been long," Martha said, rising. "Did you hear anythin' worth the tellin', or was it all wharfside gossip again?"

Hanging up his coat, Silas glanced toward Eunice before answering. "Some of it might be gossip, some might be Providence movin'." He set his hat on the table. "News from London papers brought in by packet. Admiral Rodney's left St. Eustatius. Sailed for England with a convoy heavy as Pharaoh's treasure, thirty-odd ships, they say, filled with gold, sugar, and goods stolen from every merchant and privateer doin' business on the island."

Martha snorted. "Aye, and may it sink him to the bottom."

But Eunice had risen from her chair, one hand pressed to her breast. "He's gone? Truly Rodney's gone from the Indies?"

Silas nodded. "Aye. Left what remains of the garrison under some colonel's charge. They say Rodney was so intent on guardin' his plunder that he near forgot there's a war on. French ships caught his treasure convoy off the Channel and took the whole of it, three million pounds, so the paper claims."

Martha let out a low whistle. "So greed's bitten the hand that fed it."

Eunice could scarcely breathe. "Then, if he's gone, perhaps the prisoners have been left behind. Perhaps…the captain will find some mercy without him there."

Silas' expression softened. "That's what I thought

when I heard it. I came straight back. The men in the coffeehouse said Rodney's folly cost Cornwallis his rescue. Seems he was too busy linin' his pockets to block the French fleet from reaching the Chesapeake."

Martha looked up sharply. "And if that's so, maybe the war will turn at last."

Except for the steady tick of the clock on the mantel, the flickering flames in the hearth and the faint hiss of the sea wind at the shutters, the room was quiet. Eunice drew a long breath. Then she spoke, her voice low but firm. "If the Lord can use Rodney's greed to break Britain's strength, He can use the same to free Captain Haraden. I believe it."

Martha rose and crossed to her, laying a work-roughened hand on Eunice's shoulder. "Then hold to that, my dear. Hope's as dear as bread these days."

Silas nodded. "The talk in town is of victory, or at least a turn in our favor. I'll bring any further word from the wharves. Till then, we'll keep the lamps trimmed."

Eunice looked toward the darkening harbor, where the tide whispered against the stones. Somewhere far to the south, she imagined the same sea washing up on a shore near a prison wall, and the man she loved hearing the same tide. "Hold fast, Jonathan," she whispered. "The tide's turning."

St. Eustatius, 25 November 1781

THEY HAD LEARNED to measure time by the guards' habits—which watch drank deep at dusk, which kept a steady eye on the quay, and which laughed too loud when a cask of rum was rolled by. For nearly nine months those small certainties had been the prisoners' only map of hope. Now the map ran to one last line: the hour the sentries began slurring their words.

Jon stood on the stone floor of the weighing house and watched the moon smear itself thin across the barred window. Around him men breathed in ragged rhythm, like a ship at anchor, coughing, muttering, sleeping in fits. The shackles had been eased with Rodney's departure months ago, as if the jailers had forgotten to fit them on cold wrists every night. It could have been a kindness, or more likely sloth.

Bobby slept curled against a mortar that had once held sugar, his face thin and pale but peaceful in rest. Thorndike bent over a scrap of candlelight, tracing the shadows where the tunnel had been dug toward the outer wall. Curtis listened, his jaw set. Chaplain McClure whispered a low prayer in the corner.

Jon looked at each face. "Tonight," he said, and his voice, hoarse from months of little speech and less air, carried. "We wait till the first cask goes past the guardhouse. We take two at the sentry post nearest the quay, not where the drums beat. We don't alarm the whole garrison. We move fast, quiet as an oncoming storm." His instructions reminded Jon of his days in the militia where stealth could mean victory.

Thorndike nodded. "I've watched the rounds for a week. The lieutenant at the east post always takes his cup then. He'll be slow to wake." He gripped Jon's forearm. "We can do it, Captain. We'll go like prowling wolves."

Curtis spat once and gave the list: who would take which man, where the stolen cutlasses, filched months before from a careless locker and smoothed at the hafts by Bobby's small hands, would be hidden, how the weakest among them would be carried. The surgeon had fashioned the semblance of a litter should they need it. Chaplain McClure's prayer had steadied them all. Piety and planning shared the room.

They moved in a silence that seemed a betrayal of their months of noise. Outside, somewhere down the lane, the low, vulgar laugh of a guard echoed. A dog barked and was hushed. A cask scraped and the lightest clink of tankards told them the hour had come.

Thorndike slid from the stone and bent like shadow. He passed the word with a touch: one, two, three. They were not many, perhaps ten, perhaps twelve able men who still had strength and could be trusted not to flinch. But the weak and the sick were to be helped or carried.

Jon's hand found Bobby's shoulder. The lad woke with a quick start, and was given a strip of biscuit.

They had learned to move like sailors moving aloft: steady hands, even breath, eyes fixed on a point beyond the next step. Two prisoners lay in wait just inside the narrow doorway. When the guard stooped to shift the loading ramp and roll out another cask, Thorndike dropped like a hunter and closed about the man's throat. A second hand came quick.

The other guard moved to shout, and Jon was on him. He lunged, seized the guard's wrist and drove a solid blow into his temple. The musket clattered to the stones and the guard slumped, senseless. A third sentry went down in a tangle of arms and boots before he could cry out, the cutlasses flashing long and narrow in hands made strong by years at sea.

No one meant to kill; they meant to be quick and stay quiet. A sentry dropped into a heap, breathing hard, his head bleeding from the blunt of a handspike. Another was bound with his own scarf. The air was thick with the iron scent of blood, but the night swallowed most noises. Carts loaded with rum casks continued to scrape past the post as if nothing had happened.

"Easy, lads," Jon murmured as they slipped past the corner. "No talking now unless I speak first."

They moved through the lane like ghosts with one purpose. Jon's chest hammered, and in the hollow between his ribs his anger and fear braided into a single rope of will. At the courtyard gate they found one door unbarred, a favor from a Dutch friend who had bribed a soldier earlier that week. Then they slipped through into the dark streets beyond.

The Dutch had remembered them. That was what had kept the plan breathing. Women with covered heads waited by a house along the lower quay road, bearing bowls of stew so thin Jon could have wept. One woman, who introduced herself as Anna de Graaff, handed him a bowl. "For you, Captain." Jon thanked her and made sure Bobby and Joshua ate first.

They were given cloaks and false passes and a place to lay the worst of the sick. The Dutch provided other things, too: a clever map of sentry paths, a woman who knew which sentries might be paid to look the other way, and most precious of all, a small boat hidden among the seagrass that might take them round the headland if the sea proved calm.

They had not tried to carry every prisoner. The weighing house held men beyond their strength. Those who could walk were helped. For those who could not, the Dutch agreed to bribe the guards for leniency. It was the hardest choice Jon made, one he would carry always. As they threaded the narrow alleys, men they had stood beside kissed the hands of the Dutch women helping them, leaving them to tend those who could not move.

In the gray before dawn they crouched in a thicket above a cove, salt spray stiff on their faces, the muscles of their legs drawn taut as rope. Bobby shivered and mouthed the names of his mates. Jon counted heads and found them all where they needed to be. Finally, his chest unclenched enough to take a breath that tasted of the sea.

From far out at sea, as the dawn broke, Jon heard the thrum of oars, the creak of tackles. A low thunder of sound, like surf under a storm. He and those with him watched as masts rose on the horizon, first dim and then white and bright. Jon's heart raced. It was the French squadron. "The French!" he whispered hoarsely. Their sails filled low and steady under the wind. Minutes later, guns answered with a single, rolling note as the French drove straight into the harbor.

Before long, a sharp staccato, a single volley of rifles, came from the headland, then a confused roar. Men on the ridge, a landing force who must have been sent ahead, shouted in French as the tricolor flag rose and the Union Jack tumbled. In the settlement below, redcoats scrambled, surprised and scattered as the Marquis de Bouillé's men came swiftly ashore. A cheer broke from some corner of the island, small and raw, like a voice finding its throat after a long silence.

Jon felt something loosen inside him, a muscle long clenched given back to him. He watched the French sailors coming ashore and turned to his men. They had slept in dirt-worn clothes, unwashed since spring. They had lost comrades. Yet their eyes shone with the same unsinkable courage and love of country that had carried them through broadsides and bilges. "We have prevailed."

The French officers came in small boats to the quay, and Jon and his officers went to meet them. Their saviors moved with the quick courtesy of men who had taken armies. Men in dark blue coats trimmed in gold shook hands with bandaged men of Salem and Boston as if business and mercy belonged to the same hour.

Bouillé's aide spoke through an interpreter. "Arrangements will be made to send the American men aboard French transports bound north to neutral harbors. The wounded will be tended by our own surgeons. And the guilty who plundered will be answered in due time." He turned to go and then, turning back, added, "You might like to know that Rodney's convoy with his plunder never made it to England. We captured it near the Scilly Isles off the coast of Cornwall. It will serve to help France aid America."

Jon nodded, supposing that was some comfort. "*Merci.*"

When the French were told the captain of the *Pickering* was among the prisoners, one of Bouillé's lieutenants came to Jon. "Regretfully, Captain, we cannot give you back your ship. The English have already taken her, but we can restore to you your life and the lives of your men."

Jon knew enough French to understand and to thank him. As the French officer walked away, Jon stood at the water's edge and let the wind take salt to his lips. Behind him Bobby laughed once, hugging Joshua, a single sudden noise that broke like a bell.

Thorndike clapped Jon on the shoulder, so hard it hurt. "We did it, sir!"

Curtis, wiping his eyes with a handkerchief, smiled as if he had not smiled for a year. "We are saved, Captain. You kept us alive for this day and I am once again forever in your debt."

"A strange day to be borne home," Jon said softly, thinking of Eunice, of Salem's roofs, of the girls whose laughter he could already hear in his imagination, "but a glorious one. Providence has shown us mercy."

Bobby pressed close, his voice hoarse. "We'll soon be home, Captain."

Jon placed a hand on Bobby's shoulder and felt the tired weight of the months lift a degree. "By God's grace," he answered, "we shall." Then, before the last of the landing boats scuttled to the quay, Jon took a last look at the French standard flying from the fort, the tricolor above a Dutch pennant, and sent a prayer on the salt wind, a fierce thanks for the hand the Dutch had offered in the dark and for the French guns that came with the dawn.

Haraden house, Salem, January 1782

THE HARBOR LAY iron-gray beneath a lowering sky, the tide creaking in the ice along the wharf pilings. Gulls wheeled soundless over the frozen flats. Inside the house, the fire burned low, its glow touching the flickering candles and the folded linen on the sideboard.

Eunice sat near the window with her mending, though she had stitched the same seam twice without seeing it. Hannah had just come from the kitchen where she said Martha was kneading bread. "Up to her elbows in flour!" And Polly was humming to her doll on the rug before the hearth. The day had that winter stillness when sound seemed to travel farther than sight.

Silas came in from the cold, stamping the snow from his boots. "No new post from Boston," he said, unwrapping his scarf. "But a French brig was sighted off Marblehead this mornin'. Could be bringin' prisoners north. There's talk one of them might be from Salem—"

He stopped mid-sentence at a sudden knock at the door.

Martha wiped her hands on her apron. "This hour? Who'd be callin' now?"

Eunice rose, her heart already hammering. There was something in the rhythm of the knock—firm, deliberate, with the faintest hesitation between strokes.

She opened the door.

For a long minute, she could only stare. Snow drifted in the entryway around a man in a salt-stained coat, the seams of it mended in a dozen places. His breath clouded in the cold air, his boots creaked once on the threshold.

He stood straight though his shoulders showed the weary set of long labor. The dark blue eyes were the same but his face was thinner, the skin drawn fine over the bones, and the lines around his eyes had deepened. His hair was just beginning to show gray at the temples, and his hands...she saw them tremble once before he steadied them.

"Eunice," he said softly. His voice—hoarse, uncertain, achingly familiar—broke the stillness like a wave. It was the first time he had ever spoken her given name, and it was sweet on his lips.

Her breath left her. "Jon—"

Then she was in his arms, and the months of fear fell away in a rush. He held her as if anchoring himself to land again, his face pressed into her hair. The smell of the sea still clung to him, salt, tar, and smoke, but beneath it was the faint scent of clean linen, proof that he had been cared for on the voyage home.

Hannah and Polly ran to their father to be added to his embrace and, for a moment, it was all tears and arms and the warmth of living breath. "My girls," he said, his eyes tearing up as he looked upon his daughters. "You've grown a foot."

Polly clutched his leg. "Papa! Papa!"

Martha came from the kitchen. "Merciful heavens," she whispered, half-laughing, half-crying. "Captain Haraden, we gave you up for a ghost."

Silas stepped forward, wordless, and gripped Jon's arm. "We thought you were lost, sir. But Mrs. Mason never gave up."

"I nearly was lost," Jon said. "But the French took the

island. Bouillé's men freed us. I came north aboard their transport. Landed at Boston two days ago. I could not wait another hour."

Eunice drew back enough to look at him. He'd been gone more than a year. The new gray in his hair, the hollow under his cheekbones, the weary gentleness in his eyes, each told its own tale. "You're home," she whispered. "You're truly home."

He brushed his thumb over her cheek, damp with tears. "By the grace of God, your prayers and a French cannon, yes."

"Enough!" said Silas, his voice rough with feeling. "Let the man come in out of the cold before he freezes where he stands. Martha'll have my hide if he turns to ice in her doorway."

"Of course," said Eunice, suddenly realizing he was standing in the cold. "Come sit by the fire."

Jon stepped into the parlor. Eunice took his coat, and he dropped into his chair next to the hearth. Martha pressed a mug of hot cider into his hands. "You'd best sit before you fall down," she said. "You look like you've been carved out of whalebone."

He took the cup between his hands with a shaky laugh. "Feels near to it. But I'll mend."

Eunice drew up a chair next to him and touched his hand lightly where the skin was thin over the veins and then saw the marks where shackles had been. "You've come through much, love. Rest now. You're safe."

He looked around the familiar room, the flickering firelight, the smell of bread rising from the kitchen, the

345

children's soft voices at his feet. Something in his face eased. "Aye," he said quietly, his gaze finding hers again. "Home at last."

"It appears to me, the eternal Son of God is operating powerfully against the British nation."
– Spoken by a "reputable, religious man" in a tavern in 1777 and overheard by John Adams, who sent it to his wife, Abigail

CHAPTER 21

Haraden house, the next morning, late January 1781

MORNING SUNLIGHT FILTERED pale through the frost-laced panes, glinting off pewter cups and the steam rising from the coffee. The house smelled of woodsmoke, hotcakes, and maple syrup warming by the hearth. For the first time in more than a year, the Haraden table was full again.

Eunice poured coffee into Jon's cup, her hands steady though her heart was not. "Did you sleep well?" she asked. From his expression, she could see he had not. "It may take some time…"

"Aye." He sat close to the fire, the light showing the

gray at his temples and the new lines around his eyes. But the handsome man she had fallen in love with was still there. He smiled, yet she saw how his gaze moved over the room as if testing the reality of it, the girls' laughter, the clink of plates, the sound of Martha moving around.

Martha set down a platter of fried apples. "You'll take another plate, Captain. There's plenty."

Jon lifted his head, one hand wrapped around his cup. "Aye, Martha. I'll eat what's here and be grateful. There were months when I thought I'd never smell breakfast again, and, should you be curious, the French sailors eat worse than the Americans."

The words drew silence. Even the children looked up. Eunice reached across the table and placed her hand on his, her voice gentle. "You needn't speak of it, Jon. Not today."

But he shook his head. "It's time you knew what befell us. The story belongs to all who waited."

His voice was low and even as he told it, how the ship had suffered damage taking prizes so the *Pickering* had sailed into Oranje Bay, seeking repairs under what they thought was the neutral Dutch flag; how the British guns never fired because there was no need. The island had already fallen.

He spoke of the march through the heat, the weighing house thick with hunger and despair; of the men they lost, too weak to live; of the Dutch who risked their own lives to slip them food through the bars. Of how they planned and executed an escape just as the French fleet sailed into the bay, their tricolor hoisted above the fort with the dawn. "They freed St. Eustatius," he said simply. "And by

God's grace, I am here."

"The officers?" she asked. "Lieutenant Thorndike?"

"All endured and were saved. Thorndike was particularly brave in our escape."

"The cabin boys?" asked Hannah.

"All saved," said Jon, his eyes tearing up.

Eunice felt her throat tighten. She didn't doubt he, too, had been brave, leading the other men and caring for the boys. She wanted to take his hand but didn't trust herself not to weep.

"What about your ship, Papa?" asked Hannah.

"The *Pickering* is lost to me, sweetheart. I cannot say what has become of her."

"There will be another ship," Eunice encouraged, "if you want one."

Martha cleared her throat roughly. "You'll forgive me, Captain, but I think what you're made for this mornin' is eatin'." She set another plate before him. "Tell the rest after your second helpin'."

Jon smiled faintly, the kind of smile that reached his eyes at last. "Eat first, yes. As for the rest…" he glanced at Eunice, and for a moment she saw excitement flicker in his eyes. "I've merchants to meet with and a wedding to prepare for. And after that…perhaps the sea again. But this morning, Martha, I'll take your hotcakes over any prize ship afloat."

A ripple of laughter warmed the room, light as the crackle of the fire. Outside, sounds from the harbor drifted faintly through the still air. Eunice caught his look across the table, alive and unbroken, and felt a prayer rise unspoken in her heart: *Lord, help me to help him heal.*

The London Coffeehouse, Salem, late January 1782

THE SMELL OF roasted beans and tobacco hung thick beneath the beams of the coffeehouse. Candles guttered in their sconces, their light falling across the cups and the wet shine of greatcoats hung to dry. Outside in the harbor, masts rose like gray spears against the snow. Inside, talk of the sea filled every corner.

Jon had been home scarcely a fortnight, yet word of his return had spread along Essex Street finding its way to the coffeehouse on Central Street. Merchants, sailors and shipwrights greeted him with handshakes and claps to the shoulder.

"Thought the British had you locked in irons, Captain!" one man laughed.

"They did for a time," Jon replied evenly, "but Providence proved the stronger."

At the back of the room, Elias Derby, the merchant prince of Salem, sat by the fire with a folded gazette on his knee. "Captain Haraden," he called, motioning him over. "You've the look of a man who's cheated Neptune himself. Come sit. Tell me the truth of St. Eustatius."

Jon joined him, drawing the attention of half the room. He spoke briefly, without embellishment, telling Derby how the British flew the Dutch flag to lure in ships unaware they had taken the island. He told how the *Pickering* had been taken along with her prizes, how the prisoners endured and escaped, and how the French freed the island. The men around him listened in taut silence, their cups forgotten.

Derby exhaled. "A hard tale, one the town will remember. You've done Salem credit once more. Though the British captured the *Pickering* and your prizes, you brought the men back and every family is singing your praise." He paused to take a drink of his coffee. "Now that you're home, I'll not let you rest too long. There's a new vessel being fitted out at Briggs' shipyard on the South River, a fine ship, two hundred tons, fourteen guns, forty men. She's the *Julius Caesar*. She'll carry a letter of marque in the next few months, and I'd have none but you command her."

Jon gazed into the fire for a long moment. Its light showed the faint scars on his wrists, the hollows in his cheeks, and the clear, unwavering steadiness in his eyes. "I am humbled by your confidence in me. She sounds like a proud ship," he said quietly, "and I thank you more than words can say. I am pleased to accept, but first—" he smiled faintly "—I have a wedding to attend. Mine."

Derby's grin spread beneath his dark eyes. "Then we'll drink to both, the bride and the sea. May neither be too rough on you."

Laughter rippled through the room, easing the weight of solemn talk. Someone called for a toast, and cups were raised in a ring of candlelight.

"To Captain Haraden, home again, and to the *Julius Caesar* when she's ready!"

Jon stood, acknowledging the cheer with a small nod, as he raised his cup. "To Salem," he said, his voice carrying. "To her ships, her sailors, and her faith in liberty. May we be worthy of them all."

Derby leaned toward Jon as the voices subsided. "Tell me, Captain, who might this fortunate woman be?"

"I am the fortunate one," said Jon. "She's Eunice Mason, daughter of Reverend James Diman, and coincidentally, governess to my daughters."

Another smile crossed Derby's face. "Well then, you are rescued only to be blessed."

"How goes the war?" Jon asked, knowing Derby would have his ear to the latest news.

A murmur ran through the men near the fire as another merchant, Benjamin Goodhue, folded his paper. "Despite Cornwallis' surrender at Yorktown, the war drags on."

"It's true," said Derby. "The British still hold New York, and the fighting in the Carolinas grows more brutal by the month. But St. Eustatius is not the only island in the Indies the French are taking back."

Jon set down his cup. "Then we must hold fast," he said. "Victory means little if we grow weary before the cause is secured. There are still ships to defend what we've won."

Derby regarded him a moment, then nodded. "You'll have your chance, Captain. The *Julius Caesar* will sail when the ice breaks, and with men enough who still believe in the fight."

Outside, the wind rattled the panes and the harbor bells struck the hour. As Jon left the coffeehouse, he drew his coat close, feeling the salt chill in the air. The sea would always call him, but for now, there was warmth waiting at home, and a promise made before God he meant to keep.

Haraden house, end of February 1782

SNOW LINGERED IN the ruts along Essex Street, but spring's breath was already in the air, the faint drip of melting ice and the cry of gulls farther inland than usual bearing witness. In the Haraden house, Eunice's plans were quietly underway.

She sat by the window with her mother, a Bible open on the table beside the sewing basket. A length of blue woolen fabric, the color of a clear morning sky, lay across her lap, the fabric simple but fine. "It needn't be grand," Eunice said softly. "He's had enough of ceremony for a lifetime."

Her mother smiled. "Then plain it shall be, plain, but lovely. A captain's wife's gown, meant for loving her man, for prayer and for waiting. You should know your father and I are very happy for you."

A smile she could not stop spread across Eunice's face. "None so happy as I."

They chose a ribbon for Eunice's hair the color of the dawn and talked of flowers that might bloom for the wedding in March. "Bluebells will be in the fields," her mother said. "Though for the church, it might not be warm enough for much beyond evergreens and laurel."

Eunice's longing rose for the day she would at last be Jon's wife. "A small gathering at East Church and a supper after, simple and close, would please us both."

Later that week, Eunice visited the cooper's yard near the harbor. Silas went with her. Along with Martha, they had saved money to buy Jon a new sea chest. Together, they chose one that was oak-banded and brass-hinged, its lid carved with the faint design of an anchor. "We'll line it with sailcloth," Silas said. "Your knittin' and Martha's will go inside along with other gifts."

When the chest was delivered, Eunice ran her hand over the fine craftsmanship, then filled it with care: a new shirt, a pair of wool socks, a flask of molasses, a small leather-bound Bible to replace the one the British had taken from him. On the first page, she wrote, *For Jonathan, that you may never sail without a compass true.* She'd also had a local artist paint a miniature of her and his two daughters. Wrapped in fine muslin, a note with it read, *So you know who waits for you at home and prays for you every day.*

In the days before their wedding, Jon had ordered a new coat made to replace the one ravaged in St. Eustatius, a fine navy broadcloth trimmed with gold braid and epaulets, the mark of a captain once more. When she saw him wear it for the first time, Eunice's heart ached with pride. He looked every inch the man she had loved and waited for, the sea still in his eyes but peace at last in his face.

The day before the wedding, Elias Derby stopped by the house. He carried a long parcel wrapped in canvas. Jon welcomed him into the parlor. "Elias, come in!"

Derby greeted Eunice who offered him hot cider. The merchant took a seat by the fire, as Jon opened the parcel. Seeing its contents, Eunice caught her breath. "So beautiful!"

Jon's gaze lingered long on the finely crafted sword, the blade etched with a single phrase: *For liberty and the sea.*

Derby's smile was brief. "The English took yours. Let

Salem bestow you with another."

Jon's hand closed on the hilt. "I am humbled and honored by your gift, Elias. It is truly a fine piece of workmanship. I'll wield it for liberty." Then, glancing at Eunice, he added, "And for home."

Outside, the cold March wind blew. Inside, the fire burned steady. Eunice laid her hand over his. In that quiet, the long tide of war and separation finally ebbed, leaving only the promise of tomorrow and their joy in becoming one.

East Church, Salem, 11 March 1782

THE MORNING LIGHT fell pale and pure through the tall windows of East Church, striking sparks from the brass candlesticks and the polished wood of the pews. Outside, snow melted from the eaves in continuous drops. Inside, all was still but for the soft rustle of gowns and the clearing of throats.

Jon stood before the pulpit, his new coat fitting square across the shoulders, the gold braid at the cuffs gleaming in the light. The sword Derby had given him hung at his side. He had faced cannon smoke and the rage of storms, but nothing had steadied or unsteadied him like this quiet waiting.

The door at the rear of the church opened. He turned, and the world seemed to draw a single breath.

Eunice stepped in on her father's arm, her gown of soft blue wool moving like sea-light in the stillness. There were no jewels, no veil, only a wreath of bluebells on her head woven with a ribbon. Her face was calm, but when her eyes met his, he felt the tremor in his own hands.

He had dreamed of her through hunger, through darkness, through months of iron walls. But the woman walking toward him now was no dream. She was warmth and light and the steady heart of his home.

When her father took his place before them and began, his voice seemed to come from far off. Jon heard the words, but more deeply he heard his own vow forming, not only to cherish and protect, but to *return*. Always to return.

He reached for her hand.

Eunice felt the touch of his fingers close around hers, strong and sure, and the world steadied. She saw the new lines at his eyes, and the calm behind them. She thought of the nights she had prayed, of the sea winds she had feared would never carry him home.

"—to have and to hold from this day forward…" said her father, his voice gentle with pride.

Her answer came without hesitation. "I will."

When the gold ring slid onto her finger, she felt the weight of all they had endured, each suffering the loss of a mate, the long years of working together for the good of his home, the waiting, and God's mercy that had brought them here.

The congregation's "Amen" rose softly. The bells outside took up the sound, faint but clear over the harbor.

Jon bent to kiss her, the salt of tears and sea between them. Around them, the church brightened with the smell of pine and melting snow.

Eunice thought: *This is home. This moment. This man.*

Jon thought: *This is the harbor I was meant to find.*

And as they turned together down the aisle, the winter light followed them, bright on his new coat and her blue gown, their steps matching like the rhythm of tide and shore.

Outside, the bells rang as they stepped into the sunlight, greeted by the warmth of familiar faces. Martha wiped her eyes with her handkerchief and pulled both of them into a fierce embrace. "About time, the two of you," she said, half-laughing, half-crying.

Silas' handshake was rough, his voice unsteady. "You've more than earned your peace, Captain, and you, Mrs. Haraden."

Lydia and Andrew Haraden had come from Gloucester. As Lydia embraced Eunice, she said, "We left the girls at home. Our two older ones are watching their new baby brother, Timothy."

"We were delighted to hear you had a son," said Eunice. "You must bring him soon so we can celebrate his birth."

The children ran ahead, Hannah scattering a handful of laurel leaves on the path, and six-year-old Polly trying to copy her sister's grace.

That evening, they gathered in the parlor of the Haraden house, her parents, Elias and Elizabeth Derby, Israel and Mercy Thorndike, and Lydia and Andrew Haraden. The fire burned bright, the air rich with the smell of roast fish, fresh bread, and a trace of nutmeg rising from the wine punch.

Derby raised his glass. "To Captain and Mrs. Haraden," he said, "whose courage and patience would have put any fleet to shame."

Thorndike, still pale from his months in the weighing house followed by winter's gloom, lifted his glass, his eyes brimming with admiration. "To the Captain who brought us home," he said. "And to the lady who kept that home waiting."

Laughter followed, soft and grateful.

"To our cousin, the Salamander, and his bride," said Andrew Haraden, "may God bless your union."

Later, when the guests were gone or upstairs in the case of the Gloucester Haradens, and the girls asleep, the house fell quiet. Jon stood for a long while by the window, watching the harbor lamps sway in the wind. Eunice came beside him, her hand slipping into his, warm against the chill that lingered from the harbor.

"The tide's turning," he said softly.

"It already has," she answered.

And together they watched the faint shimmer of light on the water, until the last bell of the night marked the close of their first day as one. "Come," said Jon, offering his hand, "let me show you our chamber."

Smiling, she took it without a word.

EPILOGUE

Derby Wharf, Salem, 3 May 1782

THE SPRING TIDE ran high that morning, the wind sharp from the southeast and the harbor alive with creaking lines and calling gulls. Eunice stood on the wharf between Hannah and Polly as the *Julius Caesar* eased from her berth, her new sails gleaming pale against the sky. Jon stood at the quarterdeck rail, his dark blue coat bright with gold braid, his hand raised in farewell.

They had been married a little over a month, a short season of happiness before the sea called him again. Yet she felt no fear now, only pride, and the quiet knowledge that this was the life God meant them to share. The sea had claimed part of his heart long before she had, and she would not try to keep it.

The ship's guns gave a salute, echoing over the harbor, and the crowd cheered. Eunice lifted her hand until he was lost to sight beyond the headlands. "God keep you, my love," she whispered. "And bring you home to us again."

AFTERWORD

I hope you enjoyed my story of Jon and Eunice. If you did, please post a review on Amazon. It only takes a line or two, or even a rating by stars alone.

The next in the Dawn of America will be another privateer tale, *The Daredevil,* the story of Captain Samuel Tucker of Marblehead. For notices of future releases, follow me on Amazon (amazon.com/Regan-Walker/e/B008OUWC5Y. You can also sign up for my infrequent newsletters on my website (www.reganwalkerauthor.com). I give away a free book each quarter to one of my new subscribers.

Should you be on Facebook (facebook.com/groups/ReganWalkersReaders), do join the Regan Walker's Readers group where I post special opportunities and giveaways.

For pictures of the historical places, sources and main characters in *The Salamander*, see the Pinterest Storyboard for the book (pinterest.com/reganwalker123/the-salamander-book-2-the-dawn-of-america-series). It's my research in pictures.

AUTHOR'S NOTE

Upon his return from St. Eustatius in 1782, Jon faced a court case where the owners of Captain Curtis' ship sued him for taking the ship into St. Eustatius. Such was the sympathy for Jon that when the case came on, the courthouse was filled with spectators, and the streets of Salem were thronged. When the verdict was announced in his favor, the people rent the air with their acclamations.

On Jonathan Haraden's cruise as commander of the *Julius Caesar* in 1782, the Salamander had lost none of his fight. He did battle with several English brigs and took two prizes. When he arrived back in Salem on December 31, 1782, he had yet another prize, a ship of 400 tons which had been a store ship for Lord Howe. Jon was subsequently presented with yet another silver plate by the owners of the ship, as commemorative of his bravery and skill.

With this last cruise, Captain Haraden's active service as a commander of armed vessels ended. As one of the owners of the *Julius Caesar*, he petitioned for his then First Lieutenant, Thomas Benson, to be commissioned captain, which he was in March 1783.

With the signing of the Treaty of Paris on September 3,

1783, the war officially ended. Jon became a ropemaker for ships, and made the rigging for the mainmast of the famous *Essex* at his ropewalk on Brown Street.

Jon's First Lieutenant on the *Pickering*, Israel Thorndike, became a wealthy man through his investments in the maritime trade, the textile industry and transportation. He owned and commanded ships, and became involved in politics, helping to secure the ratification of the U.S. Constitution.

In the seven years of the war, Jonathan captured sixty-six British ships and over a thousand cannon, often taking on more than one enemy ship at a time. He was the foremost privateer captain of his time, famous for his cool demeanor in the midst of battle. He was "the Salamander" they called him, immune to the flames.

It was said of him, "Captain Haraden was in his person tall and comely; his countenance was placid, and his manners and deportment remarkably mild. His discipline on board ship was excellent, especially in time of action. Yet in the common concerns of life he was easy almost to a fault. So great was the confidence he inspired, that if he but looked at a sail through his glass, and told the helmsman to steer for her, the observation went round, 'If she is an enemy, she is ours!'" His great characteristic was the most consummate self-possession on all occasions, and in midst of battle, none ever excelled him. His officers and men insisted he was more calm and cool amid the din of battle than at any other time; and the more deadly the strife, the more imminent the peril, the more terrific the scene, the more perfect his self-command and serene intrepidity. In a word, he was a hero." From *The Ships and Sailors of Old Salem* by Ralph D. Paine.

In an article by James Masciarelli, the author said, "Tributes to him from both sides of the Atlantic read like Ian Fleming's fictional persona, Commander James Bond of the British Royal Navy. The many characterizations of hawkeyed Jonathan Haraden included intrepid, cool-headed, cunning, easygoing, of dry wit, shrewd, cagey, audacious, and indomitable. His seamanship was impeccable, his judgment infallible."

In 1909, Dr. Frank A. Gardner said of him, "...his naval victories won for him a place in history above that of any other patriot who served on both land and ocean." But, as my story shows, Jonathan also knew tragedy. His first two wives, Hannah and Eunice died before him. Eunice gave him no children, but she loved his own. He married a third time in 1797, the year after Eunice died, and that wife, Mary Scallam, gave him a daughter, Lucy. All three of his young sons preceded Jonathan in death, possibly dying as infants. Jonathan's eldest daughter, Hannah, married John Ropes II, a captain and a sea merchant. They had ten children, and I thought you might like to know, one of whom was a daughter named Eunice.

Like his fellow Patriots, Jonathan was a Christian who placed his faith in Jesus Christ and God Almighty, often referred to by Americans of that time as "Providence". Both he and his first wife, Hannah Deadman, attended the First Church of Salem. When a part of the First Church broke off to become the Third Church of Salem, he went with that group and Jonathan's children were baptized in that church. In 1777, they built a new church, a copy of London's Tabernacle, and the Third Church was thereafter known by that name. The Tabernacle in London was made famous by evangelist George Whitefield, who led the Great Awakening, a series of Christian revivals that swept through Britain and America in the mid-1700s. Whitefield died in Newburyport in 1770 and was greatly mourned. Jonathan Haraden would have been aware of this. Whitefield was, like Eunice Diman's father, another of the "Black-robed Regiment" of preachers, who taught that all people are equal in the eyes of God and that individuals have a duty to resist unjust authority, providing a powerful justification for the American Revolution.

In his will, dated November 3, 1803, written in his beautiful handwriting (you can see it on my Pinterest storyboard for the book) a few weeks before he died of tuberculosis, Jonathan acknowledged he was "weak in body", but for his "perfect mind and memory", he blessed Almighty God. He was an amazing man, a courageous Patriot, an acclaimed privateer captain and a God-fearing family man. America was blessed to have him.

Most of the characters in my story are real people, including all the main characters, Jon and Eunice, the Gloucester Haradens, merchants Elias Derby and George Williams, Jonathan's officers and even the cabin boys (I have a list!). Some are portrayed on the Pinterest storyboard for this book.

When the Revolution began, Britain ruled the seas, and the naval force of the Colonies was pitifully feeble. In 1776 there were only thirty-one Continental cruisers of all classes in commission and this list was steadily diminished by the war until in 1782 only seven ships flew the American flag. However, there were one hundred and thirty-six privateers at sea by the end of the year 1776, and their number increased to four hundred and forty-nine in 1781.

The privateers captured no fewer than eight hundred British vessels and made prisoners of twelve thousand British seamen during the war, prisoners they treated much better than the British did Americans. The goods and supplies they brought back to their home ports supported Washington's army and brought food to Americans. Of the privateer ships, one hundred and fifty-eight were sent out from Salem, Massachusetts, the foremost privateering port of the Revolution.

Salem, Massachusetts was critical for both privateers and the Continental Army. Military stores, including munitions and provisions, passed through the town, and Salem's wealthy merchants, like George Williams and Elias Derby, helped fund the war. In addition to privateering, many local tradesmen and artisans produced the materials necessary to keep the war going, from shipbuilding to blacksmithing.

You might like to know that during the Revolution, slavery was abolished in Massachusetts. In 1780, when the Massachusetts Constitution went into effect, slavery was legal in the Commonwealth. However, during the years 1781 to 1783, in three related cases known today as "the Quock Walker case", the Supreme Judicial Court applied the principle of judicial review to abolish slavery. In doing so, the Court held that laws and customs that sanctioned slavery were incompatible with the new state constitution. In the words of then-Supreme Judicial Court Chief Justice William Cushing, "[S]lavery is in my judgment as effectively abolished as it can be by the granting of rights and privileges [in the Constitution] wholly incompatible and repugnant to its existence."

Some in the New England colonies (states after 1776), because of their Puritan heritage, did not celebrate Christmas at this time. However, General Washington and the Southern Colonies, as well as George Whitefield, New England's celebrated evangelist, certainly did—and with great enthusiasm. Thus, I decided to include the tradition as the characters in the story were not Puritans, and I could see them celebrating the birth of their Savior.

If you loved the story, please post a review! And thanks!

AUTHOR'S BIO

Regan Walker is an award-winning author of more than twenty historical novels set in the Regency, Georgian and Medieval periods. A lawyer turned writer, her years of serving clients in private practice and several stints in high levels of government have given her a feel for the demands of the "Crown". Hence, many of her novels feature a demanding sovereign who taps his subjects for special assignments. She is known for her deep historical research and her richly drawn characters.

The Dawn of America series is her newest venture. Set in the Revolutionary War, these stories tell of American Patriots who brought our country into being, fighting both on land and on the sea. The first three tell of the privateers, brave men whose effect on British shipping was devastating.

Regan lives in San Diego with her dog "Cody", a Wirehaired Pointing Griffon, who is dearly loved.

BOOKS BY REGAN WALKER

The Agents of the Crown series (Regency):

Racing with the Wind
Against the Wind
Wind Raven
A Secret Scottish Christmas
Rogue's Holiday

The Donet Trilogy (Georgian):

To Tame the Wind
Echo in the Wind
A Fierce Wind

Holiday Novellas (related to The Agents of the Crown):

The Shamrock & The Rose
The Holly & The Thistle
The Twelfth Night Wager

Medieval Warriors (England and Scotland 11th century):

The Red Wolf's Prize
Rogue Knight
Rebel Warrior
King's Knight

The Clan Donald Saga (Scotland 12th-15th centuries):

Summer Warrior
Bound by Honor
The Strongest Heart
Born to Trouble

Inspirational

The Refuge: An Inspirational Novel of Scotland

The Dawn of America series (Revolutionary War):

The Irish Yankee
The Salamander
The Daredevil (Coming)